The Extinction of Menai

MODERN
African
Writing
from Ohio University Press

Laura Murphy and Ainehi Edoro, Series Editors

This series brings the best African writing to an international audience. These groundbreaking novels, memoirs, and other literary works showcase the most talented writers of the African continent. The series also features works of significant historical and literary value translated into English for the first time. Moderately priced, the books chosen for the series are well crafted, original, and ideally suited for African studies classes, world literature classes, or any reader looking for compelling voices of diverse African perspectives.

CHUMA NWOKOLO

The
Extinction
of
Menai

A NOVEL

Ohio University Press   Athens

Ohio University Press, Athens, Ohio 45701
ohioswallow.com
© 2018 by Chuma Nwokolo
All rights reserved

Printed in the United States of America
Ohio University Press books are printed on acid-free paper ⊗ ™

28 27 26 25 24 23 22 21 20 19 18   5 4 3 2 1

Library of Congress Cataloging-in-Publication Data
Names: Nwokolo, Chuma, author.
Title: The extinction of Menai : a novel / Chuma Nwokolo.
Description: Athens, Ohio : Ohio University Press, [2018] | Series: Modern
  African writing series
Identifiers: LCCN 2017053684| ISBN 9780821422984 (softcover) | ISBN
  9780821446201 (pdf)
Subjects: LCSH: Nigeria--Fiction. | Nigerian fiction (English) | BISAC:
  FICTION / General. | LITERARY COLLECTIONS / African.
Classification: LCC PR9387.9.N947 E93 2018 | DDC 823/.92--dc23
LC record available at https://lccn.loc.gov/2017053684

Article 10.1
Universal Declaration of Linguistic Rights

All language communities have equal rights.

Prologue

Notes from the National Historian
Nigeria Archives, Abuja

6th March, 1990

Today, six Menai children died from the effects of the 1980 Trevi inoculations in Kreektown. A half-naked procession of a few hundred men and women carried their dead twenty kilometres to the Sontik State capital in Ubesia. Police trucks arrived to keep order, pouring out dozens of armed men, but the topless mourners were tragic, not threatening, and they flowed past checkpoint after checkpoint, chanting Menai dirges, provoking sympathy from policemen and an unprecedented empathy from the public, so that by the time the six bodies were laid out by the gates of the Governor's office in Ubesia, the numbers of topless mourners had swollen into the tens of thousands. . . .

No mass hysteria of this nature had ever been reported in Nigeria before, or since.

22nd April, 1990

An attempted coup led by Major Gideon Orkar failed to unseat the government of General Ibrahim Babangida, which had been in power since 1985. It was the bloodiest coup attempt in Nigerian history. Many of the plotters were from Sontik State in the Niger Delta region of the country, and the coup had been inspired by the feeling of exploitation of the region's minority ethnic nations. After the failed coup there was increasing talk of secession in Sontik State.

17th May, 1990

Denying any connection with the coup of April 1990 or the secession agitations, the government established several commissions and enquiries to attend to minority issues, including the Petroleum Communities Development Fund (PCDF), the Department of Research and Cultural Documentation (DRCD), and a certain Psychiatric Enquiry by Dr. Ehi Fowaka. . . .

◆ ◆ ◆

Extracts from the 1990 Interim Psychiatric Evaluation
of the Menai People

Executive Summary:

The Brief:

> As the notorious Topless Procession case demonstrated, the Menai ethnic
> nation manifests an insular clannishness and resistance to modernity. Is this
> a symptom of an underlying psychiatric condition afflicting the entire ethnic
> nation? Are those traits likely to spread to Nigeria's three-hundred-odd ethnic
> nations? Do they threaten Nigerian nationalism? Is this condition treatable,
> and if so, by what means?

The Subject:

> The Menai is a minor ethnic nation whose global population at the
> date of this interim report is about one thousand. Ninety-five percent
> of all Menai live in Kreektown, an impoverished village on Agui Creek
> in Sontik State. Although there is only one known instance of public
> nudity among them, they are pathologically incapable of adapting
> to city life. They are victims of a group indoctrination that prevents
> them from emigrating from Kreektown. This made them particularly
> vulnerable to the defective Trevi inoculations during the 1980 Lassa
> fever outbreak. They address themselves as Menai, call their language
> Menai, and (although apparently of average intelligence) stubbornly
> speak Menai to the exclusion of the official Nigerian language in their
> village square.

Extract from the Glossary:

> It is a feeble language, as I have mentioned elsewhere. There is actually no
> word for 'suicide,' which is understandable, I suppose: before this trauma of
> their imminent extinction, they had no cultural memory of Menai taking

their own lives. Their word for 'death' is a portmanteau word that opens up into the English equivalent, sleepcatastrophe. Quaint, that. Sums up their entire world view.

Chief (Dr.) Ehi A. Fowaka
M.B.B.S.–F.R.C.Psych.–W.A.C.S.–F.M.C. (Psych)–F.W.A.C.P.–J.P.

◆ ◆ ◆

Log One

SLEEPCATASTROPHES

Kreektown | March/April, 1990

Felimpe Geya
Sussie Bomadi
Filed Bomadi
Bolu Maame
Dubri Masingo
Sonnie Abah
Adje Makande
Ena Praye
Halia Gorie
Nala Nomsok
Solo Atume (aka "Chemist")

Births
Nil

Extant Menai population: 1,160
(National Population Commission [NPC] estimates)

CHIEF (DR.) EHI A. FOWAKA

Ubesia | 19th January, 1994

I was having dinner that evening at the Big Time Hotel in Ubesia, when Jonszer arrived. Apart from the bills for my daughters' school fees at

Loyola Jesuit College, nothing brings tears to my eyes like a steamed cat-fish trembling in a hot bowl of egusi. I had one such before me, and I was eating it with many prayers of thanksgiving to the munificent God that watches over Ehi Fowaka. Then Jonszer arrived. My chief regret for taking this assignment is my new familiarity with souls like Jonszer. He was half-way across the restaurant, black-clad, wild-eyed, and pungent, when I saw him. Fortunately the headwaiter was there. He is a diligent fellow from my town; I knew his godmother. He would have done well if he had got-ten his four GCEs. He was just serving my stout, and I spoke to him with my eyes—really sharp fellow, that headwaiter—and he intercepted Jonszer two yards from me and took him outside. I then, regretfully, made short work of my pounded yam.

Then I went out to meet Jonszer. This is what I am wearing today: a white linen outfit, one of the dozen I ordered at the start of Mr. Presi-dent's assignment. It is light but dignified, perfect for getting around in these wretched parts where efficient air conditioners are few and far be-tween. Jonszer was quaffing a beer. That headwaiter! He knows how to engage characters like this! When Jonszer saw me he put his bottle to his mouth and gobbled efficiently, putting it down when it was empty. 'You come, now,' he said, rising.

He did not mean to be rude, or imperious. His English was rudimen-tary, very much a second language spoken only when the other person couldn't be forced to speak Menai.

There were several good reasons not to follow the amiable drunk. Yet Kreektown's only hotel was a major apology. Working with people like Jonszer allowed me to stay in the relative comfort of Big Time Hotel, while doing excellent fieldwork in Kreektown. That appalling name alone was enough to drive my business elsewhere, but my regular hotels were full. I wanted to ask more questions of Jonszer, but we were attracting attention. This is not the sort of riffraff you want to be socially associated with. I summoned my driver, and we set off. Jonszer sat up front. I took the owner's corner. Beside me was Akeem, my PA, cameraman, interpreter, and general dogsbody.

'So tell me about this place you're taking us to.'

'Is a funeral. A Menai funeral.'

'A *funeral?*'

'Yes, Doctor.'

I sighed. This assignment was moving me closer to anthropology than pop psychiatry. I had no interests in funerals where I knew neither the corpse nor its relatives. Yet it was better that I be called out to too many things than too few; besides, it would be an opportunity for me to meet people, for the Menai were notoriously quiet, sit-at-home types. And frankly, I'd rather be doing this than be stuck at my desk at Yaba Psychiatric Hospital contesting seniority with the likes of Dr. Maleek.

'So who died?' I asked.

'Nobody,' replied Jonszer. 'Is a funeral, not a burial. Is for Sheesti Kroma, Ruma's daughter.'

Akeem caught my eyes, and we indulged some exasperated headshakings. Nobody died! Yet we were going to a funeral! This was the sort of thing that happened when you were forced to recruit a drunk as your local fixer. It was like that old joke, *It was a very fatal accident, but, thank God, nobody died.* Yet Kreektown was just twenty kilometres away, and frankly, my car was more comfortable than my hotel room. No surprise there, since the car was more expensive than the entire hotel. Which was the crazy thing about Ubesia: though the capital of an oil-producing state and cultural heart of the Sontik people, it had a local economy more stunted than the national average and has never quite moved from township into city status.

So I let my driver continue.

Kreektown was locked down when we arrived. There was a funeral under way, all right. The businesses were shut. The pool shop and beer parlours had their doors padlocked and their chairs stacked up under their awnings. The villagers had turned out in black robes like Jonszer's. Never seen that many Menai out at the same time before. They gathered at the village square. It was dark and depressing. There were none of those high-wattage bulbs that organizers of funeral parties would have thought to provide in any civilized village. It was like stumbling into the really Dark Ages, complete with traditional architecture: there were people but it wasn't a party; there was music—and it is really stretching it, to call that menacing witchery 'music,' but I am being scientific here—but no dancing. All they did was weep in song. People stood there like tree trunks and wept and sang these haunting Menai songs, songs that made you feel wretched, like the world was ending tonight, and they sang them one after the other. You don't want to be in this square for a real funeral. The most *sinister* thing was the children, some of them as small as five and six, standing and chanting like the adults. These were kids who, in normal funerals, would have been running around at play. It was clear that a severe order of group psychosis was at work here. I don't mind admitting to a most unscientific unease.

Akeem took photographs while we waited for something else to happen, but nothing else happened. They just stood there and sang.

We walked through the crowd. I recognized quite a few people that I had met in the course of my fieldwork. They were harmless, simple folk: Farmer Utoma, Ma'Bamou, Weaver Kakandu, even that old scoundrel, Kiri Ntupong. Normally these are the most polite and respectful people you will find anywhere in Nigeria, but today they waited for me to greet them first—which I did, in the interest of scientific enquiry—but even then it was like speaking to people in a trance. The wailing and the singing, it was enough to drive a fellow insane.

Then I saw their old man.

Our paths had crossed before. When I first arrived, I confused the Menai by asking for their chief. They are like the Igbos used to be, in not having proper kings. Eventually they took me to this *very* old man who has some kind of authority over them—what exactly it was, I still haven't discovered. His house was rather outside the village proper. They called him Mata, which I suppose was Menai for 'master' or something. But apart from that there was nothing chieflike about him. Had probably forgotten how to be a chief, if he ever was that. His house was probably the poorest in the village. Doubt if it was electrified. I mean, *I* won't give even my houseboy that sort of house for living quarters. I went to see him a couple of times, and all he ever did was offer me a dirty cup of water—which of course I rejected—and sit and stare at the skies. I am not exactly a guru in old age psychiatry (I despise the speciality) and without sticking out my neck—in the absence of an appropriate history and all that—I'd say this was classic dementia: answering every official query of mine with perfect silence.

He could not have looked more different today. He was playing an outsized wooden xylophone like a man possessed. Although it wasn't a very energetic performance—I mean, he was playing a *dirge*—still he was an immensely accomplished musician for a man of his age. Had his audience rapt. And even if this was not a funeral for a dead person, in my professional opinion there was going to be a dead old person in their midst very soon. It was entertainment on its own, watching him play, but it was also like waiting for a fatal accident.

Eventually I turned to go. To listen to their sad songs wasn't a problem— I could have taken that all night. But to be very candid, there are some things that I won't do, even for Nigeria. To come to a funeral and *stand!* In the past twenty, thirty years I can count on one hand the number of

weddings, funerals, or housewarmings I have attended and was not immediately invited to sit at the high table. I mean, sometimes I've accompanied
colleagues to *their* occasions and the organizers, even without knowing
who I was, have called me up to the high table, perhaps on account of my
personality, I don't know. And then I attend an occasion in a village like
Kreektown and *stand*? Really, there's a limit to patriotism. To make matters
worse, as soon as Jonszer stepped into the village square he fell under the
spell of the old man's xylophone. To talk to him was to address another
tree in the forest.

Yet after I got to my car, something about that 'funeral' kept me from
leaving. I am not much of an ethnographic investigator, but the scene un-
folding before me seemed quite crucial to the construction of a psychiatric
profile of the Menai. I was probably the only scientific eye ever to behold
this sight: 95 percent of the world population of an ethnic nation gathered
in one square, weeping and wailing. I could hardly leave a scene of such
scientific, linguistic, and cultural significance out of mere physical discom-
fort. So I compromised. I instructed Akeem to begin a video recording of
the event, which he did, fetching the kit from the boot and setting up the
tripod three metres from the car so that I could monitor proceedings from
the comfort of my Mercedes 300 SEL—at the time of writing, this is an
eight-month-old import, and I hazard a guess that there are not a dozen of
its specs within the borders of Nigeria.

This was the point at which Jonszer turned up again. I let down my
window as he approached. His hand was out, his grin lopsided, with the
effrontery that only drunks can muster. I gave him a half litre of cheap
brandy, and it disappeared into a baggy pocket—I carry this questionable
pedigree of alcohol purely for the appeasement of roughboys. It was difficult to know whether his eyes were red from weeping or from drinking.

'Just come now,' he said.

'What now?' I asked, but he was gone, walking hurriedly, in that demented gait of his, through the crowd and down a side street that led
from the square. My driver had gone to 'make water' (to use his charming
euphemism), and Akeem was tied to his recording. Reluctantly, I followed
Jonszer alone. We did not go far. We walked down Lemue Street right up
till the bend in the road that led towards the creek, and there he stopped.
He waited in the darkness beside a car, the only one on the street. When
I joined him, he tipped his head sideways, towards a small huddle in the
doorway of the house opposite. I looked, but it was too dark to make out
faces or figures.

I was angry. It was dark and stinging with mosquitoes. There was no satellite TV in my hotel room. Back in my hospital, the sly Dr. Maleek was positioning himself for the soon-to-be-vacant office of Chief Medical Director. My fellow consultants and contemporaries were attending conferences and seminars from Joburg to Stockholm, touring with escorts of polyglot, lanky ladies leaving trails of perfumes in their wake. I? I was walking dangerous streets with a drunk reeking of beer and week-old sweat.

'That's Sheesti,' he said.

'Who, where?'

He pointed with his jaw, and then he was gone.

I was afraid. This was precisely the point for me to call it a night. I urgently had to return to the safety of my car and the security of my boys— because scientific research is best conducted with two feet solidly on the ground. Any mugger looking at my clothes just then could reasonably expect to raise three or four hundred thousand naira between my wallet and mobile phones. I was a legitimate target. But the speed of Jonszer's withdrawal made it impossible for me to remove myself from the area of risk without actually taking to my heels—an undignified option, which was out of the question. I was still undecided when a man stormed out through the huddle. He was carrying a box and cursing under his breath. The scientist in me paused, warring with the human in me, which desperately desired the owner's corner of my Mercedes. 'Are you okay?' I asked, as the man flung the box into the boot of the car.

'I am a detribalised Nigerian!' he shouted, seemingly, addressing not just all of Lemue Street, but the entire Kreektown itself. 'My father is Yoruba, my mother is Ibibio!'

'Calm down,' I told him.

He only shouted louder: 'My hospital is in Onitsha! I have lived in Kano! In Calabar! In Lagos!'

'Just like me,' I told him, but he had slammed the boot shut and stormed back into the house.

I was free again to go, but by now the human in me was even more curious than the scientist. I approached the house, whose number I now saw was 43. The huddle resolved into two weeping women. The younger was begging the older, who was replying, 'There's nothing I can do, now, there's nothing I can do.'

I clasped my fingers over the gentle rise of my stomach and, using a voice developed over thirty years of clinical medicine, asked, 'Are you quite all right? I am Chief Doctor Ehi Alela Fowaka, JP. Is there anything at all I can do to help?'

I got the polite response that has been my lot, anywhere I go in this respectful country. They greeted me properly, the younger one curtseying, but before they could speak further, I-am-a-Detribalised-Nigerian stormed past, fuming, 'You are all wizards and witches! I'm sorry! Wizards and witches, that's what you are!'

'Easy, Denle, this is . . .' began the younger woman, but the man was having none of it. He had a half-packed bag in his hand, and with the other hand he grabbed the woman's arm and pulled her towards the car.

'Let's go, Sheesti, before they actually kill you. *Wizards!*'

'Is because we love you . . .' began the older, but two doors slammed shut and one very angry Honda swerved away from Lemue Street.

I was standing before the older woman when suddenly I recognized the transcendental moment of the entire research project. A river of wisdom and calm understanding flowed through me, and I understood how the gurus of the fallen religions of the world can become seduced into the delusion of godhood. I deduced the elaborate social mechanism used by this atavistic society to corral her poor members into communal compliance. 'You must be Sheesti's mother,' I said gently.

She nodded.

'She looks quite alive to me; why would you hold her funeral?'

She opened her hands. 'It has nothing to do with me. It is custom. It is all right for her to marry a foreigner—we encourage our daughters to marry foreigners—but they *must* take your name and come and live in Kreektown. That is our custom.'

'Otherwise you apply the emotional blackmail of a symbolic funeral?' I shook my head gently, as nonjudgmentally as it is possible to be without partaking in stupidity. 'This is 1994, you know, not 1794. We have laws, *federal* laws. And what does your husband have to say about this?'

'Nothing.'

'You don't mind if I have a word with him? Is he in the square, partaking of this lu— of this *custom?*'

'He's inside, but . . .'

'Oh, don't worry.' I smiled. This is one thing that thirty years of senior medical practice gives you: the ability to say grave and serious things with a smile. People are used to accepting tough news from doctors. Anyone else brings the news and they go to pieces, or go ballistic, but a doctor—with the experience—breaks it, and you see the difference. I pushed past the woman—now, this is not something I would normally do, pushing myself so precipitately into private affairs, but the things one does for one's nation . . . I stood in the middle of a large living room—desperately poor, of course, by my standards, but in the context of Kreektown, quite middle-classy, really. There was a colour television, a fancy sofa, and most bizarrely a chest freezer; and in the middle of all that sat a sad-looking man in a wheelchair. 'Good evening, sir,' I began.

He just leered at me. I began to feel vexed. I normally would not have given him a 'sir' but for the wheelchair.

'He hasn't said a word since his stroke in 1989,' she said, from very close behind me.

Munificent God! This guru thing was quite exhausting.

She continued without a break: 'He has nothing to do with this; it is custom. He himself is an Igarra man. We married in February 1973, and he moved here in April of that very same year. Since then he only visited his own town in Igarra maybe five or six times before his stroke. Is what I told Sheesti . . . Is it cold enough?'

I touched the bottle of wine she had produced for my inspection from the chest. There was a strong smell of goat meat from the exterior of the bottle, but the cork seemed intact.

'It's very nice, thank you.'

She opened it and poured me a glass, talking all the while, as her physical proximity forced me backwards and heavily onto her sofa. 'Is what I told Sheesti, I told her, "Marry him and bring him here, like I did with your daddy," but no . . .' and she went on and on.

I sat there sipping the wine, ignoring the smell of meat, and trying hard not to stare at Sheesti's father. The mother was clearly a woman's woman; her English was as fluent as her Menai and her sentences flowed steadily, brooking no interruption. She manifested the Menai custom of aggressive hospitality, which I was prepared to indulge in this case, since her offering was a sealed, if pathetically cheap, bottle of wine. A few weeks earlier I had been forced to reject an unhygienic offering of locally brewed gin invested with an eye-watering reek, only to observe the subsequent hostility and animosity, which forced my visit to end rather more precipitately than I planned.

The eyes of Sheesti's father seemed quite alive, despite the long dribble that led down from rubbery lips to a wet shirt. I couldn't pull my eyes away from this Igarra man who could not attend the funeral of his Menai daughter who was not yet dead. Yet I was a scientist with a job to do. I turned to his wife, feeling the Igarra eyes burning paralysing lasers into the side of my head. 'Who is behind this thing?' I asked, firmly, cutting off her chatter. 'Who *organized* this funeral?'

'Excuse me,' she said, and disappeared into the house, apparently to produce some documentary evidence. This was the good thing about dealing with people of a better quality than the Jonszers of this world. Documentary evidence would go down very well on a presidential report. In the meantime, I was forced to return to the scrutiny of the 'master' of the house. I wondered whether to attempt a one-sided conversation in which I would supply commentaries, questions, and suggested answers. This was usually not a problem for me. With my thirty years' experience, armed with a treatment chart, I can hold a ten-minute ward-round conversation with a comatose patient, particularly with a dozen student nurses and doctors clustered around me, trying to pick up useful hints for their viva exams. But there was something about that Kreektown parlour that threw me off my stride. This did not seem the proper forum to review the pessimistic prognoses of cerebrovascular accidents.

Then she returned. She did not have any facts, figures, or documentary evidence, but she had painted her face, and although she still looked like my mother's marginally younger sister, she no longer looked like the mother of a woman whose funeral dirge we could hear from the square. Then she came and sat next to me on the sofa, close enough for me to perceive a rather rancid variation on the eau de parfum theme. 'As I was saying,' she began, and there was something else in her voice, which was when I looked at the sadness in the eyes of the Igarra man and realised that, president or no president, this fieldwork was ending right there, right then.

'By the way,' I interrupted kindly, 'what's your name?'

'Ruma,' she simpered.

'Ruma,' I said, 'good night.'

SHEESTI KROMA-ALANTA

Kreektown | 19th April, 2000

Ruma aged suddenly and it took the villagers by suprise. It happened in the weekend her headmaster husband died. He had not said a word in the twelve years of his stroke, in the twelve years of his retirement from

Kreektown Primary. He was a presence in the house that many imagined she was better off without. Yet once he died she went to pieces, weeping without a break, in spite of how old it made her look.

I came alone for the burial, without my children and my husband. I stayed at the Kilos Inn at Ubesia, missing most of the silly ceremonies. In the evening when he was already buried, I slipped in to comfort my mother and to leave her the provisions I had bought. Then I left for home.

I had buried him a long time ago, after all—before his stroke, in fact, on that day that he flogged me after hearing about my kissing the son of Lazarus. After the things *he* himself had done to me.

And that would have been it: one more attachment to Kreektown pulled out of my life, leaving just that shrivelling root of my mother. One final visit left to pay . . .

And then I had the strange meeting with Mata Nimito.

♦ ♦ ♦

THE DRIVER had been driving fifteen minutes towards Ubesia when I remembered the ukpana leaves. By this time my anger was gone, the anger I needed to walk coldly through my old haunts. The anger I needed to look boldly at my flesh and blood, who had buried me alive.

Our first son, Moses, was prone to eczema. It had defied Denle's creams, and I had had a bet with him: Menai children did not live with eczema; they had a weekly bath with ukpana leaves for a couple of months, and that was that. Yet I did not have the Igbo word for ukpana, or the English word either. Didn't have a clue how to ask for it in any herbal market in Onitsha. I just knew where the ukpana bushes grew in Kreektown, near the abandoned church.

I had Razak turn around, and we returned to my old hometown. I could not stop thinking of my mother. We had probably had all of an hour together. Ruma had gone from dressing up in skirts to pining for her grandchildren. She did not say a word, but I knew it, now that I was a mother as well. She had made three clothes for them. She had never made me clothes and the lack of practice showed. I had thrown them in the boot, and I will throw them in the bin, but I could not stop thinking of her.

We got as far as the car could go and I told Razak to stop. It did not occur to me to ask for his protection. Safety was not something one ever thought about in Kreektown. Even in these days of the roughboys, I am not really bothered. I was nearly raped once, outside Kreektown, but he ran away when I lied about my AIDS status. Anyway, the ukpana bushes were still some distance by footpath, so the quicker I left, the better. And I wanted to walk out the silly feelings in my head, not sit in a car and let them fester.

I saw his singate even before I saw him. He stood in the path, on the bend just before the first clump of bushes. Behind him was the purple-blue of the ukpana sprays, but there he stood, not quite blocking the way, though his presence was enough to have turned me around, had I not walked so far already. Here then was the man I loathed most in the entire world.

Leaving the People for marriage was not the great unnameable offence it used to be. Too many Menai had died; the end was clear. I had had measles during the Lassa fever outbreak of the '80s and so did not get the vaccine that had doomed my people. It was obvious that I had to make a future with someone outside my dying nation. It would have been the easiest thing in the world for him to have looked the other way with Denle and me, but no, he had to bring the weight of our archaic traditions down on the life I could have had. And that was the first nineteen years of my life excised . . . and now here he was, before me.

The anger blinded me to the obvious questions: what was he doing there, why was he without the helpers who took him around in these latter days of his ancientness? His eyes were shut, as well they should be. His Menai heaven would probably fall at the taboo of a mata locking eyes with a 'dead person.' I steeled myself and walked up to him and started past him.

'Sheestumu?' he whispered. I froze. Mata Nimito named all Menai. He was an old man that the town mostly forgot, until there was a need to remember him: burials, namings, disputes . . . Nobody would ever consider him a friend. There were too many generations between him and us. But he did have that playful way with my name. He let his singate fall and lifted his arms . . . raising the bag of ukpana from his red robes, the leaves plucked just below their nodes, to preserve their potency. I took them, too. It did not seem likely he had a problem with eczema. I put his ceremonial staff back in his hand. His eyes were pinched so tightly shut I wondered if he were now blind. 'Eniemute?'

A warm glow started in me. The love for a husband comes from a region of the mind. The love for a father comes from another. There is no crossover. I felt a glow building from a hearth I had thought was terminally broken. I told him of my children, their names. He shook his head impatiently. 'Eniemute!'

With a dry mouth, I described Moses: the long limbs he owed to his father, his quick temper . . . *Ameizi,* he said. I described Cynthia, who looked so much like my baby photograph . . . *Anosso,* he said, and then I described my baby, Patricia, who had the nurses pledging their sons in marriage . . . *Ogazi,* he said.

The naming was complete.

Then he began to sing my torqwa! I that was dead to Menai! I fell on my knees, enthralled again by the antiquity of my lineage. I knelt there, streaming tears as the poetry of my identity bore me from the caravan of the exiled crown prince through the dunes and the deserts and the savannahs and the forests and creeks of their sojourn. I listened to the descendants of young Auta, trumpeter in the court of the crown prince, Xera, and his wife, Aila, daughter of Numisa, until

> *Rumieta Kroma the trader of cloth*
> *married Teacher Gaius from Igarra*
> *to birth Sheesti, little mother*
> *who, with Denle, son of Alanta,*
> *scion of Esie, built pillars for Menai:*
> *three pillars of Ameizi, fierce athlete,*
> *Anosso her mother's cunning vomitimage*
> *and Ogazi the fair, for Menai without end . . .*

I gripped my nose, as I rose, caught my breath so tight . . . Only now, hearing my torqwa in the Mata's voice, did I realise the darkling power of my funeral . . . For the first time since the arrival of my children, I felt they were not stillborn. They were named, properly *named* from the font of all Menai. I may still languish in that never-never world of a Menai who is neither dead nor ancestor, but in the land of ancestorsMenai, my children were *known*. Denle could not, could never know the burden of the crush of death.

I probably thought the Mata was going to fall, for he did sway, and frag-ile, *fragile* was the rag of bones and flesh that I grabbed as I found my feet, and held, but fierce, *fierce* was the grip he locked me in. How long we stood there, racked by dry spasms, I don't know, how long I stood, crooning over the man I hated most in all the world, until with a long breath he was stilled and the old body became rigid like a trunk. His arms fell away, but for a thin finger pointing at the singate he had dropped once again to hold me.

My eyes were red, and I was grateful he was being blind. His onion-thin skin was dry. He smelled of roasted corn. Freshly roasted corn and aged palm wine. He stood erect, implacable, like a sentinel from the past. There

was no other word, no bon mots and no goodbye, but I knew it was time
to go. What had happened was something that had not happened, could
never have happened, but I was gifted with a memory of it.

I turned and fled to the car, back to 43 Lemue Street in the old village.
She did not argue, and I felt like the mother packing the little girl off to
college. She packed her property slowly, touching things that would not
fit into the car, like she was saying goodbye. Without the anger in my
eyes I saw more of her, and although she had never said it in her letters,
I knew now that she was dying—for her to leave the living Menai and go
with her dead daughter. To break so unceremoniously with tradition.
She began to pack her thirty-year-old crockery, the set so special that
she never used it, and I sighed and stood up firmly. Ten minutes later
we were ready to go. We shut down our Kreektown house for good and
went to mine.

◆ ◆ ◆

Onitsha | 10th September, 2001

My darling husband did not throw me out, but it was a near thing. He
ran his own private hospital with a businessman's flair. Even before we
got married he had built two houses from his steep fees. With me there,
less of the fees ended up buying female handbags, and we had added a
couple more. Managing tenants and children was enough work for me.
He did not talk to me throughout that week I brought my mother home.
All he muttered, again and again to my hearing, was 'Blood is a terrible thing!' So I moved her to one of our empty flats. That compromise
seemed to work.

He never went to see her, but he never asked me to rent out the flat
either. And once, three months on, he threw a brocade fabric on my bedside, saying, 'See if that old witch likes this.' I did not tell him that Ruma
had traded in brocade and had left the largest collection of uncut brocades
at No. 43. It was the thought that counted. Even his 'old witch' was not
much angrier than the meaningless epithets he uttered in my ear after he
switched off the lights at night.

There was the day she blessed him, too. My driver had taken me to
Anam to buy yams. On my return, I stopped by her flat. I stepped out of
the car into screams from the hysterical housegirl on the balcony above.

'Which hospital?' I cried, and she stared.

I broke into the ward just as he was setting a drip. It was not something he usually did himself, but there he was. As I approached, my mother, who was just about to drift off, took his hands and held them for a silent moment. The bedlam around her ceased for a moment, as though they realised that something significant was about to happen. '*Simba tulisu. Simba tuala,*' she said, and passed out.

◆ ◆ ◆

19th December, 2001

'You could have told me she was ill,' he grumbled, afterwards. 'We might have been able to save her life.'

And it was at such times that the wise wife held her tongue, as I did.

She had started her biweekly dialysis right after her hospitalisation. I had waited patiently, with a small smile and a private bet. Yet my darling husband was a stubborn man, and it took him weeks to, casually, ask—as though it had just occurred to him—'What was that your mother said when she held my hands?'

'When was that?' I asked, playing his game. 'I don't remember . . .'

'You do,' he said, irritated. '*Samba, samba,* something.'

'Oh,' I said innocently, 'that.'

'Well?'

'She blessed your hands,' I equivocated.

'Yeah? What exactly did she say?'

At that point I was a little wary, for the words could also be construed as a curse. 'Until now, they made money. From now they will *bless* lives.'

He let that sink in a while, then he snorted. 'Well, I hope—for our sakes—that they still continue to make a little money as well!'

◆ ◆ ◆

31st December, 2001

Rumieta Kroma died on New Year's Eve. Denle thought we should bury her in Onitsha. We had a small quarrel over that, but it quickly blew over. He had wanted her in his family vault at Onitsha. Non-Kreektowners simply don't get it. I sent her body home, so she could sleep beside her husband in our empty living room. I sat in the hotel in Ubesia, seeing her sleepcatastrophe rites through my tears. When night had properly fallen,

I sneaked into the empty house to say my farewells at her grave, but the floor had not yet been broken. My people had waited, after all. And in the silence of that bereft house I sheathed my knife for good.

They sent for the Mata, and when he came, they held the second Restoration in the history of the Menai sojourn in Kreektown. Then I joined them in the burial of my mother, Rumieta Kroma, sixty-seventh descendant from Auta, trumpeter of the court of Crown Prince Xera. We moved all the furniture out, cracked the floor, and dug down a tall man's height in the earth, until soil filled the room. Then we laid Mama to sleep, sans coffin, in a burial shroud freshly woven by Kakandu. At five feet, we spread her bridal brocade. We filled another foot of earth and snapped her nuptial beads into glinting confetti on the red laterite. Then we filled the grave to its lip, packed it hard, and slabbed it over. And as we sang dirges for her sleepcatastrophe, I was mourning Kreektown as well, for I realised that the Mata had finally accepted that our nation was destined to die.

◆ ◆ ◆

Kreektown | 2nd January, 2002

When the night was as silent as the living room I went to the Mata's pavilion. He was sitting, staring at the night sky, and I sat with him. He poured me a drink of water and we toasted. As well-being flooded my body, I poured out the palm wine and we drank. Three hours passed in silence. From a distant oilfield, a single flare stack flickered. Occasionally he clucked at something he saw in the skies. Otherwise it seemed that all was well in the universe; apart from the fact that Kreektown and her last mata were all but dead.

'*Suetu maini kpana aiga she?*' I asked, pointing at the clouds.

He laughed and I laughed with him, savouring a joke I did not yet know. An hour passed and he laughed again, explaining that my grandmother, mother, and I had all suffered eczema, and he did not need the clouds to tell him that my children probably would as well.

'I can't come back. My heart is here, but I have a husband, I have a life elsewhere.'

'*Anodu tuetu siliesi.*' He smiled.

In the early hours I left him my shopping and returned home to Onitsha, salting away his words: 'You're back already.'

◆ ◆ ◆

Onitsha | 7th January, 2002

It was after that visit that I started the Menai Society (MS). My darling husband put down the seed money, but I have raised much more since then. At first it was just the language I was looking at: writing a primer, recording proverbs, idioms, historysongs, things like that. But in going around, in recording the stories, I found that what the Menai needed *now* was medicine, not tape recordings. The Omakasa Enquiry had found Trevi Biotics not negligent, so funding for medical care was a problem. So the focus of MS changed. We started registering Menai survivors, pairing them with kidney units, buying dialysis time . . . it was about this time that we sued Trevi and Megatum in London.

'We,' because my husband got involved. I had sued Trevi Biotics in the Federal High Court in Ubesia, and we were limping along, when Trevi found out that Doctor Denle Alanta was our main sponsor. They approached him with fifty times his seed money in bribes. I still don't know why that turned Denle into a crusader for the town he had once hated so much. As a doctor he loved his money; he charged even the poorest patients his fees and stopped their treatment once they stopped paying. But I suppose he also liked a good fight. That, and concrete proof of corruption, which he had always contested, in the discontinuance of the '80s litigation filed for the Menai by a medical NGO in London.

So that day I came in and there were new birth certificates for the children on the bed. 'Is that how you spell their names?' he asked, as I picked them up. My hands were trembling: he had added the Mata's Menai names to our children's official names.

'How did you know?' I whispered.

'They told me what you call them—when I'm not around. I thought they sounded quite nice.'

'You're not angry?'

He laughed. 'I'm so angry I'll leave Eddie in charge of the hospital and we'll both go to London for the Megatum hearing.'

'We?'

He showed me the hands that would now bless people. 'The curse of the dead witch,' he said.

◆ ◆ ◆

Kreektown | 12th March, 2005

'Why this Field of Stones?' I asked.

'When I rest there,' said the Mata, settling his hand almost tenderly on the earth, 'I will end the curse on this land.'

'But you said it's not even in Nigeria! It's . . . thousands of miles away!'

'This *land* . . . this *continent* . . .'

Denle arrived with a grim Jonszer behind him. He took one look at the old man. 'You have to stop now, and I mean *now*.'

I raised one finger, shielding the microphone for another five minutes until Mata Nimito slowed to catch his breath. Then I reluctantly clicked my recorder off.

Denle was standing over us, angrily surveying the Mata's home. 'We could build a house without touching the old one, and let him decide if he'll use it or not.'

'Look at it with new eyes, Denle,' I whispered. 'It's not an *old* house. It's *history*.'

I remained motionless on the bench, leaving Jonszer to attend to the old man. We'd had a marathon session: four straight hours, our longest yet. Denle always said the old man would talk himself into the grave if we let him, it was up to me to be responsible. But he saw I was upset, and he took a deep breath and put away his anger.

'Are you okay?'

'I don't want to go to London. You can represent the society at the next session.'

'It's more than a court case, Shee. You are the Menai.' He sat beside me. Softly. 'Why?'

'There's so much I didn't know!' I was near to tears. 'Behind every idiom, there's wisdom; behind every word, there's history! You know, I asked him how come all those years he never used this idiom, that word . . . and he said the *miasta* . . . the . . . need for it . . . had not come! So many stories . . . we were so blessed, we were so . . .'

'We'll be back within the month.'

I whispered in his ear so they could not overhear. 'I don't think he'll wait that long . . .'

He watched Jonszer bow as he went through the low doorway with the old man in his arms.

'We'll take him to Onitsha, with the facilities in the hospital . . .'

I laughed and he grinned with me, until he realised I was now weeping. 'What?' he asked, holding me.

'He said he won't die in a *zoo,* and he'll be buried in the original home-land of our ancestors from centuries ago.' I wiped my tears. Soberly, I added, 'He's made me promise to take his body back to the Field of Stones, and . . . and I don't have a clue where that is.'

HUMPHREY CHOW

Lower Largo, Scotland | 15th March, 2005

Rubiesu simini randa si kwemka.

Something queer happened early this morning to put me off Chinese takeaways for good. As I recall, I was alone when I retired after dinner yesterday, and I haven't drunk alcohol in days. Yet at 4:00 a.m. I woke up with a full bladder, only to find a bearded stranger snoring on the bed beside me.

Now, there are queer things and there are urgent things: I quickly used the bathroom, running a numbing jet of cold water over my head. When I shut off the tap the small room was silent. Except for the rhythmic crashing of waves on the beach outside, the gurgling as my water funnelled to its death by sewerage . . . and a ragged snore from the bedroom.

I looked carefully in the mirror, and they were there, all right: the two loneliest eyes in the world, staring back at me like solitary inmates in their psychiatric wards. 'Not so lonely now, are you?' I muttered.

He was still there when I returned, a large heavy youth lying face up in a grey trench coat. His great boots hung over the edge of my bed. A pervasive smell of stale fried chicken hung in the air. The situation was getting queerer and queerer: I snuck downstairs and found that both doors were firmly locked against the Scottish cold. The windows were fast, and there was no sign of a break-in. This was no burglar—although realistically, what burglar would stop halfway through a heist and opt to grab a snooze alongside his victim?

Now, I am a reasonable man. (My wife would argue, too reasonable. Upon stumbling across a fellow breaking into my car the other day, I'd tapped his shoulder and asked if he had mistaken my car for his. In a similar situation, Grace had broken a teenager's nose with her handbag, but I'm a reasonable man.) I made a very hot cup of tea and took it upstairs. A kitchen knife wasn't exactly my style. A scalding cup of tea was an urbane prop that could turn from beverage into portable biochemical deterrent if an Unidentified Sleeping Person turned violent.

I shook him awake, and he sat up on the edge of my bed. He looked at me. The only emotion I could see on his face was the irritation of a man shaken awake—say, on a public bench—waiting to find out why his sleep had been disturbed.

'Who are you?' I asked eventually.

He yawned and sleepily pulled a black bandanna from his pocket. As he tied the angry declaration across his forehead, I gasped. 'A suicide bomber!'

'That's *what* I am,' he said impatiently, 'not *who* I am. I am Dalminda. Dalminda Roco, ex–law student.'

Tradition is a terrible thing. 'Humphrey Chow,' I said, 'short story writer.'

He extended his hand for a handshake and when that was done, took my cup of tea with a *God, I needed that!*

He caught my surreptitious glance under the bed. 'What?' he asked.

'Are you off-duty?'

'Christ! I was sleeping, wasn't I? Do I look the sort of fanatic who carries his work to bed?' He braved a sip of the scalding tea and made a face. 'Black and bitter,' he grumbled. 'What's the point?'

That was my cue to tell him that the tea was for pouring rather than drinking. I missed it. He plunked down the cup on the bedside cupboard, spilling a dash on the wood and possibly rendering some of my holiday deposit unrecoverable. '*Chew*,' he said, apparently making conversation. 'You don't look very Chinese. In fact, you look definitely . . .'

'Chow,' I told him shortly, not believing the conversation was happening. 'And it's a long story.'

'There's black in you, definitely,' he persisted. 'Your hair . . .'

'I said it's kind of a long story.'

Yet this was meant to be a short story. I was at the end of a two-week writing break on the east coast of Scotland. Mission: write the kind of offbeat stories that had so excited my new agent when she read the manuscript for my novella two years earlier. I had done several short stories since then, but none had remotely interested her. 'Can't you write something like *Blank*?' Lynn would ask after spiking yet another clutch of tales.

Finally, I had booked the same holiday house in which I had written *Blank* in December 2003. I had come alone, in the same cold. All that remained was to remember the particularly atrocious takeaway I had eaten the day I wrote my best story ever. The food had given me a bad case of diarrhoea, and I had woken at 4:00 a.m. in a foul mood and written *Blank*. Lynn fell in love with the story, and I lost my peace of mind. I was now on the last day of my writing holiday. I had eaten dozens of different takeaways, chewed through a packet of antacids, but none of the half-dozen stories I had written was even remotely passable.

'What are you doing in my bed?' I asked eventually.

'Sleeping.' He yawned and went back to sleep.

◆ ◆ ◆

RUBIESU SIMINI randa si kwemka!

In moments of stress, Menai proverbs sometimes popped into my mind. When I was ten, a quiet, intense African stopped for a meal at Miss Chow's takeaway and stayed for dinner. Thirty months later, he was still there. It was a happy time, I guess; but it was not to last. It came to a head when Mr. Chow arrived from Shanghai unannounced and found Tobin Rani in his wife's bed. There was a fight, all now rather murky in my mind, and Miss Chow paid for her months of happiness with her life, Yan Chow got a kitchen knife in his back, Tobin moved into prison, and I went back on the queue for yet another adoption. He had good English, that African, but with me, he doggedly spoke his strange Menai language. I was a stubborn kid back then and was equally determined not to learn it, but Tobin was interested in me in a way no other man had been. Besides, thirty months was a long time in days, and . . . *urubiesu simini randa si kwemka!* There were things that really had no translation in English. They just sat there in the mind in a self-sufficient Menai phrase.

By dawn, I was reconciling myself to the possibility that I was losing my mind, again. I needed help, but the only psychiatrist I knew was my mother-in-law, whom I hadn't seen professionally in a couple of years. If I phoned to explain that I had woken up with a man in my bed in the middle of a private writing holiday, it was entirely possible that a divorce would be in progress before I returned to London.

I had to confront my demon personally.

But I was scared. I had experienced discontinuities before: I would occasionally remember something that clearly could not have happened, like me dancing in carnivals, which I wouldn't do in a few hundred years. I called those false memories my *sub stories*—since my subconscious seemed to be dabbling in the fiction business as well. But Dalminda was no sub story scripted by the deranged mind of a short story writer.

Dalminda Roco was in my bed.

ZANDA ATTURK

Kreektown | 15th March, 2005

The expression on the dead man's face was mild surprise, as though his assassin had started off with a spot of poetry. I had travelled many miles for this rendezvous with the smuggler, Korba Adevo, at a large, circular tent staked out on the grassed riverbank where the mangrove forest met Agui Creek. The tent was maybe forty feet from corner to corner and furnished like a permanent, if ramshackle, residence. The tarpaulin had been mended in several places. The ferocious dog he'd warned me about was sprawled in a broken heap by his feet, its days of ferocity very much a thing of history. Adevo's fixed eyes stared at me through the clotting blood from a head wound. He was a fresh corpse, too, with an interrupted plate of starch and banga still floating an aroma in the air. He was dressed in a lace agbada that was fashionable a decade ago, its bloodstained peak cap on the floor beside him. He sat there, alone, in his disordered tent. I let the flap fall and inched backwards into the evening sun.

Outside, my hired horse switched its tail, raising a plume of flies attached to the ulcer on its rump. An old generator sulked nearby, tethered to the tent by its cable. I looked around the mud flats skirting the creekline, searching reeds and mangroves for something out of place. Everything seemed strange and out of place: a boat berthed on mud, a jeep loaded with merchandise on a narrow beach served only by footpaths. The harmattan frisked the trees and the horse's mane. The wind was shiver-cold, but inside me, a low-grade fever boiled.

Adevo's text message that morning had just one word: *Badu.* Every now and again someone chose my number from the bylines on *Palaver*'s pages to send some bit of news or another, but this was the working journalist's dream scoop: information about the most hunted man in Nigeria. I had called immediately.

'Badu?' I had asked.

'How are you?' came the guarded voice. 'Is about that your Pitani man . . . Is Korba Adevo here . . .'

'My name is Zanda,' I had said nervously. 'Listen, my paper can pay . . . private interview . . . just me, you, and nobody else . . . how much do you want?'

There was a long pause.

'Look, I'm serious here, just talk! How much?'

'Four hundred?'

I had taken his directions and driven the few hundred kilometres from Abuja to Kreektown, but the lips of the smuggler were now sealed for good. The disappointment of losing a Badu lead was physical, almost as strong as the shock of walking into a dead man's tent. Now, my very presence in that isolated hermitage was a bad idea. The hands that had made the corpse could not be far away.

I turned to the elderly horse. I had hired it from a hotelier who also ran three donkeys in neighbouring Kreektown. All I wanted to do just then was recover my deposit for the animal and return to my desk at *Palaver* before their Roving Eye columnist—or the money in his possession—was missed . . .

Yet I was a journalist. Even though I could never print the story, the camera in my backpack craved a glance at the scene now imprinted on my mind forever. Reluctantly I pulled it out and raised the tent flap once again. I suppose my crisis started here with that failure of memory, that moment when I turned around to find something worse than amnesia's blank canvas, to find instead the present contradicting the immediate past: there was a warning snarl from the dog, and from the man, a ragged snore that ended in a yawn. 'God deliver me!' he said, in the rusty voice I remembered from the phone conversation. He looked at his wrist. 'Is that the time?'

I tried to keep my balance. 'You were . . . you are . . .'

'Adevo,' he yawned. He picked up his pristine peak cap. A joint popped and two fists strained in different directions as he stretched himself awake, large eyeballs standing out of a heavy-featured face. 'And you must be . . . *Zanda?*' He impregnated my name with a significance that eluded me.

'Yes.'

'No camera, please.' He sucked his teeth irritably. As my knees gave way and I fell into a cane chair, he said, 'Tired, eh? You shouldn't have walked; I thought I mentioned Ma'Calico's donkeys.'

'I hired her horse.' I glanced furtively about me.

He chuckled wickedly. 'That *dead* bag of bones? I swear to God, you are going to have to carry her back to Kreektown, you will see.'

There was no one else in the tent, dead or alive . . . It was just Adevo, with not a spot of blood on his old-fashioned agbada. 'You have the eyes of a thief,' he observed, with professional interest.

It was just another hallucination, then. The last major episode I remembered was so far back in my childhood I'd begun to think I had outgrown the plague. The worst thing about hallucinations was how they messed with your reflexes: back in Kreektown Primary, a snake once slithered out of my locker and I had not moved a muscle, while my classmates had broken ankles and furniture on their way to the door. They thought I was pretty brave, but I'd only thought the snake a hallucination—and I'd learned the hard way what happened to people who saw strange things. All I wanted was to see what everyone else saw—not the animals that leapt out of walls to animate my science classes. Or the dreams that continued when I was wide awake.

A woman began to laugh, and I started, but it was only a customised ring tone. He glanced at the culprit in the bank of phones on his armrest and looked away. 'Okay,' he said impatiently, 'what do you want to do about Pitani? His noise is getting too much! You said you want private interview, not so? This is me here.'

'What noise are we talking about?'

I realised that the thumb he was rubbing against an index finger was a gesture for my attention. I half rose, the better to unwind the money belt from my waist, then sat back again. My publisher, Patrick Suenu, had reluctantly paid up for the promised Badu scoop, even though I had kept my lead and his location secret. My tenure at *Palaver* was pretty shaky just then, but a Badu scoop was easily the biggest story in the decades since Dele Giwa's murder. If I had it in hand, I could sell it for an oba's ransom, and he knew it.

'You're a bit yellow,' observed Adevo in what was probably his attempt at light conversation.

I let that go and pulled out the wads of currency. My heartbeat had slowly returned to normal, but my fingers were still shaking, so I handed over the money without counting. Adevo took them on trust as well, making them disappear into various pockets on his garment. He replaced the peak cap on his head, pulling its two flaps low over his ears. There was a beatific smile on the face he turned to me. 'Correct man,' he said. 'Oya, you have one hour. Time is money.'

The financial transaction concentrated my mind.

Two weeks earlier, Badu had arrived on the national scene when he kidnapped Justice Omakasa, carried out a mock trial, and executed him vigilante-style. The video of the judge confessing to bribes from Trevi and a host of other litigants had ignited a firestorm on the Internet. The TV networks had it on an endless loop. A police manhunt for Badu was under way, but the judge's salacious confessions had turned public sympathy in favour of Badu, even as face-saving investigations against people outed by the confession foot-dragged their way through the system.

Then, a couple of days before, Charles Pitani, the inspector general of police, had also been kidnapped. The audacious abduction of Nigeria's most senior policeman had all the hallmarks of Badu's first strike, and an intensive security dragnet was under way. Yet Badu had gained such cult status that a Pitani video was feverishly awaited.

Those were the stakes I was playing for, deep in creek country.

Four hundred thousand naira was a lot of money, but not for a Badu story. The police had announced a ten-million-naira reward for information leading to the vigilante's capture. That was a powerful suggestion that the man before me was a charlatan—except that Badu was now a folk hero. Anyone who gave him up to the police had to be careful not to be lynched.

Badu had sent out his first video for free. I was more than happy to pay for the second. Perhaps he was becoming more of a media-savvy vigilante, using his contacts to sell news to sympathetic journalists to fund his operations.

I hoped I was sitting before one such contact.

I switched on my Dictaphone, rose partway, and put it on the arm of Adevo's chair. I sat back down and chewed on a nervous fingernail. 'Tell me about yourself.'

'Thank you,' he said, pocketing my Dictaphone. 'Is it me you want to talk about, or Pitani?'

I hesitated. There was no longer a Dictaphone beside him. Had I imagined pulling it out, or just the bit about its disappearance? 'We'll . . . get to Pitani and Badu,' I said, determined to get my hour's worth. I patted myself uncertainly. The recording machine was gone. I swallowed. I pulled out a pen and a notebook.

He shrugged nonchalantly. 'What do you want to know? I entered Harvard at the age of sixteen—'

'Harvard?'

'The university. You 'ave heard of it, not so? I graduated firs' class. Won the prize for my year. After my PhD, I entered revotechnics . . .'

'*Revo-* what?' I asked, writing.

'*Revotechnics.*' He sighed. 'Journalist of nowadays. So wha's the problem? Spelling or meaning?' I didn't reply, and he continued. 'By the time I was thirty I was registering patents left, right, and centre. I was chairman of UAC for ten years. Then I ran for the presidency.'

'And how was your election?' I asked caustically. I had stopped writing when he started registering patents left, right, and centre, but those shorthand squiggles that I had been silly enough to make stared up at me with pity.

'Don't mind those tribalists,' he said. He took a bottle, shook some groundnuts into a fist, and munched away. 'Anyway, that annoyed me so much that I retired here to my country villa.' His groundnut hand indicated his luxurious retirement estate. He shook his legs with barely concealed irritation. 'Any more questions?'

I did not think my crisp currency notes deserved all this sarcasm, but it was also clear that the hallucination had knocked me off-balance. I had opened an interview with a smuggler with my celebrity formula. In two and a half years of print journalism it was hard to beat a sillier opener: asking a criminal for testimony that could lock him away. I had to pull things together quickly.

Patrick's money was on the line.

He extended the groundnut bottle to me. I shook my head politely. 'This Badu, is he from this area at all?'

'No, he's from Congo.'

I stared, trying to decide if he was still being sarcastic. 'Do *you* know where he is?'

He returned my stare.

I tried another tack. 'About the second video, is it ready yet? I want the first copy.'

He sneered. 'From this money? Look, young man, I am a smuggler, not a Nollywood producer.'

I paused again: deep breath, slow exhale. 'Is the IG still alive at all?'

'What did you think will kill him? Mosquitoes?'

I paused to consider my options. Despite his fearsome reputation, Adevo did not look like a physical match for me. At fourteen, I had realised I was never going to make six feet and became the second member of the Kreektown Boxing Club. I had maintained the sport in Abuja while I hustled for my degree. I took every opportunity, in and out of the ring, to practise. Adevo did not look fit enough to yawn properly, but he had not left his chair so far, and his off-white robe was generous enough to conceal a small arsenal—a smuggler with his reputation would not get by on divine protection alone. This was a nonrefundable transaction, then. I tried again. 'Can I meet Badu?'

He stared at me.

'Are you Badu?' I asked.

'Is this a joke?' he snarled.

The harmattan howled through the interstices of the tent, sinking its chill between my shoulder blades. Fear for my money and my life seized me. I regretted coming alone, coming at all. My dreams of journalistic fame on the wings of a Badu scoop began to fade. I leaned forward and whispered, although I could have screamed in that wilderness and not been heard, 'Listen, we are on the same side, okay? Talk to me in confidence, eh? I'll use a false name for you, and a false location for Badu . . .'

He chewed his nuts quietly.

'So, is Badu planning any more strikes?'

'We pray.'

I closed my notebook. 'You want to cancel the interview?' There was a tremor in my voice, which angered me. I ratcheted up my anger. It was preferable to fear, 'Is that it?'

'No, no, the money's good,' he said, eating some more groundnuts. 'The interview's very good.'

'Because I'm getting the feeling that I'm talking to a con man who has never even *seen* Badu.'

'Is that so?' There was mockery in his voice.

'And if that's the case, just give me back my cash. Forget about my petrol, forget about my time, just give me back my . . .'

He smiled. 'There's no refund in ashawo business. You can't just tell a prostitute it wasn't sweet—'

'Listen, my friend . . .'

His smile drained slowly away. '*I know who you are.* You wanted to try me, not so? But I passed your test. Eh?'

The unspoken tract of a strange language sprawled between us. My mind gridlocked and refused to mesh. Visions of a post-*Palaver* TV-journalism career plunged into a swirling vortex. 'What are you talking about?'

'My mouth is . . .' He zipped his lips. There were bits of caked starch meal on his palm. 'I swear to God.'

I rose slowly. My mouth was parched. I prayed for a violent fit, but all I got was a roaring in my ears. I took a step towards him and provoked a belly laugh. A low growl issued from the dog, and a metal post with two black nozzles peered out from his robes. I froze.

'I'm a honest thief. A deal is a deal.'

'Our deal was for an interview. You call this an interview?'

'If you also want me to finish Pitani for you, just say so.'

'What do you mean, *finish Pitani?*' I shouted. 'What are you talking about?'

'Go and ask about me,' he boasted, getting into a clearly familiar groove. 'I am Korba Adevo.' He gestured at the bank of phones by his side. His voice rose and the tent began to billow with his bombastic rage: 'There's nothing I can't move. Me that I have sold army helicopters from this very chair. What about boats? I have six, do you hear me? *Six contraband boats!* Is it crude? I have bunkered enough petrol to flood this country. Go and check! Lamborghinis, Hummers, there's nothing that's too big for me.' He simmered slowly, then ignited again, his great eyes bulging. 'Because I'm sitting in this dirty tent! This is my field office only! My house in Ubesia is two storeys! Go to Constitution Road, Aba! Half of the houses on that road are mine! I'm the one that sold the FESTAC mask to British gov'ment, you hear me? There's nothing tha's too big for me—'

'—except the presidency . . .' I suggested.

'Leave nonsense for foolish people,' he counselled shortly. 'I sell silence as well, okay? That's me.' He picked up a phone. 'You see this red Samsung? It has the telephone of a federal minister. You know why he does business with me?' He drew his zipper again.

Beneath the bombast was some truth. I had never met him before, but the name Korba Adevo had resonance amongst the dwellers of creek country. This far from civilisation a grave would not require a death certificate to dig. A funeral would not need a coroner's report. I had lost Patrick's money. My life was still on option.

I opted to flee.

I raised the flap and backed outside. The harmattan was more insistent now. The fever inside me was gone. I was uniformly cold all over as I mounted the horse. My sore, unaccustomed buttocks connected with the craggy saddle, completing my misery. I remembered my Dictaphone, which had a few untranscribed interviews. Yet I knew that if I returned for it I would either have my head blown off at the entrance or find the fat fence dead all over again. Neither prospect appealed. I turned the horse's nose for Kreektown and urged it on.

HUMPHREY CHOW

Lower Largo, Scotland | 15th March, 2005

Dalminda Roco sang "Amazing Grace" in the bathroom. When he stepped out, the smell of stale poultry had receded somewhat. Over breakfast, I fixed him with my serious stare. 'How did you get into my room?'

He looked at me suspiciously, like someone sensing a trick question. 'I climbed the stairs and opened the door?'

'*Why?* And don't tell me you were feeling sleepy!'

'Actually, I was rather hoping to get arrested. I was here years ago for a students' beach party and I know where the housekeeper hides the spare key.'

'I am renting right now; you realise you are, kind of, trespassing?'

'Like I said, I was hoping to be arrested; instead I ended up with tea in bed.' He considered the last of his egg sandwich and shook his head. 'And a full English breakfast!'

I counted to ten with my eyes mentally closed, and asked quietly, 'Why?'

He drained his tea and yawned. '*Who . . . how . . . why . . .* look at the pedestrian issues on your mind!' He pushed his chair back. 'Me, I'm into more earth-shaking matters.'

'Like what?'

'Like bombs!' His honking laugh went very well with his macabre humour. 'Bombs shake a lot of earth!'

With that, he rose and slung his rucksack on carefully. He squared his shoulders into the weight of it and looked into the garden, 'Looks like a lovely day for it,' he grudged, scratching his beard. He was no longer laughing. 'I might as well get on with it.'

I edged closer to the block of kitchen knives. I was dealing with a plucky con man. Earth-shaking matters indeed. He was clearly anxious to make away with his swag. I hadn't seen my laptop that morning, for instance, and I couldn't afford to lose it. It had too many killer opening paragraphs with short story potential. 'That's not a bomb.'

'It's not?' He shrugged the rucksack onto a kitchen counter and offered me a cord. 'D'you want to pull-test it?'

I didn't move.

I was torn between pushing this lunatic and his bag outside and mining him for inspiration for my next short story. This was exactly the sort of offbeat material Lynn would swoon over. I didn't want to die in a bomb incident, but I felt compelled to prioritise my art—for the moment at least. After all, some authors had written their best sellers from prison, writing with boot polish on toilet paper. I was in a seaside resort, on the last day of a barren writing retreat. This seemed a chance to redeem myself: a short story begging to be written. All I needed was the gumption to interview a man carrying a bomb. 'What put you up to this?' I asked sympathetically, as he zipped up and reslung his bag. 'You look a decent sort. Did the MI5 kill your parents? Are you half Palestinian? What's your particular issue?'

'It's Google's fault.'

'Sorry?'

'Pornography isn't the only bad thing on the Internet,' he explained. 'Six months ago, my father was killed by—'

My heart raced. I was on to something: 'The CIA? Microsoft? Was that why . . . ?'

He watched me warily. 'Are you a communist or something? He was killed by a heart attack. It was right after he went bankrupt.'

'Oh. I'm sorry.'

'Don't be. We disliked each other, but at least he paid my uni fees till the end, even when I went a little off-schedule . . .'

'How "off-schedule" were you?'

'Let me put it this way, I was never going to graduate, all right? But I rather liked the student lifestyle—'

'Do you mind if I just get the facts straight? How many extra months had you, sort of, logged?'

He glared. 'Five extra years. Happy now?'

'Sorry, we writers sometimes have to be journalistic in our research.'

'So I was really feeling depressed, you understand, when I had to pull out of uni. I had no skills, no degree, no sponsor. That afternoon in the library, I googled *suicide.*'

'*Suicide?*' I blinked. 'What skills do you need to be a waiter? Did you have terminal cancer as well?'

'I was depressed and broke, all right? Anyway, I just wanted to check out my options, really. I already knew some painless ways to die, but I googled *enjoyable* and ended up on a website recruiting suicide bombers.'

'I wouldn't have put "enjoyable" and "suicide bomb" in the same sentence.'

'Well, they were paying ten thousand quid for a suicide bomber.' He patted his clothes, searching for something. 'That's plenty of enjoyment right there.'

'What is this website? Who are these people?'

'*What! Who!* Give me a break! It's just another NGO attracting more funding than they can spend. They've been in the suicide bombing business for years. They've blown up all their permanent staff—apart from the top dogs of course . . .'

'Since when did terrorist squads become NGOs?'

'Don't be simplistic. Not all suicide bombers are terrorists. This NGO is at the cutting edge of the anti–global warming lobby.'

'*What?*'

'Their carbon-footprint reduction strategy is depopulation. It's a more aggressive variation of Planned Parenthood. Not saying I buy their politics, mark you, but that's the law for you, *audi alteram partem.*'

He finally found his wallet after searching the multiple pockets on his combat trousers. He opened it. Although bereft of currency notes, he had to negotiate a drift of VAT receipts and ATM slips to extricate a weathered A4 flyer folded several times over. 'They had a backlog of volunteers. Had to wait months and months for my slot . . .'

'A *queue?*' Every time Dalminda opened his mouth he seemed to take another flight of fancy. The only thing that kept his story rooted in real life, and me listening as well, was the weight of his bomb. 'That is, a queue of people wanting to kill themselves?'

'I know how it sounds,' he conceded, 'but their conditions of service are out of this world.'

I was silent. I supposed he was now mocking me recklessly, but I knew that Lynn would go into raptures at the direction of our conversation. I wondered how it would look if I produced my Dictaphone.

'I'll tell you one of their recruitment stories: so this fellow and his family had been oppressed and exploited for generations. His—'

'How? Was he detained without trial? Were they tortured and deported—?'

'No.' He had laid the matted sheet on the counter, and his tongue crept out from the corner of his mouth as he applied himself to the task of opening it up without ripping it.

'Well?'

'They were poor.'

He was not looking, and I rolled my eyes. Halfway to the ceiling, they were snagged by the eyes of an old major in a portrait, a whiskered fellow who looked every inch as bewildered as I was at the goings-on in his short let.

'Anyway, he was married with seven children, all under ten years old, and then he had to get prostrate cancer as well.'

'Oh.'

'So this chap had three months to live when he stumbled on the website and signed on. Guess what. He blew himself up two months before he was due to die anyway, but his widow now gets a monthly pension; his kids are on scholarship. They now have a chance to break out of the oppression, the exploita—'

'How many kids do *you* have?'

He shrugged. 'None, yet.'

'Are you married?'

'No!'

'So what will you do with ten thousand pounds when you're dead?'

Smugly, he said, 'I've spent it already.'

'You've lost me.'

'You can take your money a month in advance before blowing yourself up in a crowd.' He pushed the sheet across to me. 'I have to make sure a journalist gets this *after* the blast. Can you send it out for me?'

I looked at the tattered flyer. It was issued by an ineptly named Radical Suicide Society of Global Warming Justice Phenomena. The first ten lines were an inane sort of propaganda, but my eyes fell on the bottom two lines, which were handwritten. It was the address of the corner shop down the street. It had a courtyard covered by what was probably the only CCTV camera in the village, and I had taken to parking my car there every night for the past two weeks. I folded the flyer quickly.

My insurance specifically excluded explosions—and the car financing was so new I hadn't started repaying it.

'Um . . .'

'You've got to be quick, though; there are many cash-strapped suicide squads that go around claiming the bombs of other NGOs—'

'Can we stop calling them NGOs?'

'Choose any newspaper or TV station of your choice—you can make yourself a bob or two, you know?'

'You look like you're over your depression,' I said brusquely. 'Why don't you just dump the bomb in the sea and split. The world is a big place; they'll never find you.'

'They have this Deposit-Security Programme. You should read it . . .'

'Perhaps you can give me a summary.'

'It's genius. They checked me into this clinic and put me under. They put a chip the size of a grain of rice inside me. Its biodegradable battery is invisible to X-rays and guaranteed to run for one year. Using me as an antenna, it broadcasts my location to their hub from anywhere I am in the world.' He studied his fingernails, 'They know I'm standing in your kitchen right now.'

'Why don't you take it out?' I asked, not liking the pitch of my voice. I had a sudden vision of a chip-seeking missile crashing through the window.

He ran his hand through his hair. 'That's the point. It could be in my bladder or my scalp. I have no idea.'

'If I were you,' I said, trying to provoke some common sense in the youth in front of me, 'no one could force me to detonate a suicide bomb. Think about it: the worst they can do is kill you . . .'

'Their Suicide Enforcement Team is—'

'*Please!*' I snapped. Even Lynn would not swallow *that*.

'Without that they'd be broke now, Mister Chew,' he explained patiently. 'People would just take their money and run. I know *I* would.'

'Chow?' I suggested sarcastically. It was the simplest of names.

'Thanks, but I'm full.'

'Humphrey *Chow!*'

'That's what I said, God. It's just a bloody name. Their S.E. teams abduct runaways and . . .' He hesitated before going on. 'I'll spare you the details, but personally I'd rather go with a bang than a saw.'

'Are you . . .' I cleared my throat. 'Are you still within your month of grace?'

He shook his head. 'I ran out of time and money yesterday, and they've e-mailed me the red notice. An S.E. team could be here tomorrow. I can run, but I can't hide—unless I'm arrested. I'll be safe enough in Her Majesty's Prisons.' He paused. 'Either that or I bomb the corner shop.'

'I can call the police for you,' I offered.

'That's kind of you, but this country is too damned soft. I have no prior convictions, and the best I'll get for breaking and entering will be community service.' He glared. 'This is your fault! Any other man who finds a bearded stranger in his bed would have thrown a punch, at the very least! There'd have been a major fracas yesterday—aggravated assault and battery, possibly with grievous bodily harm. By now I should have been enjoying police protection!' He sneered. '*Tea in bed!*'

The image of the chip-seeking missile had receded somewhat. In its place flared a new vision of bearded Suicide Enforcers abducting us . . . torture chambers in a dark dungeon . . . and offbeat short stories flapping inside my head like possessed bats seeking escape, but my sawn-off arms were bandaged stumps that ended at the elbows. I looked wildly around the room. 'You could break something expensive. You could . . .'

He shook his head. 'Property damage is strictly small beans. With my law school tragedy I'll probably get a suspended sentence or a month in the can. What's that? I need a year in prison. They can't track me after that. I'd rather go with a bang today than—'

'Does it have to be the corner shop? Never heard of a suicide bomber taking out a corner shop.'

He paused. 'Are you suggesting a Tesco? Whose side are you on anyway?'

'Why *this* particular shop? It's out in the middle of nowhere . . .'

He scowled. 'The owner was rude yesterday. Said I stank of fried chicken. I'll show her fried chicken!'

'That's hardly an offence worthy of the death sentence . . .'

'She's the nearest person I have a grudge against . . . unless—' He broke off and eyed me speculatively.

'Oh, come on!'

He shrugged magnanimously and turned for the door, 'Au revoir, then. I'll hang around for five or six customers and—'

'I normally park my car outside the shop,' I said casually. 'It's normally the safest place in the neighbourhood. Joyriders . . .'

He turned slowly, venting a diseased talent for melodrama. 'Your *car*? How can you think of a *car* at a time like this?'

'You dare to preach to me? *You* are blowing up corner shops for *cash!*'

'So what do you suggest?' he asked, reaching for his cord. 'Should I blow myself up here?'

I watched his hand silently.

I have not always been this timid. One winter when I was fourteen, I attempted the murder of a Queen's Counsel. I had found his name in a Hackney Social Services cabinet into which I had broken in search of the identity of my natural parents. Louis Raven, QC, retired, had signed me into care, and he seemed chief suspect for the role of Bolting Dad. I traced him to his golf club on Rounds Street. I watched him all day, following him four blocks to Poplar, where he lunched with three suits. Afterwards, we both walked back to the club; the one was well-fed, the other—following twelve anonymous paces behind—very, very, hungry. He drank till late. That afternoon when I went to confront my father I did not have a plan. By that evening, I had come to picture how different my life might have been, and it became quite clear what I had to do. I suppose the hunger was a factor. I didn't even have enough money for a knife—I slipped one off the shelf of a hardware store on Poplar East. When he left his club it was 7:00 p.m. and dark, and as he dumped his golf clubs in the boot, I approached. As he opened his Porsche he felt the point of my knife in his side and drove thirty minutes, talking all the way. He was a barrister, all right: eight inches from a painful death and he couldn't stop talking. I guess that blade kind of inspired him into the performance of his life. He slowed down along Old Kent Road, and I stepped out of the car. He still has the £7.89 knife that I got for free—and the contents of the wallet that he spilled desperately into my lap. Sometimes I wonder whether he was just a gifted liar or whether my arrival in the maternity with Negroid features truly had dissolved the marriage of his Caucasian clients, my 'legal' parents, Felix and Laura Fraser. I've never bothered to look for *them*. They can go to Hell—along with the adulterer who supplied my Negroid genes.

ZANDA ATTURK

Kreektown | 15th March, 2005

I got lost on my way back, which was ridiculous because I had spent the first eighteen years of my life in Kreektown. I was thinking too hard on my future, or the lack of it, and when the horse stopped moving I realised he was knee-deep in a swamp. I spent the next few minutes kicking and cursing, but the animal was quite frozen with fear. So I climbed down into the viscous mud myself, and the horse turned readily enough to follow me. We finally gained solid ground, the horse and I and the stink between us. The light was beginning to fail. As the shadows lengthened in the forest, my fear grew.

I heard the village called Kreektown before I saw it and followed the highlife music that led me to Ntupong's Joint, the only saloon left in the village square. It was a dramatic village surrounded by an encroaching forest. One moment I was under the canopy of trees, the next I was walking down a street of mostly empty homes where the industry of barefoot life moved in sync with the economy of mobile phones. One moment I was dragging my horse down the footpath, past a length of python curing on a grill, the next I was in a depleted village square, two hundred metres across. The earth under me was packed hard enough for cars. The roads were wide enough for cars, but all around Kreektown, the mechanicals that proliferated were motorbikes. I crossed the square where a noisy generator powered a football viewing centre. Next door, a motorbike repairer was hard at work.

The joint was just across the square. Recently, I had watched Kiri Ntupong's TV testimony at the Justice Omakasa Enquiry into the Menai Inoculation. Despite my straits, I couldn't help smiling at the prospect of seeing the old man after so many years.

He had died the week before.

I stood in the doorway, a little stunned at the news. I did not recognise the large woman who was now weeping all over again. There were only four patrons in the large parlour. Wedged around a table, they were locked in an intense game of cards. We shook hands solemnly, and one of them, a garrulous raconteur, gave me his business card. He was bearded and defiant with it. I looked at the card, puzzled. 'Hameed . . . are you supposed to do this?'

'Do what?'

'Give people cards saying you're a *secret service* agent?'

'Don't worry yourself about that. What about my boss that posted me to a village as small as this? Am I supposed to pretend to be a farmer or what?'

I turned the card over. 'This is not very . . . *secret.*'

'Is the best way,' he assured me. 'Do you know how many oil worker kidnapping cases I've solved from this very chair?' His companions nodded their corroboration as they watched him deal the pack. 'So if you hear any coup plots or secession talk, just call my Nokia, there's cool money there for you, eh?' He yelled, 'Woman! Ntupong don chop im own life finish! Wey my peppersoup?'

She wiped her tears brightly. 'Is coming, my oga!'

He gave me a 'one Nigeria' sign, a twining index and middle finger, and returned to his game.

I stepped back into the square and stared. The houses were familiar, but the faces were not. A decade had swept past like a century, and the last of the Menai were dispersed. I paused just outside the kamira, listening to the scary silence of the weavers' guild house. I had grown up to the hypnotic *chakata-chakata* of the looms. I pushed the door open, and it fell, hingeless, into the abandoned yard. A sigh of dust rose regretfully. A goat stared from a sill. Several jamayas sat in a weavers' circle, as though their owners were holding a guild meeting in an inner room and would soon return to the looms.

I walked on. Strangers lived here now, had moved into the empty homes: Sonja's shop was now Fati's 'International' Stores, Solo's Chemist was now a card recharge shop, and in Kreektown Square, instead of the Mata's beloved Menai, all I could hear were snatches of pidgin English, a curse in Sontik, and an argument in Nnewi-accented Igbo. I stood in Kreektown Square, where I had dropped my shoeshine box on December 9, 1998, to catch the ferry to Onitsha and the world. I knew no one here, now.

And no one knew me.

Instead, there was new resentment in the Kreektown air. People came here because they had nowhere else to go. Across Sontik State there was talk of secession. Indigenes of the new Sontik Republic would, with all her oil, immediately rocket to the highest per capita income in Africa. But no one would think it, to judge from the wretched eyes that followed me as I led my lame horse towards Ma'Calico's. A low-grade malice tinged the eyes that looked at me, who drove a twenty-year-old banger into town: I had another place to go after my business with the Kreektown smuggler. As I turned into Ma'Calico's yard, I felt that jailhouse grudge sink into me.

I couldn't leave, either.

It wasn't an attack of conscience because I had abandoned my doomed hometown. It was the prospect of a police interrogation. Patrick and I shared a mutual dislike for each other, but I needed his job as much as he did the only *Palaver* journalist who had ever won a Reporter-of-the-Year award. I was a difficult journalist to sack, despite my touted truancies, but after being conned by Korba Adevo, I was not going to be saved by all the awards in the Nigerian Union of Journalists.

A young woman leaned against the doorway at Ma'Calico's, eating an avocado. She was lean and angular. Her slow eyes followed me with a python's lazy grace. I remembered her bruising brazenness from when I had passed through earlier. Now, she was also wearing blood-red lipstick. 'You wan' room?' she asked with a winning smile. I supposed it was the pattern: thieves took their loot up to Adevo's for cash and the locals tried to retain as much of the proceeds for the local economy as they could.

'I'm sorry,' I told her politely. 'I don't do prostitutes.'

There was a momentary blankness, as though the sense of the words had eluded her at its first pass before boomeranging into the sacristy of her mind. Then she doubled over with the violence of a retch and laughed so hard that tears grew like translucent, animated tendrils down her cheeks. I watched her half-eaten avocado roll away in the dust. Thinking back, I suppose I was still in shock and thoughts that would normally have stopped at that were now popping through before I could rephrase them. Her blood-red fingernails gripped thighs that had locked on themselves, the way children often clamped their bladders while they rolled one more die of an addictive game. Her laughter was stirring in its nakedness—the way she laughed with everything she had. One knee found the ground, and then she was hanging onto the door handle, which was itself hanging on to the door by precarious screws.

Briefly I wondered whether to catch her before the screws gave.

Then the doorway filled up with the bored patrons of Ma'Calico's bar, their bulbous glasses in their fists.

'Wha's that?'

'Wha's that?'

'He . . . doesn't . . . do . . . prostitutes . . . See as he dirty! Which prostitute go touch am so?'

I led the horse into the backyard, away from the ensuing bray of laughter. As I tethered it, Ma'Calico strode into the yard with my deposit in her hand. I took a deep breath and exhaled. *Kaska gai muga chamu ga choke.* I was bemused. It was many years since I had begun to think in English, and here was a Menai idiom dropping unbidden into my mind. Had to be the proximity to the village. Beyond the low fence, my car sat patiently, beside a tyreless, rust-encrusted DAF truck that wasn't going anywhere either. Ma'Calico stopped three metres from me. She sniffed and blinked rapidly. She did not share her patrons' amusement.

'My daughter says you called her prostitute.'

My jaw dropped, and I was genuinely shocked, both at the lack of resemblance between the two women and at my own recklessness. 'Your daughter? . . . but I didn't know . . . I mean, I *never* . . .'

'This is *hotel*, not *brothel*.'

'I know, *I know*,' I said earnestly.

'And Amana is a graduate. And a senior DRCD civil servant.'

'I . . . I know. I . . . I'm sorry.'

'What she said,' she enunciated carefully, as though she addressed a retard, 'was that you *smell*. We have nice hotel here where you can sleep and baf before you go. Is three thousand naira for room-and-baf. You stain my bed sheet, is another five hundred naira. Do you want or not?'

I cleared my throat. 'I want,' I said, and my deposit disappeared into her brassiere. Ma'Calico seemed as tough as the fabric she was named after. She was as broad as the bole of an iroko—and just as intransigent. She made her change from the cash register of a bosom that seemed designed for commerce rather than that alien concatenation of lust and paediatric nourishment. She radiated confidence, and she gloved it with an arrogance that stemmed not just from the fact that she was the monopoly supplier of short-time and long-term beds for twenty kilometres in every direction but from the certainty that, were you the kickboxing and kung fu champion of all Nigeria, she was ready for you.

She sneered—and at that point, it seemed a biological impossibility that she was the mother of the slip of a woman whose strangled laughter was still gurgling from the front of the yard—and said, 'And if you touch my daughter, I kill you.'

'I don't do feckless girls, either,' I told her horse, long after she was gone.

MAJOR BELINJA

Lagos | 15th March, 2005

They met up in Lagos, at a private guest house in old Ikoyi. The house was an intricately gabled structure set in the rear half of a mandarin garden. From outside, nothing about the house distinguished it from neighbouring properties. Major Belinja's car nosed through the leafy driveway and came to a halt beyond the carport. The muted birdcalls from an aviary filtered down to the four soldiers in mufti.

They had spent their years at the Defence Academy jousting for the top position. In their military careers, their rivalry had not diminished, although now it was overcast by a pall of disillusionment. They were in the wrong decade, in the wrong century to be soldiers. Lamikan, for instance, had graduated with the best degree the Defence Academy had awarded in its twenty-nine-year history. He was still thirty-five, but at his age in the '60s Yakubu Gowon had already been head of state for several years.

They were in their prime, but the year was 2005 and the environment was no longer amenable to military governments. After the calamities of the Babangida and Abacha regimes, Nigerians were not going to cry out for military interventions, no matter what a hash civilians made of things. And they were making such a hash of things! There was a surliness in the young military, a sense of loss that only Belinja seemed to have escaped. Although he was the most junior in rank among them, he had become the most powerful, for he was a major in military intelligence. In a realm where titles were irrelevant, he had created—and controlled—the most subversive information database in Nigerian history. Even his bosses feared him, and he would have been redeployed long before but for fears—not wholly unfounded—that his most critical data were stored on private servers, and sacking him would be a licence to fully privatise the resource.

The hallway of the guest house was similarly unexceptional. Belinja hung back from the door and disappeared into a side entrance. Tanko, Ofo, and Lamikan looked warily around as they entered the high-ceilinged lounge. A buffet table was laid out for a small feast, and a Japanese chef brought a platter of skewered meat, which he set down to complete the tempting collage of dishes. He fiddled with a tabletop heater and then disappeared discreetly, without acknowledging the presence of the soldiers.

Belinja reappeared before his colleagues had a chance to get uncomfortable. He approached the cocktail table. 'Gentlemen, food is served.'

'And this is the meeting that will change my life?' asked Ofo as Belinja began to fill a saucer with food.

'You can start by changing your waistline.' Belinja's joke sounded forced, but alongside the logic of the buffet, it did get the others to join him at the table.

'Who owns this place?' Tanko asked as he poured himself a glass of iced zobo.

'I do,' said a voice from behind him. They turned around for their first sight of Penaka Lee. He was a wisp of a man, only marginally taller than Belinja, but his handshake, when it came, was almost as firm as his gaze. 'Sorry I couldn't receive you at the door. I spend most of my time on the phone.' He was grinning, accentuating his vaguely Asiatic features.

Belinja performed the introductions, but when it was all over Tanko continued to hold Penaka's hand. 'I usually don't like to eat the food of someone I don't know.'

'Nigerians have peculiar customs,' agreed Penaka Lee, tapping a finger on Tanko's chest. He seemed comfortable with his hand in the other man's grasp and steered Tanko easily to the drinks cabinet, where the soldier finally surrendered it.

'It's a sensible custom,' said Lamikan. 'Otherwise, you might finish a meal only to find that you can't afford it.'

Penaka Lee bowed marginally from behind the cabinet. He lined up some flutes. 'You have my assurances that this meal is completely free.' He raised a bottle of champagne and, when he got some nods, began to pour.

He passed a glass to Lamikan. 'I hear you are a champion squash player. What's your next target? The world championships?'

'My competition days are over; I'm thirty-five.'

'Really? You've got young genes! Will you stay on in the force—after your commission?'

Lamikan's eyes narrowed. He glanced at Belinja. 'I don't discuss my military career publicly.'

Belinja laughed uneasily, but Penaka's half smile did not waver. Ofo asked softly, into the strained silence, 'Who is Penaka Lee?'

The half smile broadened, and Penaka continued without any embarrassment. 'That can be a complicated question. This morning, for instance, I was reviewing my property holdings. I hold . . . quite a few assets in bricks and mortar.'

'I'd say that makes you a landlord,' said Tanko.

'And you'd be wrong,' replied Penaka. He selected a glass of champagne, turned, and headed for the room at the end of the lounge. The men took their drinks and followed, Belinja bringing up the rear. They entered a larger room, furnished like a gallery. A visually overpowering skyscape filled one wall. It was an oil painting, but it didn't seem that way at all—it seemed more like they had stepped into a room cut into a mountainside and now looked out onto a sky of incredible intensity and vividness. Penaka chuckled as he heard the intakes of breath behind him. He turned and was not disappointed by what he observed. For several seconds there was no sound in the room as the soldiers drank in the spectacle. The first dimension of its wonder was the size: the canvas was stretched over the entire wall. Then there was the sheer detail of it: one could stand close enough to inspect the feathers of the soaring kites, or stand as far back as possible, to experience the breadth of such a limitless horizon in what was, after all, a room. And then there was the magic of the colours, jumping the gap from beauty into masterpiece.

'I see you like *Open Heavens*,' said Penaka. 'If I told you I owned a couple of paintings in Nigeria it would have been just a statistic, but if I showed you one such as this, you'd feel it through your pores, won't you? It would no longer be a matter of a *number* on an *inventory*. It becomes a matter of superlatives, of scale.' He sipped delicately. 'My friends, I am a *collector*.'

'You collect paintings?' asked Ofo, stroking the rough finish of the oil on the canvas, giving the other man another cause for laughter.

'Paintings!' snorted Penaka. 'These are toys—houses, boats, aircraft— these are all hobbies. We—the club I lead—collect countries; that's my real profession.'

There was polite silence in the room. *'Countries?'* said Tanko eventually. 'Are we talking South Pacific island countries here? Hundred miles by hundred? Ten thousand population?'

Penaka managed to look insulted without letting his smile slip. 'This is not a joke, please; this is business. I'm not talking about holiday islands. I'm talking about *real* countries here. Argentina- Nigeria-size countries.'

'Oh,' said Lamikan with the dawning of understanding. 'You mean the old CIA style of getting some Idi Amin–type sergeant to bump off his bosses and take over government? Is that why we're here?'

Penaka laughed heartily and congratulated Belinja: 'Your friend is funny!' Then he said, stressing his point with firm jabs on Lamikan's chest. 'We are businessmen; we *never* do anything illegal. What we do is done at primitive levels all over the world. In Washington, lobbyists make careers of trying to influence lawmakers one way or the other.' He cranked up his grin. 'We make a success of it.'

'So you are a lobbyist?'

'In the sense that *Open Heavens* is a painting, yes. Listen, a lobbyist can deliver a senator's vote on a particular bill. I can take a particular bill—or policy, or appointment—*and deliver it*. In a dozen countries at the same time. It is a matter of the level of influence my club can deliver. We take the long view. Sometimes all we do is identify people with leadership potential in a country and build with them, sometimes over a decade. And I don't like to boast, but considering the state of our collection right now, I must say we have developed a knack for backing the right horses.'

'Or mules,' muttered Lamikan into his glass. A chill fell on the room. 'During the Orkar coup, there was a rumour of a foreign coup plotter who escaped Nigeria in the boot of a car.'

Penaka's champagne hand trembled. 'Rumours, stories, the revenge of the powerless against the powerful.'

Tanko cleared his throat. 'What you are talking about is like . . . developing connections.'

'Not connections,' insisted Penaka quietly. *'Collections.'*

'So,' said Ofo, gesturing at a political map of the world on the wall opposite the skyscape. 'How many countries are in your collection right now?'

'If you're talking connections like Tanko, there's nowhere in the world where we have none. But if you're talking *collections*—' He grinned coyly. 'Well, like my friend Lamikan suggested, there are some things that are better not said in public.'

'I see . . .' Lamikan took a deep breath and glanced pointedly at his watch.

'What's your nationality?' asked Tanko.

'Patriotism is an outdated concept. I hold a couple of passports of convenience, speak eight languages, and pay *some* tax in nine jurisdictions.'

'If patriotism is outdated, what have you replaced it with?'

'Capitalism is inconsistent with patriotism; otherwise there'd be no such thing as a tax haven. Business transcends borders. If countries can own people, why not the other way round?' He thumbed off a ringing phone. 'The most patriotic thing you can do for your country is to be very rich! Taxes win wars!'

They talked a while longer. Lamikan had fallen silent, glancing at his watch every now and then. Finally, Belinja took the hint and made their apologies. Penaka's invitation, when it came, was almost too casual: 'Some of my club members are in town for the week, and I'm giving them a dinner soon.' He waved a derisory hand to indicate his pièce de résistance: 'This painting is nothing. If they like you, you might get an invitation into the most select club in the world.'

Tanko took Penaka's hand in a farewell handshake and retained it once again. 'Let me ask you a straight question, Mister Penaka: are you planning a coup?'

'I'll give you a straight answer, my friend: I'm not crazy.'

'That's not a straight answer.'

'Touché.' He nodded. 'Look, imagine a hundred power brokers from all over the world with a hundred unique contacts each, *all in one club.* That gives every single power broker access to a hundred thousand quality contacts worldwide. That's my idea of a coup. Only it's no longer an idea. *You* can call up your president on the phone. Imagine that with me as a telephone exchange you have that kind of access to one hundred presidents. That's my coup, friends. Totally legit.'

◆ ◆ ◆

SOON AFTER, Penaka was on the patio, seeing off his guests. The soldiers were almost at the car, but Penaka hung back with Belinja until the rest were out of earshot. His smile was still intact as he said, 'That Lamikan, I don't want him back.'

'He's Obu's security adviser,' Belinja argued. 'He's critical—'

'He's out.' Penaka pushed his finger into Belinja's shoulder and repeated, 'Out.' He looked past Belinja to the soldiers talking by the car.

'Ofo is an interesting character, though. You do take risks, don't you? M.A. to the head of state. What more can he want?'

'He thinks his boss is sleeping with his wife. Guess who put that silly idea in his head?'

'Say no more, Belinja.' Penaka Lee grinned as he walked with the major toward the car. 'You're a genius with your database.'

'Thanks. When are you seeing the Sontik governor?'

'I have a plane waiting to take me to Ubesia.'

At the car, he looked at Ofo and said, 'Belinja tells me you used to write poetry at the Defence Academy.'

'Still do.'

'Who's your favourite American poet?'

'I'd say Robert Frost.'

'Give me a poem,' said Penaka. 'Any poem.'

Ofo shrugged. '"Fire and Ice."'

'Okay. I'll give you a treat from the mouth of the American president. He's scheduled to address an Island Nations conference next month. Tune in to that speech on CNN; I'll give you a practical demonstration of my skills as a presidential ventriloquist.'

Ofo kept a polite smile on his face, but as soon as they drove through the gate, he shook his head and joined in the general laughter. Belinja alone was silent.

HUMPHREY CHOW

Lower Largo, Scotland | 15th March, 2005

'I think I have a solution,' I said quietly. 'What if you refunded their money?'

'I have a cash flow situation here,' he replied.

'Let's say you refunded it; would they still come after you?'

'Of course not; it's a bloody business. Once their books balance, we're quits.' His eyes widened. 'You'll write me a ten-thousand-quid cheque?'

I had to smile at that. The week before, Grace had cut out a job advert for a dog walker and left it on my laptop. I raised my hands. 'Not so fast. I am a short story writer. I'm sure my agent can get me a decent advance on the basis of your story.'

'You'll do this? Just to save your banger?'

'Not to talk of the innocent people you planned to kill.'

The sarcasm washed over him. 'How quickly can you raise it?'

'You'll have to keep running for a few more days, if that's what you mean.'

He looked at me suspiciously. 'You can get an advance of up to ten thousand?'

'Sure,' I replied bravely.

He continued to look me up and down. 'Are you any good? I never heard the name "Humphrey Chung" before.'

'*Chow!*' I moved in polite circles where people snapped their fingers and claimed to recognize my name whenever I introduced myself as a writer, although I was sensible enough never to ask which of my stories they had read.

'Have you actually *published?* Never heard of a Humphrey Chan . . . of your Humphrey before.'

'Yes.' He was going to persist, so I continued, 'But then again, nine years of grappling with law exams doesn't leave much extra time for fiction, does it?'

'But are you any good?' he pressed on, refusing to be insulted. 'How fast can you write it?'

I shrugged. 'If I'm flowing, three to four hours.'

He stared at me suspiciously. 'If it was so easy to make ten thousand bucks, we'd all be writing stories, wouldn't we?'

'And passing law exams as well,' I suggested, 'but then you also need hard work and intelligence, talent and . . .'

His nostrils flared as he shrugged off his rucksack. His face was flushed: I had overdone the sarcasm. I hoped it would be a punch rather than an explosion, but he was only trembling with a renewed greed for life. 'This bomb pack costs another five hundred pounds,' he wheedled. 'I could destroy it. Will you pay for that as well? That would help with my train fare to Lee . . . back home . . .'

I shrugged noncommittally.

It was good enough for him.

◆ ◆ ◆

'I GET the general point,' I said, stopping him a mere half hour into the story of his life, which seemed an endless succession of drunken nights, vindictive law professors, and stinkers written to his hapless dad. I switched off my Dictaphone and switched on my laptop. We both stared at the blank Word page for several minutes. I cleared my throat. 'Ah . . . there's a TV upstairs. Should be more interesting . . .'

He studied me suspiciously. He had found a comb in one of his combat pockets and was grooming his beard. 'You write better alone, eh?'

'Yes.'

'War correspondents manage to write well enough with bombs exploding around them . . .'

'But then again, I'm not a journalist.'

'You said writers were like journalists.'

'In our pursuit of facts, not in our writing style. Newspapers are read for a day. My short stories will still be read a hundred years from today.'

He muttered something inaudible into his beard. I chose not to seek clarification. Eventually, he said, 'Can I see any of your books?'

'Don't have any here.'

'You're ashamed of your stuff, aren't you? I know this guy . . .'

Mentally I rolled my eyes. 'Only new writers carry their books around.'

'How can I trust you to write my story if I've never read one of your books?'

'You'll never read anything else either if you don't stop pestering me! Your killers are probably circling the airport right now!'

He rose with alacrity. 'Fine, I'm going upstairs. But I'm trusting you with my reputation.'

'Not to mention your life,' I muttered.

'Don't write me into a monster. Even terrorists are getting good press just now. That Bantu vigilante in Nigeria, he's all over BBC, isn't he, and it's not all bad. I'm just a regular law student who suffered a depression. D'you know how many students break down every year?'

Frankly, I said to myself, I don't give a hoot.

'And don't forget it was *my* idea to disable the bomb,' he added, jabbing at my laptop. 'Write that in as well.'

I ignored him, and he finally got the message. He turned to go, reaching for the rucksack. 'Leave that!' I said, too stridently.

'Why?'

'I need it . . . for inspiration.'

He hesitated, but I did not blink. Unless the bomb was with me, I was just going to spend all day worrying that a lunatic was about to blow me up. He shrugged and left the rucksack. Halfway up the stairs, he paused and started descending again. I steeled myself to argue some more over the custody of his bomb, but he had something else on his mind.

'Could my short story get more? Say, twenty thousand pounds?'

I frowned at his choice of pronoun. I phrased my response carefully, repossessing my intellectual property. '*My* stories have earned substantial sums before,' I said airily.

'I want half of every penny over ten thousand five hundred pounds,' he said peremptorily. 'That's my final offer.' Then he turned and went upstairs.

I thought that for a student who had spent nine years retaking law courses he was demonstrating a monumental ignorance of the basics of offer and acceptance. Still, this was not the time to quarrel over speculative royalties. Moments later, the TV went on upstairs and Spiderman, Batman, or some other rodent-human began to save the world at a disconcertingly high volume. Ten minutes later, I was still staring at a blank Word page.

It dawned on me that the possession of the bomb alone was enough to give Dalminda his year's vacation in jail. If he didn't realise that, then it was no wonder he kept flunking his law exams. My hand reached for the phone. This way, Lynn would still get her offbeat story while I got to keep all my hard-earned royalties.

Only one thing stopped me: the possibility that the police might well arrive and be unable to see either the suicide bomber or his bomb. I walked over to the bomb, unzipped the rucksack, touched it. It was there all right. And yet . . .

Rubiesu simini randa si kwemka!

I set my computer on my lap and started tapping away. I was Humphrey Chow after all, short story writer. Even if no one else saw the bomber, everyone should read his story. Upstairs, a bomb exploded on TV and I jerked, sending the laptop to the floor. Its screen winked off as its battery scooted halfway across the room. I retrieved it and put it back in with trembling fingers, then tried powering on the laptop. Nervously I watched it boot up. It seemed to remember all I had written. If this was a hallucination, the computer was hardwired into it as well. I began to write. Desperately. Lynn was going to have to change her taste in short stories. Or I'd have to take Grace's advice and interview for the dog-walker job.

PENAKA LEE

Ubesia | 15th March, 2005

'I don't want to start a war,' wheezed the obese governor.

'There'll be no war,' said Penaka Lee confidently, raising his voice over the tumult of rain.

Governor Obu pushed away his trolley of files and clasped his hands behind his head. They were alone on the veranda of the Governor's Lodge in Ubesia. The only other human in sight was the gardener bent double over a flower bed, labouring in the rain in an obsequious show that was lost on the distracted governor. The first lady of Sontik State was away in the federal capital on her minorities rights campaign, but the power of her presence was such that Penaka half expected to see her striding out onto the veranda. Sonia Obu was conscientious and charismatic—an electoral asset for any candidate—but her husband had been elected twice and had run out of electoral options. He needed other kinds of assets, like Penaka's pragmatic ruthlessness, to stay in power.

'There'll be no war,' Penaka repeated, speaking with a confidence that came from decades of successful deal-making.

'You'll say that, won't you?' The politician tipped his weight backwards until the front legs of his raffia chair left the ground. He stopped pushing back when he put his body in same precarious position as the rest of his life. 'But you can't guarantee it. Despite all the promises from your men in black, in the end, nobody can guarantee it.'

'There are no guarantees in this business, Your Excellency. But Washington doesn't want war in this delta. Every shell that falls in Ubesia will add ten cents to the price of gas in New York.'

'The Biafra War killed millions. I don't want to be responsible for another civil war.'

Penaka did not reply. He could see that the sanctimonious governor was arguing with himself, working himself up to the inevitability of secession. In the end, Governor Obu would take the decision that best suited Governor Obu. Just then, it did not take much imagination to figure out what that decision had to be. In four months, Obu's second and last term as governor of Sontik State would be over, and he was not on business terms with any of the front-runners to succeed him.

One of those front runners was the deputy governor, who had refused to take his slice of the monumental heist that liquidated the Petroleum Communities Development Fund. He could not be trusted to cover Obu's back. If the governor didn't want to stand trial for the deals he had cut with his budget, he had to argue himself into a secession decision—and quickly, too. That would entitle him to another two terms as president of a new Sontik Republic. If things panned out right, that would take him to his sixty-second birthday; ten more years of presiding over the richest oil wells in Africa would give him the opportunity to create a succession plan that would cover his back. Penaka sipped his soda water slowly. He gave Obu all the time he needed.

'They're waiting for my declaration? They'll recognise us as soon as we secede?'

'Absolutely.' He hesitated. 'Your Excellency . . .'

'What?'

Penaka looked around. He wondered how much to say, for the natives could be damned sensitive. 'The Sontik traditional ruler is a strong federalist, but he's very sick. This is the time to strike, before—'

'That's no problem. The Nanga is dying, and Elder Rantan, who will replace him, is already in my pocket. The only problem is that we don't have an army.'

'Once you give me the word, Sekurizon will mobilize—'

'I don't want mercenaries . . .'

'These are *security contractors*,' said Penaka, smoothly, 'not mercenaries. I have a planeload of them standing by in Bogotá. They are more efficient than mercenaries. They *guarantee* outcomes. We have used them before, and they will train up your military in no time.'

Obu grumbled, 'Abuja will send troops. I know they will. The president has said so. I'm not afraid, but I don't want bloodshed.'

Penaka was silent.

'How long will the American destroyer wait?'

'Five days, maybe less,' lied Penaka. The US naval exercises were scheduled to run a couple of weeks, but the lie was necessary to keep the pressure on the dithering governor. 'Once you make the secession announcement, the American destroyers will move into the Bight of Benin—which will now be the Sontik Republic's territorial waters—to protect your oil rigs, which are of US strategic national interest. You are happy to sign a security agreement with the US?'

'Of course.'

'After that, Abuja will not dare move without provoking a full American invasion.'

Obu licked his lips. 'They won't dare, will they? It's just that I don't want to start a war.'

Penaka sighed. 'I'm not supposed to tell you this, but I will, just to reassure you,'

'What?'

'The three battalions that Abuja will depend on to put down the rebellion are on our side. They will march down to Sontik State okay, but they will join up at double salary. Not one shot will be fired. *There'll be no war.*'

Obu released his generous weight, and the two front legs of his chair slammed onto the veranda with a thud. His eyes were hooded with derision, and Penaka knew he had overplayed his hand.

◆ ◆ ◆

WHEN PENAKA Lee left shortly afterwards, the rain was coming down in steady sheets and the gardener had given up. A steward followed Penaka down the long pathway to the car park holding a large umbrella, but it didn't stop him getting wet.

He slipped into the back of his limousine, allowing his PA to pass the steward a crisp note through the crack between the window and the doorframe. He dried the rain from his face and hands with a handkerchief before pulling out his phone. He opened the air conditioner vents, but his hands were wet again, this time with sweat, as he dialled his intelligence contact in Abuja.

There was a short pause as Belinja's security loop kicked in. 'Hello?'

'He's not biting,' said Penaka.

There was silence.

'He's scared,' suggested Belinja. 'Maybe next week.'

'He'll never be ready. He's a coward. He doesn't believe I can deliver Nigerian battalions to the Sontik Republic.'

'Maybe I should have a word with his security adviser . . .'

'Lamikan? Well, that's a thought.' Penaka sighed. 'Leave it with me.'

'What do you have in mind?' asked Belinja, sounding apprehensive but somewhat expectant as well.

A month earlier, when Penaka had promised to put an American destroyer in the Gulf of Benin to establish his bona fides with Obu, Belinja had been quietly derisive. Two weeks afterwards, a training exercise originally scheduled for the Indian Ocean was rezoned at the last minute, and Belinja's unwillingness to take the other man on faith had evaporated.

'I'll set up a couple of meetings with some friends,' said Penaka absently, 'organise a little escalation. Do you have a newspaper publisher on your books?'

'I have all of them.'

'I want a paper with a decent circulation.'

'How about Patrick Suenu's *Palaver?*'

Penaka was indifferent. He did not read Nigerian newspapers, 'That should do. I have a story to plant. Could you . . .'

'I'll arrange it.'

'Thanks, Belinja.'

The phone went dead, and Penaka massaged his cheek muscles. He did not like ditherers. He would be fifty-five in April. He did not have all the time in the world. It was a big country; it needed big decisions. Big decision makers. And if it burned, there were fifty other countries on the continent. He lowered the partition window between him and his staff. 'Go,' he said to his chauffeur. 'Confirm our flights for Kinshasa,' he told his PA.

He had been caught on the wrong side of a Nigerian crisis before.

It was not an experience to be repeated.

SLEEPCATASTROPHES

Kreektown | January/February, 1999

Oga Somuzo
Saint John
Allotua Allegi
Renata Torila
Jani Agams
Ariz Agams
Eddi Fadamu

Births
Ogazi Kroma-Alanta

Extant Menai population: 430 (NPC estimates)

LYNN CHRISTIE

London | 16th March, 2005

'I am worried for you, Humphrey Chow,' I said.

We had the Chinatown restaurant all to ourselves. Every five minutes, a surly waiter tacked by to see whether we wanted something more. He wore an accusing frown, as though our refusal to order extra dishes was responsible for the imminent closure of his cold restaurant. My wintry blue overcoat was buttoned to my neck. But for my black boots, I might as well not have changed out of my nightdress, for all the good my clothing did me. Humphrey risked another bite of his tacos. We had managed to find a Mexican restaurant in Chinatown, and their tacos tasted more like wafers from a Chinese menu. Still, I was carrying a couple of extra kilos, so any excuse to abandon a meal after a spoonful was welcome.

'I can't think why,' he said. 'I finally write something you like and you're worried for me?' He'd dressed with his usual absentmindedness, wearing a green scarf on top of his blue flannel shirt.

I caught myself spinning my wedding band. 'Where's the suicide bomber?'

He looked up. 'It's fiction, Lynn, remember: I don't do autobiography. Anymore.'

'Why use real names? Why set the story in your holiday home?'

He shrugged. 'I'll change the names around. It just helped me visualise, you know. It was a literary device.'

'I don't want to sell it, Humphrey Chow. I don't want to show it to a publisher.'

He stopped chewing. Now *he* looked worried. 'You said you liked it. You said it trumps *Blank*.'

'It's the strongest stuff you've written yet—speaking as your agent. But speaking as your friend, it's also the most disturbing tale I've ever read.'

'Since when did the status of agent and friend become incompatible?'

'I was looking to send it to Maximus. What if he reads it and writes you a twelve-month contract to deliver a collection? What then?'

He looked away. I could tell he did not relish the pressure either. It had taken him a year to follow up on his last story, and even though he claimed to be flowing now, there was still a huge jump from making the boast to putting fifty thousand saleable words on a ream of A4 paper. My ring was spinning fifty metres an hour and rising, though that was just every-day-grade worry. 'Humphrey Chow, I'll shop your tale around . . . but keep writing!'

'Yes, ma'am.' He grinned.

'And stay fit.' I left my worry ring and nudged his greasy plate away from him. 'I want you in good shape when Grace is done with you.' I patted his hand and pulled on my gloves.

Humphrey blew a kiss. For the past six or seven months our parting shot was usually a variation of a wedding proposal, sometimes from me and sometimes from him. It was nothing to worry about, so long as no one considered it to be anything but a joke. I don't always keep it, but my policy was *take the book to bed, not the writer.*

I left him reaching for my plate.

ZANDA ATTURK

Kreektown | 18th March, 2005

I had switched off my mobile phone and spent three nights at Ma'Calico's. The deadline for my column had come and gone. I was not much of a drinker, but I spent my afternoons and evenings at the bar downstairs. I told myself I was, like Hameed the secret service agent, prospecting for information on Badu in the most practical way. Yet I was filled with despair. It couldn't be long before Patrick Suenu's posse arrived on the trail of his AWOL reporter.

A bus arrived from Ubesia carrying a group of organisers. They came with a public address system, musicians, and a sizeable crowd of their own. They took a fortifying round of beer at Ma'Calico's and set off for the square to hold a secession rally. I thought they were pretty slow on the uptake and went along to watch the fun.

They had come the day before, played their music, and made their stirring speeches—but the not-so-secret secret agent was watching from the door of Ntupong's Joint, and nobody had joined the rally. The secessionists had given up after an hour and piled, discouraged, into their buses.

The reception this time couldn't have been more different.

Amana saw me gaping at the crowd and laughed. 'Hameed left this morning. He got an urgent summons to come to Abuja for *top secret* briefings.'

'If it's top secret, how do you know?'

'I saw them faking it at the post office.'

◆ ◆ ◆

SO FAR, I had avoided investigating Kreektown with any kind of thoroughness. For one thing, I did not want to confront the condemnation of an empty Atturk house—or far worse, an Atturk house occupied by roughboys or strangers from Ubesia. I spent my days in my rented room. By early evening, the drivers and conductors from Ubesia would begin to arrive and the bar at Ma'Calico's would grow interesting enough to bring me out of my hermitage.

The butcher brought the news of the old man's death. He didn't sell much meat in that village, so he also did some palm wine rounds, which helped him stay on the cutting edge of what anaemic gossip there was in the community. But in the land of gossip the death of Mata Nimito was a table sweeper. The butcher walked into a heated argument on the virtues of local gin and announced, raising his voice above the hubbub, 'Hundredyears don die o!'

'*Hundredyears?*' I asked.

'That dead people dia chief.'

'GodMenai!' Something like remorse touched me, manifesting as a thirst for beer. 'He was still alive?'

The butcher looked at me strangely. The timing of his laughter was off. He had not sold much palm wine that day, which was bad for his sobriety; he had a firm policy of potting his wine in his belly rather than have it go sour in his kegs. He quietened and continued, 'Everyday, I use to drop one bottle for am, yesterday's own still dey dia!' He peered at me. 'So you know Hundredyears?'

Recoiling instinctively, I shook my head. 'What killed him?'

He laughed sarcastically, his careening voice inviting other villagers into the joke. 'Old man like Hundredyears die an dis one dey ask *wetin kill am!* Okay, na witch kill am!'

They laughed generously. It was the sport of the season, mocking the Stranger That Refused to Go Home.

'He's the last of the Menai, isn't he?' asked a voice behind me,

'No, there's Jonszer . . .'

'Jonszer! We're talking of people and you're counting Jonszer?'

'And there's some sick people in their Lagos camp—it won't be long . . .'

I rose and took my glass outside, away from their raucous talk. Through the open window the laughter mocked me. I felt the traitor. Jonszer was Menai like me. Now in his fifties, he would have been in his twenties when the Trevi inoculations were administered. They had not bothered to inoculate him, considering their precious vial wasted on the drunk. That mean-spiritedness had, ironically, saved his life. Not that it did him much good. A lifetime of addictions had likely addled his mind: in the last two days, he had passed me a couple of times without recognition.

As I brooded, a limousine with the number plate "Ubesia 1" pulled off the Warri-Ubesia highway, pausing ponderously at the entrance to

Ma'Calico's. On the bonnet flew the green-crested flag of the Nanga of Ubesia, traditional ruler of the Sontik people. The windows were blacked out, so there was no way of knowing if the traditional ruler was himself in the car, but as I watched, a door opened and a greying fiftyish man stepped out. I recognised Justin Bentiy immediately, cousin and right-hand man of the Nanga.

I downed the rest of my glass and returned to the saloon as Amana emerged from the freezer with a laden tray, which emptied rapidly as she approached. I took the last bottle of beer, and she raised her voice: 'Bottle number four for Reverend!' There was a cheer all round, for I was entering uncharted waters at Ma'Calico's.

Justin Bentiy entered. It was a mostly Sontik crowd in the saloon, and they recognised him immediately, greeting him respectfully. He sat with Ma'Calico by her counter and ordered a Sprite, which he drank mincingly. In his expensive damask robe, he looked out of place in that rough bar. Then he sent Amana out to the car with cold water for the Nanga. The realisation that the Nanga of Ubesia himself was in Ma'Calico's yard hushed the room. The traditional ruler had been bedridden for months. Ma'Calico rose to attend to him, but Justin Bentiy swayed his horsetail quietly and she deferred. Amana hurried out nervously. She was gone a while, and the bar room conversation stayed on the health of the ailing Nanga until she returned. Soon afterwards, Justin rose and left, his bottle barely touched.

The news of Mata Nimito's death had breached my carefully constructed distance from Kreektown. Once again I was in the circle of death and loss. Without trying, I was remembering.

I WAS orphaned.

The new Kreektown settlers were sharper than knives. I was cut, again and again, and it was to Mata Nimito, hermit cloudcaster and stargazer, that I turned.

'Kiwami ananwusu,' he had said. 'You were nurturetaught to live among the People. It's a new world now. Now, you must not put naked fingers in a crab basket.'

'How can I live in this world, Mata?'

'Practiselearn. The lesson of the crab.'

'What is that lesson, Mata?'

'Carry your truthsweetness inside; but as for the world, show them only your crabshell.'

And I blended in.

MATA NIMITO, who had no traffic with the world, the great teacher of that world; Mata Nimito, who lived all those years only to die in the week I returned . . . No one did guilt like Menai. It weighed me down now. I had been close to the old man, until I fled his circumcision blade . . .

I rose queasily and walked towards the door again. A wave of memory rode me, and suddenly I was a seventeen-year-old, in that same bar, but it was not Ma'Calico's anymore; it was Cletus's Motel, and the language was Menai, the people were Menai . . . I fled the room, fearing another vivid hallucination, stopping only on the threshold, where I gasped.

Amana was right behind me. She was dogging me too often these days. One of these days I was going to come up against the iroko of her mother. There was the usual mischief in her eyes. 'You're throwing up!'

'I'm not drunk.'

She peered into my eyes. 'But something is wrong. Right?'

I stared.

I had tried to figure her out, without much luck. She was sprite-like in many ways, liberated from the very real things that weighed people down. Her fellow villagers discounted her from the scheme of things, as though they understood that she was outside their norm. Even the dreaded rough-boys seemed to hold her in some reverence. When she scolded them, they smiled bashfully, and they brought their quarrels for her opinions. If she had a boyfriend, he did not live in Kreektown, but she did disappear behind the treeline several times a day with a variety of men who emerged, angry and frustrated, while she followed, beaming with a transcendental contentment.

That morning, she had disappeared with a woman, Fati, for the first time.

She looked right and left now and winked conspiratorially. 'This is a secret, okay? Ma'Calico will kill me if she knows.' Then she turned for the trees.

I hesitated. I had seen Ma'Calico's hands at close quarters. They were old, far older than she was: her face looked fifty but her hands were sixty. Those hands had scraped and peeled, had squashed and soaked and burned—and they had done all that in the wet and dry, in the hot and cold, in the smoky blaze. She did not boast often, that iroko, but when she did it was always about her smart Amana, who at twenty-six would still have been station manager of DRCD's Kreektown base if rioters had not burned it down the very day she arrived from Abuja to begin her posting, and Ma'Calico's eyes would soften.

Amana reached the line of trees. She turned and gestured impatiently, and the memory of Ma'Calico waned. I followed. We walked briskly into Kreektown's shroud, which could make dusk of a brilliant noon. A clump of trees. A timeless peace. The hard-packed earth softened. I followed her. I knew the land but not the lie of it any longer. A lot had changed in a decade. We walked in long shadows, but daylight held its own—which was just as well, for I loathed the dark. Then, barely three hundred metres from her mother's parlour, we arrived at Amana's redoubt. It was a long, comfortable bench in a grove with associated creature comforts, which she clearly frequented. There was no time to talk, and she straddled the bench with an urgency that telegraphed. She spread a red velvet cloth between us, pulled out her purse, and produced a deck of playing cards.

She stared as I redid my top buttons. 'What style do you prefer?' she asked guardedly.

I was breathlessly silent.

'Okay, let's play Red Bushmeat,' she volunteered. That turned out to be a variation of a card game popularised by motor-park touts across Nigeria. I was no virgin myself and determined to teach her a painful lesson. I doubled her opening stake, and we played passionately for thirty frenzied minutes. Every time I lost a game, a grunt of frustration would slip my iron control, but her delight was ever bubbling under the surface. She had quick fingers and dealt with a croupier's skill. She had eyes only for her cards. After thirty minutes I was hooked.

Although I was sweating liberally, I could have played a few more rounds, but she was the daughter of Ma'Calico all right. A seam of discipline underpinned her greed. She reined in her flushed abandon with a sigh of satisfaction and gathered up her winnings. She folded up her red velvet cloth, her purse bulging with my money, and then she fixed me calmly with perhaps the first serious look I had seen on her.

'Do you have something to tell me?' Her voice was very polished, very much the station manager's.

I stared with angry frustration.

'I can keep a secret,' she assured me.

I rose. 'I'm sure you can,' I said, still smarting from my earlier misapprehension. 'I'm a journalist; I have a burial to cover.'

'I'm going as well.'

'Why?'

She shrugged. 'He's the last of the dead people.'

It was my chance to own up, but instead I said, 'There's still Jonszer . . . and—'

'Okay, okay.' Irritably, her accent plunging from station manager to agbero, she allowed, 'Second-to-last.'

We were walking back now. As we reached the treeline, she paused. 'Honestly, I can keep a secret.'

'That's very good for you,' I told her.

◆ ◆ ◆

AT MA'CALICO'S, I went up to my room and waited for evening and the burial. When I shut my eyes, the dead Menai I had known swam in and out of my tipsy vision. I sat up and reached for *Palaver*. A trucker passing through to Warri had left his copy for me. Badu was still front-page news; this time, it was the fact that he had done nothing for all of four days. I turned to page seven. My column was gone, despite the standby pieces I always kept on file. It was replaced by a shameless pastiche of those same standby pieces by Patience from Motoring. Oddly enough, she had a picture on her new byline, a courtesy Patrick had denied me throughout the over one hundred iterations of my column. There was no chink in the paper caused by the absence of Roving Eye. The ease with which I had dropped out of my old life—and the swiftness with which I had been replaced—depressed and frightened me. I was like a stunted shrub: a couple of tugs and up came years of growth, yanked out of the soil with one hand. I had written for *Palaver* for two and a half years, but I had dropped out and that was that. I put away the newspaper. This was, after all, how I wanted it: there was no one in my life whose loss could really hurt me.

That was why I had fled Kreektown all those years ago. I closed my eyes and tried not to remember the ninth of December, 1998. Tried not to remember every wrinkle on every lost face, every accent of every lost voice . . .

◆ ◆ ◆

I WAS orphaned.

The short hawker arrived at Kreektown Square just before noon and began to set up his stall. It was the perfect timing for an entrance. The other traders had settled into their own routines. Sisi Mari's sewing machine was singing its monotone, and the middle-aged Ruma was already yawning seamlessly. By Ntupong's gin joint, I killed time with a pack of cards and a complimentary shot while I watched for a shoeshine prospect. There were hundreds of filthy shoes in Kreektown, but few of their owners were prepared to have them shined, for a fee. My business day was half gone, and I hadn't even opened my shoeshine box.

The hawker set his portmanteau carefully on the ground. At first sight there was nothing remarkable about him. He was young and slight, the sort of man a large snake might swallow and soon afterwards go hunting rats for dessert. But he did carry his portmanteau with extreme care—that was the rather remarkable thing.

A portmanteau was no novelty in Kreektown. It was the care with which it was handled that caught the eye; that, and the very idea that a petty trader's stock-in-trade was so precious as to be ferried to market not in an oily carton or mildewed sack but in a portmanteau.

Utoma stopped ogling Etie in the adjacent stall and watched the short hawker with the suspicion reserved for a rival. It would have been rather silly, carrying eggs in portmanteaus, but Utoma sold eggs; that was the thing. He had lost a kidney and half his weight in the eighteen years since his Trevi inoculation, but he was the last surviving member of the modest Egg Sellers Association of Kreektown Market, a rather lucrative position. So he turned away from Etie's cosmetics stall and glared at the hawker.

Since his arrival, the hawker had dispensed a 'good-morning' each to the traders on either side of his stall, so he couldn't very well be called arrogant.

Yet it was a close thing.

They didn't call Etie 'Man-Magnet' for nothing and she would have felt the loss of Utoma's attention immediately. She glanced towards the distraction without skipping a strand in the hair she was braiding. The sneer she'd prepared for a woman faded. When the hawker lifted his portmanteau tenderly onto a bench, her fingers grew rigid in her customer's hair. There was one calamity Etie had lived in dread of: a real cosmetologist setting up in Kreektown.

Etie was my neighbour and fellow orphan. She was six years old at the time of the Trevi inoculation and had coped well until her mother died of kidney failure and she had her first seizure.

She held no certificates, but in her small shop on Crown Prince Street she stocked a variety of nail varnishes and lipsticks—and she regularly succeeded in plaiting a hundred and fifty Bob Marley braids on Letitia's head, which was not much larger than a grapefruit. Any other village in the world would be glad for her talents, but she knew the new Kreektown girls very well. That she was Menai counted for nothing with the new Kreektowners. Any quack with the gumption to put **cosmetologist** on a signboard would kill her business. The new Kreektown didn't have enough business for two cosmetics stalls.

Kreektown's traders watched the hawker narrowly. He had a fetish for the colour red. It was the colour of his clothes, his portmanteau, and the plastic tablecloth he spread on the rack to display his goods.

That tablecloth seemed to incense Ruma. Her merchandise was the most expensive in the market, yet she laid her fabrics out, Menai weaves and ankaras, brocades—even her imported ten-thousand-naira-per-yard Hollandis—she laid them all out directly on the wooden panels of the stall. She muttered, and it was handy that there were now so few of us who spoke the tongue in the market, '**Ayamuni jakpasi!** Just who does this upstartchild think he is, to spread a red clothshrine for his stock? Is he selling gold fabric? Or did he import his own brocades from the land of ancestorsMenai?'

Eventually, the short hawker was satisfied with the symmetry of the tablecloth. He placed an envelope on it and opened the portmanteau reverently.

Even the customers sensed something momentous in the offing and loitered around the red stall. Oga Somuzo, having haggled Ma'Bamou's size forty-eight jeans right down to a desperate four hundred naira, refrained from paying—confident that a better bargain would emerge from the red portmanteau.

What did emerge was a carton, which contained a smaller package wrapped in layers and layers of old newspapers. A drift of newsprint slowly massed around the hawker's feet as he carefully unfurled the contents of the carton. The scent of camphor filled the air. Nobody was expecting the old pair of shoes that eventually stood, pompously, in the centre of the red tablecloth.

Saint John scratched his forehead. Lesser mortals could scratch their heads and armpits, but Saint John did things his own way—and frequent perplexity, coupled with his unfamiliarity with the nail clipper, had left him with a forehead more ravaged than his fifty years would have portended. 'Ezitatu?' He spluttered, 'All this potmanto palaver for the sake of one common pair of secondhand shoes?'

'That are not even polished,' I added, hinting heavily.

There was something like pity in the hawker's eyes as he glanced at us. He probably didn't see anyone worth the trouble of puffing his goods to, because without a word, he bent over and began to gather the newspapers strewn about his feet. This was probably the moment most of us decided he was a pompous little imp.

Ma'Bamou had the only secondhand clothes shop in Kreektown. She brought in her stock of okrika monthly in huge bales that travelled six hundred circuitous smugglers' kilometres from Cotonou Port in the back of Tamiyo's Peugeot. She walked mincingly over to the portmanteau with the aid of her iron walking stick. It was really empty. There was just that arrogant pair of shoes, which to her professional eyes would have seemed grade B. She sniffed, a sound balanced delicately between relief and contempt, and returned to her stall; there was no need for a word. Oga Somuzo followed heavily, clearly aware that his old bid for the jeans was history.

Yet they were the only ones who walked away. Even Etie and her customer, whose hair was half in braids and half-afro, joined the crowd around the red stall. Kreektown might have been a village, but it was no ordinary place. We were more than most towns and cities—we were **an entire nation,** the last stronghold of Menai in the world. This was certainly not so inconsequential a place that a dirty pair of shoes should cause a stir.

So it caused a stir, the very nerve of a hawker who came to Kreektown Market just to sell an old pair of shoes. To whom did he plan to sell them? Did he take the Menai for mugus? The cheek of it! We milled angrily around the stall, although there was no violence in the air. We did not manhandle idiots of any stripe, but we did know how to ridicule a fool so well that when he got home he'd look himself very well in the mirror.

'Where the rest of your market?' began Jonszer mildly enough. A knowing wink flickered in his left eye. He knew every excuse in the book. 'They steal it for bus, not so?'

'Me, I'm not a trader,' said the hawker, pulling an affidavit out of the envelope and showing it around, 'I'm the son of Doctor Nnamdi Azikiwe's former houseboy.'

This sort of boasting was new to us. It was one thing to boast about wiping a big man's toilet seats for a living. But no, this young man was far more superior than that to an ordinary trader: he was the **son** of a man who wiped a big man's toilet seats for a living.

We were going to have fun that afternoon.

Yet around me was gathering the largest crowd Kreektown had mustered in months—which had not come for a sleepcatastrophe. It was my best marketing opportunity yet: to publicly transform a lacklustre pair of shoes and remind Kreektowners that a shoe-shiner of distinction lived amongst them.

The downside to my plan was the free shoeshine for the arrogant hawker, but it would only cost a smear of polish anyway. I sat on my shoeshine box and took the left shoe.

The hawker did not notice.

'I use to know one trader's apprentice like that,' Mukaila whispered to Saint John, in a voice that carried. 'One day like that, he miss his bus at Onitsha Motor Park, and he begin to chitchat this very nice lady . . . then they branch inside hotel . . .'

'Ajajaa!'

' . . . when they finish, the apprentice try to go but she hold him by the belt. He said he thought it was girlfriend-and-boyfriend matter, she said no, it was business.'

'Who settled it?' asked Saint John, who knew the story only too well.

'Motor park touts,' replied Mukaila. 'They said they didn't know where the boy came from, but that Onitsha prostitute don't use to wear badge . . . I swear to God, that apprentice sell all his master's okrika that day, to pay the nice lady.'

'Me, I'm not an apprentice . . .' protested the hawker, over loud laughter.

'Is it that you're stranded?' asked Salif solicitously. 'How much is your bus fare?'

'If it is a matter of ordinary bus fare,' said Ajo insincerely, 'if you ask politely, is a thing of which I can easily lend you . . .'

The hawker straightened up angrily with an armful of newspapers. The retort was fully formed in his mouth when his eyes fell on his tablecloth. By this time I'd had seventy seconds with the left shoe. It was enough. I was reaching for the right shoe when the hawker screamed in horror and leapt on me.

'It's free! It's free!' I cried, trying to dodge the hawker's blows, struggling to keep possession of the right shoe. I could be as pushy a salesman as any good shoe-shiner had to be. I knew how to seize and polish shoes still on the feet of objecting owners, who sometimes paid up when their shoes were buffed; yet, months and months of shoe-shining had not prepared me for the thing with the hawker. And it was free! I had said so myself! Eventually I yielded the shoe, but by then my shirt was torn and I was lying on my side in the dust of Kreektown Square.

The short hawker was on his knees, cradling his shoes like babies. The one was shining; the other was still grey and mottled with age. His self-assurance was gone. He rocked to and fro in the dust, muttering: 'He has cleaned it away, the very dust of Independence Day!' The throng stood in mystified silence, which turned into consternation when he sniffed and wiped his eyes.

Ruma rolled her eyes knowingly and tapped her head with a discreet finger. A ripple of nods validated her judgment: the last time the staff of

Warri Asylum went on strike, this was how lunatics had turned up in the square, bearing branches for rifles, asking for the recruitment office of the Biafran Army. Our honour was safe. This was no premeditated insult to Kreektown. This was a lunatic, pure and simple. She returned to her stall. Her own illness was advancing and did not brook much standing.

The hawker squared his shoulders and rose. He returned to his stall, straightened up the askew tablecloth, and set the shoes down carefully. He shrugged manfully. 'Okay,' he told his audience, 'because of the polish, I will off five thousand naira—but that's all. Not one kobo more. Who will buy the shoes?'

A few ruffians laughed, but we stared them down. 'First of all,' called Kiri Ntupong gently from the safety of his joint, 'what makes you think your shoes are worth one thousand, even?' He cradled a snuff hand on a gnarled knee. His eyes were red and rheumy from overindulging his own brew.

'These are Doctor Nnamdi Azikiwe's shoes,' said the hawker quietly. He recovered the circulating affidavit and waved it proudly. 'The very shoes that he wore on the first of October 1960 for Nigeria's Independence. Imagine that. These shoes are older than me! They are almost forty years old! They stood next to the Queen of England, see—' And he opened up the affidavit page of a magazine picture of a youthful queen and a grinning, dashing president for those that cared to look. 'These shoes you're looking at were inside the very same room with Tafawa Balewa and Awolowo and Nanga Saul, and all those famous people . . . you can still see the very dust of Independence Day on this one . . .'

There was polite silence in Kreektown Square. The villagers knew their own history. As Nigeria's first president, Dr. Azikiwe had been central to the Independence ceremony. He was a contemporary to Nanga Saul Bentiy of the Sontik. In the dust where I sat, the photographs from my history books came to life with a trumpeting of destiny. The red tablecloth became a red carpet. The shoes standing at waist level acquired new grandeur; the hands with which I'd handled them began to tingle.

Yet, if I was star-struck, my fellow villagers were cut of more phlegmatic cloth. They did not lose their heads. That was how a classmate returned from his first geography lesson to tell his illiterate mother how Agui Creek— this same Agui we treated with such levity—was actually called River Niger way up north, how it sprung to life more than four thousand kilometres away in Fouta Djalon Mountain, how it watered five great countries and millions of people before going to pieces in our delta, fragmenting into many creeks of which the Agui that washed Kreektown was a tiny finger, and how it finally emptied into the ocean a few kilometres from where we stood. His mother, who had lived all her life by the breadth of the creek without ever having to contemplate its length, allowed her son to finish before asking, 'So? Is it now too famous for me to baf inside?'

It was Saint John who asked the pertinent question: 'So?'

The hawker's mouth dropped open. 'So? So? These are the most important shoes in Nigeria!'

'They're old fashion,' decided Mukaila. 'Me, I can never wear them.'

'You don't buy shoes like this to wear them!'

'Why should I buy shoe again, if not to wear?'

'You buy this type of shoes to keep,' explained the hawker passionately. 'These shoes are like a pension plan; you keep them inside a glass cupboard, or trunk box, with plenty of camphor . . .'

'So you're the messenger of the latest madness, eh?' said Ntupong. He had walked up to the shoes for a closer look. His trembling snuff hand granted him easy passage through the crowd, for he was given to explosive sneezes when he snuffed. He studied the shoes at length and nodded sagely. 'First I am to burn my wooden circumcisionhead, eh? Now I am to replace it with Nnamdi's shoes, eh?' He shook his head. 'Thank you very much.' He took a final pinch and dusted off his snuff palm on his baggy shorts, but as he turned toward the suddenly thinning crowd, he sneezed. The hawker flinched as the shoes acquired a little more than the dust of independence. 'Tell those who sent you that Kiri Ntupong was not at home,' he said as he returned to his shelter.

The hawker took a deep breath and began a desperate sales pitch. 'So you didn't hear about Marilyn Monroe's shoes? One pair of shoes that sold for more than thirty thousand dollars! That's millions and millions of naira! Think about that! These very shoes you're looking at are far better than Marilyn Monroe's shoes! This is Zik of Africa I'm talking about! Even, they're better than a government pension! See: it's like having History inside your house! Then one day you bring them out, maybe when you retire, and it's worth like ten million naira! Think! Ten million naira! That's like winning the lottery—except—where's the risk? No risk! You buy it cheap, and the value is only going up and up! A pair of shoes like this is better than a plot of land!'

He stopped only because he ran out of breath.

There was a long silence in which the only sound to be heard was the hawker's heavy breathing and the commotion of a hen succumbing—

with ill grace—to her cockerel. Then Sisi Mari asked politely, 'Who is this Magdalene Mari?'

'You don't even know Marilyn Monroe?' asked the hawker in a stricken voice.

'Where's the shame there?' she demanded, taking offence. 'Does she know me?' There were nods of support from her fellow, democratically inclined Kreektowners.

The hawker realised belatedly that he had travelled too far down the Niger River and had arrived at a market that time had forgotten. He sat down slowly beside his stall as the glow of the red tablecloth slowly faded.

I shared keenly in the fading glory of Azikiwe's shoes. It was difficult to come to terms with the reality of my own exploding expectations. This was not the business turnaround I had expected. This was not the life I had expected either. I had needed a renaissance so badly. The opportunity of Zik's shoes had seemed tailor-made to make me shine. Yet right before my eyes, the precious crowd was melting away—and I had not even closed a sale.

'I knew that 419 people would find the road to Kreektown one day,' said Etie to her customer as they drifted back to her stall. 'I should now sell my papahouse and buy a pair of shoes, not so?'

'But how do they hook so many people when their scams are stupid like this?'

'You should take your business to Warri,' suggested Mukaila helpfully, 'either Warri or Lagos. Lagosians are more . . .' His words tailed off into a circular, lunatic gesture around the head. Then he headed toward his canoe at the riverside.

Utoma, Ajo, and I were among the last to leave the hawker's stall. 'Lagos people copy these foolish things better than Menai people,' agreed Ajo, not unkindly. He was an undertaker drawn to Kreektown by the bonanza of death. 'If is the bus fare that you need, just say.' He slipped away before his offer could be taken up.

Sisi Mari's electric sewing machine started up, buzzing quickly around the hem of a wavy green outfit, taking advantage of the Rural Electrification Board's generator, which ran for two hours most mornings. In the distance, a passing ferry foghorned a greeting to an empty jetty as it chugged up-creek. Oga Somuzo miscalculated a haggling gambit and called Ma'Bamou a white witch. Nearby traders rushed in to save him from the angry trader's walking stick.

Utoma was still the only egg dealer in Kreektown, and his mood was more buoyant than usual. 'Shine me,' he said, as though he were doing me a favour. He owned the poultry shed by the creek, a kilometre south of Kreektown. He had fostered me for a year after my parents drowned, and his boots, which reminded me of the muddy, smelly poultry, needed me more desperately than I needed his money. He saw my face and snapped, '**Emiko sita?** So is only the shoe of dead president that you specialise?'

'It's not that,' I said sullenly, wondering, suddenly, what it was. I stared at the mud-encrusted boots, straining for the optimism that had buoyed me when the short hawker opened the 1960 vent of glory. I wavered uncertainly between my black and brown tins of polish. 'What colour was it before-before?' I asked.

Utoma frowned, unsure whether he was being mocked. 'Before-before what? I bought it brown and is still brown, boy, wha's matter with you today?'

The money he was going to pay, less than my standard charge, was already scrunched into a parsimonious fist. I saw suddenly, transcendentally, that these terms of trade were so skewed that I would never prosper here. The suspicion had been there for a while, but right then I knew I was never going to save money for university from my shoeshine box.

I rose slowly, and the shackles of the Menai obsession with corporate existence fell away from me like a spent sentence. I would no more be Long-Lived in the land of fireflies, condemned to the Weekend Walk to Burials. I would not be a shoe-shiner for people who mostly wore slippers. I'd get to know people who weren't about to die, live in a neighbourhood whose conversation didn't hinge on kidneys, where traders prospered more than undertakers. Where the knowledge of world figures could be taken for granted. A capacious grave opened up in me. Into it slithered dead and dying Menai: Utoma, Etie, Ruma, even Mata Nimito, screaming, soundless, buried once and for all. There was something for me in the world beyond the circumscribed shores of the doomed People. Perhaps a library all of whose 359 books I had not yet read. Perhaps people whose eyes were not tinged with envy—and bitterness—that I was not like them, that I was born a few months too late to be inoculated with Trevi's death.

As I brushed the dust of Kreektown off my clothes, it was as though the dust of Zik's shoes, and the inebriating spirit of 1960, had infected me with a new and grandiose vision. Utoma could keep his custom and Kreektown could shine her shoes, but I was young and independent; and I was free of the curse of Menai.

'**Emeyama?**' he asked softly in Menai. 'What's the cryingmatter, Zanda?'

'I'm not crying,' I sniffed. 'But I don't have your type of brown.'

Then I turned and left my shoeshine box, and the square. When the ferry left that evening, it left with me.

◆ ◆ ◆

I OPENED my eyes and sat up slowly. The disturbance that had roused me seemed to come from the yard: screams and Menai phrases, shouted in a voice too distorted by rage or pain to make out properly. I scrambled to the window. In that unguarded glance I took in the roof of my dad's house halfway across the village. Then I looked down and there, in the midst of the rapidly filling courtyard, saw Jonszer.

He had a bloodied dagger, and people gave him a wide berth. A length of rope was fastened to his ankle. He leapt, pranced, screamed like one demented, hacking at his body with his blade; as I stood there, open-mouthed in the window, he stopped and pointed his broad knife at me. *Miyaka sia Menai!* In that moment I saw his grief and pain. I gagged and slumped backwards until I was on the floor, leaning against the bed, the only furniture in the tiny room. I gasped. A few seconds of silence ensued, and then he resumed, his voice hoarse, unrecognisable, fading away in the direction of Kreektown Square. In moments the yard was silent, and I knew the crowd had followed him.

I sat there and watched the sky darken. When the shadows began to pool in the corners, I rose. I closed the shutters and switched on my rechargeable lamp. An hour passed before the people started to trickle back in. Their awed comments drifted up through the shutters. His voice still rang in my ears: *Miyaka sia Menai!* I hugged myself, walling myself off from condemnation. I was independent of his hopelessness and grief. I was free. I was Nigerian, not Menai. African, not Menai. And half of me was clearly not even African anyway.

Someone knocked. I did not move, willing whoever it was to go away, but she opened the door anyway and stood there, her face bereft of its residual mischief.

'He drowned himself! Just like that! They said he tied his foot to an underwater root! How's that even possible?'

'GodMenai . . .'

'Why do you keep saying that?'

I shrugged. 'What happened to Jonszer?'

'He returned from an errand in Ubesia, and some idiot at the motor park told him that Hundredyears was dead. He just went crazy.'

'They shouldn't have told him just like that!'

'Yes. The divers haven't found his body, but they're burying Hundred-years now. Are you coming?'

I wanted to sit in that room forever, but I would stick out more by staying away. I rose. It was time to bury Mata Nimito. I had fled six and a half years before to avoid this funeral, but he had waited for me.

◆ ◆ ◆

WE TOOK the low ridge, walking through the clump of raffia trees that fringed Kreektown. The village lay to the left, our abandoned farmlands to the right, with the blackened mounds where we used to smoke our fish. Beyond lay the thickets of the mangrove swamp.

'Okay,' she said. 'I'll tell you my own secrets. She's only my African mother.'

I stared, 'Really?'

She grinned, enjoying my surprise, 'She's my mother's cousin. We first met when I was posted here three years ago.'

'It's hard to believe, the way you get along. Where's your real mum?'

'Mother, not mum. Dead. Cancer.' She raised her finger, stopping my next words. 'Don't say it. She tried to kill me when I was a baby. I didn't cry when she died.' She looked at me defiantly. 'And I'd probably try to kill my own children, so I'm not having any. It's sometimes genetic, you know?'

I stared, wondering what had brought on this embarrassing level of intimacy. I tried to stem it: 'Ah, this year's harmattan is refusing to go—'

'Have I told you I've been in jail?'

My butt clenched spontaneously. 'As in . . . *prison?*'

'I did time.' She nodded cheerfully. 'One year in Kuje Prison, Abuja. But I didn't steal the money they accused me of, honest.'

'I believe you.'

'Your turn,' she said grimly.

I opened my mouth, but nothing came out. I couldn't dredge up any confidence remotely as candid as hers, but what I had, I was now compelled to share. 'I'm Menai,' I blurted finally. 'I lied when I said I was Gabonese . . . and this is my hometown.' I shut my mouth, realizing how dangerous the ambiguous company of a woman could be.

She glared at me for one long moment. 'Fine! Don't tell me! As if I care!' She stalked ahead alone.

◆ ◆ ◆

MOST PEOPLE from the new Kreektown were there, milling about, chatting, and watching the volunteer gravediggers at work. Much had changed in the enclosure: it was much smaller. There was still the old house half sunken into the soft creekside earth. There was still the elevation from which the Mata had scoured his skies, but there was also the overgrowth that had stormed right up to the perimeters of his pavilion. Yet Jonszer had clearly kept the fight up till the end: the compound itself was as clean and Spartan as I remembered. The Menai had gathered here for festivals, but the compound had yielded acreage to the forest as the population had decreased. What was left of the pavilion was an old man's house, and it was swamped now by the new Kreektowners.

He lay there, on his clay plinth, which seemed a hundred years old as well. A low, thick-thatched sun shelter stood over him, but otherwise he lay in the open, in the shroud of his red robe, as though in yet another trance. I stopped several feet from the pavilion, reluctant to go any farther. Involuntarily, I brooded on the contrast between the straitened circumstances of the Mata of the Menai and the grandeur of the Nanga of the Sontik.

If I had come the day I arrived, I would have met him alive.

A clean-shaven man with an unruly flare of grey hair walked toward the pavilion. He wore an expensive black jacket, but his sweat was plebeian enough. His eyes were intense and piercing, fixing on me from a long way off. Then he approached and offered me a handshake.

'I'm Professor David Balsam.'

Something clicked from an earlier conversation I'd overheard at Ma'Calico's, something about a harmless black British professor of history who carried around pictures of a bronze head. The locals called him Questionnaire—because he would ask silly questions until he was shooed away. I glanced across at Amana, and she glared vindictively as she slipped away. It was too late for me.

'Zanda.'

He nodded. 'You're not from these parts.' Coming from him, it sounded like an accusation.

'Neither are you,' I countered. My mood soured further; I was spoiling for a fight. I was back in Kreektown Primary, where, for six years, a staple playground debate was the identity of Zanda's *real* father.

'Exactly.' He smiled nervously. 'You wouldn't know who's organising this, would you? The old man is not to be buried here.'

Before I could respond, he spotted a more likely face and moved away, but my mood was already ruined. It had been a mistake to come. In the presence of Mata Nimito's corpse, my remorse flared. I turned to go, but Amana had reappeared. Her mood had swung around, and she beamed excitedly. I wondered what there was to be excited about, at a burial.

'I'm going to pay my respects. Coming?'

'You didn't even know him.'

'It's not as if I didn't try. I came here a couple of times on my job, but he never spoke to me. He didn't speak English or Sontik, and I don't speak Menai. Come.'

She grabbed my hand, and I followed her through the crowd. There was an air of the carnival. Although Nigerians lived in awe of death, they saw nothing tragic about the death of an old man. Many had come with cans of beer. A grave had been sunk twelve metres from the Mata's house. The gravediggers sat on the lip of the readied hole, smoking, joking, and passing a bottle of kai-kai around as they waited for the coffin, which had been donated by the Bus Conductor's Club. I saw how, unless it was relatives who sank the grave, a burial was more waste disposal than funeral. The cheap coffin appeared, precariously balanced on a wheelbarrow. The gravediggers were anxious to be done, but the auxiliary nurse was, for once, out of his depth. They had to wait for a real doctor from the Ubesia council to sign a death certificate and write a burial licence. A bedraggled choir unloaded drums and cymbals from a minibus. The makings of a slapdash funeral were coming together as I stepped onto the elevation.

This was no way to sing a dead mata's calamity.

Two youths emerged from the Mata's submerged home dragging his mananga. My stomach heaved. That act of desecration swamped the distance I had built and nurtured since my emigration, *'Hai!'* I shouted, advancing. They looked up and fled, leaving the ancient xylophone on its side.

Amana looked at me without comprehension. 'They're just having fun. The old man is dead; it's just going to rot there.'

I kept mute. She was not to know that a mata could not be buried without his mananga.

As we watched, David Balsam ducked into the house. I turned away.

I glanced beyond her at Mata Nimito and stiffened. I took two steps closer. Deep breath. Slow exhale. Deep breath . . . I looked around.

She eyed me curiously. 'What's the matter?'

'Look at him!' I whispered.

She did so and recoiled. 'My God! He must have been at least *two* hundred years old!'

I exhaled slowly. It was another hallucination, then. I walked slowly up to Mata Nimito, philosopher-guide of Menai, and tried to see what I ought to see. He was so old, so frail, and the muscles of the thin limbs that projected out of the red robe were locked and stiff.

Miyaka sia Menai! Jonszer wasn't addled after all. He had recognised me all along. His last words for me were a disgusted *'See what's left of the Menai!'*

I wondered what Jonszer would have done.

I knew.

It was a breach of the distance I had built, but it was only a small, anonymous breach. No Menai would ever know. I went to the mananga. The arms were missing from their sockets. *3:2:1:2,* that was the base rhythm. I had attended too many calamities ever to forget it. I had never wanted to hear that tattoo again, but for Mata Nimito, for Jonszer, I would play it one more time. I turned to the Mata's home. The exterior of it was a stretched canvas for a mad illustrator: stick figures and savannahs, cattle and pyramids, tableaus painted in indelible red and black and ochre.

Inside was a large open-plan home, made small by the glut of old, inexpensive things of profound value. Questionnaire was bent over a rack of figurines, circumcisionheads, and carvings by the old man's bed; he did not hear me enter. A rage flared, but I clamped down on it. *Distance.* I ignored him. On the wall, I found the mananga's arms, the hooked mallets that gave voice to the instrument. They were dusty, had clearly not been touched in months. I ducked through the low doorway and stepped outside.

The air was noisy with the chatter of a hundred souls. The clouds were low and swift. I wondered what the Mata would have cast from such a sky.

'Zanda?'

I turned. Amana was watching me curiously.

I addressed the mananga. It was a monster of a xylophone: three dozen uniquely sized, weighted, and tuned wooden panes, built in an arc around the player. It measured five feet from end to end. I wheeled it up to a rattan bench and sat, my back to the Mata, facing the bulk of the sightseers, most of whom now watched me. *Anuesi gubu anueso gudabe:* the day's for the dead, but the dance is for the living. The tanda ma. It was the basic beat every Menai had to learn. It was the frame to which Menai history was set. Slowed down, it was also the frame on which the calamity, Menai's dirge, was hung. It surged in my heart, but I clamped my teeth on it. I would not speak or sing Menai. From the corner of my eyes, I saw her, the very arch of her body, a question; I shut my mind and my eyes and let my fingers and ears rediscover the tanda ma. The voice of the xylophone drew down a silence on the pavilion. I felt curious eyes on me.

'Amie Menai anduogu . . .'

Memory flooded me.
'It is of Menai stock I speak,' I began to play.

Near the peak of Arrawadi
is the plain of our Kantai . . .

I had not played a minute when I felt the whoosh of air. My hands faltered and I opened my eyes; for a disoriented moment I was back by my primary school locker, letting out the snake. Then I came back to the present: around me surged a stomping mob struggling to escape. Inside me, a floe of fear coalesced. A woman the size and weight of Asia plunged wordlessly past me, crushing my foot under one of her flip-flops. Suddenly the carnival was gone, leaving the enclosure like a many-limbed creature, breaking bottles, chairs, and saplings. The cheap coffin was splintered and crushed, the drums were punctured, clothes and shoes littered the Mata's enclosure, but a tinny voice nearly deafened me, and it came from right behind me. I put away the mananga's arms in their sockets.

I turned, light-headed. His voice was a note higher than I remembered. He had barely stirred, but he was coming fully out of the trance. It was no hallucination, then. I abandoned the mananga and scrambled up the embankment on my hands and feet. From the Mata's house, a thunderstruck Questionnaire emerged, bearing two singate heads like holy relics. I looked at the Mata. It seemed *evil* to call a man this old back from the grave. His eyes were milky, almost undifferentiated between pupil and whites. I searched the drawn face for a familiar expression. Then he spoke, and it *was* Mata Nimito of the Great Calm. It was not evil, then, it was *right,* to live.

'Worie.'

'Dobemu,' I replied.

He fell silent at my voice. Then he asked, *'Ama Zanda mu chei?'*

'Zanda mu chei.'

His eyes closed, and he was breathing regularly again. I bowed, condemned by the silence. When I left, he'd had a Menai nation to care for him. I had not meant for this to happen, that the Mata would face his death alone, among strangers so impatient for him to go.

'My apologies,' said Questionnaire. 'You're certainly not a stranger to the old man.'

'Yes,' I said, not looking at him. 'And where you were grave-robbing before, now you are a common thief.'

'You misunderstand me completely. Listen, this is *extremely* important.'
He was climbing up to us. 'I'd like to talk to the old man about these. Can
you interpret for me?' He took my shoulder to turn me around. I resisted,
protecting my tears from sight, but he was strong, and I turned with him,
pushing him away, sending him tumbling down the pavilion, bronzes flying. I wiped my cheeks and bent over the old man.

'*Jons miena qua?*'

'*Jonszer amie gonzi.*' There was no point in hiding anything from the
Mata. '*Minsa qua na Agui.*'

He turned towards the tidal creek, which sat lower in its bed than I had
remembered. He looked at me. His eyes were *so* milky, I wasn't sure, now,
how much he could see. '*Amazi manasi ungheu.*'

I felt the shame but no surprise at his perfect recollections, for he carried
millennia of Menai history in his head. I was away for six and a half years
and he picked up as if I had just returned from the stream. His eyebrows
lifted, and I followed his eyes to the huddle of wine gourds assembled for
the burial. He could see well enough, then.

I filled two brown glasses and brought them over. He stared. I remembered and scrambled for water. Water was primal, water was first. I gave
him a gourd, which he took with a hand that trembled. '*Amis andgus.*'

'*Andgus ashen,*' I replied and drank from the same gourd. I drank deep,
quenching a sudden thirst not for water but for custom. It was true, then:
all the healing in the world was in the gourd of water.

'This is old water,' I said in the Menai equivalent of small talk, dodging
the weighty things that had to be said.

'The sky pissed it when the world was young,' he agreed.

An age passed. The sun was going down, so I pivoted the sun shelter until
he was looking into clear skies. His hand—leathery, insubstantial—fell on
my head, and a shroud of gooseflesh wrapped itself around me, stubbling
my skin. I began to remember. Flakes of memory began to coalesce around
the water in my guts. I served his wine and joined his eyes in the skies.

There was no 'ordinary' sky. Each one was unique. Every hour's pattern
was a perfect, never-to-be-repeated arrangement of shades, wisps, and au-
guries. For a cloudcaster like Nimito, a sky—day or night—was not just a
densely scripted tome to be studied, deciphered, and decoded but a backdrop on which to project and encode a mata's legendary memories of the
past and deductions of the future. For me it was just a ceiling for life, but
in his presence it acquired a grandeur that it normally lacked.

I found myself stealing glances at his riveted face, trying to glean something of the psychosis that had kept this man so long and consistently in

this groove. His eyebrows were the most animated part of him, the one organ that seemingly refused to atrophy, gaining, instead, a second sight that stymied the first. The muscles of the brows were still as limber as a tongue. I watched the emotions course through them. A flash of sly. A pucker of small surprise. And then—thirty-five minutes after our ritual drink of water—an electrifying dilation that swamped the orbs and spread, through stiffening, corded muscles, through his wasted body.

His face fell slowly from the skies until his eyes held my gaze. There was a look of ineffable sadness in them. I knew it was time to mourn Jonszer. Yet by killing himself he had fallen foul of the great taboo. The Mata could not sing the tanda ma of his man Friday.

I went to the mananga, wondering whether I dared.

Jonszer's last words came back to me, his disgust amplified by the pathos of his suicide, by the passion of an excellent swimmer who dived into a creek with a cord and roped himself to a mangrove root under the surface.

A nervous hand hovered on my shoulder, and when I turned, Amana was standing there. Her clothes were soiled and her hair generously supplied with twigs and burrs. She was looking at the old man, who had fallen back onto the platform. I put away the mananga's arms and gathered him up carefully. He was breathing lightly, his body weighing little more than old rags. He smelled of childhood memories and brackish creeks.

I stepped down from the embankment with my burden. As I turned away, Questionnaire was emerging from the Mata's house, without the bronzes, his lips a thin, angry line.

She swallowed. 'Where are you taking him?'

'Home,' I said.

'But Ma'Calico—'

'*Home,*' I repeated.

MATA NIMITO

Kreektown | 18th March, 2005

Aiyegun Yesi Yemanagu
You see that nation in the mists
among the hills, beside the scented trees.
You see her maidens' comely walk,

her handsome sheep,
her finely sculpted men.
You hear the long language that comes like song,
and love her pleasant ways,
and do not know her name?
Her name is Menai.

We are Menai.
Our land is lost.
Our love, our soil, our soul.
But we're one clan, one nation, and one folk,
pulled by the root from the soil of our hearth.
And we are not made any more for planting towns.
We are one folk, one cloth, one destiny, one kin,
pulled by deceit from the soil of our hearth.
We are not made any more for planting towns.

Living lightly on the land,
planting crops for trees
and tents for houses . . .
Our hearts are planted
in the country that we lost,
and we will return.

We are Menai.

HUMPHREY CHOW

London | 18th March, 2005

'This could have been great, Humphrey,' said Malcolm Frisbee.

He was breathing heavily as he approached the end of his exertions. It was the week after my return from Scotland, and we were dining in the seventh-floor restaurant of Tate Modern. His final forkful of lamb paused on the lip of its plate, in the midst of the wreck of our lunch. With his other hand he tapped the plastic folder that contained my short story, which had lain bereft on one side of the table while the main business of the food was sorted. On the folder was stencilled the famous red and black initials IMX. He ate the last of his lamb and sighed regretfully. 'It could have been really, *really* great.'

I poked miserably at the remains of my Cornish haddock.

We occupied a table for four, whose surface was barely enough for the main courses that had eventually sated Malcolm's appetite. Malcolm stood six foot three in his socks and weighed a hundred and forty kilogrammes. He had won the Booker Prize at twenty-six with his first novel, *Sundance.* That early coup made his reputation, but it also put him under immense pressure for a second book worthy of a Booker Prize winner. In the six desperate years following *Sundance,* he suffered acute literary agonies, which ended in a writing vacation on a remote Greek island, where he ate a poisoned crab. He was in a coma for weeks. When he recovered, it was without his midterm memory, which elevated the challenge of a second Malcolm Frisbee novel to the level of the scaling of the Pennines by a heavily pregnant amputee.

It would have been another Greek tragedy, except that all that had taken place thirty-six years ago. Malcolm was now chairman of one of the most successful literary agencies in Europe. He was reluctantly approaching seventy but still had two unrelenting passions: the love of a good story, and a regularly indulged love of good food. In his career as a literary agent, he had represented eighteen Booker and six Pulitzer Prize winners.

He brought his passions together in his business model. Few London executives could rival his entertainment budget. He was on a first-name basis with celebrity chefs up and down the country, for he had the sort of appetite that reverberated from restaurant floor all the way to the nerve centres of the most distinguished kitchens. Malcolm snared his authors over expensive, languid dinners and sacked them over courteous, cheap lunches. In between, there were restaurant sessions to mark new books, new prizes, and the opening of promising new eateries.

For the past year I had been steeling myself to turn down a Malcolm Frisbee invitation to lunch. I was married to Grace Meadows, his favourite agent, but even that connection had its limitations. My first and only book, *Blank,* had been booed by the critics and shunned by the bookshops, but I had been picked for the Richard and Judy Show and notched up pretty good sales on Amazon. Had I received a lunch invitation during the barren months that preceded my Scottish writing retreat, I'd have declined and sent in a letter quitting Malcolm's agency with some dignity. It wasn't that clear that morning when Ruby, one of the clutch of personal assistants that he called his *memory bank,* phoned me to schedule an 'eat with the boss.' For one thing, Grace would have warned me if my representation was on the line. For another, Lynn had liked my bomber story. It worried her, but she was sure she could sell it.

She had also told me, confidentially, that Malcolm liked my story as well. Because I had written two IMX agents into my story, it had gone round in a viral e-mail on the IMX intranet. The word was, the chairman had actually read—and liked—it! When the lunch date was made, I had thought I'd written myself back into the good graces of the most aggressive literary agent in London.

Just then, it was beginning to look like his traditional terminal lunch.

'Lynn said you liked it,' I ventured.

Four fat fingers shooed away the very thought. 'I'm not in this business to *like* stories, Humphrey Chow. I'm in this business to *sell* 'em.'

'But . . .'

'And to sell a story, I have got to *love* it. *Like* is nothing. Comprehend?'

I nodded silently, filling my mouth with food, so I didn't have to say anything. Through the clear plate glass of the restaurant was a view of the Thames on a sunny day, but it was lost on me. Although I knew the score, that didn't make it any easier to bear. Literary agents needed *working* writers: young writers who were actively writing or older writers with a decent backlist. I had to accept Grace's jibe: IMX had kept me on their books because I was married to her. Presently, the plates were cleared away and I helped Malcolm drain a second bottle of a bland 2001 Gigondas.

'You must be wondering why I asked you to lunch, and here of all places,' he said finally, staring with the vague disdain of a sated appetite at a tray of steamed mussels proceeding by waitress to a patron at the far end of the busy restaurant.

It occurred to me that Malcolm had to have a streak of sadism. 'It's truly a lovely view,' I said.

His two hands combined to shoo away the very thought. 'Nonsense. Come, I'll show you.' By the time he had readied himself to rise, the bill was approaching him. It was intercepted by Ruby, who had been working her boss's phones from the café. All the same, the canny waiter persisted with a courtesy visit to our table, and Malcolm rewarded him with a superfluous tip. He made his way out of the restaurant, fielding the smiles and waves of the waiting staff like an A-list celebrity.

Malcolm Frisbee was famous for his irrational tips. The restaurant menu had warned that a 12.5 percent 'discretionary' service commission would be compulsorily added to the bill, but Malcolm had survived a crab poisoning that had ended his first career, and as a means of getting restaurant staff fully on his side, he indulged a fetish for fat tips.

We caught the lift down to the fifth floor. I followed Malcolm into the first gallery, where a special exhibit was running. It was called *Beyond Painting*. We stood before an elderly picture frame. It seemed fatally damaged, with a single diagonal slash running some twelve or so centimetres down the middle of an unpainted canvas.

'What do you think?' In his crumpled, blue linen jacket he was the quintessential arts professor examining a degree student.

I panicked, 'Of this?'

'Yes.'

I took two steps back, but the explanatory card was still too far to the left to read surreptitiously. I was between the devil of a slashed canvas and the deep blue sea of a confession of artistic ignorance. 'You mean this very canvas?'

'Yes,' he said impatiently. 'It is a Lucio Fontana. *Surely* you know Lucio Fontana.'

'Of course,' I lied, clearing my throat. I did not know much about art: my formal education had holes in it wide enough to sink a college building. To my eye it did seem like an unfortunate studio accident that had aborted a great master's attempt to paint . . . but it *was* hanging in a gallery of Tate Modern. *Not* to consider it an artistic disaster seemed safer. 'It's a unique concept, a *daring* painting.'

'It is not a *painting*,' Malcolm responded. Three female London-art-student types in flip-flops drifted closer, making no secret of their interest in our conversation. Their overlong jeans had fraying bell-bottoms as capacious as skirts and trailed loose threads, causing other visitors to give their wake a wide berth. Malcolm continued, modulating his voice to accommodate his new audience, 'If you notice, the canvas is untainted by paint. The only pigmentation on it will be the discolouration of age. It's just the slash; notice the centrality of cut to canvas, notice the new, third dimension it conveys to the previous linearity of the artwork, its boldness . . .'

'Exactly,' I said, warming to the subject. 'Its uniqueness—'

'Rubbish,' Malcolm interrupted, reaping a brace of nods from his new listeners. 'It's not unique; everyone who can afford a blade is slashing canvases these days. Pay attention, Humphrey Chow. Back in 1955 when Fontana had the gumption to present this as a work of art it was unique. It's old hat now. Comprehend? Come.'

I ignored the students' rolling eyes and followed Malcolm away from the sweep of their scorn. He took me through the huge galleries on the fifth floor of the former thermal plant. Slowed by digesting food and thought-provoking art, we browsed the hangings somnolently, with much nodding and contemplation through half-closed eyes.

Finally we stood in the amplified silence of a huge, empty hall that could have garaged a couple of articulated trucks: empty, that is, but for seven large movie screens affixed to the walls. Footage from seven grainy CCTV cameras featuring the same deserted studio at night was running simultaneously on all the screens. The exhibit was *Mapping the Studio,* by Mike Norman. Mike's studio was not a very psychedelic one. It seemed stacked with odds and ends, like someone's garage; it was a place where things were *made,* not a place designed for show. The only thing that moved in the videos were rats. When we arrived, there were only three other visitors in that room, the largest gallery by far on the floor, and they looked on with some embarrassment as Malcolm began to pace the room ostentatiously. Starting from one end of the room, he took large, measured steps in a straight line across the room. He did the same thing on the other side. Then he walked across to where I was waiting at the entrance to the room, trying to hide my mortification behind a *Metro* newspaper.

By this time, several more visitors had entered the hall and stood in a loose gaggle beside me, watching Malcolm appreciatively. A uniformed security guard procured by the surveillance cameras also drifted in through the opposite entrance. He watched us through narrowed, less appreciative eyes.

Malcolm was panting by the time he reached me. As he caught his breath, a middle-aged woman flustering her way through a handful of brochures removed the audio guide from her ear to ask, in an artsy American accent, 'I missed most of that. Sorry, what's the name?'

'Malcolm Frisbee,' said that worthy. His voice had the resignation of a B-list celebrity destined to a lifetime of halfway recognitions that had to be supplemented with the occasional introduction.

'I don't mean *your* name. I mean your piece, your performance art. It's not in the brochure . . .'

Her meaning dawned on Malcolm. 'I'm not a performance artist!' he snapped. He took my arm and turned away. We left the gallery at an angry three or four miles per hour and stormed up the stairs. Malcolm used the exercise to work off his anger at the indignity and to work up an appetite for desert. Back on the seventh floor, Ruby was waiting at the café with a prescience that verged on smugness as she nursed a sixth or seventh espresso.

Our earlier table was taken, but a waiter found us a better, if smaller, one for two, right against the glass window. We resumed our meal where we left off, he ordering a white and dark chocolate mousse and I, an ice cream. My order arrived almost immediately, but despite all his tips, we had to wait for his mousse. In the meantime, Phone-in-the-Ear-Ruby replaced the folder with the offending story in front of her boss. This time, there was also a white envelope under the transparent cover of the folder. Clearly, boss and PA had run this tag-game before. The coffee junkie did not meet my eye, nor did she return to her fix at the café. She disappeared into the ladies, like a butcher stepping back from the slab to avoid the spatter of blood.

The moment had come. The envelope was addressed to me. I did not need a BBC *Panorama* investigation to figure out its contents. I steeled myself to walk out before the final indignity. I was not going to become another IMX luncheon-termination statistic. I took a final spoon of ice cream.

Nobody did significant gazes like Malcolm Frisbee. He fixed me with one such and asked, fingers drumming a suspiciously calypsonian tattoo, 'What do you think?'

'About the ice cream?'

'About *Mapping the Studio!* Answer me from here,' he said, digging fingers into his guts. 'Tell me what you felt, standing there, watching those giant screens.'

I took another final spoon of ice cream. It was a good thing that the mind was no TV screen and that my blankness as I stood watching the CCTV footage of a deserted studio could be transmogrified into an intellectual opinion. I shook my head. 'Awesome,' I said quietly. 'At first I was like, "Nothing is happening here . . ." Then, as I looked, I realised that . . . well, something *existential* was happening before my eyes. It was like, *you know,* a Waiting-for-Godot-kind-of-happening . . .'

I trailed off.

Malcolm's chocolate mousse had arrived while I was dissembling, but he had not dived in with his usual enthusiasm. Instead, he stared. 'Are you taking the piss?'

'Sorry?'

'Come on! We were watching *seven* videos of an *empty* studio, for crying out loud!' He seized my hand. 'If I gave you a ten-hour film of an empty studio to take home, *would you watch it?*'

'Err . . .' I suspected it was a trick question. After all, this *was* Tate Modern.

'Picture this: you come home from a hard day's slog at the old nine-to-five, and there's a ten-hour DVD of an empty studio waiting for you to watch. *Will you watch it?*'

The ice cream spoon was cutting into my fingers. 'Well, if you put it that way . . .'

'Fine,' he said, unhanding me. 'Now, what if I put the same DVD up on seven cinema screens, in an auditorium measuring, what? Twenty-four paces by sixteen—say a thirteen-hundred-square-foot warehouse—what if I did that, and amplified the sound of Nothing Happening till the static was singing in your ears. What would you think then, eh?'

I said nothing.

'"*Awesome,*" isn't that what you said?'

I stared at my ice cream.

'And that is the second lesson,' he concluded.

He then attacked his mousse with gusto. The nice waiter paused by me to ask whether the ice cream was at all palatable, so I took a *final,* final spoon of it. If I left at that point, the question would haunt me for the rest of my life, so I asked it. 'What was the first lesson?'

'Lesson one: *Do something different, but do it first.* That's the Lucio Fontana lesson!' He shovelled a mouthful of mousse into his mouth.

It was a beautiful day outside. Black barges floated past on a muddy Thames, towards the Millennium Bridge. Malcolm did not notice. He was sweating in the cool room. I suppose he had a conscience after all.

'Lesson two: *Do it on a grand scale!* That's the Mike Norman lesson!' He wiped chocolate off his chin with a napkin.

I realised he was working up the anger to deliver my termination notice. I had to rise; I was cutting this too fine.

He was thundering, 'So what is this nonsense about a short story? Come on, Humphrey Chow! I wait for you, I wait *patiently* for you, for *years and years;* and you come to me with a *short story?* So where's the market for that? What's my commission in that?'

The gloves were coming off. I wanted to tell him I hadn't exactly been with his agency for 'years and years,' but I didn't. It was time to go. I took a deep breath.

'I didn't actually give it to you . . . I gave it to . . . what I mean is, Lynn and I are working on a collection of . . .'

'Give that poor girl a break,' pleaded Malcolm Frisbee, clasping his fingers dramatically.

I forced myself not to look sideways, the first lesson of drama being to affect a total lack of awareness of your audience.

'She could have walked off with her team's bonus last Christmas if your account hadn't dragged down her averages! Last quarter, every other writer on her slate grossed fifty K, annualised. You? Zilch! And now you tell me you're working on a *collection*? Humphrey Chow, are you on this planet?'

'I am a short story writer,' I said stubbornly.

'And I'm a stamp collector,' he said, 'but I know what to do with my hobby!' He set down his spoon in an empty mousse plate and counted off four stubby fingers. 'Listen, you ain't pretty, you ain't female, you ain't gay, and you ain't funny! You've basically got the odds stacked against you, so what do you have to do? You have to write a damn good novel, that's what! One hundred thousand damn good words—more, if you want to crack the US market! *Short story!*'

My ice cream was melting.

'After my Greek accident with the lobster, I could have turned to shorts, you know? My memory could have handled them. It's after page twenty or so that I began to mix up my goddamned characters. But what did I do? I got a day job, that's what I did! I left my shorts in my bottom drawer and got a day job! *Short story!*'

His 'Greek accident' was with a crab, but correcting him would have provoked him further, and he was loud enough as it was. From the corner of my eye, I saw a familiar lady enter the restaurant and look around hesitantly. She was forty metres away, but I recognized her immediately as the lady who had provoked Malcolm into furious flight from the *Mapping the Studio* exhibit. She was slim and aquiline, fiftyish from her looks, and she leaned forward with a short-sighted stoop, as she searched the faces of nearby diners.

It was well past time for me to leave, but I watched in self-loathing as Malcolm started on his 'empty' plate, so that, had it turned out to be poisoned as well, the police would not have found enough mousse for the forensic tests. He laid his napkin on the table and flicked open the folder. He pushed the envelope across to me, and my name and address stared up at me from the centre of the table, underneath the self-important initials, IMX. My dreams of a writerly rehabilitation on the wings of "Reluctant Bomber" were melting like my dollop of ice cream. I realised I was going to open the letter and become a luncheon statistic after all. There was something about the inevitable momentum of events.

Yet I have not always been this timid.

The lady from the gallery finally spotted the mound of Malcolm and made a beeline for our table. The termination letter slipped from my mind

as she leaned politely over Malcolm with an apologetic smile. 'Would that
be "Malcolm Frisbee," as in *the* "Malcolm Frisbee"?'

'Well, yes,' conceded Malcolm. He was the sort that preferred to separate himself from the scene of embarrassments, but he was not averse to
the occasional embarrassment seeking him out to apologize personally.

'Monica Parkerson.' She shot out a hand, which was grudgingly accepted
by Malcolm. Afterwards, she allowed me to shake her hand as well, although
her admiring eyes did not leave Malcolm's. 'I'm sorry about the . . .'

'Don't mention it,' Malcolm told her.

'Because it seemed such a *telling* counterpoint to the *lifelessness* in the
cinematic studios, you see.' She spoke expressively, with her fingers, her
bosom, and a muscular voice. It was like watching a stage performance.
'When you left, the exhibit seemed so flat, so drained of . . . *oomph*. Your
presence, the comportment with which you promenaded . . . the inter-
activity with the viewers . . . like a silent theatre in the round . . . do you
know the phrase that gripped my mind?' Her voice dropped into a dramatic bass: '*Of men and mice!* Someone should tell Norman . . .'

Malcolm was beginning to look distraught. 'I definitely don't want to
press this discussion further—'

'—over a public lunch,' said the lady, nodding and glaring at me, as
though it was my presence that made her confidential conversation unten-
able. 'Of course not . . .' Behind her, Ruby broke out of the ladies' room
and hurried towards us. Monica was nodding as she placed a card before
Malcolm. 'I fully understand, good ideas have wings. Do call me sometime, so we can talk things through. I'm a . . . shall we say . . . connoisseur
of good things and I see *huge* possibilities, I mean *huge* . . .'

'Yes, yes,' said Malcolm, but he made no move for the card. She turned
away, a little deflated, and drifted towards the exit, passing Ruby near the
waiter's station. Malcolm turned to me, putting the woman out of his mind.

'You're a good man, Humphrey Chow, but I'm sorry, I'm really sorry . . .'

I slowly stirred my ice cream slurry. If there had been any sorrow in
Malcolm to begin with, it had evidently been compromised by his excellent mousse. His mood seemed positively upbeat.

'This business is a bitch,' he continued, 'but you know me, I don't do
bullshit.'

As I reached for the envelope in the centre of the table, Ruby deposited
her phone bag carelessly on it. A wave of irritation swept me as she leaned
over to whisper in her boss's ear. Her black hair fell over his face, so that
when his astonished 'No!' issued, it seemed like the start of a ventriloquist's

act. She whispered some more, and then she straightened up and smoothed down her clothes. Frisbee's eyebrows were moving in for a rare, flabbergasted kiss across their nose ridge. Then the moment passed and all was well on Frisbee Mountain. He gave a belly laugh and thumped the table. 'Great!'

Ruby laughed nervously without meeting my eyes and scooped up her bag. She turned for the waiter's station to sort out our dessert bill. I wiped off a spatter of ice cream that Malcolm's thump had deposited on my arm and reached for my letter, but it was gone. It had been under Ruby's bag but now both were gone. I turned towards the retreating PA, but Malcolm leaned over and punched my shoulder. 'Tell the truth,' he said in a voice swerving with ill-fitting tomfoolery. 'There's something going on between you and my Lynn, isn't there? Go on, I won't tell Grace.'

'I beg your pardon . . .'

'She's solidly in your corner, and you know what? She's just sold your "Bomber" story—and your next eleven stories—to *Balding Wolf!* It's a pretty decent deal, too!'

'Lynn came through!' I whispered.

'*IMX* came through,' corrected Malcolm, 'as we always do. Do you want to know the size of the deal?'

'Where's my letter?' I asked, turning towards Ruby again. 'Now that I'm unagented, I should—'

'Nonsense,' said Malcolm. 'Who said you're unagented? Lynn has set up a signing at the office Monday morning at nine. Be there.' He paused, snapping open a complimentary card case. 'I have something difficult to tell you, Humphrey Chow, and you know me, no bullshit.' He chewed his lower lip as he scrawled a name and telephone number on the back of a card, which he passed over to me.

'Who's this?'

'George Maida. You must have met him at the Christmas party.'

'The Turkish contractor?'

'The Milton Street psychoanalyst. Comprehend? I've read your story, Humphrey Chow, and although I like it, it also worries me. I'm talking *very*, very worried, here.'

'I'm okay.'

'I know you are.' He opened his hands dramatically. 'But nine hundred and fifty writers have passed through these hands, and, give me one thing, Humphrey Chow, I *know* writers. Talk to Maida, ASAP. He's good. I'm talking *very*, very good, here.'

'I'm okay,' I insisted.

His voice hardened and he leaned across the table. 'I've carried you for years, Humphrey Chow,' he said quietly. 'You're not going to crack on me in the middle of a twelve-story-contract, comprehend?'

'I understand, but . . .'

'Just consider it a marketing gimmick. Writers in psychoanalysis are selling very well just now.'

I said nothing. I just sat there, seventy-one kilogrammes of intransigent Chow.

He relented. 'Okay, Humphrey Chow, forget the psychoanalysis. Just play golf with Maida every Wednesday, deal?'

'Just golf? No talk?'

'Just golf,' he agreed, putting out his great hand, which I shook reluctantly. 'Deal.' He grinned. Then he cautioned, pushing his chair back, 'You're not going to be anti-social, are you? It's quite psychotic to play golf without talking.'

''Course not.'

'You can have conversational talk, just not psychoanalytic talk, yeah?'

'Sure.'

'Then, because we're using his professional time, we'll slip him a little something for the hour, OK?' He rose. The nice waiter circled uncertainly, wondering whether twice a day was unseemly greed. Malcolm pulled at his wallet, drowning the man's doubts in lucre. I tried to rise, but he was standing beside me, holding me down with a heavy, confidential hand as he leaned over to a whisper, 'Between us, we'll know it's strictly golf, but Phil has insisted on a psychoanalysis clause in the contract. Just sign it Monday, comprehend? But between me and you and Maida, we'll know it's just golf-talk. Yeah?'

Then he was gone, and I realised I still didn't know just what my 'pretty decent deal' was. Still, after months in the wilderness, I had an important new contract. *Balding Wolf* meant new visibility. I could still go on calling myself a writer.

LYNN CHRISTIE

London | 18th March, 2005

My lunch meeting was with Phil Begg. When he got the nod to edit the new bimonthly *Balding Wolf,* he had commissioned his favourite writer,

Jenny Ely, to write him a six-thousand-word story. But Jenny, who also happened to be on my slate, had just been short-listed for the Booker for the first time and was still in the stratosphere. I had fixed the face-to-face meeting with Phil, hoping to talk him into republishing an old story of hers.

Then I heard about Humphrey Chow's lunchtime meet with the boss.

It was 2:30 p.m. The interior of The Flagon was cavernous, its upper reaches furnished by wine racks that reached up to the rafters. Phil finally made it in at 2:40 p.m. I could still feel the buzz, along with the apprehension that followed him everywhere these days. He grinned his apologies. When he loomed over me I presented my cheek to be kissed. He twisted around and kissed my lips anyway, before sitting down opposite me.

'So what are you eating?'

'Me? I've eaten already.'

He assessed me over the rims of his spectacles. 'Fine. I'm sorry I'm late; are you happy now?'

'Yes, I'll have the most expensive meal on the menu, and champagne to celebrate your launch.'

Phil chuckled. 'Now I'm really sorry I'm late . . . hey, where are you going?'

'To the ladies.' I pushed my file halfway across the table. 'There's Jenny's tale. Make yourself useful.'

In the loo, I drew on a fresh set of eyebrows and called the vet to schedule my cats. I peeked to find Phil still looking bored, but he was just opening the file. I went back in, painted my nails, and made a few more calls, burning all of twenty minutes. When I returned, he was halfway through "Reluctant Bomber." 'Sorry, Phil,' I began, but he raised a big palm to silence me. I complied happily and ordered.

Eight years ago when I was fresh out of university, we had gone out for all of one month in the heady days of the Oxford bus riots. Then he had taken a job in IVC Media Group's New York office. It was one of those 'fault-free' breakups that allowed us to meet up again and again without the undercurrents in other relationship failures. Except that he had returned from New York a brasher Phil, ever-grating, always ever taking me for granted.

It was good to return the favour for once.

By the time he finished, a steamed chicken was sitting in front of him in a bath of vegetables. I was already deep into my grilled trout. He placed Humphrey's manuscript proprietorially at his elbow and dug into his food.

'How's the launch coming?' I asked.

'Dunno,' he said through a full mouth. He sipped from his wineglass. 'I contracted out that bit. I'll turn up on the day, same as you.'

'I haven't got an invite, and neither has Jenny.'

'I can sort that right away.' He wiped his lips with a napkin and pulled his wallet from his pocket. He pulled out two tickets. He then wrote on them and pushed them across to me. 'Story's great, too. Literary tour de force. Most unlike Jenny, though. She's really reinvented herself, psychotic male voice and all that.'

'Psychotic male voice?'

He tapped the manuscript.

I pulled up my spectacles. 'Oh, that's Mr. Chow's piece.' I opened my folder again. 'Wrong story. Jenny's must be in here somewhere. I'm afraid it's a published story. She's been rather busy recently . . .'

He put down his fork and took my hand. 'Have I just read a translation from *Chinese?* It was set in Scotland!'

I grinned. 'Humphrey Chow is a British writer. There, it says HC at the bottom, sorry, my mix-up. No, Jenny has an old—'

'To hell with Jenny, it's a bloke's magazine anyway. I want this Humphrey chap.'

'I . . . I don't know . . . I'm about to ink a collection deal for him.'

'So you're not quite committed? Are you?'

'Well, you know me, Phil . . . I don't discriminate against mags; but they *are* ephemera—read for a fortnight and trashed . . . I've got to look at my client's long-term interests.' I gulped my juice, wondering whether I was over-egging it.

'Of course not,' he said sarcastically. 'We don't want this story to be forgotten like James Joyce's *Ulysses,* which was first published in a magazine, do we?' He peered at me. 'Who are you talking to?'

'Confidentially?'

He crossed his heart.

'Maximus.'

He snorted. 'Max's artsy house can push five thousand copies. Over five years. I'll sell three hundred thousand of my launch. Wake up, Babes, Max isn't even playing in my league. And you can flog him anthology rights after I'm done!'

'Well . . .'

He speared a chilli and chewed slyly. 'Has he sent a contract yet?'

'Well, confidentially, no. I was just—'

'I'll sign you a twelve-story deal, Monday, sight unseen. Six solid months of visibility. How's that for ephemeral? Next year he'll have a ready-made collection for the literary press. He may not make the hardback vanity shelf, but he'll do okay with the trade.'

I chewed through my mouthful and then pushed Jenny's old contract to him. 'Let me see some figures, Phil.'

He crossed out Jenny's name, wrote in Humphrey's, pencilled in his offer, and pushed it across. 'Don't get excited; that's for twelve stories.'

I looked at it before making a face. 'You could have fooled me. I thought you were signing the tab for our lunch.'

He crossed out his first offer and wrote another figure angrily, 'You're screwing me, aren't you? Because you know my deadline.'

I took the pen coyly. 'And Jenny?'

He took the invitation with Jenny Ely's name, tore it, and wrote another one for Humphrey Chow. He slid it across. 'Stuff Jenny. I've got no time for writers who have no time for me.'

We shook hands on it, and suddenly I had to use the loo again. This time, I called Malcolm's memory bank. It wasn't that big a deal, by IMX's standards, but the boss *was* having 'lunch' with the client, after all.

HUMPHREY CHOW

London | 18th March, 2005

I sat in my car, mulling over my twelve-tale deal. I threw my head back and laughed, until I caught sight of my pupils in the rearview mirror. The two psychiatric patients stared back balefully. They were not amused.

A cloud of gloom seemed to trail me, and if the great news did not shift it, something fundamental was going on. I let the morose memories that were so inclined flood my mind. It was all Rani and no joy. Until recently, it had been several years since I had last thought of him—and now I had thought about him twice in one week.

Kiriashi ginami ko.

One of these days I was going to have to seek out his prison and visit him. No sense in having a language that no one else but you can speak. Gaps were opening up in my knowledge of it; thoughts I could no longer express in Menai were becoming commonplace.

My mobile pinged. It was Grace. There was a tense silence. Eventually she asked, 'Have you done lunch?'

'Yes.'

'I'm sorry, Humf.'

'You knew.'

'I did drop you a hint, didn't I? All those job ads? But listen, some good news: *Balding Wolf* is buying . . .'

'I know.'

'Oh.' She sounded deflated. 'Lynn phoned you already?'

'My phone was off. She got through to Ruby, who told Malcolm, who told me. IMX didn't drop me after all.'

'Well, congratulations. I'm so happy for you, Humf.' There was another strained silence. 'Are you still doing the drug trial?'

I slapped my head. In all the excitement, I'd forgotten. I had signed up to spend the next four days at a phase one drug trial. It was worth fifteen hundred pounds. It was one of those things I did when my account went bone dry; I could still do my writing in the comfort of their lounges. With the *Balding Wolf* deal, I shouldn't have to take the risk any more. Yet I had signed contracts before and knew it would be months before I saw any cash. 'I suppose I should.'

'I think you should,' she agreed in the terse voice she reserved for financial conversations. 'I've seen the *Balding Wolf* deal. There's no up-front money.'

'What will you do with yourself all weekend?'

'I'm seeing the Hutchinsons tomorrow, and there's a Malcolm meet-up at Annie's on Sunday.' Her voice smiled. 'I'm sure we're having Chow for dinner.'

'Ha ha,' I said mildly. When she said 'Chow,' she clearly excluded herself, because she did not use my last name. Malcolm had not opposed her marriage, but our marriage was an IMX secret and she still introduced me to colleagues as 'an IMX writer.' I never missed the subtext that for someone who fished a sea of big fish writers she had somehow settled for a minnow.

♦ ♦ ♦

5:30 p.m.

By the time I packed an overnight bag, I was late for the drug trial. Several other volunteers had failed to show, so the test was about to be scrapped when I turned up. As I signed in, two more volunteers arrived. A few minutes afterwards, the trials were on. First we endured the thirty minutes of form-filling and medical history taking, in the course of which we lost one more volunteer. He couldn't quite find his photo ID, and under Sister Stuart's withering cross-examination, he confessed he was fifty-five—not thirty-nine—and was 'not exactly' the Nathan K. Smith who had attended the screening. 'This is ageism!' he muttered before stalking out.

'Wait till they retire you,' said Sister Stuart to his back.

I drew a two-man room with a nervous first-timer who joked about having written his will. The staff drew the preliminary blood samples, and I tossed two capsules down with a blasé air. After ten minutes, I knew the trial was not going to be like the others.

I felt like lying down and did. When I came to, the hands of the clock had barely moved, but the room was a bedlam. It was roiling with white coats. I was screaming, '*Sintafia, sintafia!*'

'Speak English,' pleaded Sister Stuart. 'Where does it hurt?'

'I feel fine,' I said, although my mouth was full of tongue and my voice sounded strange, even to my own ears. 'I want my computer.'

'Your *what?*'

'My laptop, please.'

The white-coats exchanged glances. 'Get Doctor Greenstone,' Sister Stuart ordered.

I had another overwhelming desire to sleep, and before I could do anything about it, I did. This time, I retained a dreamy awareness . . . *My memories were seeds. My mind was a desert in whose sand the drug had burst a geyser. The new waters pooled, soaking the earth and the parched seeds of memory, growing green shoots. An oasis of memories flowered . . . In the distance, another geyser burst . . . Another cluster of memories blossomed. A lucid past flashed through my mind. Suddenly I was remembering . . .*

I woke up in a deserted private room. My head was full of colour, brimming with images, faces, memories. I felt omniscient . . . and I had wires running from one finger, my temples, and my chest.

Within seconds after I opened my eyes, Dr. Greenstone was in the room. His hands were deep in his white pockets. 'How do you feel?'

'I'm fine. I need my laptop.'

'All in good time, sonny.'

'And where is everybody?'

'We've suspended the trials, Humphrey. Every other volunteer on Proxtigen delivered responses within our anticipated ranges, but your graphs were all over the place. You're okay now. You'll have no permanent memento of this evening, touch wood, but this requires a lot more investigation.'

'I'd like to pull out of the trials now.'

He laughed shortly. 'You've pulled the plug on the trials, Mr. Chow. Proxtigen was a promising drug, looking good for a 2007 general release— until your seizure.'

'How much of it did I get?'

'Ah . . .' he hedged, 'this is a blind trial, you understand, there's only a fifty-fifty chance you got the drug . . .'

I had said nothing, but he probably realised how silly he was sounding.

'Twenty milligrammes. But this is not a legal statement, you understand?' He continued cheerfully, 'You're going to cost us big, Mr. Chow, but if you represent the tiniest percentage of the population, you're saving us millions over the long term . . .'

'Just drop me,' I said, sitting up. 'I feel fine. I've got to be elsewhere, right now.'

'Are you on recreational drugs, Mr. Chow?'

'Sorry?'

'That's the only way I can pull your results,' he said tensely. 'Proxtigen has properties that could potentiate hallucinogenic side effects in counter-action with some recreational drugs. If you're . . . indulging, we'd be obliged to discount your results.'

I stared at him. He was sweating. I gestured at his equipment overhead. 'If I was on drugs you'd know!'

He stepped up closer. '*If* we tested, we'd know.' He pushed a trolley across to me and unclipped the sensors from my finger. The trolley had a single sheet of paper and a pen on it. I scanned the paragraph of legalese. I had never felt better in my life and my freedom to write just then was important enough to discharge myself. 'If you told us, we'd also know.' Suddenly he was rattling on: 'It's amazing the number of people who get on tests that they shouldn't be on, just because they're brok . . . ah . . . just because they want to help *break* out that cure for cancer . . . You get girls who don't know they're pregnant, you get fifty-year-olds, fourteen-year-olds—why, just this evening, one of the ancients tried to pass himself off as a teenager! You get substance abusers . . .' He watched me sign. He took the paper from me and folded it carefully. '*Thank you.*'

'When can I go?'

'How do you feel?'

'Fine.'

'I'll get them to do the paperwork. By the way, it's pretty standard to pay extra compensation in cases like this. It's not underhand or anything. You will find it all in your envelope when the paperwork is done . . .'

He was almost at the door when it opened. The signed sheet vanished into his jacket as another man stalked in, taciturn, barely acknowledging Dr. Greenstone's greetings. The new man was lean and intense. His nameplate said 'Mr. Melrose.' He had eyes only for me. 'How are you feeling now?' Melrose asked.

'Great, I was just going—'

'Out of the question,' Dr. Greenstone snapped. 'You'll be here for another week at least. We have a cascade of tests to run . . .'

'*What?*'

'Well, maybe two days. At the least,' conceded Melrose.

'Don't bother,' I said. 'I'm fine, just pull my—'

'We *never* pull . . . anything, Mr. Chow,' said Dr. Greenstone.

'But you said . . .'

'Regulations,' he answered, looking at me with inscrutable eyes. 'I said the regulations are quite clear.'

◆ ◆ ◆

AT LEAST they gave me my laptop. I shut my eyes and dived into the riot of colour, of memories. Even the recent past seemed richer, truer. But the feast was further back . . . I opened the door of a thirteen-year-old memory and sneaked into her bedroom *where she was still swinging from the light fitting. She was wearing her faded green negligee. She was heavy, so heavy, and as I watched, a sheet of plaster came down with her from the ceiling. She hit the floor and lay there awkward and twisted. And it seemed so unfair that the plaster should wait till she was dead before it gave way . . .* I sneaked further back, and . . . *Yan Chow was on the floor, the kitchen knife in his back . . .* I snapped forward, not wanting to know . . . *the white of a wedding dress beside me, my arm in hers, the swell of pride, of love . . .* Grace had not worn white for our wedding. I tried to peer into the face of my bride, but my cinematograph darkened, pulling me back into the precincts of the present. I was consumed by an overwhelming loss. The geyser was stopped, the oasis dead. The omniscience was quite gone. I opened up my laptop urgently and began to write.

ZANDA ATTURK

Kreektown | 18th March, 2005

I turned homewards, and for a while we walked side by side, up the incline from Agui Creek into Kreektown. I walked slowly, planting one foot carefully after the other. Night fell swiftly, with calming components of screeching crickets and chorusing frogs. The lone street light was a tentative moon. I realised that I had forgotten to clip my torch to my belt, and it was suddenly not so calm, the night. Only the responsibility for the old man I carried kept me from seeking light and the anchor of company.

We reached the fork in the lane. I turned away from Ma'Calico's and moved deeper into the old village. Amana hesitated and came after me.

'Where are you going?' she whispered.

'Home.'

She paused. She glanced backwards, then, when I had walked four measured paces, followed silently.

I was afraid: that the Mata would die, leaving me to bury the greatest of all Menai alone; that he would live, to judge me for my sins. I was afraid of this darkness crowding in on me, negotiating for my soul. I walked in that fear, investing my entire mind in that dangerous journey home: what to do when I got there and found it occupied by roughboys or unoccupied and in ruins? Where to go then? Mata Nimito's home was desecrated by the premature funeral. He did not need to see a grave yawning for him. He did not need the zoo of Ma'Calico's place. He would not abide a hospital. He wanted a place to die in dignity.

I stood before the Atturk house. The fear settled fully into me, lodging itself as snugly as a limb in a sleeve.

'Where's this place?' she whispered.

'Home,' I said hoarsely.

'But . . .'

'Can you fetch a lamp?'

'I've got my phone—'

'A *real* lamp? Please? And some food.'

I felt her eyes on the side of my face briefly. Then she was gone, her footfalls quick and urgent. The street was dead, from Etie's old house to Megima's old house at the junction, and all those in between, including the Atturk house and Sefi's house. The usurpers of Kreektown had contented themselves with the homes abutting the square, where they had torn up the floors, and eviscerated the family graves, before settling in, for the Sontik were too superstitious to live in homes whose old owners still lay beneath the floors. Only roughboys were heedless of the graves. They would break into a house, stay a week or month, and move on again in their rootless cycles.

The old man moaned, impelling me forward again. I crossed the road slowly. It would take Amana ten minutes, at least, to get to Ma'Calico's, another fifteen to return with the lamp. I might prefer to stand forever outside the house, but Mata Nimito had to lie down. I forced myself towards the dreaded darkness of the house; as I did so, something electric seemed to singe my nerve endings. I felt a dizziness that passed swiftly, as a darkness within me embraced the night. Something was wrong, but at the same time, *very right*. I hadn't been here in more than six years . . . yet an easy familiarity gloved the scene. My eyes slid, unsurprised, off a wall suddenly green with vines, jinked easily around the strange flare of hedges, and settled on the secured front door. I wondered how I knew about the new nail behind the old hole where the lock had once been . . . it was as though I was coming home from a day at work . . . I tried to stop, but a magnetic field drew me in. Rather than fear I felt a growing exhilaration . . .

. . . COME UP to the door. It is fast? Put a finger through the crack and turn the nail away. Push in, pass through. It is still a house, but only just. The windows and doors are there. The roof, and the masonry on which it sits. But the furniture is long gone. The kitchen is ripped out. The plumbing and the pipes that led from the well are gone. The family house in Kreektown. Ten metres wide, in its own proud yard, sandwiched between Etie's and Sefi's house. A seventy-three-year-old house built back in the day when it was a great and glorious thing to be an Atturk.

No longer. The last Atturk is not really an Atturk. My colour is wrong, far too light for this nation. My features are wrong. Guess which of my parents must have been unfaithful. It is too dark to see the photos on the wall. They hang there under a six-and-a-half-year-old film of dust, Tume Atturk and his wife, Malian, my mother, who died well before I was old enough to wring the truth of my true paternity from her.

Come through the threshold rebuilt from the hull of Raecha Atturk's boat. Step up, pass through. The smell of cassava hits you, doesn't it? It is a long time since I left, and the village is dead, but the emotional aroma of her kitchen endures. I open the door slowly, with much shaking of the ball handle, so that she gets a chance not to be there in the vent of the courtyard, skinning and chopping and soaking cassava. She never really left, Malian, never quite came to terms with her sudden drowning.

My skin is taut with gooseflesh. The walls of my ancestral home lock me in. Suddenly I understand why deep sleep exhausted me, why strange ATM withdrawals showed up in my statements from towns I had never visited. It was as though my reconciliation with the Mata was reconciling my fractured halves. I stand still; the darkness soaks into my skin. Slowly, knowledge sinks into my mind. How I **love** the dark. Hold still, let your eyes adjust. There are broken parquet sections all around, but even so, the floor is mostly sound. It is ironic, isn't it, that a house founded on wealth from the seas would fall into such landed ruin. Nobody will remember when this was the wealthiest house in the village or when it was the home of Tume Atturk, Mata-in-waiting. History and memory die together with their owners. Here is the hall. Over there's the kitchen of the making of both our laughter and our tears too. Beyond is the yard. Watch out for the low ceiling. Old Raecha Atturk was short as a stump and has given his descendants a stoop from growing up here.

I'll set you down here in the old lounge, Mata Nimito . . . I'll see that all is well.

My favourite room: Mum and Dad lie beneath. The Menai do not do cemeteries, that taking of dead relatives out with the trash. We do not tip the late into pretty landfill sites. It's their house, after all, so we rest them in it. Home burials mitigate loss: the homestead stays whole, even after the catastrophe of the long sleep . . . they continue to be privy to the family's jokes and tears. My parents drowned on a market day in 1991. I was eleven. Kreektowners were watching when their canoe capsized five metres from the jetty. They had waved and shouted excitedly for a while. The Menai on the beach had waved back self-consciously, disapproving of such boisterousness from grown-ups, it not occurring to them that somewhere on GodMenai's Earth were adult men and women who actually could not swim. Although born Menai, Dad had been raised in Bida. Like Mum, he had never learned to swim . . .

◆ ◆ ◆

I FROZE.

A sound had broken my reverie. I listened closely. It came again, the weakest of buzzing. Half cricket, half . . . telephone? I crouched and left the house, entering the courtyard that was the old kitchen. The noise faded, and I retraced my steps, following the sound to the storeroom. There was a fresh mound raised in the centre of the floor, a spade still in it. The sound ceased, but I pulled up the spade all the same. In the darkness, I carefully began to move the earth. After a few scoops, the ringing began again, the sound fainter but more urgent. I put the spade down and dug with my hands. I found the Nokia in the first pocket I searched, on the last legs of its four-hundred-hour standby lifetime. I sat on my heels, my back against the burnt-brick wall. I opened the phone. There was the pinging of a battery warning, then an agitated voice.

'Hello? Papa?'

'No.'

Anxious: 'Who is this? Where is . . . ?'

'He's dead. You know that.'

A tinny, female scream. 'Who is this?'

'Badu,' I said, as the battery died.

I sighed and broke up the phone. I restored Omakasa's mound, wondering how the body had lain undiscovered with his phone broadcasting. Badu wasn't as smart as the media gave him credit for. Neither were the police.

Then I returned to Mata Nimito. His presence seemed to swirl me until I could almost touch Justice Omakasa's killer, opposite the pillar from where I stood. When I whipped around, when I tried to catch him out, he was pirouetting just as fast, but when I shut my eyes and did not even try, I was knowing what he knew, feeling what he felt . . . without ceasing to be who I was.

I pulled up the bundled sack from the dry well in the courtyard, not wondering anymore how I knew it was there. I made up a thin bed in my old room next to the courtyard and moved Mata Nimito there. I stood motionless in the kitchen for a minute, unafraid, wearing the darkness like a second skin. I shook my head. I had done it on my own. Night was now friend, not foe.

I heard the knocking on the door.

I opened the door for Amana and an effulgent lantern. 'There's a Tobin Rani looking for you at Ma'Calico's. He was looking for Hundredyears as well.'

Tobin Rani. The name grazed the surface of an old memory, but no face came up. 'I don't know him.'

'The police were there as well,' she said tautly. 'It's the madman, Sergeant Elue. I don't know what they want, but it can't be good.'

I took the bag from her. I switched off the lantern gently. The darkness reclaimed us. 'There are no curtains on the windows; we'll be seen from the street. Shut your eyes and open them again. You'll see enough.'

'I thought you hated the dark.'

'Not anymore.'

'I'm . . . scared . . .'

'Don't be.' I took her shoulder and drew her close.

'. . . of you . . . you're different . . .'

My hand dropped to my side, and she stepped back, haltingly. 'You are *Menai?*' She made it sound like a disease. 'This is your house? Your father's house?'

'*Arue su gamu diene zi.*'

'What's that?'

'It's a Menai blessing: *May your children walk over your grave.*' I pointed. 'That's Dad's grave. Tume Atturk. He was buried above his granddad. There's space for me, too. It's a Menai thing.'

She clicked on the lamp. She hugged herself. 'It's illegal.'

'It's right.'

'This is one of the . . . *home cemeteries?*'

'Come, I'll show you round,' I said, taking the lamp. 'This is one of four rooms. Funny how rooms shrink on you. I remember when I needed fifteen paces to cross this. Now I can do it in five.'

'Why are you telling me this?'

'You wanted my secrets,' I reminded her. I could hear a noise on the street but could not clearly say it was not in my head. She was there, I thought. Yet there was a weariness in me that wanted quits with this world, where I never really knew what was there and what was an elaborate hallucination. More than anything else, just then, I wanted her to be real. More than anything else in the world, I wanted Badu to be a dream, but I knew why there was a body in the earth of my house that was no Atturk. The knowledge of a prisoner crowded in on me, a captive waiting for Badu's interrupted death sentence. I gripped my head . . . I was swirling again . . .

I was the fist of Menai Vengeance, the spirit of the Crown Prince. I was lighter than air. I crossed without boats. I read the night skies. He confessed on tape. The Crown Prince passed judgment. Pitani would die. Badu would kill. I lifted and hefted Utoma's machete. I started down towards his front room.

Emeigu tunoma. I froze. The voice and the spirit of Menai's Mata. It cut through judgment, fell like The Fisher's net over Leviathan. I was fire. I was stone. Nothing could break the power of Earth; but Tide could cover her for a time. Badu won't kill. I tempered judgment. I laid down machete. His voice, his counsel . . . **emeigu tunoma.** I left.

Cold awareness fell on me, separating me from all dreams of normalcy. I turned away.

'Are you all right?'

I took a deep breath. 'You said I could trust you.'

'You didn't . . . then . . .'

'I'm telling you now. I'm remembering things that I . . . don't remember doing . . . about Badu—'

She turned away abruptly, a flat palm in the air like one that took an oath. 'It's too much for me, now.'

My hands curled into fists. In the other room, the Mata was singing. My guilt cried out for silence. I suddenly pined for the dowry of normalcy that she could bring into my life. I whispered, 'Help me, please.'

She took an indecisive step towards the door. I let her out, turned off the lamp, and went in to Mata Nimito. He took a few spoons of jollof and pushed the food flask away. He hummed to himself. I sat next to him in the darkness. We spoke quietly, and the trickle of hesitant language inside me became a nostalgic stream. I was remembering. It was his voice and his counsel, *emeigu tunoma,* which had pulled me back from the brink of Badu. It had saved Charles Pitani's life. It was history repeating itself, the peaceful counsel of the Mata against the bloody justice of the crown prince.

'He's not hungry?' she asked from the opposite corner where she sat, hunched on her own.

'Not really.' I watched a gecko catch a moth on a moonlit sill. 'Why did you come back?'

Her teeth gleamed in the moonlight. 'I guess the graves here spooked me. I think it's a Sontik thing. I just stepped outside and I was like: *"Amana! This is what you wanted!"* You wanted help . . . I've called a doctor friend . . .'

The Mata coughed. His voice was low, and I had to lean over. I scratched my head.

'What did he say?'

I fudged. 'Many things, but he also wants us to bury him somewhere.'

Her eyes rounded in horror.

'Not alive, silly.'

◆ ◆ ◆

THE STRANGER approached the house, making no effort to be either silent or discreet. We stepped away from the door as he pushed his way in, clicking on a torch as he did so. A bluish light bathed the room. He had the heavy, drawn features of the sickly Menai, but he stood erect. He wore a fringe of grey beard.

'Mr. Rani! You followed me!'

'I didn't need to,' he said to Amana, without shifting his gaze from me. 'I know this house. *Worie.*'

'*Dobemu,*' I replied cautiously.

'*Enieme kwaya Mata.*'

I led him into the Mata's room. Even then I could feel the tension between us. He went forward to the Mata as though in a trance, and I stood there, with Amana, for several minutes as they communed in low tones. When he rose to face me, I saw that he was struggling to control himself.

'Do you know who I am?'

I nodded. The memory had returned slowly, owing more to my journalism than our common heritage. 'Tobin Rani. The Menai Legacy Group. You filed one of those cases against Trevi . . .'

He waved that connection away impatiently. 'Not that. Further back, twenty years ago, when you were a boy . . .'

'No.'

He looked up at the ceiling and down at Amana. 'Can you wait outside?'

She hesitated, glancing at me. I remembered my grand declaration. 'This is my house and she's staying.'

He smiled. His voice was gentle. '*Asie wu simini.*'

'And we're speaking English.'

His smile grew, and he took a step closer to Amana. When he placed his flat palm on her stomach, she was too surprised to react. 'Are you pregnant yet?' he asked softly.

She slapped away his hand, and he turned to me brusquely. 'If she's the one you keep no secrets from, I totally approve.' He came closer. 'We are Menai, and we don't have time to beat about the bush. Zanda, I know you've always wondered why you look like you do, despite having Malian for a mother and Tume for a father.'

I took a step forward. He raised a finger and pointed at the Mata in the corner. I took a deep breath, beginning to wish I had let Amana go outside.

'They died before they would have told you the truth: your birth mother was a Yorkshire girl called Laura Fraser. She's dead now.'

The earth beneath me gave a seismic heave.

'Who's his father?' I heard Amana ask.

'I am,' said Tobin Rani, as I struggled to breathe, '—but don't take my word for it, Zanda, talk to Mata Nimito. Come, Amana, let's leave them now.'

After turning off the lamp, he took her arm and led her, unresisting, out into the courtyard. The ground was still rolling, and I, dizzy, staggered forward, falling to my knees before the Mata. I heard a distant siren from the direction of the square.

'*Gerai torqwa mu,*' I mumbled, eventually.

He began my praisegenealogy, sixteen hundred and five years long, from the common ancestry of all Menai, the court of the exiled crown prince, Xera, cheated of his kingdom by his younger brother. I had started him off rashly and though the information I wanted was an hour away, and my mind was roiling with Tobin Rani's revelations, there was no stopping him now. There was no rushing his cadenced recital either. I sat back, thumbing on the recorder on my phone to capture a history my mind was in no state to process, just then. It was going to be a while.

The siren passed the darkness of the house and faded. I heard the barking of dogs. The minutes passed, and the Mata kept talking. I heard voices in the hallway: Tobin's voice, Questionnaire's voice.

Mata Nimito chanted on, stringing his narration with anecdotal nuggets on illustrious ancestors. His voice calmed me. I had forgotten the antiquity of the Menai heritage and the power of a recital to bring it to life. As he progressed I was moved from the apathy of my six-year exile. As the room teemed with their names, I began to *care* for these ancestors who had lived and died hundreds of years ago. The longer he went on, the more rooted I felt, the more I felt like . . . *someone*.

Deep into his recital, I was no longer alone in the room with him: Amana was sitting on her heels, as was Professor Balsam. I was past caring, seduced into another world by the song of the Mata. I knew I was probably hearing the last torqwa anyone would ever hear in this world. *Mine*. And it was by no means clear that the old man would have the energy to finish it.

His voice transported me. It dissolved the shroud of the years. I was borne away into the forests of our sojourn, through the deserts and the savannahs. Through his voice I slipped into the age that moulded not just Mata Nimito but his predecessor, Mata Doa, and *his* predecessor, Mata Djani—right up to the illustrious first mata, Mata Nara, boon companion of Xera, crown prince of the Kingdom. Mata Nara, whose praise songs fortified the devastated crown prince on the first leg of the sojourn of the People that would become the Menai. Mata Nimito's voice strengthened with pride as his narration proceeded, buoyed by the excellence of his recall.

Finally he arrived at the last century. The tension in the room grew as Etienam the zealous fathered Cature the smith with the sister of the alien, and Cature fathered Manan the poet with the daughter of Menjabi the wastrel, and Manan fathered Tobin the scholar with the daughter of Simisto the well-digger, and Tobin fathered Zanda the lost with the daughter of the alien . . .

Numbly, I put the water bottle to the lips of the old man. He drank lustily. *'Aima Zanda Atturk,'* I protested. *'Atturk.'*

'Emini Tobin Rani, ba Zanda ma mistsa sizili,' repeated Mata Nimito, in a voice shaded with rebuke; then he fell silent.

I killed the recorder on my phone. I felt my moorings to my house, to Old Raecha Atturk's house, loosening. A thought scurried in the dark crevices of my mind, refusing to be squelched: *my name was a lie.*

'Let's walk,' said a thick voice from the door. I rose stiffly and followed Tobin, past Questionnaire and Amana, into the hall. We passed on a creaking floor onto the threshold, pausing to look out for the police before we slipped into the silent, moonlit street.

'He could be wrong,' I muttered stubbornly. 'He says what he is told. He's not GodMenai. He has no way of knowing what goes on in bedrooms!'

'We have no time for this nonsense, Zanda,' said Tobin intensely, walking ahead of me into the copse that had overtaken Megima's old vegetable garden. He whipped around, taking my shoulders in both hands. 'Use your eyes. *Look* at me! *Listen* to my voice!'

I glared at him. 'I hear the voice of a liar!' I raged. 'Why have I lived such a lie?'

'Life is not convenient. Life is what it is.'

'Who are you?'

'Tobin Rani, son of Manan, son of Cature . . .'

'Spare me!' My voice was harsh, judgmental, disbelieving. 'You said my mother was a Laura.'

'Yes. It all gets very complicated . . .' He scratched his scalp. 'Zanda, we are Menai: we have no time to beat about the bush. I'll tell you how it is, as shameful as the things I've done have been—'

'By GodMenai! Just tell it! *Where* is my birth mother, and how did I end up in the house of Atturk?'

'Laura died twenty-one years ago, in England.'

'Where was I born?'

He shook his head. He crooked a finger downwards. 'You were conceived here in Kreektown, but you were born in Khartoum, Sudan . . .' He looked into the trees, at his shoes, and then he looked at me. 'Laura was married to someone else, that's the thing. And your twin brother ended up in England, fostered . . .'

'What?'

' . . . fostered by a Chinese lady—'

'I have a twin?'

'Of course.'

I was silent for an eternity. His eyes gave nothing away. He waited.

'And he's alive?'

'As far as I know, yes. His name is Humphrey Chow. You are identical twins.'

I felt my legs going rubbery again, and I leaned against a trunk. 'Humphrey Chow. *Chow.*'

He coughed. 'I had a relationship with your mother. I am not proud of it, but it happened . . . She was married to . . .'

'Where's my . . . brother?' The unfamiliar word came out eventually.

'In London . . .' He fumbled in his pockets, pulling out a slim book, much-handled. He grinned and, in a voice that sounded helplessly proud, said, 'He's a writer like you. . . . I guess that's blood for you. I've put his address on the first page. I won't get in touch with him again; I seem to mess up people's lives . . . and I've done my share for him . . .'

It was a novella titled *Blank*. He turned it over. The photograph of my face above the bio coalesced the emotions swirling in me, gave it an ugly edge of envy. I did not touch the book. Eventually his hand fell to his side. His grin slipped and he looked deflated, a baker whose long-awaited loaf was coming out flat.

'Does he know about me?'

Tobin shook his head tiredly. 'I moved Heaven and Hell to make it possible, but . . .' he shook his head again, 'he knows me like you used to know me . . . as an . . . uncle of sorts.' He grinned. 'I even taught him to speak Menai. But no, he doesn't know me as his father, and he doesn't know you exist.'

A siren began to grow in volume again, from the direction of the square. '*Why?* Why did I end up an Atturk? Why are you just telling me this? I am twenty-five years old, for GodMenai's sake!'

He shifted his weight anxiously. 'That was my deal with Tume and Malian.' He took my arm. 'We were to give you as normal a childhood as—'

I jerked free. 'They've been dead fourteen years!'

'You have to understand: for the love of Menai, I've spent most of my life either in prison or in psychiatric hospitals.'

I looked at him levelly. 'You're crazy, then?'

He grinned again. It seemed a tic he could not control. 'This is true,' he said, crooking a finger downwards, 'what I'm telling you. I'm only mad with the madness of all true Menai. The kind of madness that brings a dead old man back to life again to finish a work that must be done!' His voice grew gentle again. 'I don't know why you took that money, Zanda, but they want you, and they want you badly. Let me help you . . .'

'Mata Nimito wants to sleep in the Field of Stones.'

'He told me.'

'I promised to take him there. I will.'

Tobin grinned. 'Do you know where it is?'

'The Mata knows. He'll show the way.'

His grin widened. 'It is two thousand years and four thousand kilometres away. Nobody knows that it still exists. He will try to trace it, not from *his* memory—which I trust, by the way—but from the memory of our fathers' fathers' fathers' fathers' father . . . you get the point. He will die on the way.' He was no longer grinning; his face bore no expression, not even a faint smile. His voice was low. 'Even if he knows the way, we need help to make it to the end. Professor Balsam and I are working together on this. Our visas are almost sorted, and our expedition truck is waiting at Ma'Calico's. We'll find the Mata's Field of Stones, *if it exists*. I pledge you that, by GodMenai. But you must save your own life. I don't want you to take my place in prison. *Save yourself.*' He took a sealed envelope from his pocket, wrote a telephone number on it, and gave it to me with the book. 'Everything you wanted to ask your biological father and never could,' he said with forced lightness. 'Don't read it all at once!'

I took a step back. The book and envelope hung between us for an age.

'Save yourself, Zanda, find your way to London. Humphrey cannot deny the evidence of his eyes. He will help you. You both escaped Trevi's accursed inoculation. You're among the last of the Menai.'

'I can take care of myself.'

He gritted his teeth and put book and envelope back in his pocket. Then he turned and was gone.

Save yourself! As though there were anything left to save of my old life. I stood there for an age, swatting mosquitoes from my ears, trying to get my head around all I had heard. The book had confounded me: my face on a book I did not write. A biography for my face that was not mine. That was the icy proof of what he said.

A delayed rage engaged: two decades of jibes at my colour, my hair, and my ancestry. And here was guilt at arm's length! I felt an overwhelming urge to throw a punch—and I blundered out from the copse into the path of patrolling policemen.

◆ ◆ ◆

MY TRAINING as a boxer was useless in Elue's interrogation room at the Divisional Headquarters in Ubesia. It was unfair, because when he began to lay into me, he had not told me what he wanted and so gave me no opportunity to end my suffering. I felt myself going blind, becoming crippled and impotent. I screamed all manner of confessions before that inevitable moment when I would take a blow on my voice box and become dumb as well. Finally he thought he had softened me up enough and pulled out a notebook.

I told him every conceivable thing he could possibly want to know. I told them about Adevo's tent and the four hundred thousand naira I paid him.

He raised the baton. 'How much?'

'Five hundred!' I shouted, and when the baton rose higher, 'I mean *six* hundred!'

I told him about my hideout at Ma'Calico's and Amana's gambling retreat behind the treeline. I even told them I was Badu. At that, Elue rose angrily to his feet.

'You think this is all a *game?*'

'What I mean to say is that I will find Badu! I have paid for him! I will scoop him! You will see!'

He let that pass.

◆ ◆ ◆

SOON AFTERWARDS, policemen were piling into troop carriers for the onslaught on Kreektown.

I was unable to walk properly, so I was dragged into the cab of one of the three trucks and propped up between the driver and Sergeant Elue. A station DPO came downstairs and strutted perfunctorily for the flashbulbs of Rafael, a *Palaver* photographer, who affected not to recognise me at all, despite the meals he had eaten on my account at the cafeteria. Minutes passed in which I wondered if I dared ask leave to relieve my bladder—my retentive capacity seemed to be shot. It became too late, and a disgusted Elue gave me an elbow in the neck and debarked, joining Patrick Suenu in his car.

The ride was uncomfortable. The trucks' headlamps lit up hoardings with graffiti in praise of Badu's exploits. I cringed in shame.

There seemed to be a power failure in the village when the trucks pulled into Ma'Calico's car park. It was busier than normal: an articulated truck, several minivans, and a brand new six-wheeler off-roader that was probably Tobin's expedition truck.

Of my car, there was not a trace.

That disappearance broke the stranglehold of my fear. The realisation that another agency was at work in my affairs bolstered me, though I had no idea who it was. I still stank of ammonia and fear, but I rediscovered some function in my legs. I stumbled after my captors into the bar. At our entrance, the noisy room fell silent.

We stood there in the middle of the low-ceilinged saloon. The lanterns in the room multiplied the flickering shadows of Elue's policemen against the walls. The hotelier stared from behind her counter.

'Are you Ma'Calico?' asked Sergeant Elue, slapping his baton against his thigh.

'Tha's what they call me.'

'Where's your daughter?'

There was a snigger from the shadows around the bar counter. Ma'Calico killed it with a glare. She stepped out from behind the counter. 'Did they send you to laugh at me, or what is it? I born girl for you?'

'Where's the room you rented to this criminal?' shouted Patrick Suenu, gesturing to me, as he pushed to the fore of the posse. 'We are here to search it for my money! Listen, woman, it is over, you hear me? Your tenant here has confessed.'

Ma'Calico looked at me blankly. 'Confessed what? Who is this man?'

Sergeant Elue pushed her out of the way and I led them through the warren of rooms that was Ma'Calico's Hotel. The room that had been mine was locked and did not open to my key. Elue rapped on the door; when it opened, it was to reveal a sleepy, half-naked trucker who seemed more surprised to see us than I was to see him. Elue hummed tonelessly as they turned the room inside out in search of money, and my wounds throbbed with anticipatory pain.

He dragged me back to the parlour, my feet scrabbling to keep pace. Ma'Calico had not moved. She stood with planted feet as Elue pushed my face within an inch of hers.

'You don't know this man? He says he's your tenant, your daughter's boyfriend.'

I thought I saw a flicker of life in her eyes when the bit about the boyfriend came out, but she only sniffed long-sufferingly. 'I have to have daughter first before she can have boyfriend, not so? I have nice hotel here where you can sleep and baf before you go. Is three thousand naira for room-and-baf. If you stain my bed sheet, is another five hundred naira. Do you want or not?'

'Woman,' warned Elue, 'you may not be involved in this case, but that will change if you lie to me.'

'It's not here,' urged Patrick Suenu from the door. 'Let's go for the Korba man.'

Ma'Calico sniggered, pushing the antiquated muzzle of a Mark IV rifle out of her way as she returned to her place behind the counter, 'You're going to Korba Adevo and his roughboys this night with these your olden-days guns? I sorry for you.'

Elue stormed outside, where he ripped the tarpaulin cover off the rear of one of his trucks. He jumped behind a submachine gun and a second later released a volley of automatic gunfire into the night. The police dogs went crazy, the saloon emptied outside, and a crowd began to gather around the angry policemen. In that militarised delta, they did not seem impressed by the firepower on show. Even Ma'Calico had a submachine gun inside a bag of rice in her pantry. A second arms truck had recently been abandoned just outside Kreektown and Amana had told me how Ma'Calico had taken the submachine gun from a roughboy in settlement of his tab. The hotelier didn't like guns but she didn't see the sense of being the only business in town without one, either.

'Bring down the bikes!' barked Elue.

A tarpaulin came off another truck, ramps were fixed to the rear, and four ungainly motorbikes wheeled down. The new Kreektowners knew their bikes, and the new police issues attracted a little more respect, but Ma'Calico had seen enough tomfoolery for the night. 'You better hire my donkeys if you're entering that swamp this night . . .' she said as she returned to her counter.

Her business wiles did not wash with Elue. Within minutes the policemen were ready to march on Adevo's hideout, and there was not an equine ass in the lineup.

Hameed the secret service agent turned up, attracted by the gunfire. His easy charisma was gone and he glowered resentfully at the villagers, clearly still smarting from his humiliating trip to Abuja during the secession party. He took Elue aside. Moments afterwards, the sergeant stormed back into the bar, Hameed in tow. We could hear his roar from the courtyard.

Ma'Calico was not intimidated. 'So you're talking about Mrs. Udama? You should have said so. Siddon wait for am, she will soon be back.'

'Is she not your daughter?' asked Hameed.

'You're mad, you. All my customers call me 'Mama,' so is me that born all of them, not so?'

'Let's go for the Korba man,' begged Patrick Suenu again from the door.

'Whether she's your daughter or your customer,' warned Elue, 'you better find her before I come back, otherwise . . .' Then he turned to follow Patrick, 'You're coming with us?' he asked Hameed.

The secret service agent grinned. A grudge against Kreektown was one thing; a gratuitous gunfight was evidently another. 'No, Sarge. I'm doing one important undercover investigation like that in Ntupong's joint.'

I was assigned to the pillion of the lead motorbike, and the headlamps lit up the track into the forest. Patrick Suenu travelled on the second bike with Sergeant Elue, whining about the warning shots, which could have scared off Adevo with his money. From Elue's indifference it was clear that the sergeant would far rather avoid a shootout than die for Patrick's money.

As we left Kreektown, I heard Tobin Rani's unmistakable voice in the distance: 'Arazie, Arazie.' It took me back years. Among the Menai a woman who needed to rest—or make more babies—would send her young children to a neighbour to borrow some arazie. There was no such thing; it was a naughty adult code that told indulgent neighbours to send children round the houses for a while to buy a frazzled mother some respite.

After their frenetic barking in the carpark of Ma'Calico's Hotel, the township dogs seemed as cowed by the swamp as their owners, and I heard only whines on the outward journey. Within a few minutes we had to abandon the heavy bikes, which had become mired in the viscous earth. The policemen staggered on after me, cursing and swearing, up to their ankles in mud.

Finally we arrived at Adevo's clearing, where I sank to my knees in disbelief.

'Where's the tent?' asked Elue, playing his torch around as his men swarmed the bald spot where the tent had stood. 'Where's the generator? Where's Adevo?'

My fingers were trembling from the cold and the fear of the baton. When it rapped against my skull, I toppled over and lay still. In that night it was easy to become disoriented, but in the light of the torches, with the anchor of that dilapidated jetty—missing a boat and jeep now—with that sweeping view of the creek . . . it was impossible to be mistaken. Except that Adevo's massive tent was gone.

''Shun!' called Elue. His tired, stinking men straightened, energized by the cancelled gunfight. 'About turn!'

'You can't turn back now,' cried Patrick. 'I've mobilised you!'

'Your money has expired!' snapped the policeman without embarrassment.

The return march started, approaching me where I lay. Patrick ran after Elue, arguing, 'But she confirmed it, that Calico woman, Korba is here. This boy is hiding the real location . . .'

'Am I going to search the whole of Niger delta this night for your stupid money? What is it?' He dragged me to my feet, swearing, 'If we get lost this night, I'll bury you here!'

We returned to the head of the column. As we went, the nervousness of the policeman penetrated my own funk. I saw how exposed and vulnerable they were, walking in single file through a forest at night. Elue's fierce grip on my collar was more fear than his native brutality, and it strengthened me, giving my body a second wind beyond torture.

Arazie! This was Tobin's signal then: I was to take the policemen on a wild goose chase to buy the villagers time. Despite my memories of disabling pain, I found the courage to take a wrong turn. In minutes, I was hopelessly lost myself.

We soldiered on forever through cloning paths. One by one, the bright torches dimmed and died until we had only a few anaemic lights in the front of the march. An hour passed, and then another. Drifts of smoke came and went, and the acrid smell of burning became insistent. The oppressive darkness drew closer and the policemen grew more fearful. I fed off their fear. Elue had to have realised that our return was already three times as long as the outbound trip, but he seemed afraid to ask the obvious question. Patrick had fallen silent and had fallen back from the exposed fore into the middle of the group. Eventually, I stopped creekside, in front of Utoma's poultry shed.

Elue was trembling with rage. 'What's this meaning?'

'I'm lost.'

He swung his baton. It caught an overhanging branch and slipped from him. The torches were too weak for them to see the abandoned buildings alongside, overgrown with bushes since Utoma's death, but the stymied dogs finally began to bark. I wondered if Badu—if I—had killed the inspector general by default after all, by starving him to death. Then a hoarse voice I did not recognise bleated above the tumult of dogs and scared policemen. Elue let me go and backtracked through his milling men. I slipped back several paces until I was knee-deep in the creek.

The voice energized the weary policemen once again. There was a flurry of activity. Shots rang out, cries of 'Badu,' 'Rabbit,' 'Careful,' and 'Fool!' I had delivered the greatest policing coup in Nigerian history to an inadvertent Elue, and his sycophantic instincts were sound.

He had already stripped off his trousers to clothe his boss, but despite his girth, he was too lean for his jacket to be of much use, even for the starved Pitani. He ran around in his boxers looking for the fattest of his policemen to strip. Presently, Charles Pitani emerged in all his shrunken grandeur. He had inspected hundreds of parades in his life, but the filthy, exultant band of policemen, with a commanding sergeant in underwear, was clearly the sweetest his eyes had ever seen.

I backed further away, into an amphibious curtain of mangrove roots. The main body of policemen stood between me and Kreektown, which was less than a kilometre away; it might as well have been a world away, for I had burned my boats. I shut my eyes as Elue shouted my name, his voice an exultant threat. I heard the yelp of tired dogs. I edged deeper into the creek. My heart pounded. Then a shadow separated itself from the trees. He wore the string vest of the roughboys, and rubber boots came up to his knees. He was armed: machete in a waist sheath and automatic rifle on shoulders. He was shiny with sweat, and I realised he had been following us all night.

'You fit swim?'

I nodded silently.

He pointed across the stream. 'Adevo dey wait you.'

I looked across the creek. It was nearly dawn. The opposite bank was still in darkness, but the middle section had no tree cover and the moonlight glinted off the surface of the creek. When I looked back there were two others with him. He made a dive gesture with his hand, and they melted into the trees once again.

I shed my shirt and sank into the creek, breast-stroking away from the shoreline toward where the creek was deeper. Suddenly, the flaccid night was stretched to garrotte tautness by the excited barking of dogs. I had not been silent enough. I felt like the last Menai, bedding down for eternity in a watery tomb as I took a gulp and dived. There were shots, then I was kicking, stroking deeper and deeper.

I had not swum the Agui since it drowned my parents; I had not swum any river or pool. Yet when this moment came, I dived without a thought into waters that had lately drowned a grieving Jonszer. I stroked, blind, into the creek. As an eleven-year-old I used to swim across the creek regularly but had never done so underwater. My lungs were larger now—and my reasons more desperate. As soon as I was underwater, I changed direction, swimming with the current that emptied into the Atlantic. I came up two minutes later, downstream from the poultry shed but on the same side of the creek. I treaded water and refreshed my lungs. It was exhilarating to be in the water again, and the adrenaline rush masked the pain from my torture. I took my bearings, reassured by the fainter barking, and dived again. This time, I made for the farther bank.

I lay panting on the sandbank for an age, until the red tint of my eyesight returned to normal. I heard the rustle and sat up moments before Amana reached me. She hugged me fiercely, while I tried to bite down the pain from my bruises.

'Why did you bring them here?'

I panted wordlessly.

'You're human after all. Come.'

Exhaustion arrived with a vengeance, and I fought to retain consciousness, missing my shirt and shoes badly. I stumbled after her for 150 metres up a narrow footpath until we gained a crowded clearing. Perhaps a dozen faces from Ma'Calico's were there. The iroko herself stood, hulking over a fire. Her eyes were warm for the first time in our acquaintance. And there was something like capitulation in her lips, although I would be stretching things to call it a smile.

Adevo was there too. He pushed a bundled-up robe into my hands.

I pulled it on gratefully, too breathless for the profuse thanks that were due. It smelled of kaushe soup and singed hide, not a particularly unpleasant combination of things to smell of, just then. I followed Adevo to the fire, where several Sontik villagers from Kreektown snatched a communal meal, looking far more cheerful than refugees had a cause to be.

'Eat,' he commanded, as he turned away, phone to ear. It was a welcome order.

We were on a narrow spit of land between two creeks, and a ceaseless stream of people hurried past the clearing, carrying property toward speedboats on the far bank.

'Small man devil,' said Fati proudly, beaming at me. She gave me a chunk of venison.

'He will kill elephant and carry in head pan,' agreed a face from Ma'Calico's, putting a can of warm beer in my hand.

'But he didn't kill that snake, Pitani,' grumbled Ma'Calico, keeping things in perspective. There was the silence of mastication, as roast tubers and a small antelope were quickly shared. I struggled to keep my eyes open.

Furious shots rang out from across the Agui. I looked up as Korba Adevo chuckled. 'I've collected all their trucks and motorcycles!'

'And we burned down my hotel,' added Ma'Calico. 'Everything we couldn't carry, we burned to the ground.'

'What?' I was stunned.

'They would have locked me up and demolished it anyway,' she explained.

'As for,' said Adevo. He sucked his teeth morosely. 'Farmers burn their farms after harvest. It grows faster next time.'

'Mouth!' said Ma'Calico. 'Oya, bring petrol, let's burn your boats also!' There was bravado in her voice; there was also pride in the hands she lifted to the fire. 'This is my hotel. Anywhere I plant it, it will grow.'

'Amen,' agreed Fati. 'Is a big delta. We will find another town.'

Ma'Calico hesitated. Her eyes bore through me in a return to form. 'You should have killed that snake.'

I was taken aback by her venom. 'There's been enough blood already.'

'He's a snake,' she insisted. Now that she was liberated from her job, she was sounding more schoolmistress than local hotelier. 'They have destroyed our country. I don't mind burning my business, but you kill a snake before he bites you, that's nature's law. You should have killed him.' She rose and lumbered away.

There were grunts of assent from around the fire.

'If you said, I could have finished him for you,' complained Adevo, 'but me, I don't like poke-nosing into another man's business. Drink.'

I did. I leaned over to Amana. 'Mata Nimito?'

'He's okay, Tobin took him.' She gave me a large envelope. 'He said I should give you this.' She held my eyes in a steady gaze. 'He told me about Humphrey Chow. Are we going to him?'

It was easier, at that point, merely to nod.

There was some excitement in the shadows; when I looked, I saw a figure emerge and approach the fires. When he was close enough, Amana jumped to her feet. There was a grin on her face, and she pulled me up to meet him. She took his hand in a fervent handshake.

'Thanks for coming.'

He was unsmiling, guarded. 'You said it was a matter of life and death . . . and I met the whole place burning . . .'

'That's how they welcomed me too, Dr. Maleek. Fire is a Kreektown tradition.' She lowered her voice soberly. 'I couldn't get you to break my mother's confidence, Doc. Can you keep my own secrets?'

He shrugged ungraciously. 'So long as . . .'

'Zanda,' she cut in as I struggled to keep upright, 'You said you needed help. This is Dr. Maleek.'

'Thanks. I just need painkillers and sleep right now,' I began.

'No, he's a psychiatrist,' she explained. 'Dr. Maleek, Zanda also likes to call himself Badu.'

His brows furrowed. 'Badu . . . as in *"Badu?"*'

What I saw in his eyes was another variation of Sergeant Elue's incredulity earlier that day—the gap between my spineless reality and the Badu of urban legend. I'm not sure why it got to me this time. Perhaps it was the absence of guns. To the southeast, a flare stack belched explosively. From behind my eyes, stars also exploded, and I think I stumbled forward, slipping deeper into sleep than I had ever fallen before.

SLEEPCATASTROPHES

Kreektown | April, 2000

Etie Nomsok
Sisi Mari
Gaius Kroma
Clema Dadie
Salia Kakandu
Haji Megima
Baby Megima

Births
Nil

Extant Menai population: 350 (NPC estimates)

CHARLES PITANI

Abuja | 19th March, 2005

I wake before her. I stay in bed with my eyes closed till she dresses and leaves home.

This life is a bitch. I am gone for a week, and her wardrobe has expanded and expanded until my own clothes are in a *Ghana-mus'-go* in the bathroom. Buys designer black with my money to prepare for my own burial. And a cow and bags of rice in the backyard for the funeral jollof . . . is that the first thing? When they haven't even seen my corpse?

It's not her fault. I have moved all my money abroad now. If this thing takes my head she has to start all over again . . .

Yes, I let her go. Talking is not what I want to do now. Now is time for action. I get up and shower. I am hacking and spitting like a pregnant woman. It is this smell of chicken shit that I can't get out of my nose. But that is neither here nor there.

I don't shave. I want something sharp on my body, to resemble the broken bottles all over my mind.

There's a new housegirl too. Downstairs in the bar, I take her. She is better than the last one. *Oga, please, don't,* she whispers, but her free hand holds the door shut. Yet when it is over, the siren that was blowing is still blowing.

I leave the TV on, but I don't answer the telephone. That's the compromise I have made. At least I am not totally out of touch. Every newscast has something about me. That's their business. Last time I pass the phone, I see the housegirl has recorded seventy-four messages on the notepad. They can wait.

There are things you think you have passed in life, then *gbam!* They are looking at you face to face! *Suspension?* A whole inspector general of police? Okay. They can keep their job for now. I have enough personal police work on my hands. So many people have offered me the video. Each time, it is just as I suspected: another fool trying to make quick money. This country is terrible. They've paid dearly for their greed, but that is neither here nor there. I am still a prisoner of that Badu bastard, as long as that video is out there somewhere. Maybe this is what he planned. To have my own business partners execute me themselves. But I will get him first.

Unless my name is not Charles Pitani.

There is food on the table and I am hungry. Until I see the chicken in the stew. I don't know if I can ever eat chicken again after my experience in that poultry shed. There was a dead man in a cane chair. I watched Badu bury the man in the room and tie me on the same bloody chair! The smell of dead men and rotten eggs and chicken is now the same for me.

Being suspended has its advantages: it opens your eyes to alternatives. With fifty thousand policemen my deputy could not find Badu. With my money and my motivation, I have much better alternatives. And I am going to get that Badu, if it is the last thing I do.

Especially if it's the last thing I do.

'You've got to watch your liver, Charles.'

I turned. I tried to fake a smile but nothing happened. This disaster has frozen my face like panla, but that is neither here nor there. Jude Fijaro is the last person I want to see now. 'How did you get in?'

'That's not very friendly. You won't take my phone calls and I come in person and you won't even offer me a brandy.'

I walked across and parted the curtains; the gates were unmanned! Did they withdraw my security staff? That my deputy is a viper. He uses the files on my desk to take my job from under my feet, and he won't even leave me an ordinary gateman detail. I turned. The light opened up the large room, but Fijaro filled it with his poisonous personality. He was dressed in his usual white brocade. He wore that smile of his that was not really a smile, that sat on his face like a painful wound. By the time I came back from the window to shake his hand, I was smiling like him. 'Welcome. Coke or rocks?'

'None.'

I poured him a brandy and he sat down. He had not shaved either.

He did not waste any time. 'Am I safe?' he asked.

'I don't know.'

'What kind of answer is that?'

'I don't know! Please! I hope you haven't come to add to my problems. I've just spent the worst week of my life—'

Fijaro pushed himself up. The brandy spilled on his brocade and my carpet. He did not notice. He came over very fast. I hope he gets physical— no, I *pray* the fat balloon gets physical today, because I am angry enough to give him the surprise of his life. But he only came to kneel beside me with an elbow on my armrest and to whisper angrily in my ear, 'And I'm *still* in the middle of the worst week of my life! *Am I safe?*'

He has watched too much Nollywood. Through the brandy on his breath, I can smell fear and an unwashed mouth.

'By the grace of God.'

'Let's leave God out of this! Did you talk? Did he video you like Omakasa?'

I feel a spasm in my crotch. Every time I think about the video, it is the same.

Fijaro saw my face and did not need an answer. He slid away on the carpet, spilling more brandy. *'Mo gbe! Mo gbe!'*

I've never seen him like this, even though he's a hard drinker and a worse curser. When he's drunk he likes for us to call him Judas. If I was not in such shit myself, I would be enjoying his pain.

By the time he reached the sofa he had recovered. He set the brandy down on the glass coffee table and dried his fingers with a handkerchief. He sat down properly. 'Okay. What exactly did you say?'

Idiot. Thinks he's in court. 'They drugged me. I can't remember exactly.'

'They? Are we talking about Badu here or a committee of kidnappers?'

'You think only one man could have done this to me? This was an organised gang!'

'They didn't drug Omakasa,' he said suspiciously. 'I saw the video. The judge was confessing with his full senses.'

'I'm a trained policeman, I'm not Omakasa,' I said angrily. A text had come that evening a week ago as I left Force Headquarters. It was from Fernandez, a name I vaguely remembered, and asked whether the balance of my money was seven or seventeen thousand dollars. It gave a hotel room where I could send an aide to pick it up. As if that was the sort of errand one ever sent aides on. Especially where both deal and balance were so uncertain.

The hotel was on my way home, and my convoy pulled in there. Armed escorts waited at the entrance of the hotel. My armed aides stood guard at the entrance to the room.

Room 32 was opened for me by a uniformed housekeeper whose trolley stood just inside the room. As I walked past him, the door closed behind me and I was karate-chopped on the back of the neck. When I dropped to my knees, a steel hand clamped a damp towel over my face. I remember being paralysed, before losing consciousness.

I must have been carried past my aides stuffed in a laundry trolley! And dumped in a boot in the car park! Right under the eyes of my idiotic escorts!

I am homicidal with shame, but that is neither here nor there.

Fijaro poured himself another brandy, neat. He took a gulp. Quality brandy was always wasted on people like him. 'Did you . . . did you . . . ?'

'Yes?'

'Did you mention my name?'

'Yes.'

He hissed like a snake. 'Where's the video?'

There was something in my throat. When I finished coughing, he was still glaring at me.

'What?' I asked.

'I said, "Where's the bloody video?"'

'I'm not sure there is one.'

'Why?'

'If there is, it would be out by now, wouldn't it? This is what we call the modus operandi. With Omakasa it was out within—'

'You're not Omakasa.'

'I know, I'm talking about the *modus operandi* now. This is Policing 101. With Omakasa it was out in twenty-four hours. That means—'

'Drop this modus operandi baloney; I'm not a recruit in your freaking Police College. All I want to know is whether there was a tape of your confession or not!'

'His video recorder was—'

'*He?* Or *they?* Where's our "organised gang" now?'

I gave him a sidelong glare. 'They had a video recorder all right, but the battery was dead or something. Because if not, by their modus—'

'What are you going to do, Charles? Sit here moping in your living room till they arrest Badu? Is he going to repeat what you told him in court? Is this how my daughter in Cambridge will hear her daddy's name on BBC?'

'Don't worry, Badu will never go to court. My mercenaries are coming.'

He looked at me for a very long time, then he swore. '*Iro*. Airy baloney. That Zanda wimp whose picture is circulating could not have done this to you and Omakasa. That's not Badu. All the men in your force could not catch Badu. Your white boys are just coming to eat your money. I have to go into damage limitation now, Charles. For all I know, the video could be uploading on the Internet right now.' He shivered and snapped his fingers. 'Hah! *Mo gbe!* Tell me everything you said. I have to know what to expect.'

'You know everything. I told the truth, that's all.'

'You told the truth?' He lost his temper. 'That's more than you told me! All I know is the hundred thousand you gave me—'

'What more do you want to know?'

'Everything!' he snapped. 'Those blank permits I backdated and registered for you, what did you use them for? There's no record—'

'Was that not the point of the bribe? If they wanted records all over the place, wouldn't they have paid the official fifty naira fee?'

'So what were they for?'

I cracked all my knuckles, one by one. He waited patiently.

'The Menai case in London.'

'*What?*'

'What's all this drama?' I demanded. I was never this rude to Fijaro before, but I don't care anymore. With all his connections as a prince in the palace, what more can he do to me? I am already suspended. But as for me, I can still do plenty of pulling down. 'I arranged their backdated vaccine-testing authorisations. And I *paid you very well,* so what are you making noise about?'

'This is what you dragged my name into? My God!'

'So God can now come in, eh?'

'Don't you have any *principles?* Don't you have any *conscience?* People *died* in that inoculation! *Women and children!*'

I stood up. My legs were shaking but not from fear. I'm not sure what it was, but I was not afraid. '"Women and children!" Always women and children! When you want pity it is *women and children!* As if men that died there are donkeys! Okay, so people died! Is it more than what can be settled? When your nephew killed that *innocent* Kanuri woman in the hit-and-run and you came running to me—'

'*Thousands of people died . . .*'

'Thousands of people die every day! Go to the roads! Go to the mortuaries! You're preaching to me now.'

'All right.'

'Okay, so they didn't get permission to test. . . . am I supposed to shoot them? Those thalidomide doctors, who shot them? Tell me that. All those tablets you take every day, were they tested on human *beans?* When your drunk nephew killed that pregnant Kanuri woman and you came—'

'I said it's *okay!* Hah!' He paused. 'How much did they pay you?'

'You mean to me?'

'Yes.'

I sat down just before my legs gave way. I didn't know what was happening to me. 'Is that what we're talking about now? Or are you now working in the tax office?'

'Omakasa said everything on the tape. If you told Badu, you might as well—'

'Okay! Do you mean everything together?'

'Yes, everything. Because that Trevi case in London is also against Megatum. And those companies think in foreign exchange, those people. They don't even have a naira account.'

I sucked my teeth. Still, I said it on the video, and there's no point in swallowing my own words. What I have eaten, I have eaten. 'One million US.'

I saw the whole six-mile length of his tongue. Plus all the gold fillings in his mouth. Then he flung his brandy glass at my coffee table—*wicked man!* Pieces of brandy glass and coffee table glass scattered in every direction!

From my head to my toes, I was full of pieces of glass! The man is a maniac. With all his American education, Yaba Psychiatric Hospital is what fits him.

He screamed, 'Bastard! Bastard! *Were! Aje!* You take one million US dollars and give me a hundred thousand *naira!*'

I am angry myself. 'What did you bring? Was it not ordinary photocopy form? Hundred thousand for a fifty-naira paper, was that not enough?'

'And you kept one million US dollars? You alone?' His voice cracked. *'Am I your houseboy?'*

'It wasn't for me alone,' I said calmly. 'And I also had to give police protection . . .' but he was not listening, just screaming all over the place. I let him shout. I don't care; he can shout from now till kingdom come. That money is now part of my pension.

Without being called, the housegirl ran in with a broom and packer, her ears flapping like an elephant's. Bloody gossip, looking for news to sell to that useless *Punch.* Where she got the temerity, I'll never know.

'Get out and close that door!' I screamed, and she leapt out of the room like a frightened rabbit.

That's the problem. They see your prick once and the fear's gone forever.

ZANDA ATTURK

Limbe | 19th March, 2005

I was stretched out on creaking boards. Someone was shaking my shoulders and speaking in long and rambling sentences. I was suffused with a sense of loss greater than the sum of all my current woes. I realised I was mourning my parents all over again. When I thought 'Dad,' the image of Tume Atturk no longer materialised unequivocally in my mind. Tobin Rani had broken down a house he could not rebuild. I shut my eyes and drifted off again.

I WAKE in a world the colour of watermelon, where people were turtles. There is a party in progress whose music is a dirge and whose dancers are dressed in mourning white. The natter of conversations in strange tongues washes over me. I wade through the bloodiness of the world, until I find a waistcoated grey turtle, the patterning of whose shell was vaguely familiar. I offer a handshake and find it is a paw.

I am also a turtle.

'I see you're new,' drawls GreyShell, ignoring my paw indulgently. He speaks a manicured Menai whose verbs are conjugated in the ancient style. 'I am Grand Menai; you're one of mine.'

'Where are we?' I ask.

'The Council of Dead Languages.'

'That's why I cannot understand a word!'

'No one understands anyone. That's the beauty of our conversation.'

'There's no communication,' I marvel.

'And no disagreement either.'

'Is this a party, then?'

'It's a party as the dead call parties. It is my induction night.'

'You still look quite good to me,' I say, 'not dead at all.'

'You said it,' he replies genially. 'You said it, yourself.' He kicks his limbs slowly, proudly, but when I look up again, his head is sinking gently into his shell and a soft, good-natured snore replaces his cultured Menai.

I wade away disconsolate. I am sleepy as well, but I am now the last chance of Menai. I will not capitulate. I try to dance but the dirge is worse than a lullaby and the dance floor is cluttered with sleeping turtles.

In the centre of the dance floor a brave geriatric entertains with a spot of break-dancing. When he is done there are drowsy nods of applause. As we help him gather the broken pieces of his shell, I try to strike up another conversation but every turtle will only speak his own tongue. From across the hall I hear a well-lubricated duffer deploy a perfectly turned proverb in Menai. I promptly buttonhole him. 'You speak Menai,' I say.

'Only in the area of untranslateables,' he concedes in Menai. 'But I am the last repository of Esha'—at which point he continues his conversation with himself in Esha.

I find myself by a bar, whose maid gurgles with a seismic laughter reminiscent of Amana's; because of that association I accept a drink offered in a tongue so guttural that I do not wonder that it is dead. I sip her drink in sympathy and feel its soporific draught leaden my limbs. My head sinks into my shell.

I WOKE again to the smell of food. I was in a dark and listing cellar. Hollow footfalls rang out overhead, the ceiling so low I could barely sit up.

Disembodied voices and the clang and whir of machinery, none of it as pressing as the burnt fish whose smell had roused me. I was vaguely aware of a benevolent giant ladling out watery beans from a saucepan, but I took three mouthfuls and faded away.

WUIDA ATTURK (ANCESTORMENAI)

Kreektown | 12th January, 1980

Wuida's first funeral took place in 1956. For the next twenty-four years, she lived in exile in Bida, where she raised her sons and lost her husband. In January 1980, already suffering the ailment from which she died, she arrived at Kreektown Square with Tume, the younger of her sons. There was the pathos of a woman who had literally returned to be buried in her family house. All that week the Mata had been predicting an eclipse. When she arrived, the Menai stopped looking skywards for the cosmic aberration.

Her story was well-known, even to the Menai born after her funeral: A charismatic Fulani trader had arrived in the early '50s. He had fallen in with the Menai and set up his stall in the village square. He had a gift for languages and quickly picked up enough Menai to prosper as a shopkeeper and to woo and marry Wuida with the blessing of the Mata, for he had no problem with the oath to give their children his wife's name and make a home in Kreektown. They had two sons in quick succession. Then Wuida's world was blasted apart by the rocket of a message from her husband's hometown: his father and elder brother had died in a crash, and a thousand head of cattle were looking for an heir.

The Menai were not easily tempted by wealth, but even they recognised the lure represented by a thousand head of Fulani cattle and saw that he had to go.

She and her husband quarrelled nightly over their children. She was ready to yield her marriage but not her children—and of course it was impossible to give up her people. Then came the night he slipped away with the boys.

What followed were two weeks of a death that was life, until the Mata called her in for a sky-gazing. That was August 12, 1956. Her funeral was held that same night, and she was sent off with sadness and prayers, never to see her people again.

Until she returned that January.

All that history would have made no difference, for the living had no truck with the dead; but Wuida sat there at the square and wailed for someone to dig her a grave, until the Mata ordered a new festival, a Restoration, a celebration muted only by her imminent death; but it was as much about her son, Tume, as it was about her. The Menai had last seen Tume as a two-year-old. He was a young man now, a little too loud, a little too brash, and a little too dreamy for life in creek country. But all his flaws were neutralised by his flawless Menai and his unnerving knowledge of the way of the Menai. He had come to stay, and he spoke like a native.

In that sense, his mother had ruined him for life in the real world. She had arrived in Bida to find her husband fitting out another shop. The father and brothers were still alive, and there were no cattle. The message had been a ruse, and the move from Kreektown was for his career: he had decided that Kreektown was too small, after all, to build the prosperity he craved, so he had relocated to a real town. Years passed. A Muslim, he went on to marry two other wives, which enabled Wuida to retreat even more into the Menai of her mind. Her first son did not follow her there. He would understand his mother but would rarely reply in Menai. Ahmed belonged to the Bida of his father.

It was Tume who was sold on her fables of the homeland, the remembered stories of her childhood, related from the earliest days of his own childhood. She reconstructed the texture of the Menai in their rooms in Bida. He knew Kreektown in the map of his mind; he knew the names of all his relations and knew an anecdote, sometimes three, on each and every one of them. He knew a dozen historysongs, which was more than quite a few born and bred Menai. Although he was uncircumcised, he knew how to carve a mean circumcisionhead in whitewood with closed eyes. He also pined for the mananga, whose sound he had never heard, for that peaceful land of the tom-toms, and for the stories that always ended in the good trumping the bad, and the weak the strong, of justice winning out and the evil getting their just recompense.

His father had mapped out Tume's destiny as second assistant shop-keeper in a prosperous provision store that had swamped the street, swallowing up a house on either side and swarming daily onto the sidewalks with vats of beans and rice and millet and pumpkin seeds. Yet Tume did not want a life locked in by shelves; he did not want to sell grain from dawn to dusk, to snatch three meals a day from the same countertop. His father delighted in things like that—in the 55 percent margin he managed to make on the batch of soap he picked up cheap.

Such commercial coups did not excite Tume. As he neared his majority, his father despaired of teaching him the basics of business, regretting his overfamiliarity with Wuida, who had infected him with a dreaminess that was anathema to the businessman. Tume lacked even the most rudimentary greed. He was so popular with customers that he was a liability to a shopkeeper.

Their father's sudden death left Ahmed in hostile charge of the shop, with their mother ailing of the sickness that had killed her husband. Ahmed ran tighter purse strings than his father, but Wuida was not as dreamy as the world imagined. Her father was Raecha, a seafarer and herbalist of the first water, and she knew enough herbal remedies to be consulted by womenfolk in the locality. She never charged for her services, which caused her husband to discount the business potential of her gifting. The grateful donations pressed into her hands were rarely disturbed, and over two decades they had slowly built up. When she counted them into Tume's hands, he had more cash to start their new life in Kreektown than his brother had to run the family shop in Bida.

CHIEF (DR.) EHI A. FOWAKA

Yaba | 19th March, 2005

We are ruled by frightened politicians. There are a hundred and one health care priorities more deserving of research funding than the psychiatric fate of this doomed ethnic nation, but they are afraid that the Menai will become another Ogoni and that the Menai Society will become another Movement for the Survival of the Ogoni People. Yet, Tobin Rani is no Ken Saro-Wiwa. Neither is Sheesti Kroma-Alanta—bless her pretty soul. This thing will end in a whimper, not a bang.

And if the extinction of Menai is such a tragedy, we should all go and plait nooses! None of the children of my Urhobo, Igbo, Yoruba, Hausa, and Efik colleagues can ask for water in any language besides English. If the instructions of Life were written in our ancestral languages, our next generation would be doomed. It will take a few more years, but even our bigger languages are heading for extinction with a psychedelic accent.

With my own daughters, I have tried to change things, addressing the odd comment to them in our language, but they just give me this pitying look, and I have to admit that, at ages thirteen and fourteen, I may have left it too late.

The Menai are facing a double whammy, of course: they will die out with their language. It is rather outside the terms of reference of my psychiatric enquiry, but I shall be recommending a symbolic state funeral when the last ethnic national dies. For them and for the dozens of other languages on the brink of extinction.

Right now, though, I have a job to do and consultancy fees to earn: and I am earning them. I have had untrammelled access to Kreektown—at least to the areas where my Mercedes 300 SEL can now safely go—and no year has passed, since my appointment in the wake of Gideon Orkar's abortive coup, that has not seen the publication of an Annual Interim Report on the Menai. (And as long as my connections in the Ministry of Health endure, long may it continue.)

◆ ◆ ◆

I AM, of course, the most important academic authority worldwide on the Menai. In this connection, I have to mention, for the sake of completeness, the recent frenzied outpourings from ex-Oxford don Dr.—or is it Professor—David Balsam. (His affiliation with Oxford University ended three decades ago under cloudy circumstances, which I will not advert to here—beyond the brief observation that intellectual honesty is the lodestar of academic aspiration—but he seems quite incapable of resisting a dropped name.) He has rushed to blog with an interesting perspective, but his work appears bedevilled by a certain Indiana Jones approach. And as for the sincere work of Mrs. Sheesti Kroma-Alanta, who is like a daughter to me, it is while reading her maudlin pages that one best understands the benefit of objective distance to scientific enquiry.

But as for me, my research project has enjoyed and survived the patronage of no less than five presidential regimes. I am not one to drop names, but I worked for the general, Babangida (stepped a little too far to the side and fell off the plot); the company man, Shonekan (nice, harmless fellow, my old boy as well); the generals Abacha (the less said about this one the better) and Abubakar (brevity was the name of his game, poor fellow); and our dear military-civilian loose cannon, Obasanjo.

Sadly, by the time my final report is published, it is clear that the Menai will have become history and their psychiatric condition will be of only academic interest to scholars. So I might as well make the interim observation that in my considered opinion, the problem with the Menai is a focus on the past at the expense of the future. I mean, in most parts of Nigeria, all a five-year-old will know of his ancestry is that his father is called Papa and his mother, Mama. The average Menai five-year-old will name five or six generations of his maternal and paternal ancestry without breaking a sweat. And I have seen Menai gatherings with forty, fifty adults reciting hour-long, word-perfect historysongs in tandem. All that investment in remembering their 'glorious' past was clearly at a cost.

Their future.

In my trained opinion, the chances of this 'past-psychosis' infecting other Nigerian ethnic nations is nil. My compatriots have buried their own glorious histories and slabbed over the graves. Concrete cities have replaced our earthen homes, even if they mostly end up slums. New religions have replaced our old ones, even if they're still mostly idolatrous cults.

My enthusiasm for fieldwork has received a considerable fillip with the arrival of my 2005 Mercedes W220 S500, but at the date of this writing, the registered numbers of the Menai have dropped below two dozen. It does appear that this illustrious chapter of Chief (Dr.) Ehi Alela Fowaka's life may be drawing to a close. (No, I am not afflicted by the malady of false modesty: I have worked hard for my distinctions and only a handful of my 140 million fellow nationals have the skills and perspicacity to shadow my achievements.) I do not at all relish returning to the envious stares of Dr. Maleek and my other colleagues in my old hospital or leaving the field of my latter-day speciality to the overzealous expatriate scholar David Balsam.

DAVID BALSAM

Great Milton | 22nd December, 1979

It was the first meeting between professor and peer, and their conversation tapered off as they approached the bronze in the glass cabinet. Professor David Balsam had been promised a private viewing of a major antique that had been in the Risborough family for ninety years. As he reached for it, he knew the same thrill of expectation that had sentenced him to a lifetime in antiquities.

'One second,' warned the Ninth Marquis of Wye from behind, as he entered a combination on the keypad by the light switch. A red light in the ceiling winked off, disabling the proximity alarm. He nodded, and David lifted the glass guard and took the bronze head in his hands.

It was exquisitely worked, mesmerising in its coldness. There was the usual disconnect between compact size and heavy weight. He raised it to the light and traced the irregular lines of the base. As he interrogated the piece, he felt he had entered into a separate universe with it. Unconsciously, he was matching it against the vast categories in his mind; the tiny holes were a dead giveaway, the stylistic distinctions notwithstanding. It was of Benin provenance, perhaps from an earlier period, in the light of its divergences from traditional Bini art. The bronze seemed unfinished . . . the dome of the bald head had a shine and perfection that the stylized beard lacked, as though the work had been separated from the craftsman by death or boredom before being completed. He nodded as the gears of recognition suddenly meshed.

Under his professional veneer, he was deeply disappointed. He was not looking at anything new after all. He must have been delusional to believe he would discover a new, thousand-year-old African bronze in a castle in rural Oxfordshire. He set down the bronze head, still nodding, and pushed his hands into his pockets. Although he still stood there, he had disengaged mentally. Lord Risborough read his body language.

'You don't think it's—'

'Excellent,' he said, turning away. 'It's an excellent imitation.'

There was a small Constable landscape on the wall, among grand pastorals of idyllic English villages, but there was nothing in the room to hold his interest. The voices of the boisterous party filtered over from the hall beyond, but he had accepted the invitation only for the chance to see the bronze behind him. He drifted towards the large double doors that opened onto a balcony, followed by his anxious host.

'How can you tell so quickly? You barely looked at it . . .'

'It's an unfinished piece,' said David, parting the drapes and peering out into the premature darkness. 'Still, it has a couple of unique features. I saw the original years ago in the Grant Collection.' He hesitated. The balcony looked inhospitably cold, but it offered a temporary respite from the compulsory good cheer of the Christmas season. 'I do hope you didn't pay a lot of money for yours.'

'As it happens, I did,' said Conrad, Lord Risborough, with a grim smile. He was tall and silver-haired, with blue, haunted eyes that set off what seemed to be a kindly disposition. 'But my granddad must have paid a lot of other people's blood for it.'

David paused, his hand on the large doorknob. 'What do you mean?'

'It's been in the family's collection since 1899, when he returned to this castle from the Benin Campaign. He brought back a good many trophies, but this one he liked too much to sell.'

'So the piece at The Grant . . .'

'. . . was sold to them by my brother five years ago. When he died this year, I paid to buy it back.'

'I'm sorry about your brother.' David opened the doors. He was indeed very sorry, for original or not, the piece was already catalogued. While it would be valuable to collectors, for curators and academics like him it was artistically insignificant. He hesitated again as the cold barrelled in.

'Maybe tea will help?' suggested Conrad. 'Or cognac, perhaps.'

'Tea sounds good, thank you.'

◆ ◆ ◆

TEA WAS a wintry affair. In warmer months, it would have been a pleasant view, even in the moonlight, but the trees in the orchard were bare and the view from the balcony was a featureless sweep of snow-covered fields. A bracing wind strafed the balcony, and David looked out on a prospect as bleak as his own future. From a bright and meteoric beginning as the don to watch in his small cubicle in Baliol College, he had acquired his PhD at twenty-five, producing an influential monograph every year for seven years and building a reputation respected on both sides of the Atlantic.

Then, back in June, while he was in the middle of a messy divorce, his last book, *Genesis of Mythical Africa,* had debuted with a first paragraph that doused his career in petrol. A reviewer in College Historian had lit the spark by discovering the unattributed, word-for-word, source in a two-year-old article by an unknown Nigerian research student.

Six months had passed since the College Historian article, and the bonfire was yet to die. He still marvelled at how quickly his hard work of the previous decade had gone down the toilet. He knew he was guilty of the crime of carelessness, but it took a charge of plagiarism to demonstrate the superficiality of his friendships and the cutthroat environment he worked in. His earlier books were now the most borrowed in academic libraries. Students and lecturers alike were keen to share the instant celebrity status of the College Historian reviewer by showing how his Genesis episode was not a one-off gaffe. His lecture tours had collapsed in a deluge of cancellations.

The invitation to Wye Castle, and the titillating note attached to it, had been difficult to resist: for a start, it was the only one he'd had all month, which was depressing enough in December. For another, it promised a project outside academe. He was due for a year's sabbatical, but all the prospects he had lined up six months ago had melted away. He needed something to absorb his energies for the next year or so. His lifelong aversion to fieldwork had vanished in the light of his current predicament. In his circumstances, his ideal sabbatical was miles away from academia and from the sort of people who read books like *Genesis of Mythical Africa*.

David took his second sip of a now-tepid tea and locked eyes with the other man. 'Why am I here?' he asked.

Conrad put his cup down on the balustrade. He smiled thinly. 'You mean, apart from the Christmas party?'

David did not bother to reply.

There was another silence, in the course of which the professor sipped his tea and the peer's cup grew colder. Set beside David's experience, Conrad's life had been one of sheer privilege: he had been born in the same thirty-room castle in which they stood, where Risboroughs had been born for several generations. His grandfather had sat in the House of Lords, and the family wealth and title had been established at least two hundred years earlier. They held family estates in five counties, from Berkshire to Wales, and they still owned 22 percent of the equity of Smythes Private Bank.

But there was a deficit side: he was also the last of the Risboroughs and walked as though he carried the very stones of the castle on his shoulders. David had read somewhere of a rare and, as yet, undiagnosed genetic problem that had kept the male heirs of the lineage from living beyond their fifty-fifth birthdays. Conrad's elder brother had died on schedule, leaving the castle and title to him. And he was a couple of years off the mark himself.

'Please come,' said Conrad, turning on his heel. He returned to the warmth of the castle's reception rooms, followed by his guest. They walked through the cocktail room, through the midst of chinking glasses and laughter, exchanging smiles and handshakes, nothing dissipating the gloom of their personal clouds.

David could not help noticing the only other suit at the party, worn by a pale, smallish man with a permanent smile who stood aloof from the carefree crowd and followed the peer with a fixed stare. 'I'm keeping you from your friend,' murmured David.

'Penaka will wait,' Conrad said shortly. He led the way up a spiral staircase to another level of the castle and entered a room where their heels rang an echo on a stone floor, whose intricate patterning was too valuable to be covered with anonymous carpeting. Wall-length tapestries draped the high walls. An Edwardian suite crouched in a corner. The opposite corner was dominated by a crest, under which was sketched an intricate family genealogy tracing generations of the Risboroughs. Conrad stood before the chart and shrugged apologetically. 'I'm sorry to inflict this on you, but you need to see it, to appreciate where I'm coming from.'

'Shoot,' said David.

'My grandfather, Laddie Anthony Risborough,' said Conrad, pointing. 'He was thirty-eight when he served the Queen in the Benin Campaign. That was one of the wars of pacification that brought the peoples of present-day Nigeria under British rule. He survived the war only to die in his sleep, at the age of fifty-five.'

'I know of him.'

'My father, Paul Christopher, inherited everything, including that bronze. He was born in 1890, and he died on his fifty-fifth birthday. Now it gets interesting. Here's my brother. He was two years my elder, and he inherited the castle and the peerage. He died this year, at—'

'—the age of fifty-five.'

Conrad paused. He bit his lip, then he continued, 'I used to take that flippant tone with my mother. She was the one that drew up this chart. But my brother was unmarried and childless. I am now the owner of Wye Castle and all that is in it.'

There was a little more gravity in David's voice as he said, 'I read something about your genetic predisposition in a local rag many years ago, but why are you telling me this?'

'Because all the medicine money can buy hasn't diagnosed a genetic condition that can explain the coincidence.'

'Conrad, I'm sure you know I'm no expert in these things. I am just a historian with a special interest in antiquities.'

There was a final hesitation, then Conrad blurted, 'I read one of your papers on the ancient Benin kingdom. You wrote that their kings were god-kings, that their court art was almost always used in spiritualist rituals. I know what you are an expert on, and that is why I asked you here today. My mother found my grandfather's diaries. She won't let me read them, but she is convinced that our early deaths are linked to that infernal bronze!'

'And you?'

Conrad hesitated. 'I am fifty-three. That's enough to make a believer of anyone. Look at the evidence.' He indicated the chart. 'This

early-death-syndrome only afflicts Risborough heirs, those who inherit the
peerage and the castle—and, by implication, the bronze. My father's two
bachelor brothers died in their eighties. Yet Risboroughs have been inher-
iting Wye Castle for the past three hundred years.'

David shook his head. He looked around theatrically, trying for a
jocularity he did not feel. 'This is the Christmas party trick, right? This is
the point at which the candid camera comes out of hiding?'

There was a moment of puzzlement, before Conrad said with cold
fury, 'Do you imagine for one moment that I am sporting with you?'

'Listen, Conrad, pull yourself together. I've articulated the belief systems of a pagan ethnic nation. That's my job. I don't subscribe to it.
This is twentieth-century England, for goodness sake! There may be an
explanation for your fifty-five-year syndrome, but you won't find it in a
centuries-old hex!'

Conrad stared wordlessly at David, and the professor realised—with
sudden apprehension—that the peer was not merely frightened; he was
terrified. David had heard similar stories from his colleagues in cancer
research: otherwise intelligent terminal cancer patients with millions of
pounds in assets who descended into shamanism as the veils of despair
came down in the terminal stages of cancer. He sighed, beginning to wish
he had declined the invitation. 'What do you want from me?'

'I want you to take this on as a project. Research this bronze, David.
Where does it come from? What is it? Does it have any . . . occult powers?
Is it behind the premature deaths? What can be done to . . . break its power
. . . ? All the experts I've spoken with tell me that I should look to medicine,
not hocus-pocus. But my mother has this gut feeling, which I also share,
now, that the bronze is at the root of it. David, I'm begging you, please
take this up as your sabbatical project. Money is no object.'

Indeed, thought David. The last nail he needed for the coffin of his reputation was a new article on the occult powers of centuries-dead craftsmen.
He decided to say no, nicely. He knew where to hit rich men: where they
lived. 'Your bronze is worth a fair packet on the block. It could cost you a
quarter million to fund my research for a year. Are you prepared to return
it free of charge to a Bini king? Just for a stab at a fifty-sixth birthday?'

Conrad Risborough did not blink. 'Of course.'

The professor swallowed, feeling a little of the chill from the death sentence the peer had lived under, ever since he was old enough to realise that
his brother might predecease him just in time to pass him their poisoned
chalice of a heirloom.

'Fifty-five years, that's better than half the third world . . .'

'I don't live in the third world,' snapped Conrad, 'I live in England, and fifty-five is twenty years below the national average. Thirty years below my family average. This is the bloody prime of my life!'

'Why don't you just sell the damn bronze? Or melt it down! You've set up an idol, for crying out loud!'

'Sell it!' A lady hovered tentatively at the door, but Conrad waved her off impatiently. 'That will be music to Penaka's ears. He's been trying to buy it off me, ever since he saw it, but my brother sold it, didn't he? Fat lot of good it did him.' Conrad bit his lip. 'That's why I got it back. Better have the bugger here where I can keep my eyes on it, eh?'

His attempt at humour fell flat. David turned away from the chart. He felt insulted. No one would have dared present a project this crackpot to him six months ago. Now it was open season on Professor David Balsam. As he explored that train of thought, his hackles rose. What made him so eminently qualified to exorcise a piece of tribal artwork, after all? His black skin?

He suddenly tired of it all. He wanted to get into his empty car and drive the sixteen miles of empty country roads to his empty house. He stuck out his hand. He had no more time for niceties. 'I'm sorry,' he said.

Conrad took a while before he accepted the handshake. 'So am I,' he said eventually. 'You will, of course, keep this between us,' he said as he walked his guest to the car. 'I should hate to read about our conversation in the Daily Mail.'

'That would embarrass me more than you,' David snapped.

The peer stopped in his tracks, and the professor walked to his car alone.

◆ ◆ ◆

London | 28th April, 2004

Twenty-four years was a long time in any career, and Professor David Balsam had used the two dozen years since his plagiarism embarrassment to turn his moribund career around. He had joined the Stroud Institute for Humanities Research and, finding himself particularly gifted in its insular brand of politics, had risen over the years to become executive director. He found himself in the very satisfactory position of stinting paymaster to hundreds of academics, many of whom had persecuted him during his travails in Oxford. David Balsam had a long memory for things like that. But even that memory was sorely tested when he received an envelope taped to a heavy gift-wrapped box from a law firm on his birthday.

His desk was busy, and the mail sat unopened until the end of day, when he took a cognac to the suite of easy chairs in his office. The envelope contained a birthday card, the only one he had received that day. Not that he expected any: he had never married again and had no close relations. The name Conrad on the card did not ring a bell. A letter accompanied the card, but he opened the gift-wrapped package first. The sight of the bronze struck a chill in his heart, bringing back to his mind, for the first time in two decades, his meeting with Conrad Risborough in Wye Castle.

He reflected that perhaps he had taken offence too quickly at the end of that meeting, but at the time he had been too wrapped up in his own problems to make allowance for the state of other people's minds. With growing disquiet, he sat back and read the letter.

Happy 54th birthday, David,

If you are reading this letter, it will mean that I never got the chance to change my will, and that I did not survive my fifty-fifth birthday. I am the end of my line, so I had to think hard about my estate. It may be that we Risborough heirs do have a genetic defect that kills us at fifty-five, in which case you have no reason to fear this valuable bequest of our eighteenth-century Benin bronze. I am passing it on to you, in the same way I got it, by inheritance, for the sake of scientific research. My friend and business partner, Penaka Lee, would have killed for it, but I can think of no other person better qualified to test your genetic defect theory. I am giving you this in time, so that you can, if you choose, take the one-year sabbatical I had so anxiously requested, to investigate the occult powers of your new inheritance. Of course, you may be too busy to do so, in which case you may wish to sell, throw away, loan or melt down the bloody lump of bronze.

Many more birthdays,

Your friend,

Conrad.

DAVID PUT down the letter. He had concluded, after having met Conrad, that there probably wasn't a genetic defect to start with: just that overwhelming death wish of a fear. He had died because he believed he would die. David stared at the bronze for a long minute, then went home. He slept well.

The next morning, the cleaner had moved the head to his desk. It was beautiful, in an ominous sort of way, and an inexplicable dread settled on David. There was an intensity to the bronze that was unnatural. He felt an overwhelming desire to get rid of it, but that, he told himself, would be irrational. It was an exquisite work of art, as every visitor to his office re-marked. He resolved not to make the slightest concession to irrationality.

The months passed, and he behaved with utmost rationality. He even moved the head from his desk to a plinth in the common room where it could be admired by even more visitors to the institute. Still, he rationally observed that he had lost six kilogrammes since the arrival of the bronze and that he spent, on average, one sleepless hour each night, picturing Conrad settling into the chair in which he was found on the morning after his fifty-fifth birthday.

Things came to a head in January 2005, when David arrived at the institute and the head was missing from its plinth. He hurried into his secretary's office. 'The bronze,' he said, 'was it stolen overnight?'

His secretary looked at him curiously. 'No, David, it's in the safe.'

'Why?'

'The broker just left. Our insurance policy won't permit art that valu-able on open view.'

He took a deep breath and considered his situation rationally. He real-ised that he had subconsciously hoped a twenty-first-century equivalent of Anthony Risborough would steal the bronze and take on the fifty-fifth-year death sentence. He decided he was firmly on the slippery slope after all. He then sat down to book his annual vacation and an open ticket to Nigeria.

◆ ◆ ◆

Lagos | 1st February, 2005

He told himself it was just a holiday—in the course of which he would make some enquiries into an artefact that happened to be in his collection. He did not even travel with the bronze: he left it at home and took some photographs with him. He checked into the Sheraton Hotel and Towers in Lagos, three hundred kilometres from Benin City.

He was well-travelled, but apart from a couple of Nairobi stopovers when he had booked a Kenya Airways connection to the Far East, it was his very first trip to Africa. He was overwhelmed by the physical proximity to so many people of his skin hue, but he felt no sense of kinship. Instead he was consumed by self-loathing at the secret reason for his presence there. He did the touristy things and spent a couple of days on a golf course. After the casinos closed he sat for hours in the darkness of his room, not thinking about Conrad, Lord Risborough.

Then he met a persuasive advert rep at the bar. Halfway through his second whiskey, David gave the rep some cash and a photograph of the bronze. A newspaper ad appeared soon after, offering to pay for information on the artefact. His first call was from Penaka Lee—who, by some crazy coincidence, was in Abuja. Because of the recent reference in Conrad's letter, he was able to dredge up the memory of their brief introduction and the man's cloying smile.

'Are you selling?' Penaka asked.

'No, no, I'm just . . . researching a paper on the impact of tribal art on the ontology of—'

'I'll pay twenty-five percent over independent valuation.'

'No. Not yet, anyway.'

'Fifty? Sixty?'

'Mr. Penaka,' he said, sharply, 'it's not a matter of price.'

'Can I at least hold it again? Haven't touched that lovely bronze in twenty years! I see it in my dreams you know, most peculiar . . .'

'I'm afraid it's in my house in London.'

'You now live in London?'

''Fraid so. I work for Stroud Humanities. I'm more manager than academic, these days.'

'It's called "follow the money," isn't it? Oh, well, you'll give me first option if you change your mind, won't you?'

'Naturally.'

◆　◆　◆

Lagos | 7th February, 2005

After Penaka, he got several calls from craftsmen wanting to sell him living room art, as well as from more-dodgy businessmen offering 'genuine Nok' artefacts dug up 'last week.' Yet the calls did snap him out of his depression. He booked a taxi and left Lagos for Benin City. Once he made that move, he threw himself fully into the enquiry.

He found no joy at the palace, the guild of bronze workers, or the museum, where the curator was on his annual vacation. His enquiry was crippled by his inability to bring himself to ask the relevant question: excuse me, but how do I go about lifting a curse from this bloody bronze? He walked around the sleepy museum, ending up before a case of bronzes, thinking that he had seen more-impressive collections of Benin bronzes in London. He pulled out his photograph.

'Interesting. May I?'

He turned around. The man behind him was probably in his sixties, but he had not aged well. Red blotches were seared into his light skin. Bright eyes darted from behind thick, round lenses. 'Hmm. You must be the man behind the advert.'

'Yes. Professor Balsam,' said David, taking back the picture. He offered a handshake. The other man made no move to take it.

'We haven't met, but our careers have crossed. You blighted my career, and yours, by stealing my intellectual work.'

It was several moments before David could breathe, more still before he could turn and follow the other man. He found him about to enter an office, 'Dr. Omaruyi!' he called, closing the gap in a few paces but finding himself unable to say anything. Instead he followed Omaruyi into a dimly lit office with dusty metal shelves and a cluttered table. Against the far wall were stacked columns of paper wallets.

'Mister Omaruyi,' said the other man, leaning on his desk. 'I never did finish my PhD.'

'Sorry, I assumed . . . look, about that book . . .'

'Aha, a personal apology after twenty-five years? This should be good.'

'I just want you to know it was an accident; I never intended—'

'I have a measure of respect for you, despite everything, which I will lose, if you continue along this line.'

David took a deep breath and shrugged. 'I'm sorry.'

There was a long pause, then Omaruyi offered his hand. They shook hands solemnly, 'I'm not bitter,' said Omaruyi bitterly, 'not at all. It's just seeing you there in the middle of another conceited crusade. You have framed your theories, haven't you? Now you're cherry-picking data for your next book—am I wrong? But no, I'm not bitter at all. So what brings you to my bronze gallery? Nobody needs to come here to see the best of our art. You've got them out there in London, in New York, in—'

'Look, it's nothing. I . . . am glad I had this opportunity to—'

'Nobody advertises a photo of a Menai singate head for nothing.'

'. . . A Menai singer . . . ?'

'You did not really think that was a Benin artefact, surely?'

'It was acquired from the palace in 1897.'

'"Acquired." Interesting choice of word. We would have received it in tribute . . . or else "acquired" it in war. The knowledge of metallurgy was not exactly encouraged outside the Oba's court.'

'Well, the carbon-dating did place it around 1200 AD—'

'That would be consistent with a Menai provenance. But I won't blame you, Professor; you have not had the privilege of seeing a wooden Menai singate, as I have. Of course, I cannot be certain, until I see this bronze. A hollow under its base for the head of a staff would be conclusive.'

David did his best to mask his amazement, but his voice was hoarse. 'There is a hollow in the bronze . . . that would be the casting process—'

'But quite atypical, is it not, Professor? Not like other Benin bronzes?'

'I'm quite prepared, of course, to pay for this information—'

'To hell with your money! If I wanted your money I would have phoned the number on your advert, am I wrong? Don't get me wrong, I'm not bitter, not at all! It has been twenty-five years and six months since your Genesis book appeared, has it not? A man who keeps a grudge that long is asking for a stroke. I'm not bitter. You've been publishing, haven't you? Other books?'

'Um, actually . . . yes.'

'How many?'

There was a small pause.

'Because I know you didn't even publish an article for ten years after—'

'I've published four books in the past four years.'

'You see? You've moved on finally. You're back to your old form now. Am I wrong? But what about me? Was I even able to submit my PhD thesis? Do you see that stack? Manuscripts for articles, monographs. I have visited several psychiatrists, but have I lost my fear, my phobia, for submitting my intellectual work to peers?'

'Look, this is my card. I don't mean to patronise you, but—'

'So don't try to, David. I am fifty: what do you imagine your institute can do for me? Let me patronise you instead. What can I do for you?'

'What, if you don't mind my asking, is a . . . singate head?'

'It sits on the head of a staff. The spiritual leader of the Menai nation carries it as an emblem of authority. The singate head I have seen is a wooden replica of this. They have an oral tradition of a bronze singate, but their knowledge of bronze-working died out with their last bronze smith a hundred years ago or more.'

'Where is this nation?' David asked respectfully.

'On its last legs,' Omaruyi answered. 'But there's no point in looking for their spiritual leader. He never speaks English, and he doesn't talk to strangers. You probably should see Tobin . . . Tobin Rani. If he is still alive.'

◆ ◆ ◆

Ubesia | 9th March, 2005

David finally found Tobin Rani at the offices of the Menai Legacy Group in a bungalow in Ubesia. He had waited in the reception, which was a thin wall away from the office of the director. Eventually, he was sitting opposite Tobin, who took a glance at the picture.

'Omaruyi was right; that's a singateya. We lived under the sway of Great Bini. This might have been tribute a century ago, perhaps even from Mata Nimito's predecessor.'

'Singateya?'

'A singate head.'

'And a singate is a staff?'

Tobin shrugged. 'In the same way that a throne is a chair.' He returned the picture and waited. He seemed preoccupied, anxious to get back to his affairs.

David was at a loss. He had not expected such nonchalance. He cleared his throat. 'Your nation's leader wouldn't . . . want it back?'

Tobin was surprised. 'Whatever for?'

'I . . . hear he has a wooden . . .'

'Have you ever lifted that bronze?'

'Yes.'

'The Mata is over a century old, and right now the singate is also a walking stick. The last thing he wants is to be lugging a block like that around the place.'

'And you? Your people?'

He laughed. 'You are welcome to it, Professor. It is not unique, and we have rather more important things on our mind than an old singateya.' He stood up. 'I'm sorry to be rude, Professor, but I'm in the middle of a crisis right now—'

◆ ◆ ◆

HE SAT in the stationary taxi for several minutes before he returned to Tobin's office. Tobin was back on the phone; he put an impatient hand on the receiver and raised his eyebrows. 'Sorry,' said David, 'but I couldn't help overhearing: this custom truck you've been trying to fund for the last few minutes—'

'Last few months, more like!'

'Would it be used principally for the purposes of an ethnographic investigation?'

'No, it is basically for—'

'Perhaps I am not explaining myself properly . . . let me put it this way. The Stroud Institute for Humanities Research will be able to fund this truck if it is intended to be used principally for an ethnographic investigation. Well, will it?'

'Oh, absolutely. Definitely.'

'That brings it within the purview of my institute. I may be able to help.'

Tobin replaced the phone abruptly. 'Please sit down, Professor . . . sorry, what was your name again?'

ZANDA ATTURK

Gulf of Benin | 20th March, 2005

The hatch opened again, and I came awake. I was still one monumental ache, but I was also hungry for food, and for life. A strange face filled the hatch. With some relief I saw that he was smiling.

'Aha. You don sleep belleful. Come.'

On the deck of the modified barge I saw a moonlit horizon in three directions and the comfort of a distant shore in the fourth. This was not the delta I had fallen asleep in. I washed my face and rinsed out my foul mouth as an impatient speedboat pulled alongside the barge. Beneath my feet a tired engine crooned. I stared, transfixed by the placid lights on the horizon several kilometres off.

'Limbe,' said the voice from behind me.

'Where be that?'

'Cameroon.' He shook his head at my ignorance. He slung a waterproof handbag over my shoulder. 'Hide dis bag like ya blokoss, o,' he warned. 'Oya!'

'Who . . .' I began, but the pilot of the speedboat was as short-fused as the bargeman had been easygoing. I was overboard and stinging from the flying spray before I could muster the appropriate thanks. The bag contained Humphrey Chow's book, the sealed envelope from Tobin, and more comfortingly, some CFA francs, though not quite as precious as my genitals.

I tried to talk to the boatman, but his engine was an angry, loud backdrop that sapped my energy just to hear it. I stared at those stiff shoulders for what seemed an eternity. Then the voice of the engine broke and we began to lose speed. Within minutes he was circling in a quiet cove, apparently waiting for some signal from the benighted shore. It came by way of a blinking flashlight. He sounded with a pole and gestured for me to jump. I did and found myself up to my neck. Holding my bag over my head, I waded ashore, feeling desperately alone and disoriented. The speedboat was now far away, but the captain's jumpiness had been infectious.

Two men were waiting. They emerged from the bushes. They were not uniformed, but their manner was supercilious and formal. *'Réfugié! Où est votre passeport!'*

I gabbled incoherently for a desperate minute in a language that was not French and barely English. They badgered me till I was reduced to a stutter, then they cracked up; and I understood from the fit they were throwing on Limbe's sandy beach that I had been the subject of a practical joke.

My new friends were two brothers, Claude and Pokas. Bar their fiendish humour, they seemed regular enough slum kids who wanted above all else not to clean the toilets their parents cleaned for a living. They ran a smuggling sideline, and so long as I paid my keep, they did not seem too discomfited when I arrived in place of a consignment of contraband. They lived in their stall in a tourist village just outside Limbe. The sprawling market sold everything from wooden carvings to leather goods. It bustled by daytime, but after dark it resolved into three or four locales where the nightlife centred on the braziers of the open-air restaurants. I spent the next twenty days in that market. The days were passable, and I made myself useful stuffing leather pouffes for the brothers, but when night fell they made my life a misery, pumping me for intimate accounts of Badu's adventures.

I took a passport photograph, which I sent to Adevo via barge mail. He had broken up and sold my car, and he sent some forex to prove it. Things were getting hotter and more uncertain in creek country, but it seemed that the more dangerous things grew, the healthier the margins in his black market.

A week passed before I received the fake passport from him. I was now the twenty-eight-year-old Nelson Kara Ogunde, a Nigerian trader with a UK visa. Claude and Pokas clicked their tongues as they looked over the passport with what appeared to be professional eyes. I pressed them anxiously on the point, and for fifty pounds of the sterling proceeds from the sale of my car, I became a Cameroonian named Nelson Ndoya with pristine visas for the US, Japan, Brazil, Canada, the UK, and the Schengen countries.

I thought the Ogunde papers looked rather more convincing.

◆ ◆ ◆

WHEN WE finally spoke on the phone, Amana's news was not as upbeat. She could not join me until Ma'Calico was settled, and Ma'Calico was taking some settling. The hotelier had grown moody at the thought of losing her daughter and seemed to reject every opportunity that came up.

Amana was still upset that I had punched Dr. Maleek before passing out. The punch was news to me, which seemed to mollify her somewhat. 'So would you be happy to see him again?'

'Of course!' I lied smoothly. 'But you know that's impossible, I can't possibly come—'

'He's actually anxious to see you. He's happy to fly into Cameroon.'

It was too late to back out then.

CHARLES PITANI

Abuja | 21st March, 2005

The 'mercenaries' arrived this morning, all eight of them. Their leader calls himself Rudolf. If he's a mercenary, then I am Chaka the Zulu.

He is the size of two fat women, and he is always either just finishing a club sandwich or just starting a peppered chicken. Because he always has a bottle of beer in his right hand, his answer to a handshake is his left fist. He seems to think he is Twenty Cents. Is this the biggest mistake of my life?

I met them in a quiet guesthouse in Gwagwalada. I was in the room with Rudolf, still wondering whether to waste any more money on them, when we heard a man screaming. We rushed out: a waiter had tried to keep the change of the mercenary that called himself Amit and the madman had thrown him downstairs! The money did not even amount to a hundred naira.

I like the idea of somebody throwing Badu out of a ten- or twenty-storey building. I decided to use them, but from now I will only do business with them on the phone. These people are animals.

◆ ◆ ◆

I AM beginning to enjoy this situation. I have put down my money, and it is burning like matches, but if I say I am not enjoying this, I would be lying.

I have spread the word. And any checkpoint policeman that hears *pim* about Badu would be stupid to report to the station, when they could call my number and collect their pension up-front. Twenty policemen already have joined my mercenaries, with more coming every day. And why shouldn't they take sick leave and make some good money? I am paying double, and they have families.

The problem is these bad eggs I have to deal with every day. I have to finish this Badu business and return to my normal life.

ZANDA ATTURK

Limbe | 22nd March, 2005

I got panic attacks when I considered my future prospects in any kind of detail, so I took things step by step. My next goal was London. My feelings for my twin were more than ambivalent. Our genes were probably all we had in common; our ideas about life were likely worlds apart. I thought I would engineer a street meeting. If I liked the sound of him, we would take it from there.

Adevo had also given me the phone number of a certain Frederick Eghwrudjakpor. He had been the smartest hustler in Warri in the '80s, but the city became too small for him. He was now making waves in London.

I had options.

HUMPHREY CHOW

London | 24th March, 2005

I felt strange in the wheelchair. I was strong enough to walk, but they insisted on wheeling me everywhere. I sat in a pokey office in the research centre. The attendant had withdrawn, leaving me alone with Dr. Greenstone.

He seemed reluctant to start. I got up nervously. 'I can leave today, right?'

'Oh, yes,' said Greenstone. 'You're fine. You've been fine for days, we just had to keep you under observation. The good news is that the trial will continue.'

That was *his* good news, but I didn't say that. I had been busy writing, and come Monday, Lynn had brought my contract with Phil Begg for signing, so it wasn't a total waste of time. There was a rack of vials and bottles on a wall. I recognised a row of Proxtigen, the drug that had caused so much drama.

'Mr. Chow,' he said, and I turned to look at him. 'Your results checked out pretty much until we ran your genome profile. I am afraid there is a problem at gene level.'

'What problem?'

'A mutation. An extra chromosome. You probably don't need to worry about this—your average DNA carries some three billion components. You can pack in quite a few mutations that won't get in the way of a healthy life.' He shrugged. 'You're twenty-five years old and have done well enough so far. I'd advise you to give drug trials a miss from now on, though.' He grinned. 'We've sent a note of this hypersensitivity to your NHS surgery. Otherwise,' he shrugged again, 'continue your life as normal.'

'What caused the mutation?'

'There's the ten-quid question, isn't it?'

I could see that his attention was now downstairs, at his drug trial.

'We don't have your parents' histories. It could be anything, really. Mutations can be spontaneous, they can be induced by teratogens . . .' He walked to the door ahead of me.

Without reflection, I took a bottle of Proxtigen and pushed it slowly down my jeans pocket. It was almost like taking a bottle of shampoo as a memento from a hotel washroom.

I did not ask him what a teratogen was. My medical history since childhood had made me something of an Internet medical researcher.

♦ ♦ ♦

2:00 p.m.

I sat in my car and shut my eyes. The feast of memory was over. I opened my laptop and read what I had written.

Tobin Rani confessed to killing Yan Chow, and went to jail for it. He lied. Previously, my recollection of Yan Chow's death had come mostly from the Social Services file I had read. Now, an authentic memory flowered in my mind, as dense and detailed as a movie image.

I had opened the door for an angry immigrant of Chinese extraction. He had just arrived from Shanghai, the long way, at the end of a six-year-old dream to join his wife. He was tired and hungry, and his mood did not improve when he discovered an African in Mum's bedroom. He was small-bodied but his rage was monumental, and he was getting the better of the fight with the African, who had taught me songs and funnies in a strange language—until, that is, I sank a kitchen knife in Yan Chow's back.

It was a twelve-year-old's stab at preserving the happiest of his many families, but it was a grown-up world, and Mr. Chow died before the ambulance arrived. Miss Chow hung herself before the police arrived. And the African took the fall and did the time.

That was it, then, the grave of my happiness. I had known it in my bones, even if I didn't remember it in my conscious mind. He had probably gone in for life, leaving me to get on with mine as best as I could, untainted by the calumny of a murder. But I knew, now.

Now, I knew.

◆ ◆ ◆

I CLOSED the laptop. I couldn't *own* the memory anymore, but I had written it when it was raw. That was enough. A drizzle had started as I arrived at the prisons. I tried to get a prisoner's number for their visitor's booking form and ran into the first hurdle: they did not have a Tobin Rani on their books.

There was a change of duty as I left, and the new desk officer, an older man, frowned at my enquiry slip. 'What's with this? This bloke's been gone three years and suddenly everybody's asking for him!'

I turned. 'Everybody?'

'Who are *you*?'

'Humphrey Chow, short story writer.'

'Don't give a damn if you're a long story writer,' he said genially. 'What's your relationship to this fella?'

'He's my, sort of, foster father.'

He hesitated and turned to the younger warden. 'Oi, take him up to the guvnor.'

The 'guvnor' was considerably more forthcoming. He did not refer to his computer, or to the folder on his desk, as he spoke to me. 'He was a pretty straightforward case: he got a fifteen-year sentence, got time off, did ten, got out. Probably still in Nigeria now.'

'Why Nigeria?'

He looked at me curiously. 'If he's your foster father you should know he held Nigerian nationality, shouldn't you? It's standard procedure: a convict like him is put on a flight home after his sentence, courtesy Her Majesty.'

'I see.' I looked at my nails. 'The officer downstairs said *everyone* was looking for Tobin these days.'

'I don't know about "everyone,"' he said, finally opening the file, 'but this man will certainly be interested in speaking to you.' He took a card from the folder and brought it around his desk.

'Professor M. J. Reid.'

'Yes, he's an archaeologist from Bristol Uni. Two months ago, one of his students got carried away in a nightclub. He spent a month as our guest. The first night, he was shaking the bars all night. Seems he recognised some of the graffiti on the walls from his lecture notes. Next morning, he finally got to make a call, and this prof was down here like a shot. I let him make a cell visit, and there's been five more university dons coming and going—with cameras and notebooks.'

'What does this have to do with Tobin Rani?'

'I've had to track down the last few occupants of that cell. There's a consensus that it first appeared on that wall after Tobin's occupancy. That was when the mirror first went up.'

'What was this graffiti? What was so special about it?'

He leaned over and pulled out a couple of pictures from the file. He put them in my hands. It was a photograph of hieroglyphs on a wall. Most of the hieroglyphs had been painted over, but there was a square in lighter paint that had line after line of the close-lined script. I recognised it immediately. Tobin had had notebooks full of the stuff.

He was watching me carefully. 'Have you seen it before?'

I shook my head carefully, reluctant to be drawn into all the excitement over stick figures on a wall. 'And this has been on the wall for three years, at least?'

'Yes. The mirror was being replaced; that's how the student noticed it.'

A pause developed, and I rose slowly. 'Thank you,' I said sincerely. I was at a loose end. I had been prepared to confess to a thirteen-year-old murder to free a convict, but it was a little too late for that now. There was still the little matter of clearing his name, but I definitely wasn't going to Nigeria to do that. I was free to be happy.

'Give the prof a call, will you?' he urged as he walked me to his door.

'I will,' I lied.

While I waited to be let out, I dropped the card in a nearby bin. Seconds afterwards, the administrator hurried over with an open diary. 'I found his private mobile number. Gimme the card; I'll copy it out for you.'

I checked my pockets with rising embarrassment. Then a gate detail leaned over the bin and retrieved Professor Reid's card with two supercilious fingernails. The guvnor's face frosted over. He snatched the card and stalked off.

I walked to my car. I'm free to be happy, I told myself.

I had not spoken to Grace since I went into the lab. It seemed a marriage by terse text messages just then and she knew nothing of my little excitement. I would normally have phoned, but this time I had waited, perversely, for her to call first. I remembered how we had first met in the reception of an elderly psychiatrist closing for the weekend:

'Not sure I can squeeze you in today, handsome. What's the matter?'

'I don't remember anything from my last few years . . . the last I . . .'

'You look good for another fifty, young man, why bother about the last few?'

'I . . .'

'Listen, Grace here has just been stood up—'

'Mum!'

'—take her for a drink, and if by Monday you're still worried about history, I'll see you at eleven thirty. Deal?'

ZANDA ATTURK

Limbe | 26th March, 2005

I did not leave the market during the days but spent the daylight hours cooped up in the leather workshop in the rear. Come night, to avoid the moonlight-tales hour, I took long strolls.

HUMPHREY CHOW

London | 1st April, 2005

On April 1, "Reluctant Bomber" appeared in the first issue of *Balding Wolf.* The magazine sold a respectable 140,000 copies, but four out of five newspapers panned it. The *Herald Scotland* called it a flaccid *GQ,* but most reviewers singled out my story for praise. Grace decided it was worth celebrating, on balance. That evening she cleared her diary, and we took in a concert at the Royal Festival Hall.

Afterwards, when we found my car, there was a policeman examining its registration with a torch. 'You will find it's perfectly in order,' I told him cheerfully, pulling out my keys.

From the other side of the road, another policeman opened the rear door of his car. 'You'll find this faster, this time of night,' he said, as we were escorted brusquely to the squad car.

Grace's mascara was running. She was mumbling something about it being just a bloody expense account.

Kaiba tanimi ma sonke!

I knew she was worrying about nothing. They had found out that I killed Mr. Chow. I was rubbery with relief. I wondered if this was how murderers felt when they were finally arrested with ancient killings on their consciences. Then the cuffs clicked shut on my wrists for the first time in my life.

As Grace and I piled into the back of the police car, I was suddenly oppressed by the statistic of fifty-six deaths in police custody from the year before. Visions of black men like Michael Powell with mental health issues dying in the back of a police van . . . *Roholiabu menta! Roholiabu menta!*

At the Charing Cross station, we were separated and I was fingerprinted, photographed, and issued receipts for everything in my pockets. Then I was issued a receipt for all my receipts and processed into a windowless police truck. We must have driven for hours, leaving traffic noises behind, and I was hopelessly disoriented. We could have been close to Scotland or crossed the Chunnel into France. Eventually, the doors opened and I found myself in an underground car park. I went through a warren of lifts and padded corridors with numbers rather than names on their doors.

I was led into a table in a windowless lobby. After a minute, I realised that the sandwiches and soda were for me. It was probably a subtle form of torture: in the hours since my arrest and processing, no one had spoken to me. I ate perfunctorily, conscious that this was not exactly the postconcert dinner I had planned with Grace. I wondered where she was, how she was. Another short walk, and a security-coded door opened into what looked like a traditional interrogation room.

My heart leaped with joy: someone to talk to at last!

I found myself sitting across the table from a dark-haired woman who clasped her hands and tapped her thumbs patiently, one against the other, as she waited for me to settle in. 'I'm Inspector Hannah,' she said eventually. Her voice was deep, pleasant to listen to.

'Humphrey Chow, short story writer.'

'I am to inform you that your responses are being recorded, and that anything you say may be used in evidence against you in a court of law. If you want a lawyer . . .'

'I don't *need* a lawyer,' I said.

'Tea? Coffee?'

I shook my head.

◆ ◆ ◆

SHE HAD full eyebrows and lips that pursed often. Her thumbs kept tapping, suggesting their readiness to wait as long as it took for the truth. 'Did you write the short story, "Reluctant Bomber," in the current issue of *Balding Wolf*?'

'Yes.'

'Did you personally write *every* word in the story?'

'Not *every* word; there's the editorial process. Word count. They wanted a six-thousand-word story, and my story was seven . . .' I paused. The thumbnails were clicking neurotically.

'Yes?' Her voice was as kindly as ever.

'So I had to cut. That's where I got some help from Lynn . . . we had a deadline to hit.'

'Who's Lynn?'

'Lynn Christie, my agent.'

'What did she add?'

'I'll need to check my laptop to confirm.'

She shrugged fluidly. 'In a rough way—we can go into specifics later.'

'Well, this and that, really. Like cutting out my *"then again"*'s. She says I use them far too much. But I checked out the final version. It was my story. Sort of.' I had clasped my own hands underneath the tabletop and tried to

mimic her thumbnails; it was unsustainable. She had probably been prac-
tising for ages. She didn't look that old, but it probably took years and years
to make inspector, hundreds of interrogations, thousands even . . .

Her head was cocked uncertainly. My thumbs froze under the table.
'Are you okay?' she asked.

'I . . . think I'll have the coffee.'

'Milk, sugar?'

'Yes, please.'

She nodded. 'So you take personal responsibility for every word in
the story?'

'The coffee . . .'

' . . . is on its way.'

Somewhere in the warren of corridors, then, was a room where my
interrogation was being monitored, where a hospitality detail was pouring
my cup as we spoke. Her thumbs were back to tapping, impatiently now.
'Well?'

'I do.'

'Did anyone suggest the story to you?'

I paused. It was always going to be a rather long pause. Fortunately the
door opened at that moment and my beverage arrived by policeman. He
placed a coffee at my elbow. I had asked for tea, but the aroma was suddenly so much more appealing than tea. I reached for it and lifted it slowly,
breathing deeply and thinking desperately. Just what sort of a question was
this, and how could I answer it *truthfully?* The truth was that Dalminda
Roco had suggested the story to me. Or was that really the truth? Even so,
it would be madness to own that to the paranoid police. But then again, it
was also folly to lie to the machinery of justice. The cup was millimetres
from my lips when it occurred to me that strong coffee was an excellent
mask for a truth serum. I paused again and studied the coffee.

'Are you *okay?*'

I looked up. The thumbs were frozen five centimetres apart, and real
worry was etched on Hannah's face.

'I'm fine.'

'You don't want the coffee anymore?'

'I asked for *tea.*'

Her eyebrows edged together and she touched a finger to her ear. 'I
seem to remember you said *coffee.*'

'I said I wanted *tea*—you can play back your tape or something and
check.' I put down the cup. 'Anyway, I don't want anything anymore.'

She deployed an indifferent shrug. 'Did anyone suggest the story line?'

'No.'

'And the characters? Did anyone suggest your characters to you?'

'Yes.'

She picked up a pencil. 'Who suggested what?'

'Well, my agent suggested I should change Lynn to Bessie and Grace to Rebecca and Humphrey Chow to G. G. Phipps.'

She was scribbling as I spoke. 'Why?'

'Grace insisted that she didn't break the nose of the thief, so Lynn suggested that I change everyone's names so it would be clear that it was fiction.'

She leaned forward. 'So it was fact originally? The characters were real?'

'Um . . . they are fictional characters *inspired* by real people.'

'And Dalminda Roco?'

I sipped some of my rejected coffee, to buy some thinking time. 'What about Dalminda Roco?'

'You didn't change his name?'

'He was already a fictional character. There was no need to change his name.'

'Wasn't he based on a real character, like the other characters in your story?'

'Come on! Have you ever met a *Dalminda*? A Dalminda *Roco*?'

'I'm asking the questions.'

'No. He was a totally fictional character.'

'Have you ever met a Dalminda? A Dalminda Roco?'

I was in a panic. Inept crime was hopelessly outflanked by police wizardry. What manner of software had they wired into her ear? Why had she picked up on Dalminda? What did they know?'

'I've never met a Dalminda Roco! I already said that!'

'What if I told you that there is in fact a Dalminda Roco, who just so happens to be a terrorist like the hero of your story? As you have admitted, it is a rather unusual name.'

I paused. This was dangerous territory, if only for my own mental health. When I finished writing my story in the kitchen of the Scottish holiday house I had looked up to find that the rucksack was gone. I had gone upstairs and there was no Dalminda either. No failed law-student suicide bomber. The story was done and the powerful inspiration was gone. Dalminda Roco was clearly an incendiary figment of the fevered imagination of a desperate writer. Or yet another psychotic episode in the life of

Humphrey Chow. That was all it was, and that was all it had to be. She was bluffing—why on earth, I had not a clue, but she had to be bluffing. I shook my head. 'I'd say that was completely impossible.'

She closed her binder. Her thumbs tapped, slowly, contentedly. 'Thank you very much, Mr. Chow.'

◆ ◆ ◆

ON CUE, a heavy hand fell on my shoulder. I stood up as bracelets were clipped onto my wrists. We stood there for two minutes like actors waiting for a cue until the door opened and another man stepped in, smiling genially. He was about my height, which was too bad for him, but he radiated a confidence that made him seem to be looking down on the policeman he was looking up at. 'That will do, Harris,' he said. 'Take his cuffs off.'

'Mr. Chow,' he gushed, when we could finally shake hands properly, 'I love your writing and I've been looking forward to meeting you. My name is Ram Gupta. I'm leading this investigation, and there's a friendly discussion I'm hoping you can join.'

'Can I see my wife?' I asked, halfheartedly, expecting a refusal.

'I thought you'd never ask.'

He turned away, and I followed him next door into a larger, better-appointed, room. A yellow light from the ceiling lent a sulphuric tint to the silent glares that welcomed me from Grace, Lynn, Phil, and Malcolm Frisbee.

By then it was pretty clear that my arrest had nothing to do with the death of Yan Chow. I was in deeper trouble than mere murder.

The room was blandly furnished. Prints of *Mona Lisa, The Scream,* and *Dancing in the Rain* reinforced the tedium of beige walls. A suite of cream sofas lounged. Two potted palms and four policemen—who seemed chosen from an American mall for their bulk—were planted around the room. I got the uncanny feeling that I was on a TV set for a special production of the *Jerry Springer Show*—such was the apprehension of violence in the air. Savouring my circumscribed freedom, I kissed Grace Meadows's cold cheek gingerly and lurched into an empty chair.

Ram Gupta panned his cheerful smile around the room. 'I'm glad you could all join us for this friendly conversation—'

'Thirty-five years,' began Malcolm Frisbee, 'nine hundred and sixty writers, five continents, seventeen countries, and I have never, *never*—'

'Let me start with you, Humphrey Chow,' said Gupta hurriedly, slipping behind a desk whose surface bristled with pink Post-it Notes. His hand hovered as he selected one, which he stuck onto his steaming mug. '*Somebody* has *insisted* that in fact you did know Dalminda Roco, long before you wrote "Reluctant Bomber." Is this true, Humphrey Chow?'

I came to the edge of my seat, propelled by a mixture of fear and fury. 'False! And if I may add, whoever said so is a bloody liar.'

'You're calling me a liar?' Grace asked coldly.

'*You?*' I was shaken. '*Grace?*'

Gupta folded his hands smugly and sat back.

'Don't take that tone with me, Humf, you know you talk in your sleep.'

'That was *years and years* ago!'

'We haven't been married for *years and years!*'

'And then again, how would you know? We don't even sleep in the same room anymore!'

'Any why did I change rooms? Wasn't it to get a good night's sleep?'

'—And I mentioned Dalminda in my sleep? Is that what you're saying?'

'Dalminda, Estelle, Padre . . . it was always crowded in your bed, Humf!'

'*I* mentioned *Dalminda?* I?'

'The subconscious mind can be very talkative,' said Gupta smoothly. The door opened then, and a young policeman brought in a green Post-it Note for his mug. We watched apprehensively as the investigator studied his new intelligence. 'Here's the real question I need help with,' he said as the door closed quietly. 'Why would you go all the way to Scotland for a fortnight, if it was not to rendezvous with the secretive Dalminda Roco?'

'It was a writing retreat . . .'

There was a snort from Phil Begg's general direction, but I had a twelve-story-contract with the editor, the first story of which had thrilled critics across Britain, so it probably came from the policeman behind him.

'The housekeeper remembers clearing two breakfast places on the day you checked out,' said Gupta.

'I was very hungry.'

'In your story, there's talk about dumping the bomb in the sea . . . is that what happened?'

'No.'

He leaned forward. 'Where's the bomb, Mr. Chow? Is it still live and dangerous? Bear in mind that concealment of terrorist materials is a serious offence.'

'It was just a story!'

Gupta gave me a sly look, 'You quarrelled with Dalminda, didn't you? You were hard up, your bank confirms this, you were trying to blackmail

Roco and he didn't bite so you exposed the most secretive terrorist in Western Europe in your story. Is that what happened, Mr. Chow?'

I shook my head helplessly.

Gupta glared at me. 'This group of yours, this . . .' he pulled up a note, 'Radical Suicide Society of Global Warming Justice Phenomena, I looked it up on the Internet and—'

'—of course you won't find it. It's fiction!'

'Precisely. What's their *real* name?'

I was silent. With hindsight, I saw that Grace's dog-walker job advert had been an act of love.

'I must say I'm getting no cooperation from this conspiracy,' said Gupta, glaring around the room. 'You all *conspired* to give comfort to a dangerous terrorist. Then you outed him publicly, thereby increasing the risk of a pre-emptive strike. Our intelligence suggests that an attack is imminent. Unless we make immediate arrests, there will be casualties. And guess who's heading for the dock on terrorism charges.'

'Tell them what they need to know, Humfy dear,' pleaded Grace tearfully. 'They have these deals they can offer, don't you, Mr. Gupta?'

Ram Gupta kept his lips sealed, and his powder dry.

'*If* there is a real-life Dalminda,' suggested Lynn in the first helpful comment of the day, 'maybe it's just a horrible coincidence. It's happened before, you know, writers create characters and somewhere in the world there's somebody going exactly by that name. I remember—'

'What are the chances that the only two Dalminda Rocos in the known universe are both ex–law students, dangerous terrorists, and personally known to Mr. Chow?' asked Gupta.

'Nil,' said Malcolm Frisbee poisonously. 'Clearly "Reluctant Bomber" is not fiction but *faction,* a well-known literary genre, a conflation of jejune truth and fecund imagination, with the line between blurred, in this case, by psychosis—'

'I want answers, not theories,' snapped Gupta. He looked at me. 'You have a twelve-tale contract with *Balding Wolf,* don't you?'

'I do.'

The policeman behind Phil Begg appeared to snort again. I began to worry about my twelve-tale deal.

'Have you written the second story?'

'No.'

'So, what other escapades *will* Dalminda get up to,' he asked delicately, 'over the next eleven issues?'

I realised that my mouth was open. 'I don't know that I am going to write about him anymore. The character is rather clapped out . . .'

'Was he taken out? Do I have your assurance that he's dead?'

There was a longish silence, then he began to lay out a multiple-choice scenario. 'Did he die in a solo suicide? Was he terminated by your cell leadership? Were you romantically involved . . . *was this a crime of passion?*'

'No! I'm talking about a *fictional* Dalminda! Look, I'll probably just use new characters for the other stories.'

Gupta reached swiftly for a blank slab of Post-it Notes. He nodded encouragingly, pen poised. 'Go on.'

'Go on with what?'

'Your new characters.'

My coffee, tepid before, was now cold. I sipped it slowly. I knew I ought to shut up and get a good lawyer. 'I tell you, it's fiction. I *create* the characters.'

'The way you created Dalminda Roco?'

'Exactly!' I thought he was beginning to understand.

'That's fine with me,' said Ram Gupta, drawing a line down the middle of his blank note block. 'Go on, create me a character.'

I shrugged. This was crazy. Lynn cast me a warning look, her lazy left eye toeing the party line, but I had gone on and said, 'Okay. Damien Higram.'

'Spell,' said Gupta, and I obliged. Lynn's eyes were closed, and she was twirling her wedding ring in a gesture I knew too well. Gupta was on cocaine or something, hyperactive with excitement, talking into a radio and a telephone at the same time. 'I have a name: Damien Higram, not Ingram, Higram, H-I-G-R-A-M. Read that back. Super. Move. *Move . . .*' His eyes dilated and he seemed to remember us. He swivelled to the wall, spilling a file to the ground heedlessly. His voice dropped into a warble of excitement, indistinct but for words like 'CIA files' and 'Mossad.' I considered speaking up with a caveat, but his momentum was pretty scary. Another minute of this passed and he put phone and radio against his chest and turned to me, hopefully. 'Do you have an address for me?'

My heart was pounding.

'Fictional, of course,' he conceded with a wink. Lynn was humming "Three Blind Mice."

'*This* is the address,' I said tautly.

'Sorry?'

I pointed at the policeman to his right. 'That's Damien.' I pointed at the policeman to his left. 'That's Higram.' I had combined the first names on their badges to create a character. 'Look, this joke has got to stop right now—'

'—*this joke?*' roared Ram Gupta, leaping to his feet. He slammed phone and radio down and raged, '*This joke?* Does five hundred thousand pounds strike you like a joke? Does thousands of overtime hours, leave cancellations, transatlantic plane trips . . . do they sound to you like *a joke?*'

'Maybe it's the quality of the investigation that you need to improve,' said Phil Begg, walking to the water dispenser. 'I read "Reluctant Bomber" and realised that my readers would like it, as they have. But it was also clearly a cry for psychiatric attention—'

'There's another thing,' said Gupta, reaching for another Post-it Note. His hand was trembling. 'How's your psychoanalysis going?'

'I am not under psychoanalysis,' I said sharply.

They stared at me.

Malcolm Frisbee lumbered to his feet. 'Where's the goddamned loo?' he asked, and a policeman held open a door for him.

'You saw Dr. George on Wednesday,' said Phil, 'he told me so, and it's there in our contract.'

'I play golf with Dr. George Maida every Wednesday,' I said loftily, 'and as for the conversation that passes between us, I might as well have been playing golf with my window cleaner.'

'That's a breach of contract: the twelve-story deal is dead!'

'Hallelujah,' I muttered, bravely.

Malcolm bounded back into the room. 'You can't take legal action based on anything you learn here!'

'I don't get my legal advice from you,' replied Phil. 'My God, I should never have allowed myself to be blackmailed into publishing this claptrap.'

Gupta pricked up his ears. '*Blackmailed?* What—'

'You keep out of this,' snapped Frisbee. 'This is a business matter.'

'Phil,' said Lynn, quietly.

'Blackmailed?' asked Malcolm Frisbee derisively, walking over to Phil, 'Somebody jog my medium-term memory here—who blackmailed *you?* Who left that *prostrate* message with my PA asking for my personal commitment on "Reluctant Bomber?" That story is the only thing worthy of review in your . . . your flaccid rag!'

'See who's talking!' shouted Phil, rising to his feet. 'No wonder you couldn't get out the word! The only reason I read that mad hodgepodge was because I thought it was a Jenny Ely story. It was a hodgepodge. *A hodgepodge!*'

'Calm down, everyone,' said Gupta.

'What's he saying, Lynn?' Frisbee demanded.

'On the day I . . .' began Phil.

'You keep out of this,' snapped Frisbee. 'This is a company matter.'

Lynn shrugged. 'Well, maybe he did start reading the Bible thinking it was the Quran . . . but it should have dawned on him at some point—'

'*You* were out of line,' snarled Phil. 'It was thoroughly unethical. And as *I* recall, the contract that I signed had a psycho clause . . . which he has obviously breached!'

'Humphrey Chow,' said Gupta, cutting to the chase, 'will you submit to a psychiatric evaluation?'

Phil opened his hands and looked upwards in mock thanksgiving.

'Never,' I said, categorically.

TOBIN RANI

Kantai | 3rd April, 2005

We walked slowly through the ruins. Here and there, we found waist-high remains of adobe homes enclosed in swathes of grass. Slabs of red clay in a sea of green, a scrubland cropped with dwarf trees. In the distance, we could just make out the black ribbon of a trunk road. A grey duiker surprised us, springing from cover and breaking across our path as we turned towards the expedition vehicle where it stood under a tree, up to its axles in grass.

On the tailboard of the truck sat the Mata, lost in thought as he stared up into the Jinn Hills where he had once lived.

'This is it?' David asked eventually. 'Kantai?'

'Yes,' I said. 'The Menai lived here seventy-two years. In 1920, Mata Nimito led our migration from here to Kreektown. He was born here, and he was in his twenties when we set out.' I turned and looked north. 'It gets interesting now: from here we head out into the desert, on a path *he* has never seen, trusting in the accuracy of our historysongs.'

'We're being romantic here, aren't we?' David said genially. 'The desert is featureless. How can you map a journey across the Sahara and then lock it up over hundreds of years in the ethnic memory of . . . *songs?*'

'The songs are written. He knows them by heart, but there's a written text.'

'Yeah, yeah.' He said absently. His eyes were far away, fixed on the distant road, 'We could have come here faster on the trunk road. The GPS could have brought us here a day earlier.'

'There were no roads when we left Kantai, David, and we have no coordinates for these locations. The Mata's maps are mostly in the sky. He can tell us *how* to get there, not *where* they are. Do you know what a starmap is?'

'No.'

'It's like a map of the night sky. The matas were cloudcasters and astronomers.' I paused and glanced at the last of the matas where he sat, and thought that they were also philosophers, and priests, and historians, and living libraries . . . I turned back to the professor. 'When we migrated from Kantai to Kreektown the route was encoded in a songline that combined star patterns with geographical features like rivers and cliffs, encoding travel directions that can survive centuries. The desert is not "featureless," David. That was how the Mata brought us here.'

'And that is how he plans to take us to the Field of Stones?'

'Precisely.' I looked around slowly. In one of these ruins lay my grandfather's grave. It was one thing to hear it in Mata Nimito's songs. It was another to actually stand here. 'Each migration has a songline. Our migration was meant to be temporary, so accurate route maps were critical. The Mata can recite all eight songlines from our historysongs.'

'But we don't need to go to all eight settlements, right?

'Of course not . . . what are you thinking?'

'We can plot the next songline from here to the next settlement on a map. If we do that for all eight place-names, we'll end up with the "X" that marks the Field of Stones. Then we can drive there as the crow flies.'

'That will probably save weeks and tanks of fuel . . . worth a shot!'

'You bet.' David sighed. 'We could also save tons more fuel by turning back now. Um . . . run this by me again: why aren't we looking for a premium plot in a nice cemetery?'

'You can't really get how big a deal this is. There's an Original Sin in the history of the Menai that must be rested—'

'I'll just steer clear of the religion, if you don't mind.'

'Okay, it's a crazy journey, David. A ninety-eight percent chance of failure—'

'Make that ninety-nine point nine.'

'Fine! And I'll possibly die on the trail as well. You don't have to come along. Thanks for the loan of the truck and all . . .'

'I'm in. I'm just surprised you gave yourself a two percent chance of success.'

I stopped and looked at him. At times like this the professor was difficult to read. He was hiding something; what it was, I had no clue. 'So what's in this for you? You're not risking your life out of gratitude that I identified your singateya.'

'Dunno. Research, I guess. Maybe I smell another book coming. With you here, it's a chance to interview the Mata . . .'

'You have to be *alive* to write a book. Listen, we may never find the Field of Stones. I may just have to dig a grave for him in the desert. Go home. If it's all about your damned research, I'll phone you when I find the Field of Stones and you can fly into the nearest town or something.'

'Sometimes the journey there is the most important part of the trip.'

I grinned. 'Then quit bitching.'

ZANDA ATTURK

Limbe | 4th April, 2005

I called one of Adevo's numbers, and he gave me the unexpected news of Ma'Calico's arrest. It was a fluke: one of the policemen from Elue's Kreektown raid had recognised her in a bus at a checkpoint. Unfortunately, her relatives had now looked for her at every police station in Ubesia without luck. She seemed to have disappeared into thin air.

I was speechless, imagining Amana's state of mind.

He sucked his teeth morosely. 'Remember what I did once I heard that Elue had arrested you?'

'You moved your tent?'

'Is good you also move your tent now,' he said. 'Everything Ma'Calico knows about you should be a lie. I'm sending Amana tomorrow.'

◆ ◆ ◆

AMANA ARRIVED unexpectedly in place of another bale. That night, when the brothers came back from the drop, they took me halfway across the market to another stall, where she had been installed. It was neither the reunion I had looked forward to nor the woman I remembered. She had arrived less her effervescence—and it was not just the seasickness.

She had brought a copy of *Palaver,* and I found that my column was back, at least for that issue. Under my Roving Eye byline ran a strange story: I had apparently interviewed the man who was used by the government to eliminate over a hundred soldiers in a 1992 plane crash. He claimed to have been approached by an agent of the current federal government to eliminate certain 'enemies of state' by similar means. Since he was now born-again, he had refused and was going public with the information in the hope that the government would be shamed into shelving its plans . . . It was a bizarre plant of a story. Patrick Suenu was certainly getting his money's worth. First, he had got the scoop on Charles Pitani's rescue. Now this . . . the longer I thought on it, the more puzzled I grew. In all the years I had written Roving Eye for *Palaver,* we had never had to publish an apology or retraction. He had resurrected the column to use that reputation to plant a complete fabrication.

And it worried me.

Yet other things came to occupy my mind: Amana's passport did not arrive for another three days, and the bad news did not let up.

CHARLES PITANI

Abuja | 6th April, 2005

I've got news about Badu. It is difficult, these days, to tell truth from lies, but this one looks good. The woman died saying the same thing, and people are usually too religious to take a lie to the grave. But *Limbe!* I don't even know where that is on the map! That's eight plane tickets, plus expenses! I'm not enjoying this anymore.

ZANDA ATTURK

Limbe | 7th April, 2005

We were in the backyard having a dinner of sweet potatoes when Bete arrived. He was the customs officer cousin at Douala Airport who was supposed to smooth our way through, but he was sounding flustered that evening. He had been raised in Bertoua and defaulted into French in his nervousness, rattling on and on to his bilingual cousins. When he was done, I read the fear in the faces of the usually cocksure brothers.

'Interpol posters, all over the airport,' Pokas said, unnecessarily; I had picked up that much.

'Don't worry,' Claude responded, 'we have people in Congo. There's a boat leaving . . .'

'No more boats,' said Amana, firmly. She had not sailed well.

We all looked at Bete. 'Unless on ninth . . .' he suggested. 'I have my boys on shift on ninth April.'

That gave us two days.

'Dr. Maleek comes tomorrow,' said Amana quietly, long after Bete had gone. There were friendly villagers around, and bottles of palm wine circulating, but we managed to feel left out. We had taken our misery to the beach.

'Do you trust him?'

'Of course. He thinks I'm screwed up, but I think he loved my mother . . . the way he talks—'

'Coming all this way . . . the reward money for Badu . . .'

She considered that point, then shook her head. 'He was bending over backwards for me, before he knew about you and Badu.' She smiled wanly. 'I suspect he wants to make sure you won't butcher me some night. I rather like the sound of that: he's coming to give you an MOT.'

'I thought you said you never missed a father figure.'

She grinned and I saw a flash of the old Amana. 'An MOT does not a father make.'

◆ ◆ ◆

8th April, 2005

I met Dr. Maleek in a palm-fronted café on the Atlantic beach. The Café Noir was attached to the Hotel Obix, and as I walked slowly into the foyer, an aroma of frying green peppers filled my mouth with saliva. I followed the signage to the café. There was a theme of stained teak panelling, and he was sitting at the bar with a lonely barman.

He was dressed in a jean jacket over stone trousers. A cautious smile lurked in a lush moustache streaked with grey. He rose, and we shook hands stiffly. After I refused a drink, he picked up his coffee cup and we walked to a booth on the other side of the café. As we sat down, I cleared my throat. 'I'm sorry about the punch. It's all those boxing lessons I took as a child. Sometimes I punch before I think.'

He grinned. 'That's all right.' His eyes narrowed, and he looked past me. 'What's that?'

I looked back. The bar was still empty. The barman was polishing a tap, and he gave me a friendly nod. There was nothing to see. I turned back— into a stinging slap. I gasped, more in shock than in hurt.

'You're crazy!' I spluttered.

He took his spectacles off and blew on the lenses. 'No, just angry. In case you were wondering, this payback was the main reason I travelled from Lagos to Limbe! Excuse me!' He pushed back his chair and walked out of the café.

I watched him go. I knew then that Amana was wrong and the police were waiting outside, but I didn't rise. It was a thirty-minute taxi ride to the brothers' market stall, and I didn't have a taxi waiting. Besides, I was tired of running.

The barman who had witnessed the 'unprovoked' assault was yet to close his mouth, and he brought me a pint of beer. His face was clouded with indignation and he waved away my wallet. 'Those Nigerians are *crazy!*' he marvelled.

It was difficult to convince him not to call the police on my behalf. I was halfway through the commiserative beer when Dr. Maleek returned to his coffee. He cleared his throat. 'I'm sorry about the slap.'

I laughed, partly in relief that he had no police escort, partly because I suddenly found it comical. He grinned widely and we shook hands; my cheek was no longer stinging and I found the handshake warmer than I expected. The barman was too far to overhear what we said, but he watched us with a deepening frown, and I wondered whether I would now get a bill for his beer.

'There should be something illegal about a doctor slapping his patient.'

'It's a matter of timing. You're not my patient, yet.'

'What is it between you and Amana? You didn't come all this way, either to slap me or to treat me.'

'No, I didn't,' he admitted. 'She's a special girl.'

'I know.'

'No, you *don't* know.'

'I'm listening.'

'I'm not here to talk.' He sipped his cold coffee. '*You* are. If she's worried about you, then I am. Let's talk about your relationship with this Badu.'

'Is this the point at which you call the police?'

He waved his hand angrily. 'If I was going to call the police you'd be locked up by now.'

A pause developed.

'Have you ever seen a psychiatrist?'

I shook my head.

'Amana says you don't recollect everything you do as . . . Badu.'

I nodded.

'Can I get some contribution from your tongue or something? How long has this been going on?'

'All my life. Well, obviously not the Badu thing. But I have been . . . different for as long as I remember.'

'Define different,' he said.

So I did.

We talked for an hour, with him asking cerebral questions and taking close-cropped notes in a book that emerged from his jacket. Finally we went upstairs to his room. It was a large, luxurious room with a suit carrier that sat, unpacked, on the bed. It was a far cry from my present lodgings. He opened his bag, and the smell of hospitals caught up with us. He drew some blood.

'I guarantee you I don't do drugs.'

'Then I guarantee you a drug-free certificate.' He continued his examination. Eventually, he sat back. 'Hmm.'

'So what do you think? Am I good enough to see your daughter?'

'My daughter?'

'There's no other reason why you would come out to Kreektown, and now Limbe, to see me. She doesn't know who her father was . . .'

He was laughing. '. . . and that makes me her dad? Well, nice try, but that won't make me give up my secrets.' He laughed again. 'Listen, give me a call when you settle somewhere. I'll run some tests on your specimens and I'll let you know.'

I got up.

'Why didn't you kill him?' he asked abruptly.

'Kill who?'

'Pitani.'

I stared. '*What?*'

'The hanging of that bent judge has done a lot more for that country than my forty years of medical practice,' he said bitterly. 'You should have hanged that bastard Pitani. We need a revolution in that country.'

I left without a word. At the end of the corridor I waited for the elevator, wondering why—if so many people wanted the man dead—they didn't just go ahead and lynch him themselves. It wasn't as though they didn't know where he lived.

Then Dr. Maleek opened his door and crooked a finger at me. Back in the room, he paced the room, wiping the lenses of his spectacles with the recently liberated tail of his shirt. Finally, he turned to me. His eyes were small and deep-set. He replaced his glasses and pushed them up the bridge of his nose. 'Do you love her?'

'How is that your business? You're not her father. You're not even her doctor.' We glared at each other for a season, until I shrugged. 'Yes.'

'Will you protect her with your life?'

I remembered Elue. I sighed. 'I'm a coward. I can't promise that.'

'That doesn't sound convincing, coming from Badu.'

'This isn't Badu speaking.'

'Some honesty at least.' He sighed. 'You'll probably keep her safer than a brave idiot. That will have to do for me. I'm going to tell you something you must promise never to tell Amana.'

I nodded without thinking.

'She could be next in line for the throne of the Nanga.'

'What?'

'Her mother was Saul Bentiy's concubine. There were problems, and she had to flee the kingdom, never to return. Unfortunately, by then, she was already pregnant with Amana.'

'Why are you telling me this?'

'You know, of course, that I am Sontik. Our traditional ruler is dying. In a few weeks, or months, the kingmakers will have to choose a new—'

'No woman has ever been Nanga . . .'

'No jailbird either, and she's both. But the kingmakers' current preference will be a disaster. For the Sontik, for Nigeria. I'm telling you this because I want you to keep her safe, Zanda. I didn't like to see her out there in the creeks . . . gunshots, fires . . .'

'You've just given me a little extra pressure, Dr. Maleek. If I crack again it will be on your conscience.'

'If you do crack,' he said, and there was no hint of a smile on his face, 'don't miss Pitani.'

I turned and walked out a second time. This time, I took the stairs.

◆　◆　◆

10:00 p.m.

It was our last night in Limbe. All four of us were huddled in the leather store, sorting out stories and identities. The phone rang in my hand. It was Adevo. 'She dey there?'

'Yes.'

'Leave her side. Now.'

'What's the matter?' she asked as I rose to my feet.

'Poor reception,' I said, slipping out.

Outside, the sandy aisle was deserted. I walked several metres away and put the phone to my ear again. My heart was pounding with dread. 'I can talk now,' I said tightly.

'Is about her mother,' grunted Adevo. 'We found her, finally-finally.'

I knew the answer to my next question, so I was silent for a while, stretching out that season of normalcy when all was well with the world. 'Will she be fine?'

'Yes, now. If person like Ma'Calico can't enter heaven, they have to close the place . . .'

I flung the phone down with an oath, just as Amana hurried up.

'What happened?'

I faked a laugh as I bent over to retrieve the pieces of the phone. 'It fell down. Now the reception will really be fantastic! Come, let's see Limbe for the last time.'

We walked the beach. The prospect of the trip made her more cheerful than she had been in days. My hollow laughter rang false beside hers. I could not break the news.

That night I opened the covers of my brother's book for the first time. His address was scrawled in pencil on the first page, with a telephone number beneath. I read the blurb on the back, read the first few pages, then I closed the book slowly. I shut my eyes. It was incredible; he was even crazier than I was.

◆ ◆ ◆

9th April, 2005

By the time we left for the airport at Douala, I had not mustered the courage to tell her. I told myself that such news would endanger our lives. After crying all night, her face would be too puffy for the passport image.

Or she might refuse to travel, and where would that leave us? It sounded logical enough, and I didn't have the nerve, anyway.

It was the smoothest boarding ever. We left it until the last minute before presenting ourselves at the check-in counter. At the last boarding announcement, we left our friends and boarded the London-bound Boeing with a stopover in Paris. My last image of Douala was a frightened Bete trying to make his shoulders broader than they could conceivably be as he stood in front of an Interpol poster of the most-wanted.

The jet was almost empty. We had a three-seater row all to ourselves. I suppose that gave me ideas. '*Ma'Calico*. Why do they call her that?'

'She used to sell the material, back in the day. It just stuck.' She looked at me, blinking rapidly. She whispered, 'She's dead, isn't she?'

When I didn't answer, she said, 'You must *never* keep secrets from me, Zanda. For me, secrets are worse than infidelity.'

'*Really?*' I said, mischievously, trying to lead her as far away from Ma'Calico as possible.

'Do be serious! That was the call you got yesterday night, wasn't it?'

I stared at her.

She took my hand, caressed it softly. Her fingernails bore her favoured blood-red paint. 'When my real mother died, I didn't even shed a tear. I can take it. She's dead, isn't she?'

But her hands were trembling, and I was no fool. 'I'm going to tell her how much you wanted her dead,' I said, and that shut her up. 'You know,' I said, to distract her, 'the only thing I know about your past is that you did time. And that's a shame.'

She took a deep breath. 'Do you have a few hours?'

We were less than an hour into our eleven-hour journey. 'Maybe fifteen minutes,' I said. 'I have a dental appointment in half an hour . . .'

That time she managed a faint smile.

AMANA UDAMA

Abuja | 4th February, 2002

That morning, I arrived at my desk at DRCD in Wuse and found Dr. Ologbon's memo waiting for me: it was the Kreektown posting we had been dreading for months. I must have dropped too heavily into my chair, because through the glass partitions I felt the communal flinch of conscience-stricken staff pretending not to be looking my way.

I am not beautiful, so I have had to be tough. I learnt that lesson from my mother's flower patch: root out the weeds and they grew right back but step on a pretty bulb and it died right away. Pretty things always find a gardener. Survivors need to be tough. I was not feeling especially tough on that morning of the Kreektown posting. The real Amana would have confronted Dr. Ologbon right away, but in my state of mind I would have broken down in the course of any confrontation. It was the domino effect, I think—I had only been out of jail two months. And I will never start a confrontation that will leave me in tears.

Never.

It was over, then. I set my lips and started to clear my desk.

The messenger stopped by on another mail round and didn't try to pretend ignorance, which was good for him. There were other posting slips in his mail basket, including the prized foreign assignments, but what he brought me was a clumsy attempt at consolation.

'You'll be fine, Amana; take it like a man.' He gave his honking laugh, which did not come in a whisper mode, and moved on to the next cubicle.

Well, I wasn't a man, I thought bitterly. There were a dozen so-called men in the office, and I still ended up with the most dangerous posting in DRCD. Kreektown had gone from 'most crime-free village in Nigeria' to 'highest incidence of gun violence per capita.' I was busy writing up my handover notes and clearing my desk, right up till lunchtime.

The staff canteen was full of whispered conversations that tailed off when I came within eavesdropping distance. I felt as though I'd stumbled into my own funeral; I bolted my meal and left. By 1:30 p.m., my handover notes were done, and I wrote my terse resignation in time for what Dr. Ologbon supposed was a briefing on my new posting. I sealed and addressed the envelope. Then I sat back and tried to work up the anger to deliver it.

It wasn't easy. Eight weeks earlier when I finished my jail sentence, my boss was the only one waiting at the prison gate. I wasn't expecting anyone, not my mother, who had died during my stint in jail, and definitely not my old boyfriend, who had never visited but had sent me a wedding invitation just to make things clear. Yet Dr. Ologbon was there in his blue Mercedes, offering a lift to the Halfway Hostel.

I remembered his uncommon chattiness, which resulted in a singular circularity of speech. It had taken him two hours to spring the news that brought him to the prison gates in the first place: the missing funds that put me in jail might have been an accounting error after all. The silence in the car afterwards lasted another year or two. There were many things I could have said, but none of them would have come without tears, and above all things, I like to keep my composure. Then he mentioned how an ongoing external audit investigation would confirm it one way or the other. In the meantime, Headquarters Personnel would expect me at 9:00 a.m. the following morning to clear me provisionally, not for my last accounts job, but for the cultural desk, if I wanted it.

I still remembered his cowardice at my trial, but I was fresh out of jail, facing destitution, and it was the wrong time to rehash old grudges. Back then, I had kept the 9:00 a.m. appointment.

Just as I was going to keep this 2:00 p.m. appointment.

Until the external audit was concluded and I was cleared, I couldn't remove the stigma of my conviction. That year-long 'sabbatical' was as far as most new employers would go on my CV before filing away my application in a shredder.

I had to go to Kreektown.

Reluctantly, I tore up the resignation and went to Dr. Ologbon's office. No confrontation, I reminded myself, sinking into a chair. I waited while Mercy flounced in and out to air her killer red shoes/red jacket combination and other gossipy colleagues toed and froed, faking errands in the boss's office . . . and all I could think was, why me? By the time his office was finally empty and he turned to me, it finally dawned on me, and my resolution collapsed. 'This is why you picked me up from prison!'

Dr. Ologbon's eyes narrowed. He was a smallish, balding man whose surviving hair was an unrealistic shade of black, considering the grey hairs on the back of his fingers. He did not cut a strong image, and he rarely got in the last word, but he was the kind of man that got on well in Abuja's civil service: he knew his job, knew the right people, and knew how to write memos with a combination of obsequiousness and cunning—which his ministers finally understood once they left office and were writing statements at the Economic and Financial Crimes Commission. 'What are you talking about?' he asked, rapping a Biro nervously on his tabletop.

'With my prison record, I'm the only person in this office who can't afford to resign!'

'You've got this all wrong,' he said, walking to the door.

'Why else would Personnel have cleared a jailbird for a civil service post? Akpan resigned over this posting. Everyone else threatened to; that was the only reason why you were at the prison gate.'

He shut the door quietly. We were still visible to the rest of the office, but we could speak privately. It was an odd kind of privacy. To encourage me to keep my voice down, he took the visitor's seat a foot away from me. He folded his hands and stared, trying his silly silent-chastisement thing.

Dr. Ologbon could have done a little more to keep me out of jail in the first place, like the small matter of a character reference my lawyer had asked for, to attack the circumstantial evidence that had put me away. I had gone to jail for foolishness, not for crime: back then I had been struggling financially. My mother's cancer treatments had thrown my rent into arrears. The cancer had gone into remission, but then, so had my finances. The office had turned down my desperate loan application. Then I stepped out one morning for my regular jog to find a heavy envelope containing eight hundred thousand naira by my door, with a note: 'This is from God, for your rent.'

Now, I was no fool: God would have bought me the house rather than clear my rent arrears and would certainly have done better for stationery than a Post-it note.

Practically all my friends knew about my rent crisis, but none of them had the spare cash—or the modesty to have given it anonymously. By the next morning, I was no nearer to explaining the mystery, so when the caretaker's walking stick came banging on my door I just muttered, 'Thank you God,' and paid the Shylock off.

Stupidly, I bragged about my miraculous deliverance to my half-dozen friends in the office. A week or so later, when I opened the door for my morning jog it was to let in some large men crowding the landing. They turned out to be CID investigators pursuing some missing money at the DRCD. They were working on an anonymous tip-off and wanted to search my house. Payday was still three days away, and (not being silly enough to produce God's Post-it note) I couldn't explain the fresh rent receipt.

I became the prime suspect in the case of DRCD's missing millions. When I tried to narrow down the people who could have tipped off the CID and came up with the same half-dozen possibilities, I knew it was time to change my friends.

But that lesson came too late to keep me from jail and cost me a full year to learn.

'Is this how you thank me for promoting you—and giving you a raise?' he said finally. He was aiming for the jocular tone, but he wasn't quite there yet.

I had noticed the promotion. They couldn't very well have posted a clerical officer to do Old Ira's job, so I was now Acting Research Supervisor with allowances to match. 'I'd rather be a living clerk than a dead supervisor.'

He sobered. 'You have nothing to fear, Amana; we've succeeded in getting a police post opened on the same street with the DRCD station. The roughboys have been tamed. You'll have a mobile phone and a radio. You'll be safer in the DRCD house in Kreektown than in your hostel in Abuja.'

'Ira was kidnapped on fieldwork. Do I get an armed police bodyguard on fieldwork?'

He blinked rapidly. 'I'm sure you can sort out the details with the Kreektown Police, Amana.'

I pursed my lips. It was a novel experience for me, fear as a physical tremor running through me.

'One day you're going to look back to this day, and you're going to recognise it as the biggest opportunity anyone ever gave you.'

'I'm too young for the opportunity of heaven—'

'Shall we get serious here? A station manager role is one that you'd normally have to wait another ten years to qualify for. Focus on that.'

I clamped my teeth as the fear became anger, and I focused instead on the single reason why I could not rise up that moment, like Akpan had done months earlier, and leave the job. 'When will the external audit report be ready, sir?'

He sighed, recognising my total capitulation. I understood his relief: I had seen my personnel file. They still fear the rebel who mobilised fellow students to shut down their uni and sack their corrupt vice chancellor. But people grew up. I left uni with a third-class degree rather than the second-class upper I worked for. I can never register for a PhD in this country, but my old VC is still a prof—and was appointed a VC elsewhere. Rage had to be systematic, not instinctual. 'I've known audit queries that dragged on for years,' he said, pushing the black case across to me. 'Your Kreektown paperwork. Questionnaire pads, manuals, and briefing folders, everything you need. You've got your job. Focus on that.'

'I don't do questionnaires, sir,' I said, wondering how far I could risk insubordination.

He grinned. 'I cleared it with the director-general. Run your station how you like it.'

I concealed my shock by going through the bag as he lined up the requisition dockets for my signature.

'Just deliver the annual report within a fortnight,' he ordered.

'How can I . . . ?'

'Ira hired a local as a cultural aide to help him drill down into local dialects and cultures. Find a translator who knows his way around, and I'll put him on the sessional payroll. Okay?'

I signed for my allowances, and in minutes we were heading across Abuja to the Federal Secretariat, for the obligatory pep talk with the director-general. It was only my second time in the DG's office, and I prepared myself for the magnetic insincerity of his presence.

He met us at the door, which made it unnecessary to sit down, as he made a brief variant of his Christmas Party speech: 'Our cultures will not survive, Miss Udama. Not in their present form, and maybe not at all. In a hundred years, these soulless, bastard urban streets will be all we have left. We must scour the land, capturing, photographing, and documenting culture for posterity. We're not interested in how it was, we're not historians, or how it should be, we're not futurists; our business is with how it is. Today. That's the sacred role of the Department of Research and Cultural Documentation, and you've been called to the front line. Congratulations, Amana.'

It was over in minutes. How different it had been two years earlier when I first entered his office. I had been touring Nasarawa in central Nigeria, administering oral literature questionnaires to the indigenes. It was a low-literacy neighbourhood, and although I found many willing respondents, I had to fill in each questionnaire personally. By 10:00 a.m. that morning, I was ready to climb the nearest telephone mast. And jump. In a sense, it was self-preservation, really: I could have gone crazy, had I continued to do the job by the book. Instead, I met the most incredible beard I ever saw. He agreed to do a questionnaire, and I recorded him as DRCD's Sample NAS2393, but his first responses hinted at far more valuable anecdotes on oral literature than any report that had come out of our bureau. I knew that the flesh and blood of his story would tell the DRCD more about orature in Nasarawa than the skeletal statistics from another hundred samples. So I let him talk . . .

Back in my hotel room, I was in serious trouble: I was a hundred questionnaires short of my target. So I did the only thing I could have and entered Beard's story across the DRCD 090 grid normally reserved for questionnaire results.

My report caused a small crisis at our head office. Dr. Ologbon treated it as dereliction of duty and sent off a photocopy to Personnel for the attention of the disciplinary panel. Personnel interpreted it as a resignation. They were familiar with the genre: when Idris won the lottery, instead of his regular weekly report, he'd had his nine-year-old daughter copy her homework onto the DRCD 090 grid form. To further confuse matters, the Apo Health Directorate claimed jurisdiction, interpreting the form as a transparent plea for psychiatric intervention.

Finally Beard's story went right up to the DG for a decision. That was my first time in his office. I'd expected a tongue-lashing, but instead he asked me a lot of strange questions. I told him what he probably wanted to hear: that my greatest desire was to end my career at his desk (well after his retirement, of course). He told me that when I got to sit in his chair I would see that although NAS2393 would give the department better insight into Nasarawa's orature than all the other work my department had done that week, it was an inspirational approach that could only complement, never replace, the tried and trusted 'perspirational' questionnaires of DRCD.

'You're the one who applied for a compassionate salary advance?'

'Yes, sir,' I had said, hoping for a miracle. 'It was for my mum's hospital bills, but it was turned down.'

'You won't solve your financial crisis by writing stories on my DRCD 090 forms.' He mused, with the many distracted nose palpations of the closet gold digger. 'I'll see what I can do for you.'

What he did was transfer me to the Accounts department. There were no provocative questionnaires on that beat, but I didn't stay there too long. Within a month I had received my note from God and another couple of weeks afterwards I found myself filling out a questionnaire for the Ministry of Internal Affairs at Kuje Prison in Abuja.

◆ ◆ ◆

5th February, 2002

I was feeling more upbeat in the morning. DRCD's protocol office had printed my itinerary, which I broke as soon as I arrived at the Abuja Airport. Instead of the flight from Abuja to Ubesia, I boarded the first flight to Lagos. The plane arrived within the hour, and I caught a cab to the psychiatric hospital at Yaba. I left my bags with a friendly receptionist and joined a long queue to see Dr. Maleek.

His table was cluttered with files, but he had made enough room for two elbows and a cup of tea. There was a suspicion of aloofness in his eyes, a man used to putting distance between himself and the relentless stream of suffering in which he worked. 'Where's your card, young lady?'

I shook my head quietly. 'I'm not a patient; my name is Amana Udama. It's about my mother.'

'What's her name?'

'Evarina Udama. She lived in a tiny village near Abuja, but you used to be her doctor . . .'

His smile seemed to become warmer, less professional. When I didn't continue, he asked, 'How can I help you, Amana?'

'It's about . . . I need to talk about her . . .'

'Do you have a letter from her?'

'She's dead.'

'I'm sorry.' He paused for a beat. 'I am. But a doctor's confidence isn't released by his patient's death.'

'She was my mother. I . . . came all the way from Abuja . . .'

'I hate to sound callous . . . Miss?'

I nodded.

'Miss Udama, but it doesn't matter where you came from. These rules have a purpose.'

'The confidence is already broken. A medical report was sent from here to her doctor in Abuja. I was at home when the letter arrived, and I read it.'

'Then you don't need me.'

I rose. Suddenly he didn't seem that warm anymore. 'You'll have to use the information in my mother's file'—I knew I was sounding melodramatic, but I couldn't help myself—'whether you help me now, or when they carry me back here screaming and kicking!'

He smiled and offered me his complimentary card.

I ignored it and walked out, managing not to slam the door. Later, I was glad I didn't. I was waiting for a taxi outside the hospital gate when a green-clad orderly I had noticed outside Dr. Maleek's office hurried up to me.

♦ ♦ ♦

12 noon

He took me to lunch in a Montgomery Road restaurant whose proprietress played the same Rex Lawson track all afternoon. He no longer looked indifferent or warm, merely tired. I was now sorry about my outburst, and rude exit, and spent the twenty minutes while I ate and he made small-talk trying to muster an apology. By the time I put down my fork I had given up the struggle. 'Thanks for lunch,' I said, instead. 'I'm sorry to take you out of the hospital.'

'It's fine. I had to grab the opportunity to enjoy lunch with Evarina's daughter—before she becomes my patient.'

I recognised another cue for an apology and sidestepped it swiftly. 'You remembered my mother after so many years without looking up a file . . .'

He nodded. 'She was a . . . special case—I'm still not discussing her, by the way, I'm discussing you. Did you have a good childhood? Stepfather?'

I shook my head. 'No father, whether real or step. My mother didn't have much luck in the marriage pools. As for my childhood,' I hesitated, 'it's over.'

He groomed his moustache. 'She wasn't a good mother?'

I shook my head. 'But then again, I wasn't a good child.' I hesitated, 'I finally understood, when I read the medical report and saw that she tried to kill me as a baby . . .'

Dr. Maleek sighed and ran his hand over his bald spot. He suddenly looked years older. 'I was hoping you were bluffing about reading the report. But you have to understand, she was ill. It was involuntary, what she did. It's like a mum having a heart attack and dropping her own child; she deserves pity, not hatred.'

'You know a lot of medicine, Dr. Maleek, but you obviously don't know women. My mother was no loony. The thing with my father didn't work out, and I was a hindrance for the next eligible man to come along . . .'

'And you are the woman expert, aren't you? Diagnosing an event that happened when you were two days old.'

'I'm analysing a woman I lived with all my life!'

'She was suffering a well-documented medical condition!'

'Oh, yes? Was she still suffering from it when she packed me off to boarding school, to get me out of her way? She had so many relationships—and none worked out. She forgot to pick me up on three holidays, but she never, ever made another mistake.'

'Another mistake?'

'I was her only child.'

'Did it ever occur to you that she didn't marry again because she didn't want the pressure to have children . . . and that you didn't have siblings because she was afraid of another breakdown?'

'You're not just her doctor; you're her advocate as well.'

'You force me into that role—by deciding to be her judge and jury as well. Look, since you've read the report, why did you want to see me?'

'Will you now break your Hippocratic oath? Or is this just a rhetoric question?'

He smiled wanly. 'Amana, I've been a doctor for thirty years. I am fifty-eight years old. I've got two years for every year of your life. First time I met you, you were small enough to sleep in that purse around your waist. Do you understand what I'm saying?'

'You loved my mum too, didn't you? She had that effect on men; they took her side every time. Her only failure was my biological father.'

He gulped down the rest of his tonic water, spilling some on his coat. He put down the glass angrily and said, his voice cold and bitter as he slapped at his clothes, 'Maybe you should register as a patient after all. I thought I'd have lunch with a success story and it turns out a busman's holiday!'

I shut my eyes and struggled with my own anger. Temperamental was the most consistent adjective in my annual assessments at DRCD.

Eventually, he relented, pointing a finger at me. 'Listen, your mother had postpartum depression with a major psychotic episode. From what you're telling me, it had an impact on mother-child bonding.'

'It certainly did.'

'It happens. But she was ill. Not you. This doesn't have to happen to you and your children. It's difficult, but you must get over your bitterness toward her and get on with your life.'

I shrugged and said lightly, 'I'm not bitter, just stating a cold fact.'

'Look, what do you really want from me?'

'She wrote me a letter, from her deathbed, asking me never to seek out my father or visit her hometown . . .'

'About your father, I can't . . .'

'I don't care about him,' I said sharply. I bit my tongue. 'I just want to know why she had this thing about her hometown. She's Sontik, from Ubesia, but she's never been there since I was born. Now, I've just been posted to Kreektown, which is just a few kilometres outside Ubesia . . .'

He stared. 'You don't care about your father, but you're interested in a town?'

I opened my purse and pulled out a mirror and a small plastic tube of lipstick. 'He rejected me, so that's easy. I'm not one of those clingers who pine for fools that have rejected them . . .'

The bill arrived, and he pulled out his wallet and paid, again offering me his complimentary card, which I accepted this time. His voice was level, measured. 'As it happens, fatherhood is one issue bigger than parent/

doctor confidence. There was nothing about your father on the files, and I can't tell you anything now, but in the near future . . . what's so amusing?'

'I am twenty-three years old. I have a degree, I have a job, and I pay my way. Why on earth do I need a runaway father?'

'So what do you want to know about Ubesia? Are you hoping to track down your mother's relatives, is that it?'

I grimaced at the small mirror and relaid two tracks of lipstick in two economical strokes. 'I'm alone and happy,' I said, clicking the mirror shut and put away my concessions to femininity. I leaned forward, counting off my fingers. 'I don't want siblings, I don't want relatives. I don't want parents. Why is this so difficult for people to accept? Is this a psychiatric condition, Dr. Maleek, being satisfied with your aloneness?'

'Not by itself, no.' He was studying me narrowly. 'So what is it about Ubesia that brings you to me?'

I hesitated. 'I don't have my mum's beauty, but I have her last name. If she made enemies, if there's a feud or something . . . well, I'd like to go into things with my eyes open. Kreektown is dangerous enough as it is . . .'

He was staring at me with pursed lips.

I shrugged. 'Besides, it's also my hometown, isn't it? I'd just like to know if there's any sane reason why I should stay away from it. I've lived in Abuja all my life, and that might be long enough already.'

He took a cocktail stick. His fingers were trembling, but his voice was cold. 'Amana, I'm Sontik like you. Ubesia is my hometown, too. There's a very traumatic reason, but the trauma only concerns Evarina Udama and those who loved her. That leaves you in the clear, I suppose?'

I glared. 'So you know, but you're not telling me, is that what it is?

The cocktail stick broke in two. The crack seemed to startle the psychiatrist, but he deliberately broke the remaining halves as well. He arranged the pieces into a tiny, self-assured square. 'I want to tell you . . . some of it, Amana,' he said gently, 'but do you want to know? It requires some affection for your mother and it contains some information about your father. So, do you want to know?'

I struggled to get out the words. He was a mind doctor all right. In a few sentences he had served me a plate of humble pie, which I would rather die than eat.

I pushed my chair away and grabbed my bags. I blundered out. I was sweating by the time I found a taxi, but I had missed the second and last flight to Ubesia for the day. Soon I was heading for the Ojota motor park, where I caught a bus bound for Ubesia.

• • •

2:15 p.m.

It was a beautiful day to be going to one's hometown for the first time. I slept most of the way, but by the time we passed Benin City and the fast bus started down the road to Ubesia, I was awake and alert. As evening fell, a party of school children in the bus started singing songs that lopped some years off my life. I began to enjoy the detour through Lagos.

It was 7:00 p.m. when I arrived at the Ubesia motor park. After Abuja and Lagos, the city seemed positively provincial, and I felt the strangest pride to hear Sontik, a language I previously had only ever heard in living rooms, spoken in the public spaces. I was tempted to spend the night in an Ubesia hotel, but in the end, a lifetime of my mother's antipathy had its way and I loaded up my bags into another taxi, this one bound for Kreektown. The driver was septuagenarian, his taxi not much younger. He drove with such care and compassion for his undercarriage that the twenty-kilometre drive over the potholed roads took us an hour.

We smelled the smoke as we approached Kreektown, and as we drew nearer, we saw the thick pillar of smoke climbing into the clear, moonlit sky. The driver, fearing for his car, was reluctant to go farther, but passersby assured us that the latest rioting by roughboys had been quelled, and we drove on. When we arrived, what was left of the looted DRCD station was in flames.

• • •

9:00 p.m.

I was so spooked that I was prepared to return to Abuja that night, if there was a car to take me; but all my taxi driver could promise was a drive back to Ubesia, where he lived—and that, after his dinner. He took me to a bustling hotel at the outskirts of Kreektown, where he drank a beer with his jollof to steady his nerves. The saloon was crowded and pulsing with gossip about the fire. I sat aloof from the rowdiness with folded arms, waiting for him to finish. When he was done, he walked unsteadily to the loo, bumping into people who were doing their best to avoid him. When he returned and started on a second beer for the road,

I lost my own nerve. I went to the severe woman at the counter to ask for a room for the night.

She looked me up and down, from the supercilious corners of her eyes. 'So you will manage my room now, not so? Proud Congo!'

I returned her look stolidly. We were not in the same class, and all the diplomacy in the world could not change that. Eventually, she relented and pushed her book across. I filled out my name on the grid and put down her deposit. She counted the money carefully, holding the bills suspiciously against the light. Finally, she folded the money into her brassiere and reached for a key in a cane basket. That was when she first glanced at the register. 'Udama?' she broke the name into speculative syllables, 'Amana Udama? Ematu Sontik?'

'Sia,' I agreed, not sure where that was going.

She wagged a finger threateningly. 'I've been looking at you.' She rose slowly to her full height. Her voice trembled. She was several inches taller than I was, and her voice was aggressive and masculine. 'Ematuni Evarina Udama?'

I took a step backwards. I remembered my mother's warning, but I was too proud to say anything but 'Sia.'

She attacked me—but she was also whooping with an explosive kind of joy, taking me in a bear hug that swept my feet off the ground. No one had ever done that before to Amana Udama. She was loud and blue-collar dirty and I was upset and quite embarrassed, but by the time my feet touched the ground again . . . I was also grinning helplessly. And that was the beginning of the end of my old life. She was my mother's 'African sister,' although I've never quite figured out the precise relationship. She was not much put out to learn that Evarina was dead—as far as the family was concerned, Evarina had died when she jumped off a Lagos bridge two decades earlier. Yet Ma'Calico had recognised Evarina's walk in me, which mystified me in all sorts of ways. And she threw out the occupant of the best room in the house and installed me there.

I suppose I was unprepared for the presumption of a Ma'Calico, for her gargantuan generosity. She introduced me as her daughter. There were no complicated stories. The only quarrel we ever had was once when she overheard me describing her as 'my mother's cousin' . . . It took me a week to call her 'Mama,' and by then, the transformation of Amana Udama was complete.

◆ ◆ ◆

15th November, 2004

The DRCD never rebuilt their Kreektown office and were happy for me to run the project out of the Kreektown Guest House, as we called Ma'Calico's hotel in the monthly invoices we sent to Abuja. I found a Sontik lad, Domu, who knew enough to show me around the degraded community even though he didn't speak a word of Menai. When our work for the day was done, he pulled out a pack of cards to supplement his sessional wages with my salary.

I was a fast learner. Within a fortnight he lost interest in card games.

Come Christmas, I got the letter I'd been dreading recalling me to Abuja. The numbers of the Menai had grown statistically insignificant for DRCD sampling. On our classifications register, the Menai were now extinct and the project was shut down.

That's life, I guess.

Dr. Ologbon eventually made good on his promise to clear my name with an audit, but I never did figure out which of my tattling 'friends' had sent me to prison. Between returning to my 2002 post (Ologbon did have a mean streak) and going full-time into the hotel business, it wasn't that hard a decision.

SLEEPCATASTROPHES

Kreektown | December, 2001

Rumieta Kroma
Dudu Mpaya
Mukaila Dede
Ajo Munije
Owma Maraje
Cletus Anieme

Births
Nil

Extant Menai population: 290 (NPC estimates)

CHARLES PITANI

Abuja | 10th April, 2005

A few days after Rudolf left for Limbe, he was back in my living room with a fat case. A leather sofa that had never complained in its life was creaking under him.

'I thought you were supposed to be in Cameroon.'

'Badu is now in London,' he said, looking around hungrily. 'Boy, it's a fucking hot day . . . any lager?'

'London?' I looked at him suspiciously. This club sandwich graveyard apparently thinks he has found a free travel agency. He should just ask for Paris–New York–Wellington at the same time. 'So you want a return ticket to London, eh?'

He must have noticed my tone, for he forgot about the beer, for the time being. He pulled out his laptop and set a video to play.

I stared. I swallowed. My crotch burned. *And the boy looks so innocent!* Unless he was possessed by demons, how could a boy like that do all this to me? All on his own? 'Which airport is this?'

'Douala.'

'What flight?'

'He went to London.'

'And they let him through? With all those Interpol posters everywhere? What kind of police force do they have in that stupid country?' But I am not really angry. This is the closest yet. This fat pig is not totally useless. 'You're going to London immediately!'

'It's bloody hot here,' he said, wiping his face.

It was near freezing in the air-conditioned room, but I knew what he meant. 'Tina! Bring beer!' I shouted. 'London is difficult, isn't it?'

'London is no problem; I have my Romanians on him already.'

'Romanians?'

'They're not as arrogant as the Russians. I have sent them this video, and they've already picked up his landing card at Heathrow immigration. Do you need a corpse for lying-in-state?'

'What are you talking about?'

'The Romanians specialise in bombs, but they can use bullets if you need a corpse for lying-in—'

'Bombs,' I said. 'I like the sound of *bombs*. Tina! Are you deaf?'

HUMPHREY CHOW

London | 11th April, 2005

'I agreed to psychoanalysis,' I said, flipping through Dr. Asian Borha's profile, 'but I don't believe in hypnosis.'

'He's one of the finest therapists on our books,' said Gupta, 'and he doesn't come cheap. But we need to get inside that head of yours.' He paused delicately. 'How's your marriage counselling going?'

None of your business, I told him, mentally.

'I'm in your corner on that point, okay?'

I ignored him. We had traded a two-week detention for a consultation with a police psychiatrist, but friendship was not part of the bargain. Grace had filed for divorce soon after our arrest. Phil had also threatened to scupper my twelve-story deal, but it seemed that the more notorious my first story grew, the more interest there was in the second. My contract was safe for the time being. Unfortunately, with all the tension from the police investigation, I was a day from the deadline and still didn't have a story. I was meeting with Lynn in less than an hour, and I didn't have good news for her.

I waited. Gupta himself seemed to cast about for something to say. We were sitting in a cubicle of an incident room in his local station, waiting for Dr. Asian Borha to make an appearance. Then the door opened . . . but the man who stood there shared no resemblance with the Dr. Borha in the profile. This man was elderly and lanky, and his joints cracked and snapped as he walked across to shake Gupta's hand. 'Let me introduce you to Sergeant Andrews, retired now.' said Gupta, 'He investigated Dalminda's aborted London bombing in 1991.'

We shook hands solemnly. Andrews sat on the edge of the desk. His voice was quiet and deferential. 'We never met, but my name may ring a bell . . . ?'

I shook my head.

'We didn't interview you in 1991. We thought you were too young. A big mistake, as it turns out.'

'Exactly what are we talking about here?'

'In 1991 Miss Chow's boyfriend, Tobin Rani, phoned the police to report a terrorist plot. A certain Dalminda Roco was trying to recruit him into a scheme to blow up the offices of Trevi Biotics. They'd met at a demonstration outside Trevi's office. Roco had more violent plans. We knew he became close to Tobin, he was a frequent visitor to your house. That was where he made his pitch to Tobin. That's where he must have started grooming you.' He opened a large file, slipped out a picture, and placed it before me. 'Does this look familiar?—Of course, he'll look fourteen years or so older today.'

I was staring at my Scottish Dalminda Roco, and not a day older. My head ached. My mouth dried up. I shook my head.

'Are you sure? This Dalminda, like yours, went to law school but didn't finish. Like yours, this Dalminda lost his father in his mid-twenties. Like yours, this Dalminda wanted to blow up people . . .'

'Never seen this Dalminda.'

They exchanged glances. Andrews plucked at his lower lip briefly. 'It is not in your interest to be obstructive, Humphrey Chow. The gap between a witness and an accused person can be a very small one; and it comes down to how cooperative you are.'

There was a knock on the door. This time, Dr. Borha entered. He looked the part of a successful London doctor who charged six hundred pounds an hour, and I shook his hand as coldly as I could, but his self-effacing grin neutralised my antipathy. He nodded at the profile in my hand. 'I see you've done the background checks on me. I hope I passed muster!' He took the chair on my side of the desk. 'We have an hour, Mr. Chow, and we can start as soon as we're alone.'

'Don't mind us,' said Gupta, sinking into the chair on the other side of the desk.

'I'm afraid I do.' Dr. Borha smiled politely. 'You get to read a medical report, but not to look over my shoulder.'

I felt considerably warmer towards the doctor as Gupta glowered.

'Well, let me just run this by you both, so you know where we're at.' Gupta took a Post-it Note from his folder and walked around his desk to prop himself up alongside Andrews. 'Fact: Dalminda had the opportunity of unsupervised meetings with an eleven-year-old Humphrey Chow. How long this grooming continued, we don't know. Fact: Humphrey dropped below our radar at age fourteen, when he went to the Ivory Coast with his foster parents at the time. Fact: he was there till . . .'

'I've never been to the Ivory Coast.'

Gupta slammed a palm on the desk and swore. He caught himself and pointed at Dr. Borha. 'One hour!' He gathered up his papers and stormed out of the room. Andrews followed more sedately, sad eyes lingering on me.

Dr. Borha cleared his throat and crossed his legs. 'It is a matter of public record, Humphrey,' he said gently. 'It's in the brief they sent me. You left Britain at age fourteen and turned up at age twenty-two at the British High Commission in Abidjan. They fear your amnesia may be a tad too convenient. They . . .'

'Are you Gupta's lawyer, or my doctor?'

He seemed to consider that for the first time. Then he chuckled. 'To be perfectly honest, Humphrey, I'm here because I'm intrigued by the reference from your surgery, which was backed up by your latest lab tests.'

'What was there to intrigue you in my medical records?'

'Nothing worrisome on its own, but together with the history from the police, well . . . I'd like to test a hypothesis, but I'm still waiting on your genome report. The Met is sparing no expense on you, Humphrey, and I've reached that point in my career when I can afford to indulge myself in matters that pique my interest.' He rubbed his hands. 'If it's all right with you, we can start with a session of hypnosis to seek any subconscious associations you may have with the real Dalminda Roco.'

'I signed up for psychoanalysis,' I told him. 'I don't respond to hypnosis. My first psychiatrist—'

'Then forget it,' he said easily. 'I'll just give you some hypnotic suggestions to relax you . . .'

'Whatever you want to do. But I don't have an hour. I have a lunch appointment in thirty minutes.'

'Oh, you can leave anytime you want.' He reached into a case on the ground and brought out a digital recorder with a fat microphone. He set it on the table beside us, apologizing: 'Less distracting than taking notes.' He stripped the cellophane off a new pack of microcassettes, labelled one with an 'A', and slotted it into the machine. He clicked on the recorder before pulling his chair closer to me. He clasped his hands, cracking a few knuckles in the process. He crossed his legs, notching up his voice into a hammy, mellifluous cadence; my mental sneer became a snort. 'It's good to relax, isn't it, to feel the worries of the world slip away from your shoulders, to feel the muscles loosen in your neck . . .' He went on and on.

I watched him, warily, wondering if I was going to lose thirty minutes of my life in a shamanic séance officiated by an expensive doctor; then something weird began to happen. *He* began to relax visibly. His voice slowed, and he sank deeper into his chair. Presently his arms were hanging limply. He was still talking, but there were now distinct pauses between his broken sentences. I realised I was about to have a hypnotized psychoanalyst on my hands.

I glanced at my watch, wondering if I should just leave. My own hands were clammy with imminent embarrassment. It was definitely not relaxing.

His sonorous voice droned on, like a tape, although he seemed nearer to snoring than hypnosis. 'It is good to relax . . . you are feeling lighter and lighter with every breath . . . the resistance you have is melting away . . . melting away . . .'

I decided he was more likely performing. I was bothering myself over nothing. I sat back, folded my arms, and shut his twaddle out of my mind.

Just then my telephone rang. It was a wrenching sound in the isolation of Gupta's incident-turned-hypnosis room, and I sat up. Dr. Borha seemed as flustered as I was, staring, disoriented, at my waist where the offending instrument was clipped. ''Scuse me,' I said.

'That's all right, I should have reminded you to switch off the phone . . . but we were just about done anyway.' He switched off the digital recorder as I took the call. Lynn sounded cross.

'Thanks for standing me up!'

'It's still on,' I said. 'I'll be there in fifteen.'

'Don't bother, I've already done lunch. Can you e-mail the story?'

'Well, I've got some ideas,' I began.

'Ideas won't cut it, Humphrey Chow; you've got a day to deliver six thousand words to Phil. They go to press on Wednesday, and they hit the streets on Friday. I did warn you about the pressure.'

I was listening to a dead phone. Lynn had never hung up on me before. I glanced at my watch and did a double take.

Dr. Borha was smiling privately as Ram Gupta returned. He was still carrying his file. 'So how did that go?'

'Very well indeed,' muttered Dr. Borha. 'I haven't seen a better hypnosis subject . . .'

'You haven't?' I said in some confusion. I had lost an hour—and all certainty as to whether I was going or coming.

For answer, Dr. Borha rewound a few seconds of tape and played it back. My voice issued from the digital recorder in a monotone that curled my toes. Then my phone rang so convincingly that I reached for my waist again, before I realised that it was ringing on the tape. Dr. Borha thumbed off the digital recorder. 'Plenty happened.'

My throat constricted. I felt tugged towards a past I had escaped, a past of turmoil. I wanted to get out of that room, and I knew I was never going to put myself in this situation again, whatever the conditions of my bail.

Gupta stretched out his hand for the microcassette, but Dr. Borha had other ideas. He slipped it into his shirt pocket and hefted his case. 'There's plenty here, like I said, but first off, I've got to determine whether we were listening to Humphrey Chow's memories or to Humphrey Chow the storyteller.'

'I'll figure that out for myself,' said Gupta, stepping forward. 'That's what I learned in detective school.'

'Let me finish what *I* learned in medical school,' insisted Dr. Borha, following me towards the door. 'This is still a work in progress; his referents are psychometrically incoherent. This material falls short of forensic standards; I'll finish my own investigations, Sergeant. I'll call you tomorrow.'

I left the police station with the doctor on my heels. My jaw was set. I showed him my wrist watch. 'Your hour is spent. Haven't you noticed?'

'You intrigue me, Humphrey Chow,' he said. 'I owe you an apology for your lunch with your girlfriend . . .'

'I'm married. That was my IMX agent, Lynn.'

We were standing outside the Green Man pub. A scruffy blackboard on the pavement proudly announced two eight-ounce steaks, and spuds, for a fiver. He looked from the board to me. 'Tell you what, I'll buy you lunch.'

'I'm not hungry. Goodbye, Dr. Borha.' I turned to go, and he pulled out the microcassette from his pocket.

'You have an amazing story here, Humphrey Chow. To my mind, more interesting than what you had in the first issue of *Balding Wolf.*'

I stopped dead. He had got me; and from the look in his eyes, he knew it. 'I'm not saying another word today.'

'As it happens'—he laughed—'I'm in a garrulous mood myself. This lunch is on me, and I promise, you won't be getting a bill for this hour!'

He pushed through the door of the pub, presumptuously assuming that I would follow. He led the way through the bar proper into the dimly lit interior, where five gnarled oak tables were set for four and a cloying spice of tobacco hung in the air. He plunked his case down by a table in the corner and shrugged out of his jacket. On nearby tables, a smattering of diners watched a football match on a muted screen. 'I'll order,' he offered. 'Steak for you? Beer?'

I sat down gingerly. I didn't mind a steak, but I certainly minded a rich psychoanalyst acting like a pimply, hard-up youth on a first date. I glanced at the menu. 'I'll have the risotto and cream,' I said casually, picking the most expensive item, which was barely fifteen pounds anyway, 'but I'll have the king prawn entrée as well.'

'Okay,' he said. 'And a beer?'

'Any good champagne will do.'

He grinned. 'I can see you're used to dining well, Humphrey Chow, but this is a humble pub. Perhaps a house wine?'

That was probably when I relaxed. We had a passable meal, if it was possible to do passable with a divorce on the horizon, a cross agent on my case, and no story for my deadline. Dr. Borha was as garrulous as he had promised, becoming even more so after three pints of Stella Artois. I had seen that trick before, and I knew he was probably more in control of his faculties than he let on. I stuck severely to my glass of wine and ate my risotto mincingly.

Eventually, the plates were cleared away; he took a deep breath and put the microcassette on the table.

'Can I have a listen?' I asked tightly.

'Not now,' he said, waving a hand to take in the diners on the other tables.

'Well, was there anything . . . ?'

'Incriminating? Perhaps potentially. But it depends on whether you take the contents of this tape as gospel truth or as the product of a novelist's subconscious. That's where further investigations come in. And I need you to trust me, to open up to me . . .'

'You promised,' I warned. 'You said you'd do the talking.'

He laughed, raising his hands in surrender as he sat back. 'Fine, but I was just filling the vacuum. You've shown a singular lack of interest in me.'

'I guess I was being polite,' I conceded. 'Where were you from, originally?'

'I'm Trinidadian,' he said. He took a sip, showing me the bottom of his glass. 'Although I have travelled widely in Africa. About Ivory Coast—'

'I've never been there.'

'I think you should listen to this, Humphrey,' he said abruptly, opening up his doctor's case to pull out the digital recorder. He slotted in the cassette and passed it to me. 'Go on. The toilet has thick enough walls. I'll wait.'

I took the machine, but I didn't rise. The memory of the voice I had heard in Gupta's office returned, and a strange fear filled me. 'I don't want to listen to it in a pub toilet. I don't even want to listen to it in your clinic. I want to listen to it in the privacy of my own rooms.'

He hesitated for a beat. 'That's fine,' he said, taking me completely by surprise. 'You're my patient, and while I won't lie to the police, my ultimate loyalties are to you, not the police. I do have one condition, though.'

'What is it?'

'We must get to the bottom of this. You have these strong screen memories that you use to shield traumatic histories, but your medical records suggest organic triggers for your condition at genome level. Call my secretary and make an appointment. Is that a deal?'

'Sure.' I hesitated. 'Do you have a diagnosis? My last psychiatrist said—'

'I read her notes,' he said arrogantly. 'Don't bother with her opinion.'

'And you?'

He shrugged. 'Early days. The categories of dysfunction are never closed, but for a working diagnosis, I'd plunk you into the dissociative fugue box. Ever heard of that?'

Dissociative fugue. I shook my head.

'Google it,' he advised. 'It's usually less stressful if you can put a name to your condition.'

'Is it curable?'

'God, I don't know, I'm not in the DNA uncrimping business. But'—he rubbed his hands together gleefully—'I'll get richer finding out.'

I laughed in spite of myself.

♦ ♦ ♦

I HURRIED home from my meeting with Dr. Asian Borha to listen to the tape. Within the hour I was inside the small flat.

Grace was long gone, of course. The breakup itself had been sophisticated. After our row at the police station, she had checked herself into her mother's clinic because she was having panic attacks, brought on, she said, by a fear of what I could let into the house while she slept. The improbable Dalminda Roco had become an invisible presence between us. When the week in the clinic was up, she moved back into her mother's house. The moving truck came later. We did not even have an argument about breaking up.

Our flat was in Putney Village, above a pub called the Cricketers Arms. I wasn't hungry when I got home, but I buttered some toast while I sorted my mail. I binned the junk mail and left the bills unopened. I opened one letter, bearing the crest of the House of Commons, after I made and drank a mug of soup. It was the second summons to appear at the Sub-Committee on the Pharmaceutical Industries. The invitation to testify had started arriving after my near-death experience at the drug trial.

I binned it as well. I was about to pull out the vacuum cleaner for the crumbs on the kitchen floor when it struck me: I was dodging the confrontation with the voice on the tape.

Reluctantly I went to the flare in the corridor that the estate agent had described as 'the lounge,' where I had left the digital recorder. I sat before it. All that was left was for me to press the Play button, but the memory of that voice released a weight of fear that paralysed me. I was still in that funk when the doorbell rang. It was Lynn.

'I thought you were mad at me.'

'I still am.' She smiled. 'But I got a call from a Dr. Asian Borha, who said he was worried about you. That made two of us.' She pushed past me. 'Have you listened to the tape?'

'I was just about to, actually.'

She stood in the middle of the tiny lounge. Her black bag was slung across a shoulder, strap held captive in both hands. She had picked up Grace a couple of times but had never been in the flat before. She had eyes only for the digital recorder on the stool. 'Well, what are you waiting for?'

'Let me get your coat . . .'

'Thanks, but I'm not stopping long.'

'I . . .' I hesitated. I supposed some small talk was in order. 'Won't you sit down? Do you want a cup of tea?'

She picked up the machine and pressed the Play button. Dr. Asian Borha's dreamy voice filled the room, coaxing, cajoling. Just to hear it again made my knees weak, and I hurried into the kitchen and out of earshot to make some tea. I took my time. When I returned with two Chinese teas I was relieved to find Lynn still awake and alert. A strident male voice was now talking. I vaguely recognized myself, but I also knew it was not *me*. It was a different voice, a voice that belonged to a man who could, should his wife arrive at a marriage counsellor's with a boyfriend, throw them both though a window. Lynn was sitting down, and she reached for her teacup wordlessly.

I listened from the door.

♦ ♦ ♦

WHEN THE tape finally ran out there was a dread silence in the room. I put down my cold cup of tea by the digital recorder and sat beside her. Eventually the silence became more unbearable than the prospect that my voice would break if I spoke. I cleared my throat. 'That was your phone call, by the way. Cut me off in full flood. So what do you think?'

'What happened when Bamou hit the wall? Did he . . . die?'

I was blank. Listening to the tape had not rekindled any memories. I could not *own* the narration as personal history, could not picture myself as the narrator in the uniform of a prison warder. I could not see the prison, could not picture Bamou beyond a young, anguished face . . . The recording had told a stranger's story, so I did what I always did when people asked me what happened to characters at the end of my stories. I smiled and shrugged.

'I'm worried about you, Humphrey Chow.'

'You don't think it's as "edgy" as "Reluctant Bomber"?'

'Come on, Humphrey'—there was irritation in her voice—'this is not a *story*. This is your life we're talking about!'

I shrugged again. '*Blank* was basically my life, as well. We could change the names around, like before, just to be sure.'

Lynn stared at me. I looked away. She spoke quietly, intensely: 'Humphrey, this is no joke any longer. Did you hear your voice?—Did you hear your *voices*? What's going on inside you, Humphrey? You're a writer, you're supposed to *imagine* things, not *live* them.'

'This is my imagination in, kind of, overdrive.'

'You're no dramatist,' she insisted. 'I've never heard you do anything this sustained with your voice. You were doing *characters!*'

'Then again, hypnosis does things to you . . . you lose your inhibitions, that sort of thing. Have you ever been hypnotised, Lynn?'

'No.'

'Me neither. But I'm glad I was today. I think Phil will like it.'

'You really want to write this up for Phil?'

' . . . if you think it's, kind of, strong enough . . .'

'Were you involved in this plot to . . . kill the endangered monkeys?'

I thought before answering. 'Don't think so.'

'You still have twenty hours to the deadline . . .' She squeezed my shoulder. 'We can't risk publishing another story that brings Interpol, the UK and the Ivory Coast police down on you. I'll call Dr. Borha and tell him you're fine. Yeah?'

She walked towards the door as a slow panic seized me. I dried my hands. 'So, what are you doing tonight?'

'How do you do *that?*'

'What?'

'Sometimes you have this strong Oriental accent, sometimes it's very East Midlands, just now it's rather . . . African . . . just not as sustained as what you have on the tape'

'I had these domineering foster parents . . .'

'Usually people just blend their accents into one twang. You seem to have them all parcelled out.'

'Children of immigrants often do.' I smiled. 'But I guess it's open season on Humphrey Chow. Now it's your turn to psychoanalyse me.' I took the empty cups to the tiny kitchenette. I saw the grimace on my face from the reflection in a glass cabinet and stopped smiling.

Something was going on, that much was obvious. A face had suddenly materialised in my mind, associated with the name Bamou. It settled there, intransigent, nonnegotiable, and at that moment I was exercising all my self-control not to turn around to see if he had materialised like a latter-day Dalminda. I placed the cups in the sink but made no move to wash them; instead I stood watching a grey squirrel at the root of a tree in the base of the garden. I couldn't see a squirrel face, but there was a bobbing tail as expressive as any face, and I stood there, trying to draw the peace of the garden into my roiling life. Lynn's footfalls stopped at the door of the kitchenette.

'Beautiful,' she said.

She took two tentative steps, which brought her beside the sink. We had never been in as intimate a situation before. We stood shoulder to shoulder, and I noted that hers were a clear inch higher than mine.

Grace and I often stood shoulder to shoulder at the sink. In the mornings when she came down on stockinged feet and we drank the first coffee and talked through the day ahead, it was usually a dead heat. For the last coffee of the day, when she stood in high heels from a party outing or a late day at the agency, hers were usually two or three inches higher. Lynn folded her arms and stared out through the window as well. She cleared her throat but said nothing.

There was a long silence. I could see that she was building up to saying something, and the very effort of that buildup was stressing me. I was in the comfort zone of my flat. I had been through hypnosis, and depth charges were still going off in my mind. She was also a comfort zone, a person to be silent with, a surrogate everything, and she was building up to something else, and whatever it was, I didn't like it already.

'Humphrey, I can't do this anymore.'

'Do what?' I tried a laugh. 'Agent, friend, or shrink?'

'I feel like I'm in a slow-motion car crash. I want out.'

My mouth hung open for a beat. 'I don't understand; we're doing well just now. You've waited . . .'

'Not from where I'm standing, Humphrey.' She took my hand, smiled. 'I'm no shrink. So that's sorted. But as an agent, I want to work with a *writer,* someone who creates a world from imagination . . . not from memory. What are you going to do when you run out of edgy . . . *memories?*'

'I'm . . . exorcising my demons. Once my memory is sorted, my imagination . . .'

'And as your friend, I don't want you *ever* in a police interrogation like the last. I don't want to sign off any more stories from your memory, Humphrey. Shaun has agreed to take on your account.'

'Look, Lynn—'

'I've made up my mind.' She was suddenly speaking very fast, a cyclist pedalling uphill quickly to get through a hard patch. She was close enough for me to see the darting of her lazy left pupil, anxious enough not to consciously still it. She played with her scarf until it was looped once around her neck and round and around her wrists. Her bunched-up fists bounced in their scarf suspensions. 'I've read that people with bad experiences with their natural mothers—'

'I didn't know my natural mother,' I said hotly.

'Exactly. That such people look for replacement mothers in close . . . female friends.' She paused. 'Well, I'm not, you know.' There was probably more to say, but her jaw was clenched, and I had gotten the point anyway. She leaned forward and kissed me, not on the cheeks as was our wont, but full on the lips. It lingered, as though to atone for her curt words. She drew back and said, 'Goodbye, Humphrey.' Her voice was as cold as the kiss had been warm. Then she nodded and walked away.

I listened to her footfalls and their final punctuation with the snap of a closed door.

LYNN CHRISTIE

London | 11th April, 2005

I stopped at the entrance of his apartment block. I'd smoked my two sticks for the day, but I lit a cigarette anyway. I smoked it halfway through and crushed it into a bin. I entered the Cricketers Arms and ordered a gin I didn't need either.

The break with Humphrey gutted me, and yet I'd only given him half the picture. The subtext between us had always worried me. With Grace out of the picture it would only get worse. I was a sucker for the helpless male. The ease with which I made a home visit, the magnetism in the room with him . . . there was nothing to prevent the incipient affair from breaking out.

My marriage was rocky just then. It probably always would be, but it was also five years old and two sons wide. It would not survive a Humphrey Chow mistake. Besides, Humphrey was so damned fragile! I could never go out with someone who would go crazy when I left him. I had made the right decision, then. I drank down my gin. But why did it have to be so bloody wrenching?

HUMPHREY CHOW

London | 11th April, 2005

I listened to the silence. Suddenly I realised I was half dreading, half expecting Bamou's voice. I pushed away from the sink, snapped on a radio, and filled the flat with the silly banter of a DJ more scared of silence than I was.

I went through the small flat. I was alone; but my confirmation did not come with any relief. I sat in my tiny study and wrote doggedly. Thirty minutes passed, and I had to check to make sure I was still alone.

An hour passed, and I reviewed the paragraphs I'd written. It read like wooden reportage. A stenographer's account. A transcription from tape that lacked the electricity of life. I shut my eyes and tried to imagine the prison, to place myself and Bamou within its walls; I tried to plumb emotions into the tale, in vain. *Ivory Coast*. Was it possible that I had spent so many years there without recalling a single night? I rose and stormed into the bath, where I showered and shaved. I ate a tub of ice cream.

After returning to the computer, I deleted the story. I tried to write a sequel for Phil Begg that did not have anything to do with bombs, suicidal psychopaths, or prison cells. I put my hero on a golf course, had him run a cruise ship, stuck him in a polyandrous triangle . . . it was all in vain. By the second paragraph I would find my lips curling into a sneer and would lean on the delete key.

Finally, I opened up the kitchen cabinet and took out the bottle of Proxtigen capsules I'd swiped from Dr. Greenstone's office. I stared at it for a long minute, trying to weigh the risks. I had no idea what the medics had done to bring me around after I passed out. Perhaps I would have come around without medical intervention. Perhaps not. It seemed crazy to take the risk just to find out the end of a story—or to tell it more sympathetically. Yet I remembered the lush sweep of memory that accompanied my last Proxtigen, like a talking movie after a silent, like a colour film after monochrome . . . It was like the coupling on of a sixth sense. It had given me a rush like I had never experienced before.

I wanted it again.

I needed to recall the Bamou chapter of my life with the vividness with which I recalled Yan Chow's death . . . I tossed a capsule in my mouth and sipped some water. I shut my eyes and tried to swallow . . . but then again, Bamou might return with the physicality of Dalminda Roco and his bomb . . . I spat the capsule into the sink, slamming my palms on the draining board with a force that brought china crashing down. I ignored the broken plates, pushed the bottle of capsules into my pocket, and called Dr. Borha's secretary. She offered me an appointment in six days.

'It's really *really* urgent,' I said.

'All Dr. Borha's appointments are really, *really* urgent,' she explained. 'I also have another opening in two weeks, if you prefer.'

I switched off the phone, pulled on my jacket, and broke out of the flat.

◆ ◆ ◆

I WALKED hard till I was exhausted; my fog lifted and I found myself in the commons. I loitered, wondering what to do when it was too late to loiter and I had to return home. Homelessness acquired a new cachet: the state of having a house that wasn't home, where I was afraid of being alone. Marriage, even a bad one, acquired a new allure: the guarantee of companionship through the lonely hours when old faces stalked in to visit, from an unrecalled past. The streets teemed with life. I tried to lose myself in it, but the faces were securely locked down. The only open faces were seeking narrow things. Where there was a smile she was peddling flowers, or taking an opinion poll, or signing up direct debits on behalf of a charity . . . I slumped on a park bench and watched night fall. The bottle of Proxtigen burned in my pocket, and I chafed at my cowardice. I strained at the gate of my *screen memory,* interrogating what I knew and all I had taken for granted. Every time I came close, the memory slipped further away.

I was overwhelmed by a sense of loss.

The shrill of my phone cut through my thoughts. It was Doctor Borha. I glanced at my watch in surprise. He offered to meet, and we agreed on the

Cricketers Arms under my flat. I rose and started for home, surprised at my relief. When I arrived, he was draping his coat on the back of a chair and the table was already furnished with two pint glasses of cider. I pulled a mug of beer at the bar, joined him at the table, and sloughed off my own jacket.

'Thanks for coming out. You got my call?'

'What call?'

'I called your secretary for an appointment as you suggested.'

He shook his head and gestured at the envelope on the table. 'I got a police package on you; that's why I'm here.'

He was looking more serious than he had been that afternoon. I met his gaze. 'You're putting in some serious overtime on my case. Is it the terror angle, then?'

'You intrigue me, remember? Listen, Humphrey, have you ever had a genetic counselling session?'

'What's that?'

'I guess that answers my question.' He sipped his cider.

'The boffins at a drug trial told me I had an extra chromosome, if that's what you mean.'

'It's that as well,' he agreed. 'Gupta used his clout to dig up your biological mother's medical, welfare, and police records.'

'Laura Fraser,' I said quietly, conscious that I had never spoken the name aloud before.

'Yes. Her gene records checked out fine, by the way. She had a long history of drug abuse, but her drug of choice was a designer narcotic that didn't fit any known profile. Your paediatrician picked it up in her breast milk soon after you were born, but her husband was a brilliant chemist, so that's probably one mystery solved. Now, listen here, Humphrey, your juvenile records have some odd psychotic episodes. My suspicion is that your problems stem from this mutation that dated from birth.'

'I got a high in the womb, and the pusher was her husband?'

'Exactly. Marijuana has that effect; this drug might have been even more toxic to the embryo.'

'Should I be worried?'

'There's not much you can do about it.'

He scratched his head and pushed the papers back into the A5 envelope. He looked out on a pedestrianised street full of harried workers and distracted tourists. A spatter of rain appeared on the window. A couple hurried in and settled at the table beside ours. The man was brash and loud and carried a large, heavy briefcase. The woman was burdened with a crying baby. He met my eye as they settled in. There was a stony defiance there, as though he challenged me to complain about his baby; then he went off to place an order at the bar. His raised voice came back to us.

A comprehensive downpour soaked the street. Dr. Borha watched as though mesmerised. The bar filled slowly. The man at the next table was back from quarrelling with the barman and was quarrelling with his partner in a language I'd never heard before. Some people carried their rage around like an open wound. The woman seemed the most clueless mother ever. Something about that crying baby reminded me of my life with my many foster families: the way the colour of husband and the colour of wife did not quite add up to the colour of child.

I placed the digital recorder on the table between me and the pensive Doctor Borha. He glanced at it with little interest. He had barely touched his drink. The avidity with which he had gone at his beers in the afternoon was gone. In its place was a certain introspection. I had come worried that he would grill me about Dalminda Roco. As the minutes passed, I began to worry that the evening would end without him grilling me about Dalminda Roco. So I told him about my Scottish holiday. 'I'm almost . . . kind of . . . afraid to be alone, particularly after this.' I gestured at the digital recorder. 'It's like . . . wow, where are these people coming from . . . are they inside? Will they come out . . . you know?'

Another minute passed in silence between us.

The argument at the next table stopped abruptly. The man rose and stalked out of the establishment. The child wailed on. The woman craned her neck anxiously as the man passed her window, swearing as he crossed the road and went out of sight.

'I used to be able to go home Christmases,' said Asian, as if I hadn't spoken. 'Then this sycophantic journalist on the island wrote an article about me. He said I had stables in Kent where I parked my two dozen flash cars, that sort of nonsense. Now my mailman—who used to come on a bike— he's got a small van because of me. It's like I won the lottery or something, the sacks of begging letters I get from home . . . You won't believe how much I'm hated now. Those I used to help out now think my gifts were miserly. Those I don't help think I'm the devil incarnate.' He shrugged. 'I haven't been home in years. In a sense, I have blanked home the way you blanked the Ivory Coast . . .'

He took a long swig and put down the glass empty.

At the neighbouring table, the woman's alarm had grown, rivalling her ward's. She rose with her baby and hurried toward the door after her fuming partner. I studied Dr. Asian Borha, wondering if he had overplayed his hand with the afternoon beers. He pulled up the second glass, and I tried again. 'Do you think Bamou will jump out of the woodwork? Like Dalminda?'

'Conversation is an elliptical art, Humphrey. There's a big world out there beyond your problems, you know, let's explore it!' He took a leisurely sip. 'I understand abruptness when you're paying ten pounds a minute to talk to me, but we're chilling in a pub . . .'

A leggy female had gone down on a knee in front of us, and the flash of a camera went off in our eyes. It was my first paparazza moment, and she was chatty into the bargain. Fame would take some getting used to, not having to correct *Chew* to *Chow*. As she walked away, I looked around in embarrassment and noticed the briefcase under the neighbouring table. He had stalked off angry, she had hurried off anxious, and they'd both forgotten their briefcase. Unaccountably, I thought about Felix and Laura Fraser abandoning their brown package. I left Asian to his ten-pounds-a-minute cider and hurried towards the door to see if I could catch a glimpse of her down the street.

Then the blast hit me, and I lost some more pages of my life.

ZANDA ATTURK

London | 11th April, 2005

I had wanted to seek out Korba Adevo's contact first. Amana resisted that one-way ticket into the real London underground of false identities and dodgy businesses, so after we had checked into the bed-and-breakfast in Bermondsey, we went to track down Humphrey.

He was entering the pub on the ground floor of his apartment block when we arrived. Amana gripped my hand fiercely. It took that sight of my brooding mirror image to make it real: I'd had company in my mother's womb, twenty-odd years ago, and he was having a drink, not fifty metres away. We had made no elaborate plans, but she now insisted that a public house was not the ideal venue for a first meeting between adult brothers.

We might cry, she said.

We waited indecisively on that sidewalk for fifteen minutes, but the sky was growing incontinent. A couple of pedestrians had already greeted me familiarly, and we were now the object of the surreptitious interest of a couple with a wailing child. I pulled up my hood, and we walked in. It was a large, three-lounge pub. We saw Humphrey immediately, engrossed in conversation with a bearded, older man in the sports bar. We slipped into an alcove in the shadows from where we could watch them.

We waited awhile, but all they did was talk.

The minutes passed. It was getting later. My own tension grew. There was no guarantee that he would go up to his flat when he left the pub. I rose.

Amana was grinning with excitement as I crossed over to the sports bar, negotiating tables, pillars, and people as I went. As I approached my clone, I was filled with dread rather than excitement.

I felt around for that surge of whatever brothers were meant to feel for brothers. It was there, all right, drowning in the stew of emotions swirling inside me. Despite my best efforts, my face was frozen. I couldn't smile. What drove me across that genteel bar, that ground floor of Humphrey's easy life, was despair. He'd had everything: our real parents, the opportunities, the fame of the published writer . . . and I, ex-shoeshine boy, ex-journalist, I wore the infamy of Nigeria's most wanted criminal.

What I most wanted just then was to flee the pub. To hide away for the years it would take me to approach the table of brotherhood as an equal to the twin in front of me. Instead, I plodded forward, propelled by Amana's excitement. I approached him from behind. The hand that he ran over his hair wore a wedding band. There was a wife, then. I probably had four nieces and nephews upstairs . . . the resentment that had driven me after Tobin on my last night in Kreektown broke out in a green rash of envy and sibling rivalry. The black-and-white moment was upon us. I tried to smile as I reached for his shoulder, thinking how odd it was that a trained hand was the one anarchist's weapon that airport scanners could not interdict.

And I wondered whether the therapeutic demon Dr. Maleek had exorcised when he lashed out at me in the Limbe bar was a Badu moment. And I saw how the Badu in everyman could do not only those things that one ought to but didn't . . . but also those things one ought *not* to do but did anyway . . .

Then there was a flash. In front of us, a trigger-happy Amana crouched in that stuffy English pub, photographing the first meeting of brothers.

Spooked, I swerved away for the loo. I barged through the double doors, accelerating until I collided with a washbasin. I clasped my fingers behind my head. A frightened old man at the urinal hurried away, not looking left or right. I shut my eyes and, swaying, gripped the sink to steady myself. I opened my eyes and stared at the mirror.

In that splitsecond I saw that it was not Humphrey I loathed but myself. The one who had abandoned his flesh and blood, all the years of their desperate need. Who had cut himself off from land and language. Even Badu had judged me, had split from me . . . if he could, perhaps he would have served me Omakasa's sentence . . . Suddenly I saw Badu arriving at Farmer Utoma's poultry shed with Pitani in his boot, to find the poultry man long dead in his front room. Utoma had raised me as an orphan, but he had met his death alone . . . *Badu would have killed* . . . I struck then, smashed my hand into the jaw of the man in the mirror. I ran a stream of cold water over my bloodied fist. My red eyes were inches from a shard.

The sting of pain made things crystal clear: this was nothing more than a barroom meeting. We would share a drink and exchange numbers. And goodbyes. There would be no expectations. Perhaps the phone would ring again, perhaps it would not . . . Life would elaborate, step after step.

At the doors of the loo, I paused to compose myself. The double doors slammed inwards with a force that knocked me into the wall. I blacked out momentarily. When I came to, the hinges had lost their doors and my forearms were numb from the concussion. I was on the ground, staring, disbelieving, at the carnage in the pub. Broken furniture was strewn all over, and as the dust settled, screams filled the air. Humphrey's bearded companion lay on his back across a table that had lost its legs. I rose and stumbled across the room, coughing as I crunched through broken glass. A pillar walling off our distant alcove had taken the force of the blast and Amana emerged, dusty, shaken, but unhurt. She grabbed me from behind, wordlessly, as I stared at my motionless brother by the doorway. I leaned over his body. I felt a dull ache where the emotions had swirled just a few minutes before. This grief was just as real as the previous resentment, and as meaningless. I touched his—my—stubbled cheek with a tenderness I did not need to feign.

Then I heard the first sirens. I straightened and walked Amana unsteadily out of the pub.

That night, as she mourned Humphrey, I thought how much more honest a bomb was than humans at breaking bad news and told her about Ma'Calico's death.

FARMER UTOMA (ANCESTORMENAI)

Kreektown | 18th February, 2005

The stomach is a worm of which it bites when it is hungry. This is a thing of which we know very well. But nowadays it is biting all the time.

Normally, is my chickens that will wake me up at this time. Once their lamp is on, they will eat. That's the thing. And normally at this time I must give them food. And water too. Because, nothing sweets the belly of a poultryman like chickens eating and growing fatter and fatter.

Today there is no noise of chickens at all at all. Not even the smallest *quoi quoi quoiiii* of baby chickens struggling to near the lamp. Is the habit of doing the same thing for thirty-something years that wakes me up. Is dark in the poultry shed, like the inside of stomach. There's kerosene in the lamps, but I have switch them off. What's the need?

I go to the kitchen. To cook eku is just to mix eku and water on the fire and turn and turn it. And yet . . . eku does not taste like eku since my wife died . . . I don't know . . .

From the window I can see the hungrymoon shining on the poultry shed in my yard and on the faraway zinc roofs of Kreektown—or Ghosttown, as Daudi use to call it. May GodMenai rest his soul. Is funny how the sleepcatastrophe of Daudi and Clama and their daughter Netia happened on the same day. After singing their calamity, my voice disappeared for many days. Many, many kilometres away, I can see the gas chimneys of the oil companies firing and farting, lighting the night like Christmas knockout. Is nice. But is like the smile of the teeth of a dead man. Is still a sad night.

The stomachworm has start to bite again. My feet are so fat they cannot enter any of my shoe again. I sit down. Yet, I want to do something. There is nothing to do, except wait. So I wear my rubber slippers and walk around, slow, slow. Zanda's old room. Strange boy. To prefer shining shoes to raising chickens. Maybe is the smell that drive him. The first thing my visitors use to say is *hai! The smell!* Me myself, I can't smell anything anymore. The smell of chicken shit and the smell of frying chicken smells the same to me! This life of a thing. When Tume and Malian died, is just one years that Zanda live with me before it was Ruma's turn to look after the orphan boy. Maybe if I really took him as my son instead of all that one-one year fostering, maybe he would not have run away . . . but I cannot lie:

after I buried my bloodson, there are two things I cannot bear: the sound of singing, and the sound of another child calling me Daddy.

I cannot lie.

I go outside. I don't know, but I will just walk around the poultry shed. All of them are died now, my chickens. Apart from the few that I leave to stroll the compound and feed themselves. Just to keep me company. Is not difficult, or sad, even, killing the rest. Killing chickens is a thing of which I did everyday. And is better for them to die at once, instead of them to suffer. If I don't wake up, the worst thing for me is to know that my chickens will suffer and die in their cage.

Like the Menai in their town.

Is funny that after singing hundreds upon hundreds of other people's calamity, nobody will sing my own. This life of a thing. I walk around the compound slowly. Maybe this is how a chicken feels, walking round his cage, waiting for Christmas, or Easter. I don't go behind the poultry shed. There is a strong smell now, from all the crates upon crates of eggs I couldn't sell, that have now spoiled. That particular smell, that smell of rotten eggs, even me I can't stand it. That's the thing . . . when your customers have die even before your chickens . . . that particular sadness is very hard to bear. I arrange the chairs in the yard.

This life of a thing.

I go back to my front room. I am jealousing Daudi, how he died with his family. My whole family is now in the circle of ancestorMenai and I hungry to go there. But to hurry there before the time GodMenai whispers in your ear is taboo. Is to jump the wadigulf of death, and miss the other side.

I have to wait.

So I sit down in my cane chair.

I wait.

DAVID BALSAM

Chad Republic | 11th April, 2005

The best part of his days were the sunrises. Opening his eyes to a tangerine sun suddenly at his feet, with nothing between him and the early warmth but a horizon of sand and sky. The worst part was usually the moment afterwards when he asked himself what he was doing there in the middle of the largest desert in the world, putting his life on the line to bury a man who was not yet dead.

And yet, there was something about the honesty of this loneliness, out there in the Sahara, where nobody was going to stop by and visit, compared with his life in the midst of millions of Londoners, where, if he stayed home for months on end, nobody was going to stop by and visit. He liked what he learned about himself in the deafening silence of the large bedroom in which he nightly watched the moon walk the sky.

He was now into the second chapter of his monograph on the Menai, but it shamed him that he could not be honest with Tobin and his Mata about his true motivations, how much more with his future readers. He wished he had the forthrightness of a Conrad Risborough who confessed his superstitions head-on. He remembered his twenty-five-year-old "pull yourself together" speech to the late peer, and sighed.

He sat up. He had slept outside his tent as usual, and he saw that Tobin had beaten him to the gas fire by the truck and was returning with two cups of coffee. He studied the other man as he approached. They had been three days into the trip when he figured, from the drugs Tobin was taking regularly, that he was also a victim of the Trevi inoculations. David wished he could ask the direct question. He took the coffee gratefully. 'How are you? Keeping up?'

'Holding it together. You?'

'Doing okay.'

And with those meaningless words, they swept important issues under gruff manhood and regrouped around the map on which they had managed to plot their journey. It was still lying open from the night before. They had spent days map-making with Mata Nimito, pairing their topographic survey maps with the Mata's 'historysongs.' In the library of his mind, the map to the Field of Stones had not been filed in one volume. Sometimes he would recite an hour-long historysong for the clues in the geographical stanza at the end of it. And then there were the interminable translations from English to Menai and back . . . yet they had done it in the end. All the place-names the Mata described had disappeared; and where they had not, they had moved; and where they had not moved, they had changed names. Still, there were enough clues on the ground and stars in the sky to orient the Mata's description of a migration path that crisscrossed the Sahara.

The Mata claimed a precise location north of Khartoum, Sudan, for a Field of Stones that he had never seen. It would not have been so bad if they were finally making a straightforward safari to the X that was supposed to mark the spot, but no. The Mata was like some gregarious corpse on the way to the grave who wanted to say hi to some homies on the way home.

They were now making tracks for one such nostalgic stopover: the Keep of Njakara.

David thought it was a good thing he was growing a beard, for he could no longer recognise himself.

HUMPHREY CHOW

London | 11th April, 2005

I woke up between two policemen in a hospital ward and caused a minor commotion just by opening my eyes. I asked the time of a nurse, who didn't seem qualified to look at her watch. Instead she fled to fetch a doctor, whose voice sounded like a prescription to calm bomb-blast victims.

I was stretched out, and a dull pain throbbed in my back. I could see my limbs splayed before me, but I had not tried to move them and had no idea whether they still worked. I had no idea who had tried to kill me, whether it was the real Dalminda or the Scottish ghost version. The thought that filled me with dread was the possibility that I had missed Phil's deadline and lost my twelve-tale deal.

'What day is it?' I asked the doctor, not recognising my own voice.

'You were very lucky, Mr. Chow,' said the calm voice. A nettle stung my right arm. At least that part was still alive. 'Don't bother about clocks and calendars just now, just focus on getting well . . .' Then he faded away.

ZANDA ATTURK

London | 12th April, 2005

We knew right away that the bomb at the Cricketers Arms had been meant for me: clearly the British took rewards more seriously than Nigerians. We changed lodgings right away and holed up in a dingy block in East

London. The street was clogged with black bin bags. The landlord, who lived on-premises, offered to take my rent in marijuana and was miffed when I passed. We did nothing but play cards and follow the bomb story on TV. Two patrons had died from the blast, but Humphrey was not on the list. On that day after the blast, a list of three critically ill people was released. He was not on that list either. We didn't dare go looking for him for fear of setting off another bomb. The brotherly reunion wasn't cancelled after all; it was on hold. Yet we had only a few more days before we ran out of money. We couldn't stay holed up forever.

I made the call to Adevo's contact and, that evening, went over to see him. It was a council flat near Elephant and Castle. There was a whiff of urine in the elevator. It didn't look like the residence of a man who, according to Adevo's description, was taking London by storm.

'Are you Frederick Eghwrudjak—' I began, doubtfully.

'Freddie Jacks, Freddie Jacks,' he said irritably. He was fortyish and sported a walking stick with a silver head. He did not let me into his flat. We talked on the balcony of his fifth-floor apartment, which had poetic graffiti running across the walls. Next door was a boarded-up flat in which a breathy clandestine transaction was in progress. He was balding, but his beard and what hair remained on his head were dreadlocked. He wore a tracksuit and bounced from foot to foot, as though we were chatting in a boxing ring.

'Yeah, man,' he said without preamble. 'I'm breaking a Felixstowe container this night. They're packing right now; are you in or out?'

'What are you packing?' I asked. He had a mostly Cockney accent, but when he got excited it betrayed a strong Urhobo undertone.

His eyes narrowed. 'Stuff. Yer a curious chappie, innit?'

'Adevo said I could trust you.'

'Everybody knows Freddie Jacks,' he said, 'but it's rude, man. You don't go asking people what's in their containers.'

I paused. 'How much?'

He stopped bouncing and stared.

I glanced around. 'What?'

'*How much?*' he repeated incredulously. 'Brotherman! Ah been in this business twenty years, man, nobody never started by asking Freddie Jacks how much. You gotta watch ya greed, man; it ain't cool to be greedy in this business.'

I told him I would think about it. As the transaction next door reached an orgasmic conclusion, he took my photograph and 'Nelson Ogunde's' details. We shook hands, and he promised to call me about other job offers the next day.

◆ ◆ ◆

WHAT WAS real was Amana. She was the anchor I had wanted, but responsibility for her now weighed on my conscience. I had ended her old life, and she was an outlaw on my account. I didn't know how long I could go before I went off the rails again. If I sleepwalked in this land I would be caught on camera before I went a dozen paces. Badu would not thrive long here. I had to get a job, tighten the loose nuts in my head, and set up proper house with Amana . . . the interminable corridors of normalcy stretched out before me, bland, pedestrian, featureless.

I knew it would drive me crazy.

I walked on.

HUMPHREY CHOW

London | 12th April, 2005

When I woke again, Grace was standing there, in a dress I did not know, and she was holding my hand. A picky resentment flared, then, that I had to take a bomb in the back to bring her to my side. I began to pull my hand away childishly. Then a thought occurred to me. 'Where's Dr. Borha?' I asked her.

'He's dead,' she said tragically, 'but don't worry, Mum has agreed to . . .'

My two hands were working well then, because they seemed able and willing to grapple. She fell back, jolted, as policemen and skittish nurses held me down, waiting for the sedative to kick in.

I do not think there will be a reconciliation, after all.

ZANDA ATTURK

London | 12th April, 2005

She stared at me.

'You're not saying anything,' I said.

'I don't know what to say to you,' she replied eventually.

'You could say, "That's a great idea, dear—"'

'Let me get this straight: someone is trying to kill you and you want to get a job flipping burgers? I thought we should see Humphrey, start a political movement—'

'We've got to be realistic here—'

'Realistic? *You're Badu.*'

'Only when I'm crazy. We're two illegal immigrants, that's what we are . . .'

'I can't just turn my back. They killed my mum. This is personal. You started a revolution and you ran out. Give us leadership, Zanda! I trusted you, I loved you!'

I looked at her bleakly. *'Loved?'*

She took a deep breath and looked out of our bed-and-breakfast window. 'Story of my life,' she muttered. 'I like a record, I buy it, and I play it till the sound of it disgusts me,' she hissed.

'Disgusts?'

She tried not to laugh and gave up. 'You're a glutton for punishment, aren't you?' She kissed me, but I didn't blink, and she sighed. 'I don't know, Zanda, I've never loved before. When you start flipping burgers tomorrow, I don't know how I'll feel.'

'It's not that long since you were serving beers at . . .' I bit back my words, but the reference to Ma'Calico didn't bring on the blues as I feared.

She laughed shortly. 'Okay, so I sell beer for my mama beer parlour, so therefore? This na your papa house? What am I supposed to feel when my own Badu starts flipping burgers?'

A sullen silence reigned. I looked around the room. The walls were thinner than my room at Ma'Calico's, the floors creaked with every shift of weight. When other tenants used the toilet, we had to raise the volume of the TV to drown out the sound of their business. There was no help for the smell of it. And at forty-five pounds a night, we'd be broke in days. There was a mouse in the couch that didn't realise *I* was paying the rent— and that *it* was supposed to do the fleeing when our paths crossed. I had to start flipping burgers the next day so we could stay in a place like this . . .

'You could feel grateful,' I said through gritted teeth. I walked out.

◆ ◆ ◆

IT WAS too cold to go far, and I had left without my jacket. She brought it to me, on the bench across the road. I pulled it on wordlessly. It was technically spring, but we were miserably cold. We sat silently. In days we had grown grey, like our clothes, like the weather, like the country. We watched the swirling leaves and passing boots in the light of streetlamps. 'I'll say I'm sorry if you'll say you're sorry,' she offered.

I clenched my teeth on my mirth. She had a sheaf of papers under her arm. The game wasn't over. This was the Queen's Gambit Deferred. 'Don't be. You said what you felt. I like that.'

She opened up her papers anyway. They were printouts of Nigerian dailies, which she had downloaded from the Internet in the library. One of them was a story on the Badu movement. 'So who leads them?' Asked Amana, 'What's a revolution without its leader?'

I skimmed the story. A judge had arrived in court to find details of a bribe he had taken in the case before him pasted all over the courtroom. Copies of the poster were folded into pamphlets and fastened under the wipers of cars in the court's car park. He had stayed away from court for a week, but when he finally appeared, it was to peals of laughter. He had resigned ahead of his disciplinary hearing. Another reluctant judicial enquiry was under way. 'They're doing very well without Badu,' I said. 'All communism wanted of Karl Marx was the push of *Das Kapital*.'

'Well, see where it landed them,' she snapped.

I left her on the bench and went back to our room.

HUMPHREY CHOW

London | 12th April, 2005

Next time I came up, the drapes were drawn, but the gloom of the ward suited me fine. They must have shot vials of black ink into my veins because my mood was sooty as sin. Ram Gupta was sleeping in the chair beside me. His head was lolling, practically touching his shoulder, and a string of saliva extended halfway down to his lapel. The two policemen at the door were gone. In their place was a screen on which was pinned a dozen colourful get-well cards.

His newspaper had slipped down his lap, but I reached it easily. It was the day after, and the bomb blast at the Cricketers Arms was still front-page news. I was fifteen minutes into the newspaper when the door opened softly and a man I had never seen before entered, carrying two

paper cups of coffee. Ram Gupta came awake grumpily, sitting up when
he saw me.

'About time, too,' he grumbled, wiping his lips. 'Never saw a man who
slept so much.' He took back his newspaper.

'Did he die immediately?' My voice sounded hollow to my ears.

'Yes.' He pulled his chair forward. He took a coffee from the other
man, who went over to the other side of my bed. Gupta looked tired and
unshaven. 'We've lost too much time, Humphrey. Give me names. Who
could have done this thing? They clearly don't share your loyalty.'

'I don't know them. I can give you a good description though . . .'

The other man pulled out two pencil sketches, accurate enough artists' impressions of the murderous team, less the baby. He held them
out to me. His feet were two feet apart. His coffee hand was held at
chest level, and his head projected two inches behind the rest of his
body. I almost looked around for the movie camera. 'We don't need a
description. We have thousands of these in circulation,' he said. 'What
I want from you are *names*. We have witnesses who saw you chasing
after the woman. Did you recognise her? Did she give you a warning?
What's the deal?'

'I chased after her,' I said wearily, 'because they left the briefcase.'

'The bomb.'

'I didn't know that then.'

'So why did you run away just before it exploded?'

I stared. I decided to become too ill to answer questions.

'This is my colleague Rob Dawes,' said Gupta. I could sense the tension
between the two. 'Rob is a member of the International Terrorism Contact Unit based in Seattle . . .'

'I'm *director* of the ITCU,' clarified Rob, 'and we suspect Dalminda's
cell is trying to silence you, to stop more revelations about them. Your
"Reluctant Suicide" story, by the way, ruined years of detective work.'
He waved the sketches, maybe to keep my drowsy eyes open.

But I let them close anyway. I had a right to be ill after taking a bomb
in the back.

Rob said, 'I have a team of memory experts on the way . . .'

The door opened again, and a nurse pushed in a trolley, followed by an
elderly doctor in a sports jacket. His face was lined and creased, and the
smell of tobacco went ahead of him and hung around when he left.

'Today is a done deal,' he wheezed. 'You've got more questions? Tomorrow is another day.'

'Fine,' grumbled Gupta as the nurse pushed my finger into a sleeve and took my readings.

'We'll be here at seven tomorrow,' said Rob.

The doctor grinned. 'The cleaner is here at seven, the nurses are finished at nine, and you can come at ten, how's that?'

The American locked eyes with the doctor for a moment, then yielded with ill grace, following Gupta out of the room. When the door had shut behind them, the doctor turned to me, as I gagged on his large tablets. 'So how's the wife-beater today?'

'How's Grace . . . when can I see her?'

'She's no longer on your visitor's list.' He lifted me with the assistance of the nurse as he examined me. He spoke as he worked. 'Not very gentlemanly of you, Humphrey, to attack the messenger?'

'I lost it . . . I'm sorry.'

He came around my bed, stooping until he was at face level. 'Open up.' I did, and he checked the mobility of my jaw.

'Will I live?'

'You got off easy, Humphrey, just a concussion and a few minor lacerations. But with your history, we are watching that bump on your head. Dr. Asian Borha wasn't so lucky . . .'

He went on for another few minutes before I found a pause. 'Can I call my agent, Shaun Jones?'

'Do you have a number? We'll give him a call tomorrow . . .'

'Tonight! Please . . .'

His brows climbed upwards. 'It's eight p.m.'

'I feel like I've been sleeping for days.'

He shrugged. 'I'll see what your minders have to say about that.'

ZANDA ATTURK

London | 12th April, 2005

The heating had gone off. We got over our pride and huddled together for warmth. She sighed wearily. 'You know that bomb in the pub?'

'Yes?'

'Remember that couple with the child? It was in the man's briefcase.'

'Likely, but how can you be sure?'

She put a photo envelope in my hand. 'I wanted a photograph of you and your brother, so I had this one printed.'

I glanced at the photo I held, with my thumb over my own face.

Humphrey was sitting across the table from the bearded man whose face had been in the papers. He was grinning so vitally, it was hard to believe he was dead. In the lower background of the picture was the briefcase carried in by the man in the street.

'They must have followed us into the pub. They clearly mistook Humphrey for you.'

I was silent. I didn't thank her for putting my thoughts into words. Death and destruction had followed me all the way from Kreektown to London.

'Our government didn't do this,' she said. 'Was there a Pitani video?'

'I . . . can't remember.'

'For our sake, please remember,' she whispered. 'They don't want a trial for you. We'll all be safer once the video is published.'

I nodded. She tried to take back the picture, but I held onto it. She prised it away gently and held it up to me. The lenses had caught the tortured expression on my face.

'You were going to strangle him?' There was no condemnation in her eyes, just curiosity.

'Of course not!'

She shrugged. 'So I said to myself: If Badu wants to kill someone, he will, eventually. So I thought I should get to know Humphrey before he died. So I talked to him.'

I sat up. 'You did?'

'Yes, when you went into the toilet.' She laughed. '"You should be a model, not a paparazza," that's what he said to me. You didn't mistake me for a model that first time we met, Zanda. Did you?'

I bit my lips, remembering how I had mistaken her for a prostitute. The differences between identical twin brothers were emerging: the one put his foot in his mouth, the other had a knack for unforgettable first lines. She stared at the photograph for ages. Then, starting at my face, she tore it in two, and then in bits. 'My biological mother . . . had this veil of secrecy over her life,' she said bitterly. 'Small things, big things . . . when she died, I found her diaries were written in code! Two years with Ma'Calico's changed me. I want no secrets between us, Zanda. Please. I'll forgive anything, but don't keep secrets from me.'

I nodded.

She held my face, forcing me to look at her. Her brows were knit, worried. 'He's your twin. I'd be excited. I'd be . . .' she paused. A shadow passed over her face as the hypocrisy hit her, and she let me go. She sighed and sat back. 'I suppose it either happens or it doesn't. I didn't love my birth mother either. Didn't shed a tear when she died . . .' She sniffed. 'With Ma'Calico, I . . .'

I held her closer. 'I know. I don't feel . . . negative about him. Anymore.'

'You still find it hard to say his name, though. No, I understand.' She got up tiredly. She measured a smile to reassure. 'I won't judge you,' she said.

Yet I felt judged, condemned.

HUMPHREY CHOW

London | 12th April, 2005

He was in my room before 9:00 p.m., a young Glaswegian with a shock of red hair and a permanently dishevelled air. He had a box of chocolates, which he carried with some embarrassment. I reached for it. 'Relax, Shaun, it's okay to be happy; I didn't die!'

'That's the point.' He winced, hunching his shoulders and hanging onto the box. 'It's a gift for my girlfriend's birthday. There was no one outside to leave it with. Sorry.'

'Oh. I hear you're stuck with me.'

'Yeah,' he said, setting his chocs safely on my bedside locker. 'Lynn's a wee bit indisposed.'

'What's the state of play with *Balding Wolf?*'

'You had till today.' He spread his hands and said, 'But don't worry about it, I'll find you something.'

I nodded. I knew that whatever he found me had to be less trouble than a box of chocolates. 'I have a story,' I said.

'You do?'

'On my laptop. I just have to clean it up and e-mail it overnight—if I can find a signal. Can you push the deadline by some hours? '

He looked around dubiously. 'Where's your laptop?'

'At home in Putney. You could pick it up and be back here in, what . . . ? Thirty minutes?'

He looked at his watch. 'I don't know . . .'

'I hate to drag your books down from the beginning . . . and I'm sorry about your girlfriend, but once they run another writer from this issue, my twelve-tale deal is dead . . .'

That decided him. 'I'll call Phil. Where's your key?'

I pressed the bell for the nurse. She brought the box of personal effects from the clothes that had been cut off my body. I gave Shaun the keys and my address and he left. After the nurse carried off the box and I was alone again, I opened the bottle of capsules I had sneaked from right under their noses.

Something was taking shape in my mind, some sort of dynamic for the crisis of an imagination that had seized up too many years ago. Either I had no imagination worthy of a writer or my constipated memory had clogged up the pores of my mind. I had to *boil out* that memory, *write* it out of me.

While Dalminda and his bombs had stayed in the realms of hallucinations, I could always drop my writerly pretensions and find another job. But with bombs going off around me, I no longer had a choice in the matter. Dr. Borha's death had closed the hypnotic door to my memory. I now had to give it a boost any which way. It was a dangerous path, and my heartbeat quickened, just to contemplate it. Yet I was in a hospital ward and there was no safer place to attempt what I was about to do. I simply had to know who was after me, before they got to me. Bamou's story and a liberated imagination that could write other stories would be a bonus, really. I selected two capsules of Proxtigen and waited.

Shaun was back within the hour, with my laptop and a pack of CDs. His chocolates were gone, and he was considerably more at ease. 'I can wait and pick it up,' he offered.

I shook my head. 'Still a few T's to cross, I'm afraid,' I told him. 'I'll leave it for you at the reception. Say, seven a.m. tomorrow?'

'You wish.' Said the nurse who had come in with him, 'You're not crossing any T's on my watch.' She stowed my laptop in a wall cabinet. He grinned as she shooed him out. Shaun had brought a few more things from my flat: a toilet bag and a change of clothes. He was not going to be a bad agent after all. I let the ward quieten down for the night; then I sat up gingerly. Slowly, I let my feet take my weight. I rolled my drip stand across to my laptop and carried it back to the bed, where I hid it under the duvet. I took a deep breath and swallowed the capsules with a glass of water, then lay back.

It was 10:00 p.m.

IN AUGUST 2002, I started a new job in the prison. I was a newly wedded twenty-two-year-old in my eighth year in Cote d'Ivoire. On the night shift, I heard a song in a strange language that cost me my peace of mind. By some linguistic osmosis, I seemed to understand the words of the lyrics without knowing anything of the language of the song. Night after night, as I stood there at my sentry post in the prison yard, the same voice floated his love song to his mother from the silence of the darkened prison block. Haunting and unforgettable. As I listened, the strange language flowered in my mind, growing in lexis, in idiom.

One night, I followed the voice into the prison block and found him by the window in his cell, serenading a clear night sky.

> *Ejue Ma'Bamou*
> *atuemi ga ju*
> *ejue, ejue gaju eni . . .*

The words slipped like eels into my mind. My memory writhed in the dark, translating them . . . 'Ma'Bamou, eyewitness to my birth, bear witness to my grief . . .' I understood the language but nothing else! Not the name of it, not the first idea how and where I learned it. When he turned around, I was unprepared for the sight of the bearded giant, some twenty years older than I was but as vulnerable as a teenager.

'What's your name?'

'Bamou Geya.'

'What language was that?'

'Menai!' laughed his fellow prisoners.

I was on the prison's censors team and took to calling Bamou into the post room for mail queries. The first time, I dumbfounded him by speaking to him in Menai, and he burst into speech of such speed and passion that it was impossible to follow him.

Since I could speak the language, he began to send and receive his mail in Menai. He only ever wrote to a sister called Rubi, in Kreektown, Nigeria. There was nothing to take issue with in his letters—I could barely read Menai, to be fair—but the prison was more interested in what might be smuggled in the post than what the letters had to say. I took that opportunity to see him regularly to learn his story.

He was a widower whose wife had died in childbirth, and he had three years left on his fifteen-year sentence. In those weeks that I got to know him, I grew a kinship with that Menai man, which came not just from a private, shared tongue but also from his story and the story of his endangered ethnic nation.

In 1990 he was working for a CITES project breeding the rare white-naped mangabey monkeys for reintroduction into the wild. The parallel between his people's fate and that of the animals had drawn him to the work of the Convention. The white-naped mangabeys were a special case: the beautiful humanoid primates had been sighted in only two locations in the world. The project had advertised for an intern, and he needed to earn some money after his commonwealth-funded course in Ottawa. He was in the Primate Camp that evening when news of the Topless Procession came through on the radio. One of the six dead children was his daughter, Felimpe.

It was the loss of daughter, the disconnect between the care and expense invested in monkeys and the world's indifference to the extinction of his ethnic nation that drove him into a five-minute fit of madness with a handy machete. He would spend the rest of his life ruing the death of those two dozen mangabeys in his frenzied slaughter.

His remorse counted for nothing. He was sentenced to fifteen years in jail. It was difficult for me to reconcile the convict of the slaughter of protected monkeys with the gentle giant in the Abidjan prison. Yet the real tragedy of his life was the subterfuge that he practised on his parents. In the month he was due to finish his internship and return to Kreektown, he had started his jail sentence and swore his sister, Rubi, to secrecy. It was far preferable to him that his parents thought him a cad who had forgotten them than that they suffered vicariously with him throughout his jail term.

We mostly spoke Menai. Or rather, he mostly taught me, for my knowledge turned out to be quite rudimentary. We were never able to figure out how I could have learnt the language. Even then, I knew there were pages of my life that were missing. The more time I spent with Bamou, the more I fretted about those pages, about that earlier home in which I had learnt Menai. My parents could not help. They were elderly Ivoriens who had chosen to give a troubled teenager another start in life when they decided to retire home to Abidjan. They knew nothing of my earlier adoption history.

His remorse had been so total that he had never mentioned the provocation of his dead daughter and dying nation, either to the lawyer who defended him or to the court that sentenced him. I brought his story to the attention of the Commandant. It was a very short campaign. He had some time off due to him anyway, and soon after I first met him, his release was scheduled in a matter of weeks. It was a heady achievement for a young prison officer on his first job.

OUR LAST day together had been busy for me. I had several convicts to see, but I scheduled Bamou for last, as usual, so that I could spend some extra time with him. We were alone in the office. I usually would read his letters first, but that day, I didn't. While I cleared my desk, he read a few lines and then let out a roar that was more buffalo than man. He rose, threw my heavy desk across the room with a sweep of the hand, and charged at the far wall, head lowered like a battering ram!

That was my last clear memory from that life. My friend, Bamou, the pleasant Menai who did not have a single enemy in the world—bar the ghosts of his hapless mangabeys—went from a man looking forward to his release within the fortnight to a convulsing body, bleeding from head fractures as he died on my office floor. I remember my spastic hands picking up the letter, seeking an explanation for the horror I had just witnessed . . . but my mind was already fleeing, again. It was Dr. Borha's trauma-triggered dissociative fugue all over again. I fled the scene of Bamou's death into another darkness, never finding out what inspired his terrible suicide.

ZANDA ATTURK

London | 13th April, 2005

We were next in line to be served at the fish 'n chips shop. 'A bag of chips and four sausages,' she said.

The vendor looked askance. 'Say what?'

'A bag of chips and four sausages!' chipped in a voice from behind us.

He served us tentatively.

'You want some gravy on them?' he asked.

'What's he saying?' she asked me.

'I think he's asking if we want gravy,' I said.

She shook her head, and we went off with our food. She was vexed. 'I don't think I'm going to like this country. It's the same language but I'm needing interpreters.'

◆ ◆ ◆

WE FOUND a park bench to eat on.

'There's no future in this, you know?'

'What?'

'False papers, flipping burgers.'

I was silent for a beat. I had taken my passport, NI card, and CV into the employment office. The consultant's brows had risen as she examined the fake documents. She had done a double take at the NI card and had taken it to her boss in the glass cubicle behind. I had watched them doubling over with laughter and hurried out while they were still incapacitated. That was the end of the road for 'Nelson Ogunde' and his papers. So much for Freddie Jacks's expertise in alternative documentation.

'It's a bridge,' I said doggedly.

'A bridge to nowhere, Zanda. They've tried to kill you, so you can ask for asylum. What have we got to lose?'

I stared at her. 'How do you figure that out? They try to kill me and therefore I can ask for asylum? By GodMenai, I'm a wanted terrorist!'

'Remember Umaru Dikko?' she asked. 'Back in eighty-four, he was wanted for corruption in Nigeria. Our government tried to smuggle him out of London in a diplomatic crate and failed.'

'I remember.'

'So they finally brought a repatriation request, and the UK rejected it. He's still living in London right now.'

'Badu's different. Corruption is a different ball game from terrorism.'

'We didn't blow up a pub, Zanda. *They* are the terrorists now.'

I looked at her speculatively. 'You get some really weird ideas.'

She punched my arm. 'You are *soooo* timid! I wish I could talk to Badu!'

◆ ◆ ◆

4:00 p.m.

We walked home. I knew she had something on her mind. 'What are you thinking?'

'Humphrey,' she said quietly. She stopped and looked at me.

'I was thinking the same thing. Tomorrow?'

She nodded. We held hands and walked on. She watched young people milling about. 'Things are even worse here,' she said solemnly, crumpling her can and tossing it into the trash. 'Most of their youths, they also got fake vaccines.'

'How so?'

She nodded at a group of teenagers with trousers halfway down their buttocks, hips swinging violently in the latest fashion, as though to some unheard music. 'Meningitis, much worse than ours.'

I stared at her. It was sometimes difficult to know when she was clowning.

◆ ◆ ◆

6:10 p.m.

Freddie Jacks phoned. He said he had a job for a smart young man who didn't ask too many questions. It would take an hour or two and there would be a few hundred pounds at the end of the day for the smart young man.

I told him I had just one question, and he hung up the phone.

Amana listened solemnly as I recounted our conversation.

'Probably a few years in jail, as well, for the smart young man,' she sniffed.

◆ ◆ ◆

9:45 p.m.

The world was suddenly full of exploding bombs. That night, listening to the BBC world service, we picked up news of Nanga Saul Bentiy's death. He had died the day before at his palace in Ubesia. The breaking news, however, was about the plane carrying Sonia Obu, the first lady of Sontik State, which had crashed soon after takeoff in the federal capital, Abuja. Witnesses had reported an explosion, but there was no news yet on casualties. We remembered the *Palaver* edition Amana had brought to Cameroon, and a black disquiet filled our room. For the first time in days, my thoughts jerked guiltily to the Mata. I found Tobin's envelope and called his number. When I got a recorded message, I called yet another number. This time I got David Balsam. He passed the phone to Tobin, who said the Mata was in one of his trances. I was unprepared for Tobin's effusive warmth or for the chill that followed when I told him I had not yet read his letter. He hung up. I was silent for a while.

◆ ◆ ◆

'ARE YOU okay?' Amana asked.

'I'm fine,' I lied. I was haunted by the call, tempted to call back to mend fences, but I didn't. Since my flight from Kreektown in 1998 I had lived a clear emotional strategy: never to let people in who would wreck me when they left. I had seen Tobin's face. He was one of the short-lived Menai. I was a stopover on his way home. I sat still and let him go on alone.

I watched Amana carefully. She was Sontik and had received the news of the Nanga's death with a groan, but I saw no personal grief there, nothing in her mien to suggest that she had just received news of her father's death. I toyed with the temptation of telling her what Dr. Maleek had shared with me, but something caused me to keep that strange secret to myself.

◆ ◆ ◆

10:20 p.m.

The TV fell silent, and we ate dinner in the dark as we held back yet another coin from the gluttonous meter. We were homesick in a visceral way. The Internet radio was set to the Voice of Nigeria, and we sieved the flood of opinion for scraps of hard news: there were outbreaks of violence in Ubesia and a few cars had been burnt, but there was no sustained rioting.

I probed her gently. 'Are you sorry he's gone?'

'Who?'

'Your Nanga.'

'I barely knew him: I'm not your typical Sontik. I was raised up north, lived there all my life. I've only been in Sontik State for the last two years.'

'You did meet him . . .'

'Just that once, when I served him at Ma'Calico's. It was the oddest thing, though.'

'You spent quite some time with him, as I recall.'

She smiled, remembering. 'He was a curious old man! Really frail, but he couldn't stop asking questions!'

'What kind of stuff did he ask?'

'Oh, all sorts. Politics mostly—did I think we should secede? What would it take to solve the roughboys problem?—that sort of thing.' A small smile appeared on her face. 'But he also wanted to know if I like kentu soup . . . and I never had someone ask me so much about my mother . . .' She laughed embarrassedly,

'What?'

'I don't know, he might have been a dirty old man, if he wasn't so ill! He was very tactile—he held my hand after the handshake and didn't let go.' She fell silent. 'This is the worst time for him to die.'

'Why?'

'He alone had the authority to keep the Sontik in Nigeria.'

'And you? Do you support secession?'

She raised her right hand and flexed her digits, murmuring with playful thoughtfulness, 'Tricky. Should the thumb stay on the palm? Hmm . . .'

◆ ◆ ◆

WE SURFED the Internet gloomily for Nigerian news. The country was getting more than her fair share of coverage, thanks to the downed plane, a dead traditional ruler, and a restive delta. 'There's going to be trouble,' she sighed, 'mark my words.' She gathered up the scraps of our dinner and carried them out to the bin. I hesitated a moment longer, then took my phone out to the balcony and called Dr. Maleek. I got an answering machine and left my telephone and address and asked him to get in touch. I began to kick myself as soon as I ended the call.

She fell asleep. There was nothing else to do then but to read Tobin Rani's letter, after all. It was only a few pages long, but once I started it I realised I would get no sleep that night.

TOBIN RANI

Ubesia | 2nd February, 2005

My Dear Son,

I am writing this in case I don't live long enough—or find the courage—to tell it.

I remember this as if it happened yesterday: I was in Dundee, studying for my PhD. I was also running advocacy for Menai culture and prospecting a twin city for Kreektown . . . but that PhD, that was the main thing.

It started in Umunede, sixty-nine kilometres from Kreektown: six Lassa fever cases at the General Hospital. By the following week it hit Illah and Patani. By the weekend there were five dead patients and ten new cases. By the time it reached Ubesia, it was all over CNN. The BBC's correspondent in Benin City was flown out by air ambulance with the fever. Seventy dead patients within three weeks! By that time it was officially an epidemic. There was one thing I couldn't do, and that was sit in front of the TV in Dundee. My spirit was in Kreektown so my body followed.

At the height of the epidemic, seventeen people were dying daily. Medical teams were coming from all over the world. Red Cross, Medecins Sans Frontières . . . The World Health Organisation was there, helping the Ministry of Health. Field camps were going up all over the place. That was how Felix Fraser came into the picture.

He was the head of a volunteer medical team from Trevi Biotics Ltd. They camped out in Kreektown Square. He came in, set up camp, and went off to a more virulent outbreak in Congo, leaving his wife to run the camp. By the time I arrived, the epidemic was at its height. The ironic thing was, Kreektown never suffered a single Lassa fever case. The virulence of the virus was scary: in the epidemic phase, one in two infected people would die. That was an outcome we were not prepared to risk. Trevi was administering a Lassa fever vaccine. GodMenai! The things you realise from hindsight! I arrived and jumped right into the action. You are Menai, and you know how this thing is. I was not a volunteer, I was Menai. I was there with Trevi, doing the public information, the infection control, isolation precautions, everything. And when the vials arrived, my son, I also helped to administer them.

Laura Fraser was the lab tech who ran the site in the absence of her husband. She was as diametrically opposite to Felix as it was possible to be and still remain one species. She was female and he was male. She had six GCEs and he was a professor of biochemistry. She was twenty-five to his fifty, tall and blonde to his grey and balding. She pined for company the way he pined for the sagacious loneliness of a book-lined study—and the only cement I could find for their three-year-old, childless marriage was his wealth. For Felix Fraser owned 6 percent of the stock of Trevi Biotics Ltd., which made him a millionaire many times over, and Laura Fraser loved all the things that wealth could do. And then, of course, there was her addiction to his custom drug.

Proximity to death impairs judgement. Our affair lasted a night, ending there on the bed of our first love-making. She had a post-sex routine that involved a drug of her biochemist husband's invention. They called it XP9. I told her I was not into drugs, whether experimental or otherwise, and she laughed and said I was, now: I'd taken the vaccine, a trial drug probably more dangerous than her own fix.

I ran back to the project office and looked with new eyes at the consent form that I got every Menai to sign. Something happens to small print in the thick of an epidemic, doesn't it? The details tend to disappear . . . but it was there on the back of the cards: it **was** a trial vaccine with a long slate of potential side-effects. I returned to Laura. She was over her high and tried to play down her words. I travelled to the WHO base in Lagos. I read the literature. There were no known vaccines for Lassa fever. I went to the Health Ministry in Ubesia and the Federal Ministry in Lagos. No one could track down authorisations for the trial vaccine Trevi had injected into the Menai. In the heat of an epidemic it seemed bad manners to ask too many questions when people were dying so quickly. At any rate the health hierarchy did not like my questions. The epidemic was over and things had to move along.

I began to pray.

At first, it seemed that GodMenai had heard my prayers. The epidemic blew over. Not a single Menai had sickened. Not a single soul had died. But things had soured between Laura and me. In another week the camp was broken up. Trevi Biotics went on to another African trouble spot to play with their bag of tricks, and my professors hauled me back to school to my books. I celebrated my twenty-seventh birthday in The Orchid, Dundee, on the first of November, 1980. You were born on the fourth. I got the call out of the blue from Laura. She was in hospital in Sudan. I had not spoken with her since she left Kreektown.

Her babies had arrived six weeks early, she wept, and they were too dark to be her husband's.

I was shattered. Didn't know what to do. But she had a plan. She didn't want to lose her marriage, and two black sons would certainly do that. She had made arrangements for two death certificates. I was to come and get you and your brother, and she would fly on to London with her lies and your death certificates, to meet her husband.

I did not hesitate. Between leaving my sons to be adopted by strangers, and taking them, there was no real choice. I left my studies once again, but I made one mistake: I flew to Sudan through Nigeria. Tume's wife, Malian, had a still-birth a week earlier. They did not hesitate to come with me. It was too late. When we walked into the hospital Laura was red with rage: her husband had just been there.

He had seen the boys on the bed beside her. He had not said much, had simply turned and walked out of the hospital, but her marriage was already on the ropes, and there was not much point in death certificates anymore. Yet, by then, Malian had carried you and had fallen in love. We tried to persuade Laura to stick to the plan, but she was afraid: he had seen two healthy children. Two death certificates would have been too suspicious. That evening she left the hospital with your brother. By the next day she was off to try to save her marriage.

It wasn't that Laura loved you less, but she had a god: her XP9. And Felix was its high priest. That was why divorce was not an option for her. But she couldn't save her marriage. In the end she lost Felix and started off on other drugs.

She overdosed in 1984. She's buried in Kent.

And let me assure you, Zanda, it wasn't that I loved you less, either, but Malian and Tume were the best apology I could make for the way you came into the world. Her breasts were primed for a suckling child. Their hearts were open too. And Tume was the Mata's chosen one. That is royalty, as Menai counts it now.

Still, I was haunted by your brother, Humphrey.

I felt I had done my duty by you. But as for your brother . . . I could not sleep at night. Laura was in no state to raise a child. By then she bore me a grudge for breaking her marriage, so she cut me off, spitefully. Her husband had managed to leave her penniless, and in her state she could not keep a job. When she lost your brother to the care system, I did not have a clue. She knew I would have done anything to have him, and that was her way of hurting me.

You know how it is with us Menai. From birth we have that duty wired into us: get married, have children—and that as quickly as possible. But with us, it is not just the having of the children. There is no point in having children, if they are not nurtured into the way of the Menai. I was getting on, in my thirties, but it was different. I ended my PhD studies. There was no point any longer, you see. What was a degree to a dying man? I had fallen ill, and I knew then that Laura had told the truth.

I obsessed about Felix Fraser and Trevi . . . I followed his interventions around the world. He never went to another Lassa outbreak, but anywhere there was a meningitis epidemic, a yellow fever regression, an Ebola strike, he was there. I boned up on the background of Trevi Biotics. The definitive way the atomic bombs ended World War Two persuaded Britain that all weapons, however horrible, could be put to good use some day. After the war, biological and chemical weapons research continued, but it was a very expensive business, and the work of reconstruction was also tasking Britain's resources. They decided to terminate weapons research and rely on the US for future BioChem needs under NATO and bilateral treaties.

But a complete break was undesirable. What to do?

By a series of invisible transactions, most of the BioChem heritage of the old R&D was transferred to private companies. Trevi is one of those inheritors. In return for the research assets inherited, the company was structured to act as an unofficial quick response arm for the Ministry of Defence. MoD contracts were discreetly funnelled through subcontracting arrangements, and Trevi maintained two faces. The stock exchange face developed and vended consumer drugs. The secret face conducted and tested pure research into offensive BioChem weapons and antidotes.

Especially antidotes. Antidotes are pretty critical, whether you are weaponising a biological or a chemical agent, or building a defensive shield against one.

So the vaccine that we got was the cutting edge of the invisible germ warfare. I did not know when I started to build a dossier, but suddenly I had one. Press cuttings, brochures, bios, commentaries . . . it grew into a portmanteau. I threw myself into the whole anti-war campaign, five years of my life, Zanda. I lost my Menai focus. I took on the big picture. I fought my disease, I fought my war . . .

Then the Menai started dying. People had started grumbling that the Menai Health Centre had not delivered a single child since 1980. Then they noticed a spike in nephritic cases. We started dying in 1985. Ugom was the first to go, nine years old, the son of Farmer Utoma and his wife, Megani. He had the worst stammer in Kreektown—but when he sang? When Ugom sang, his stammer held its breath and even angels stopped to listen. 1990 was the year that six children died in a day. That was the year of Ma'Bamou's Topless Procession, which put Menai on the world stage.

Then the test results arrived. Scientists were flown in from all over the world. We were the ethnic flavour of the season. It was pundit galore, an open season on hypotheses. What was clear was that everybody who had taken the vaccine was ailing. It was a double whammy: sterility and renal disease. And our children were dying first. There was still a Menai homeland, but it was no longer a viable community. The schools were shut. Chemist was gone. Toyota Doctor was gone. Half the market stalls in Kreektown Square were empty, and it was hard even to buy the ingredients for a pot of soup. Kreektown was a ghost town, and the morale of those left behind was gone. What the civil war could not do to us, what Lassa fever could not do to us, Felix and Laura Fraser, with the help of Tobin Rani, had done to us.

It was a big thing for a man to have on his conscience: the responsibility for the extinction of his own nation. Menai's herbal medicine is legendary. There were hundreds of people who would never have taken that vaccine if I had not been on that front line, urging them on. I was the star Menai, you see: the scholarship kid. I had the best GCEs in Kreektown history, aside from Bamou's. I was an expert in our ancient text—I was the one the Mata chose to copy his leather scrolls. I had even thought I'd be the new Mata, but he had cast the skies and he said that future was in neither the clouds of the day nor the stars of the night. My lineage was wrong. Still, with me, the Mata had not needed much persuasion to bless my journeys from Kreektown. I was the one chosen to go and bring home the strategy, the means of the Menai's survival. But I had allowed myself to be distracted by Laura . . . and my nation was paying the ultimate price.

I did not plan to kill Felix Fraser or anything like that. I am not an anarchist. The Mata schooled all Menai in peace. Much later, when that roach, Dalminda Roco, tried to get me in on the plot to bomb Trevi, I called the cops on him. Yet Felix had gone on TV, denying the link between his vaccine and the first Menai deaths. He was lying. I still remembered Laura's words. All I wanted was to tell him things I couldn't say . . . openly . . . to save his face . . . my face . . . your face . . .

But it got out of hand, didn't it? It degenerated into a stupid brawl. He came at me with the pent-up fury of the cuckold. He broke my nose. But he was an older man, and he had nothing to compare to the pent-up fury of the endangered national.

I broke his back.

I didn't get what I deserved: they put a spin on the Menai-extinction angle, on the fact that throughout the trial I could only speak Menai . . . I guess I got too intense, had too little sleep, something or another, so I broke down, didn't I? For a month or so I couldn't speak a word of English. They say I raved on and on in Menai. I guess I was saying goodbye to the spirits of our people, to the breaking lineage, to the naan of the totem, to the language of the stories . . .

I was packed off to a psychiatric hospital.

I got out after two years, but it was not until 1990 that I traced your brother down to Miss Chow's takeaway in Battersea. I watched him two Saturdays in a row . . . and she got the impression I was watching **her**.

Well, she was a good woman, too.

But it was always about your brother.

I lived with them until it was time to go to jail again. I am proud to say that your brother can speak Menai. At first he did not know what language he was learning, but throughout the time I lived with them, I affected an atrocious English until they learnt a flawless Menai.

Yet Miss Chow was hiding a secret from me: there was a Mr. Chow. He arrived from Shanghai without warning one Sunday morning. Your brother opened the door and there he was. There was a lot of angry cursing in Mandarin when I stepped out of his wife's room half-clad. He was on my neck, head butting, punching . . . he was half my size and no real danger, but my hands were, you know, weakened by guilt . . . yet another married woman . . . Then your brother put the kitchen knife in his back.

He was twelve years old.

Mr. Chow died there in the flat above the Battersea takeaway. I called the police and told them I had killed him. There was no one to contradict me: Miss Chow had hung herself in the bedroom, and your brother was catatonic. He never said a word to me again until the Social Services came to get him.

I spent ten years in jail in England. In a sense it was the worst time of my life. It was the Hell of being locked away from Kreektown. It was the knowledge that Tume and Malian had just drowned: I had the two of you out there, and I could not do anything, anything to help you. I started my renal treatment in prison. By the time I got out in 2002, half the Menai were dead and I had to get into the mindset of campaigning, not for an endangered culture, but for an extinct one. To work, not to keep a language spoken in a village square, but to get the name of an ethnic nation so imprinted in human memory that, so long as men walk this Earth, they will remember that the Menai once did.

I am fifty-two. The lesson of the Menai is to live your days, to walk in acceptance, not in regret. They are not your **last** days. They are your days. In prison I lived every day. Under the sentence of death, I finished the degrees I never could finish when I was carefree and free. I started the Menai Legacy Group. I built the Menai web. And although there were many times I thought back to that night I crossed the line with your mother in Kreektown, there was also that day in 2004 when I read your column, and his book, and I understood why the Mata says **ai gbono di, gbona dabi**: a curse in one language is indeed a blessing in another. So, no, I regret nothing. If I didn't reach out to you earlier, it was that fear of destroying everything I try to fix.

I do love you both.
Tobin, son of Manan,
Father of Zanda & Humphrey,
Spawn of Menai.

MAJOR LAMIKAN

State House Squash Courts, Ubesia | 13th April, 2005

Ordinarily, it wasn't difficult to play a game of squash with Governor Obu. He was a generous winner and a petty, vindictive loser. Playing him—at least for anyone in his service—was a matter of simulating a desperate game that the governor would win by a slim couple of points acquired by the sublime experience of an old warrior. It was the responsibility of the opponents to avoid the impression that they had thrown the match.

Unfortunately, a preliminary session with bowls of fish pepper soup had sapped the governor's physical resources. A competent player could have dispatched him while sitting on a stool. The governor seemed incapable of the short dash that defined squash and couldn't keep the ball under the out-of-court lines. Major Lamikan had never played worse in his life, and he had won the first game. By faking leg cramps at three critical points, he had managed to give Governor Obu the second game.

It was the third and decisive game of the match, and despite Lamikan's efforts, the governor was already an underdog at 5–7. The governor was serving, incompetently, and Major Lamikan was watching his carefully built rapport with his boss going down the toilet. He was wondering whether he dared fake another cramp when the door into the court opened and the governor's aide entered. He was wearing a sports outfit, and he offered his boss a mobile phone. 'It's important, sir.'

'For goodness sake . . .' exploded Governor Obu, finding a legitimate vent for his frustration.

'Brugges, Geneva,' said the aide, inches from his boss's ear.

The governor's anger drained away, and he lost interest in the game. He waved his apologies to the obsequious gallery and gave the aide his racquet. 'I've a good game here. Better don't mess it up.'

As the door closed behind the governor, Lamikan felt like hugging his saviour.

GOVERNOR OBU

State House, Ubesia | 13th April, 2005

'Five minutes,' Obu said to the other party and switched off the phone. He strode to the lift, which he rode to his office on the third floor. He waved away the brace of salutes and went through the darkened ante-chamber to his suite at the end room. He stripped quickly and showered, humming cheerfully, his squash annoyances forgotten.

He remembered his first meeting with Pierre-Verdonk Brugges. It had been three years earlier in the reception of the Abuja Hilton Hotel and Towers, soon after the Petroleum Communities Development Fund bonanza had opened. He had been walking to the lifts, on his way to a rendezvous in the privacy of an eighth-floor suite. The beefy Belgian had sprung into his path, spouting a sales pitch on banking.

Obu had brushed him off curtly, although he did accept Brugges's com-plimentary card. He was already down to his undergarments in the suite under the admiring gaze of two pairs of Fulani eyes when he glanced at the back of the card and read details of his last three deposits into his Swiss accounts! He struggled into his clothes while shouting instructions to his security staff on the mobile phone. Fifteen minutes later, Pierre-Verdonk was in an impromptu interrogation room in the Sontik State liaison office in Abuja. Because of the sensitiveness of the issues, Obu was alone with the Belgian. Pierre-Verdonk was in the hot seat, but it was Obu who was sweating. 'Talk,' he had snapped. 'Who are you and where did you get this information?'

'I'm a creative banking consultant,' the man had said, calmly. 'The in-formation I put on that card is what any halfway smart auditor from your country's corruption commission can find out within twenty-four hours of arriving in Europe with the necessary authorisations from your govern-ment. The secrecy laws have changed, you see.'

'I'm listening,' Obu had told him.

'I've worked in private banking for two decades. The goal of my team is to stay ahead of regulation.' The man brought out another card and passed it over to Obu. 'If you make your . . . investments through us, this is what the smartest auditors and financial investigators will be able to trace after years of hard work.'

Obu had turned the card over. 'It's blank,' he had said.

'Exactly,' Pierre-Verdonk had said. 'It's a very complex process, but it's simplified by computer technology. We work with some six hundred and fifty digitally enabled banks in tax havens all over the world. We have automated the account opening process; our computers in Berne can open thirty numerically coded FX accounts per hour. If we're passing a million dollars through the system, for instance, I simply transfer it to our source-code account. Within sixty minutes the money has been wired through hundreds of separate accounts. Each of those fund transfers are holding accounts beneath the reporting threshold, so they're essentially invisible. The computerised, automated transfers continue for the next four to six weeks, and every time a transfer is made, the necessary invoice/remittance paper trail will be generated. My staff follows up the paper trail. The funds will spend between forty-eight and ninety-six hours in each account, defeating trace-back regulations in each fiscal jurisdiction. By the time it reaches its final investment destination in Ireland—'

'I hate the Irish.'

'What do you think of Singaporeans?'

He had made an iffy gesture with his spread fingers.

'Fine. By the time it reaches your final repository account in Singapore, the money is totally untraceable.' Pierre-Verdonk had grinned at this point. 'I'm talking *totally* untraceable.'

Pierre-Verdonk had gotten a new client that evening.

◆ ◆ ◆

OBU WAS changing into a caftan when the phone rang.

This Belgian was time-conscious. Their hotels were something else. The governor picked it up on the fourth ring.

'Hello.' He listened briefly, then frowned. 'Listen, Penaka, I can't see you tonight. I have very urgent affairs of state on my desk!' He ended the call with a curse. Perhaps it was time to get another *private* private line.

He didn't have to wait long before the phone rang again. 'Thank you, Obu,' said Pierre-Verdonk. 'The latest PCC funds are in.'

'Good,' Obu replied coldly. It was the first time the other man had addressed him without the title "Your Excellency", and he did not like it. 'What's the balance? Ballpark.' He had a good idea of the ballpark figure, but he never tired of hearing it.

'It doesn't matter.'

Obu frowned. 'What?'

'I'm closing your account, effective now.'

Obu looked at the phone in puzzlement. 'Pierre-Verdonk Brugges, are you drunk?'

'You're slow this evening, Obu,' said Pierre-Verdonk. 'You know all those Singaporean investment certificates I sent you?'

'You mean my SICs?'

'You can call them your ITPs or international toilet papers for all I care. Anyway, don't take them near a bank, all right? I don't want you ending up in jail and this story appearing in the press. I have a dozen political thieves like you who are still depositing.'

'I'm flying to Singapore tomorrow! This very night!'

'Sure. Come with your trainers. The gym that we normally redecorate into your "private bank" will still be a gym.'

Obu realised he was on the floor; he did not know how he got there, but there he was, struggling to hold onto the phone. 'Let's talk about this. Is it the commission? What do you want? I'll give you three percent, Pierre-Verdonk.'

The other man laughed. 'Try another name. I just love this bit!'

'Please, Pierre, okay, six percent!'

'Nah, I can't give you six percent of my money. That would shave a nasty six feet off the length of my new yacht. Listen, use registered banks for your loot next time. They're not more honest than I am, but they can afford to take the long view—when you die, they usually inherit. As a natural person I've got to take the shorter view of things. And in the short view, you're out of office in a few weeks, and the aspect of private banking that I hate most is the withdrawal phase.'

'Pierre? Pierre?'

PENAKA LEE

MMI Airport, Lagos | 13th April, 2005

Penaka was waiting for his plane, his mind already enmeshed in the Congolese political economy, when his PA brought him a mobile phone and a red Post-it Note. He might have rejected the call, after Obu's rudeness earlier, but he understood that emotions had no role in business. He took the phone immediately, walking towards the sweep of windows in the executive lounge for more privacy.

'Your Excellency?' he said quietly.

'I'm ready.'

'For what?'

'Are you deaf?' The rude voice on the other end had a hysterical rattle. 'Let's go. Now!'

Penaka Lee looked at his watch. Had the plane gone down already? That was impossible. He shook his head. 'Are we talking about . . .'

'Look, this is not a telephone discussion. Come in now.'

'I'm due for a meeting in Kinshasa in—'

'More important than our country? Are you joking with me, Mr. Lee?'

'Ah . . . I'll be there.' The phone was already dead.

♦ ♦ ♦

HE SAT down and closed his eyes. The second boarding announcement came. He blanked it out of his mind. His special gift was decision making, and he practised it like a science. Something had happened, something potentially catastrophic, to push the Great Ditherer onto the path of express action, even before the unfortunate catastrophe Penaka had prepared for him. Penaka's instincts of personal preservation screamed for him to get on the plane. Yet he had also cultivated a special instinct of financial preservation, which counselled otherwise. Plus, he did not have all the information. Good decisions could only be made with quality information.

He speed-dialled Belinja, who was his usual cagey self until his encryption kicked in. Penaka went straight to the point. 'Our friend just called me. He was . . . very upset. Ready to go. Do you have any information?'

'I just spoke to Lamikan,' Belinja replied. 'The poor man has been conned. He's lost his Swiss egg. Everything.'

Penaka closed his eyes as thoughts crowded in, thick and fast. By his estimates the governor had stolen half his state's budget over the past year alone. It was criminally stupid to lose it all just like that. 'Is that possible?'

'He fell for the Belgian Reverse.' Penaka had never heard sympathy in Belinja's voice before. 'If he retires now, it will be on his civil service pension . . . poor bastard.'

Penaka broke off the call. His PA, not daring to interrupt him even for the final boarding call, was standing three metres in front of him.

Sonia's plane was scheduled to leave in two hours. There was still a chance to prevent some unnecessary deaths.

Penaka had no problem with hard decisions. If something had to be done, he got it done. Yet the slow governor was now ready to roll and it was unnecessary for his wife's plane to go down. Penaka wished there was a simple way to stop the bomb, but he had structured a complex web to ensure that there was no traceback.

He used his disposable phone to make the first call. The man had come highly recommended, and Penaka knew next to nothing about him except that he used an MTN number, a BVI bank account, and a fake American twang, which became a fake Canadian accent when he spoke too fast. Today he was shouting, coming across more Yorkshire than the relevant pudding: *'You think this is a joke?'*

'Just do it, okay? It doesn't affect the payment.'

''Course it doesn't affect the flipping payment!' He snorted. 'What's the problem—did you suddenly become born-again or what?'

'Just do it!' Penaka snapped.

There was music, and children were laughing in the background. Was the assassin at a family barbecue?

'I don't know. We're talking less than two hours, and I'm not doing it myself, you know, I subcontracted . . .'

'Then I suggest you get off the phone and call your subcontractor. I'll call you in ten.'

The man hung up rudely.

Penaka saw that his PA had taken a seat. The flight was gone.

He had a gift of being able to smile under most conditions. He was smiling now. The elderly woman next to him was trying to get her wooden carvings into her duty-free bag. Penaka helped her, and they chatted about the terrible traffic over the Third Mainland Bridge that morning. She was off to Kuwait to see her brother-in-law. She told him that her name was Mrs. Kafaru. Penaka did not volunteer his.

He did not like his current position. He was not sure why he was so concerned about Sonia's fate. She had always been expendable. It must have been something about the wastefulness of it. Besides, she was a particularly nice woman, as charming as her husband was boorish. Penaka had met her a few times. She threw a terrific party. She was the only person he had told the story of his ex-wife, and six months afterwards she remembered to ask whether Christabel had returned Penaka's Pekingese after the court judgment. (She hadn't.) If Sonia died, it would be her blasted husband's fault.

But Penaka would definitely be sending flowers.

While he waited, a text came in from Monica Parkerson. Her team had tracked down the professor's London house and acquired Penaka's bronze, which was on its way to Geneva. They'd had to take a few other things to make it look like a regular break-in. Penaka could not believe he had tears in his eyes.

Eleven minutes had passed. He pressed redial.

The man's voice was angry. 'It's too late.'

'What do you mean, "It's too late"?' Penaka was angry as well, even though he was still smiling. The elderly woman was looking at him. He rose and walked away. 'You still have one and a half hours. They haven't even boarded . . .'

'It is over, okay? The plane left early.'

'Scheduled flights don't leave early. Go and check—'

'If you are an airline that cancelled your flight from the night before, your scheduled flight can bloody well leave early.' There was a sullen pause. 'So what are you saying? You promised a bonus if it went without a hitch. Are you saying . . . ?'

Penaka smiled angrily. 'You'll get your bonus.'

There was no emotion in business.

◆ ◆ ◆

HE PUT away the phone and reviewed his situation. The old lady dropped another carving, and he stepped over it on his way out. He was still smiling, but he had maxed out the day's quota of courtesies to Old Women Travelling to Kuwait. His PA was hurrying alongside with his case. 'There's another flight for Nairobi in three hours. We can—'

'Scrap Congo,' Penaka told him. 'Call ahead to Aero Contractors in the domestic wing. Charter a plane and have them file a flight plan for Ubesia.'

'Sir?' The PA was no fool. He had picked up Penaka's vibes. He also seemed anxious to be anywhere but Nigeria just then.

'You heard me.'

And that was Penaka. He made his decisions the way the stakes fell. The bigger the risk, the bigger the payoff. Obu was right: Sontik Republic was the biggest single stake he had ever played, and he would not get a bigger shot as Corus chairman. Thirty billion barrels of oil reserves, a hundred and fifty trillion cubic feet of gas. Twenty billion dollars in annual potential income. The richest petrochemical resource on the bloody continent, politicians as crooked as fusilli, and citizens as cowardly as sheep. The game belonged to the daring, and Penaka saw himself a bloody eagle in a coven of bow-legged crows.

The fat governor had two crutches: his money and his wife. The federal murder of his wife would push him onto the highway of a revenge secession. But being broke and widowed on the same day? He might well implode. Penaka had to be in that bunker to protect his investments.

He just hoped the situation wouldn't turn out to be 1990 all over again. Blasted Belgians.

SLEEPCATASTROPHES

Kreektown | August/September, 2002

Namodi Geya
Bamou Geya
Salima Geya (Ma'Bamou)
Sonja Abene
Masingo Awaka

Births
Nil

Extant Menai population: 210 (NPC estimates)

HUMPHREY CHOW

London | 13th April, 2005

I shivered. The silence of the NHS hospital was mediated by the hum of medical machinery. It was not quite 3:00 a.m. I didn't know how long I had been out, or how long I had been writing. I could not remember the period since 10:00 p.m. as a continuum. I only remembered snatches of intense, vivid colour, of memory as lush as present tense. I had lost my drip line and was fully dressed without remembering the act of dressing. I had come to the end of my new recollections, but it was not enough. I did not yet have a story. Even my old self had no idea why Bamou killed himself. I had to invent a satisfactory explanation for my readers.

I began to write.

An hour later, I found a stray wireless signal winking in the icon tray and e-mailed the story to Shaun. If he checked his mail like a good e-mail junkie, it would save him a trip to the hospital.

I put away the computer and crawled into bed again. My mind seethed with all but the details I sought. I tried to put a face to a suddenly insistent name, Estelle, but a darkness was beginning to seize the borders of my mind again, and I was fighting a craving for another capsule. I tried to fall asleep, in vain. In despair I broke open the bottle of Proxtigen, poured it into the washbasin, and opened the faucet. I climbed back into bed, panting. An age passed. I tiptoed back to the basin and turned off the tap. Most of the capsules had run down the drain, but a few had been caught at the vent. Their casings had melted, leaving a whitish sludge on the bronze ring of the drain. I carefully scooped some into my mouth. It was definitely more than two capsules, but I couldn't let the last of my Proxtigen go to waste. I slumped there, next to the sink.

Then I remembered my drug addict mother, Laura, and I was sick with disgust at myself. Perhaps she had overdosed in a corner much like this, with Felix, her chemist husband, handing her the pills. Perhaps I was nothing more than a junkie looking for his substance. Then my mind began to bloom as I sailed beyond regret.

I waited.

FELIX FRASER

Southend | 4th August, 1985

On the first floor of the nursing home, Louis Raven, QC, paused outside his old friend's room for several minutes, steeling himself for what was on the other side of the door. Eventually he had to go through. It was a large, overly warm private room. The one bed was empty and unmade, with bedclothes on the floor. His eyes followed the trailing blanket to the window, where Professor Felix Fraser sat hunched in his wheelchair.

Raven feared and detested infirmity in equal measure. Now seventy-three and retired, he played golf four times a week, drove his 300SL gull-wing at Silverstone Marque Shows, and immersed himself in the company of people decades his junior. The visit was a trial for him precisely because of the identity of the man in the chair.

'Go away,' said Fraser.

At least it was the same, cynical voice. Raven had feared a slurred conversation full of misapprehensions and 'beg y' pardons.' He picked up the blanket and walked over, turning the chair around firmly.

They looked at each other, the one not hiding his anger and rage, the other smiling gently, keeping his shock and revulsion from his face. 'How's tricks, Felix?'

'Bad.'

'Won't say I told you so, though I did, didn't I?' Raven draped the blanket over the chair, covering the unsightly legs of the invalid and tucking the cloth around his neck. 'Stubborn old crank.'

'Get your hands off me! What are you playing at?'

'It's time for my walk,' said Raven as he pushed the chair toward the door, 'and you're coming along.'

There was a poisonous silence, then, 'My pouch is almost full.'

'Full of what? What pouch are we talking about?'

'Urine. I have a urostomy pouch.'

Behind the chair, Raven winced and scratched his head. 'I'll get your nurse,' he said.

♦ ♦ ♦

SOON, THEY were at the edge of a grotty car park in which Raven's blue, low-slung Porsche 911 stood out like a beacon for vandals. Around them, pigeons scavenged for food. It had been hard going, pushing the basic, NHS-issue wheelchair, and he had early given up and paused for an extended breather, seating himself on a bench. He pulled a newspaper from his coat pocket and opened it expansively.

Fraser cleared his throat uncomfortably.

'Don't mention,' muttered Raven into the *Financial Times*.

♦ ♦ ♦

PRESENTLY, A few spots of rain appeared on the newspaper. Raven folded it up and left it on the bench. He looked at his watch. He sighed. 'What are you going to do with yourself now?'

Felix rolled his eyes at the boughs of an ash tree overhead. 'Lunch.'

'You know what I mean. Your silly fight broke your spine, not your brain.'

'You're a lousy life coach, Louis; don't go there.'

'You heard about Laura? She's ODed, and the lad's in care.'

He laughed bitterly. 'Who's Laura?'

'She messed up five years ago, Felix. Your pity train ran out of rail miles ago.'

'Get me out of the rain, and go home to your swank life, QC.'

The retired queen's counsel took off his spectacles and carefully wiped away the rain spots. He held them up and squinted carefully at them. They remained clear. 'What rain?' he asked, replacing them on his nose. He took an envelope from his pocket and half pulled a cheque out of it. He let the other man see the payee and amount, then he put it back into his pocket. 'Oh, well, I'll get you back into your cell now.'

'It's a room, and fine, you've got my attention. What's that cheque about?'

'Depends. Are you through with self-pity? It's down payment for an entrepreneur, not graft for a charity case.'

'Whose money is that? You're not that generous.'

'I'm not a thief, either. It's your money, Felix.'

There was moment of shock. The man in the wheelchair swallowed. 'What?'

'Remember the second casino? The night after you came in from the Sudan?'

'St. Cloud, West End. Six hundred thousand pounds plus. Three-way poker.'

'You have a good memory.'

'Well?'

'I knew you would come to this, and I rigged that game. It was actually seven hundred and twelve thousand pounds you lost there, but the owner of St. Cloud was also a client, and I had a contract signed before I took you there. He's kept this half million ever since.'

'And you never told me.'

'So you didn't have to lie at the divorce proceedings.'

'That's why you refused to represent me? You said you were too close to Laura.'

'I am that, too. Remember the private club on the first floor of the Hotel Philippe?'

Felix ran a hand through his thin hair. 'Four hundred thousand pounds . . .'

'Half that money went to Laura.'

'Traitor! I'll sue . . .'

He laughed. 'Shut up, Felix, you're too broke to knock on a lawyer's door.'

'You played me for a fool.'

'You played yourself, old friend. You still don't see it? Look at you, Felix. From chief executive of Trevi Biotics to room fifteen in a pathetic nursing home . . .'

'None of your bloody business!'

'Fine.' He got to his feet. 'I did preserve an option for you to buy back some of your Megatum shares at original offer price, but it expires tomorrow. Well, I'll leave you to your life. I'll tell your nurse to come get you. I have to watch my seventy-year-old waist.' He turned to go.

'Where's my money?'

'What money, Felix?' Raven's voice was cold. 'I have no money even remotely connected to you. I retired three years ago. My client accounts have passed scrutiny, my personal accounts are above board . . .'

'Okay, okay, okay.'

They glared at each other.

Felix sighed. 'Okay. Get me out of here, all right?'

'I'm waiting.'

'Damn you! Please and thank you!'

Raven sighed and sank back onto the oak bench. He suddenly looked older than his seventy-three years. 'I'm not interested in your Ps and Qs, Felix. I'm tired of playing God. Your wife died ten days after I gave her the money . . . Maybe I should leave you to enjoy a long life here . . .'

'I'm not Laura.'

'Glad you know who she is now.'

Felix studied his palms bitterly. 'I brought this on myself. You want total abasement, don't you? Okay, I, Felix Fraser, promise I won't end up like Laura. I will turn my life around, so help me God.'

'And the kid? Turns out the adoption—'

'Keep the goddamned money!' swore Felix, jerking his chair away. 'That kid's got nothing to do with me!'

Raven seized a wheel firmly. 'Keep your shirt on, old friend.' He sighed. 'I was just making conversation. Remember, I'm not playing God anymore.'

HUMPHREY CHOW

London | 13th April, 2005

etiem baba kaini ga moye i said no i dont want a big tea just put the small tea in a big cup and fill it up with water *rumbie chaka sumienogota* i have walked so far away i cannot return before dark i cannot harvest all i planted before night cannot finish all i started just have to up and go home and go CHANGE HERE FOR WATERLOO i have lived so long that the people i know are gone so who made these rules anyway? that i cannot go back to the past? well here i go and one finger to OPEN ALL DOORS i may not speak mandarin like a mandarin but i am miss chows boy i speak it like a boy raised on pea soup and love by the best MIND THE GAP BETWEEN THE TRAIN AND THE PLATFORM she healed my stammer until mister cho cho cho you must not stammer you must ta ta take a deep breath and not stammer until mister cho cho chow came DO NOT PASS GO DO NOT connections are better on the tube *hiramba kuti che* I AM IVORY TAKE ME TO MY COAST i like your wings can i fly too? my name ist omfry show short story writa this is what i do for better or for worse *kurie gai faifa fo soke* stop begging my pardon and CHANGE HERE FOR YOUR WATERLOO you dont need a ticket to hell you just turn up and travel MEN DONT CRY go away from me go far far away from me this is i that bin the ones that love him most in the trash can of forgetting do you take this woman for your lawful wedded wife? who is this woman? PLEASE ATTEND TO ALL BAGS AT ALL TIMES they loved me in sudbury they called me nath she liked pumpkins he liked his papers with his morning milk then their wombborn baby came and they returned me and their extra pumpkins to tesco *ajoeke na tofe* EVERY UNATTENDED CHILD WILL BE REMOVED AND DESTROYED IN A CONTROLLED EXPLOSION this is i of two dads bearded daddy sue and breasted daddy phil i called sid in the house of the chanting cult called dwayne in brixton i am nath not dwayne yer noim is dwayne so shut yer trap an lissen up i'm the daddy ain't no one telling me wot ter call ma boy go far away from me because i am coming home your name is izak baptiste as in john the baptist and THE WAR IS coming after you with a cho cho CHECK THE SEATS IN FRONT OF YOU FOR YOUR PASSPORTS *rugudu simabi nubi* around jericho was not one word spoken by israelites when circling mountains best to zip it until it is time to find the voice for a shout then let it rip so the walls come tumbling

down unless you are humpty dumpty or buffalo bamou then your brains
come tumbling out MIND THE GAP BETWEEN THE STRAIN AND THE
OUTCOME my name was humpney chow snort story writer and i sure am
peased i sure am prised i shure am pleased to meat you

◆ ◆ ◆

Abidjan | 8:56 p.m.

'*Izak, tu vas bien?*' She was studying me anxiously.
'*Je vais bien.*'
'You sure?' This was another youth with what seemed like size thir-
teen boots fifteen inches from my head. 'You look bad, mister. Do you live
around here? I could call a taxi for you or something.'
'It's okay,' said the woman, 'he's with me.'
Indeed, I thought. I sat up. I was surrounded by a sea of young faces lit
up by strobes. We were in what looked like a nightclub. There was a hub-
bub around me but no music.
'I said I'm fine.'
'What he needs is an ambulance, not a cab, that's what he needs,' said
another woman, in between the snaps and clicks of her chewing gum.
'Where am I?'
'Club Fuju.'
My heart started thumping. Soon it was pounding like I had just fin-
ished a race. I was sitting on the edge of a dance floor, the centre of attention. Over the public address system, a DJ yelled, '*Ce qui se passe là-bas?*'
'He's stoned out of his mind, but he's fine!'
'Then get him off my dance floor!'
'I'm not stoned, I'm fine,' I protested as two men took my arms and
helped me to my feet. I stood readily enough as a storming *soukous* belted
from the speakers at full blast. The dance floor filled up quickly as they led
me out into a cool courtyard. She stuck with me after they left. Her smile
was friendly, bemused. Her name was at the tip of my tongue. My heart
began to slow. 'Where is this?'
She laughed uncertainly. 'Have you become epileptic or something?
You've never freaked out under disco lights before . . .'
I took her hand and squeezed it lightly. '*Where* is this?'
She threw up her hands. The gesture registered distinctly. 'This is Club
Fuju's back entrance, through which they usually throw out troublemak-
ers. Come, we'll find a quieter place to celebrate.'

She led the way out, and I followed. I had on leather trousers and a three-inch buckle that mystified me. I had wound dressings on my chest and an ache in my back that I couldn't explain either. I pulled my jersey lower as she pushed the side gate open onto the street. *Treichville, not Brixton.* For some reason, I was proud of that knowledge. The sky was lower, the clothes louder, the smells earthier . . . *This was Treichville, not Brixton.*

She was suddenly very close to me. *'Alors, ta mémoire te reviens?'*

'Yes, but I'm also forgetting more,' I replied. The memories were coming back. With big holes in them. This was Treichville, but *where* was Treichville? 'Where are we and why are we speaking French?'

Her smile faded. 'We are speaking French because we are in Abidjan,' she said sharply. 'That's what people do here.'

'But I don't speak French,' I whispered, in French.

She threw her hands up in frustration. A window opened in my mind, and I opened my mouth with her name, but the sound did not come. She grabbed a handful of my jersey. It was a friendly gesture, but I recognised the edge in her words. 'You've forgotten me again, haven't you? I can see it in your eyes.'

'Of course not, Estelle. How can I ever forget you?'

'But you did before, didn't you? So what's your wife's name, Humphrey *Con Man* Chow?'

There was a warning in her eyes. At my side, my fingers did the check. I had on the only two rings I ever wore: my mother's and Grace's. It was too much to think I could ever forget I was married to Grace Meadows. It was, probably, not in my nature to go telling people I was single. I shrugged. 'Obviously, we're going through problems right now . . .'

'*Who is* your wife?' Her voice was undeflectable steel.

I shrugged. 'Grace Me—'

Her hand struck my cheek with a shock more electric than physical, snapping me back into a church where I was taking the vows . . . which was wrong, because Grace and I had gotten married in a county hall with nine witnesses, yet there I was in an all-black all-singing all-dancing church that used to be a nightclub in Cocody, Abidjan, and I looked around and that *was* Estelle beside me.

The relief came with the pain.

She punched a fist into my shirt pocket. I staggered backwards, nearly pushing a cyclist into the sewer. '*Attention!*' he swore, deftly swinging his pannier of baguettes past. I looked around. She was gone as well. I sat in an open bistro and sank my head in my hands. *I was a bigamist!* The memories began to come thick and fast, no longer standing in isolated clumps. Mishael, Padre, Tomas . . . my Ivorien foster parents who had been lost in an early skirmish of the war . . . the job at the SCALA Prison.

Always the job at the prison.

I worked hard in the theatre of my mind, piecing together, piecing together.

He was sitting on the idling scooter, watching me with a thin smile. 'Hallo, Mishael,' I said.

'At least you remember me. She says you've gone crazy again, you speak English again. I'm to bring you home.'

'I'll find my way. I've got to make a call.'

'To who?' he sneered. 'Your wife?'

I was silent. He got off his scooter and joined me at the table. He waved away the waiter. He took off his glasses and wiped them slowly. 'I knew where you were all along.'

'You did?'

'Six months after you disappeared, my friend at the British Embassy saw Estelle's wedding pictures and recognised you. She told me. It made perfect sense: the war was coming, you were British—'

'That's not how it was,' I said quietly.

'This Grace, has she thrown you out? Is that it?'

I looked away. 'We broke up, but that's not it.'

Mishael was silent for a long time. 'I like to believe the best of you, Izak, but I'm going to protect my sister. Okay? I didn't tell her you were alive. Or that you escaped to Britain without her. I let her think the best of you. Okay, so it didn't work out for you, and you swallowed your shame and came back with this stupid story . . . mon dieu, Izak, if you've found your memory, now, damn well keep it!'

I took a deep breath. 'I'll do my best.'

He rose. 'You can find your way home?'

I nodded. 'By the way, why do you keep calling me Izak?'

He stared hard at me. He turned away without another word.

I watched him ride away. I reached into the chest pocket of my jersey for her ring. It was a smaller clone of my coal-black ring. It was not my mother's, then. I was a . . . *bigamist?* I pulled the rings off my fingers. I went through the rest of my pockets carefully. I was carrying 34,400 CFA. I also had a bus ticket, a map of Abidjan . . . and my Humphrey Chow passport.

My name is Humphrey Chow. My name is Humphrey Chow . . . I gathered
up my things, dropped Grace's wedding ring in a beggar's bowl, and left
for home.

◆ ◆ ◆

11:00 p.m.

The ground floor of Le Moyeu was a chaotic fifteen-station Internet
café with a raft of add-on services offered by Estelle and her younger
brother. Mishael lived on the first floor, adjacent to the open-plan office
from which they ran their business, and Estelle . . . and I . . . had lived in
the loft apartment, which had a deep verandah that opened left of the
premises. Le Moyeu opened early and shut late, and there were usually a
few inveterate surfers and gamers who kept at it until midnight.

But it was a slow Wednesday night for Abidjan. The last of the patrons—
a party of students—were outside, exchanging interminable adieus. I sat
in a pew on the first floor, overlooking the front of the house, watching
them leave. At midnight the lights began to wink out downstairs, one
after the other. A neighbour's music player was belting out a Lingana
song as she mounted the wooden steps. Her footfalls paused on the landing. 'Mon dieu.'

I closed my eyes. 'Tough day, eh?'

She was silent. There was still no visual contact, but the timbers of the
house were thin. I heard her exhale and sink down. We rested against the
same wall. She yawned.

I tried again. 'Did you make a lot of money?'

'And what business of yours is that, stranger?' She said tiredly.

'I remember now,' I said, softly.

'Hallelujah, bring the champagne, Padre, the husband remembers his
wedding day!'

'Padre's gone home,' called Mishael from his room.

'Was I talking to you?'

'Oh, sorry!' he shouted sarcastically.

She pushed herself upright, and the stairs creaked again as she mounted
the short flight up to the loft. She rounded the banisters and looked in on
the veranda. On the wall behind her hung the small square of our wedding
photograph. Her voice was no longer tired. 'You remember now, don't
you? And that's supposed to erase the disgrace, the pain of the last three
years? To erase your adultery, your callousness, your . . .'

'I was ill,' I whispered, trying to cue her to lower her voice. 'I'm still ill, but I'm getting better.'

'You were not ill,' she said in the same voice, and I understood that in a sense she was not just talking to me, she was talking to the bones of the house that had witnessed the disgrace of the jilted wife. 'You were calculating. You are here now, why? I'll tell you why, Izak, why is because you have no money for hotel. Telephone Grace Chow, let her send you money and leave me alone! Let me be!'

She crossed into the room and shut the door. I listened to the angry snap of the belt snaking from her waist, the chink of bracelets plonked into her jewellery box . . . I listened to her stalk from one end of the room to the other as she undressed . . . until finally she sighed onto her bed like a ball deflating.

There was something eerie about a café out-of-hours. It was the ghostliness of the bustle that had soaked into the walls . . . but now there was so much resentment in the mix as well. I walked downstairs. Across the deck, large windows faced the street, and their vertical slats divided up the moonlight. Out in the yard, mongrels gathered, drawn by the resident bitch coming into heat. One howled at the moon, and the others followed suit. From upstairs, Estelle threw a curse and an empty can, and they broke up, for the moment.

I opened the door and stood on the threshold. The car and the flat in Putney were waiting. I would have a few days' worth of junk mail and overdue bills to sort. I had a laptop to rescue from the hospital. I had a flagging career to attend to. Fingers crossed, my memory was healed and the pieces of the jigsaw complete. The work Asian Borha had started was painfully done. I could pick up my life, and when Ram Gupta came into it, tell him of the young Dalminda Roco whom I had met at age twelve and who had crashed out of my memory on that psychotic day in Scotland, grist from a tired writer's mind. I stood in the doorway for several minutes, filling my lungs again and again.

I could not leave.

I was not healed after all. Despite her words it seemed to me that there was only one person in the world that my life or death could stir. It was difficult to leave such a woman . . . for a flat and a year-old car . . . especially with the emotions rekindling in me. I had travelled three thousand miles from an English hospital bed to an Abidjan nightclub, recovering memories that had stymied psychiatrists for years. I did not know how, but the woman upstairs had something to do with it. Our wedding photograph was still on her wall. My clothes were still in her wardrobe. She was the anchor I needed now. I shut the door securely and mounted the stairs to the top. At the door it was a struggle to get out the words, and she asked if I was going to watch her all night.

'*Je t'aime.*'

She stared me down. 'Try something more original. I can get five hundred men between here and the Palais Omnisport to stand at my door and tell me "I love you."'

'I'm getting better, Estelle,' I whispered, 'but I'm afraid of sleeping—I don't know who I will be when I wake up.'

'You can always turn to . . .'

'Please don't say it, Estelle.'

'*Dee.*' She sat up. There was an edge in her voice. 'That's what you used to call me.'

'*Dee?*' Long pause. Tentatively, 'Is that your . . . middle name?'

'No. But that was what you called me, and I rather prefer that to "Estelle."'

The dogs began to howl again. 'Why did I call you that?'

'That's for you to tell me, isn't it?' She held my gaze for a long second. 'Tomorrow, we'll go see our uncle Stephane.'

'Is this a test? We don't have an uncle Stephane.'

'He's a new one. He married our cousin Bintou, last August.'

'I remember Bintou!'

'Hallelujah!' she replied, this time with a smile.

ZANDA ATTURK

London | 14th April, 2005

7:30 a.m.

London was full of nice people. On the bus to Humphrey's flat we met a lovely lady carrying more books than was good for her back. She did not look very British, but Amana recognised one of her textbooks and fell into conversation. A few bus stops later, she introduced us. We shook hands solemnly, with me filing her name in a temporary slot for people I would see for a few minutes and never again.

Amana exclaimed, 'Japan! That's a long way to travel from, just to read history!'

A dreamy look entered the young lady's eyes. She stroked her textbooks with delicate fingers. Her voice was music to sleep to. 'I wanted the *opportooonity* to study under these *prooofessors*.'

She struggled off the bus with her books at the next stop, and Amana shuddered theatrically. 'I sorry for the wives of those *prooofessors*.'

◆ ◆ ◆

8:00 a.m.

I wore dark glasses and pulled the hood up over my head; this close to my brother's haunts, there was no sense in flaunting my face. The police ribbons we had seen on TV had given way to builder's scaffolding, which now surrounded the pub. A white mask now covered the charred gash in the face of the building. The rest of the building had escaped without much damage. It was a five-storey block of flats, and the entrance to the upper flats was several metres away from the scaffolding. We entered the stairwell and mounted up to the first floor. We rang the bell and waited.

I sighed. It was turning out like the last time. 'Wait here, I'll check the restaurant.'

'Let me do that. Someone might recognise you.'

She went downstairs, opening the door for a woman in uniform who was halfway up the stairs when an elderly woman entered the stairwell, struggling up with a basket of shopping.

It was suddenly a very busy building. I stood aside for them to pass, but the uniformed lady stopped in front of Humphrey's door and leaned on the bell. The elderly woman was fitting a key into the flat opposite Humphrey's. I knew it was time to go. As I stepped towards the stairs, the older woman looked up. 'Oh, hello, Humphrey. Beautiful weather today, isn't it?'

'Uh,' I said, and the uniformed woman tapped my shoulder.

I turned around and she put a letter in my hand. 'You're served, sir.'

'I am not Humphrey Chow,' I said.

'There's really nothing to be afraid of,' she said with some exasperation. 'You're just needed as a witness. They do pay expenses, you know?'

I looked at the envelope. It bore the crest of the House of Commons. I shook my head. 'I'm really not . . .'

'This is your fourth summons, Mr. Chow,' she scolded. 'The subcommittee is in session right now and we have a courtesy car downstairs. Do you want to use it or not?'

I was conscious that the old neighbour who was responsible for this particular predicament had entered her flat and 'forgotten' to shut the door. I was even more conscious that any moment Amana would return. If I drew this out, she would become involved. I sighed and walked downstairs. The uniformed woman followed.

◆ ◆ ◆

SHE READ *Healthy Times* and offered me some of her chewing gum. My phone buzzed with Amana's desperate *Where are you?* I opened it up to reply, and the phone buzzed three times and died.

By the time we arrived at the venue of the Parliamentary subcommittee, I had read the summons carefully and understood that I was not under arrest, either as Humphrey, Nelson, Zanda, or Badu. I did not *need* to have gone with her. I could have answered her with a curt 'No thanks,' but I had been overawed by her uniform, the officialdom, and the rank illegality of my own situation. Yet compliance had a momentum that carried me through the corridors. It was not quite on the scale of the Apo complex at Abuja. They led me through an anonymous door, which opened into a small purpose-built chamber in session. My heart sank still further as a name badge was pinned on my shirt.

I was pressed onto a pew in the audience. The crest on my summons was replicated on the order of proceedings, *Parliamentary Sub-Committee on the Pharmaceutical Industry*. In the chairman's seat sat a dapper man with a handlebar moustache. The card before him read, 'Hon. Dr. Clem Harper, Sub-Committee Chairman.' He sat at the centre of an arched panel, with two committee persons to his right and three to his left. Facing the panel was the table for witnesses. One of them was testifying when I entered. Two bored men in baseball caps manned the TV camera in a well in the centre of the room.

I sat down, worrying about Amana. I steeled myself to rise, take a toilet break, and flee. Yet the longer I sat there, something about the process under way—and the stray barbs from Amana—imbued me with courage that would have become a Badu: I decided to throw off the Humphrey Chow misapprehension and claim asylum! Then I heard Humphrey's name on the public address, and I started to my feet with the men around me. By the time I was installed at the witness table with two others, the beast of my courage had bolted again.

'I see Mr. Chow is with us finally,' observed the chairman drily. He spoke in a stagy whisper that was more Corleone than parliamentary. I cleared my throat and was startled by the magnification of the microphone. 'Dr. Jim Stewart, Dr. Jan Brill, thank you for coming.'

The men beside me muttered with a little more composure into their microphones.

'We will take your submission first, Dr. Brill.'

The secretaries had placed new name cards before us. Dr. Brill's card identified him as 'Executive Chairman, Megatum GmbH.' He made an expert's presentation full of statistics from an electronic reader—without once removing his left thumb from its anchorage in a multicoloured suspender. My brain was too exercised by worrying over what I was going to say to pay much attention to what he was saying . . . then I heard the name Trevi Biotics Limited. I returned with a start to the present, but Dr. Brill was just wrapping up. Two members addressed respectful questions to him, which he fielded decorously, and the chairman turned to me. 'Mr. Chow?'

The moment had come. I was conscious of television cameras and of the fact that I was certainly the most casually dressed in the room. I was usually on the other side of the cameras, writing the news reports. It was definitely the height of foolishness to inform a UK Parliamentary subcommittee that I was a terrorist seeking asylum. Besides, the reference to Trevi had woken me up to the bigger issues at stake. 'What?' I prevaricated.

'You did get our invitation?' he asked.

I nodded my head. An irritable woman to his left removed a pair of spectacles and folded it into a tidy square, which she slotted away into a silver case, speaking all the while, faster than I'd ever heard a human speak before. 'Your case was thrown up as one of the most dramatic human-drug-test accidents in the last year, Mr. Chow. We are interested in the public health repercussions of these drug trials. Our terms of reference are wide, but you might want to advert your mind to . . .'

I stared.

The chairman smiled and intervened in patronisingly slow words. 'Do you have a perspective you want to share with this subcommittee, Mr. Chow?'

'I do have a perspective,' I said quietly, turning Humphrey Chow's name on its face. I stood up slowly. The rage in Tobin's letter was twenty-five years old, but cold rage was good for oratory, I found. I felt it stir slowly in me, consuming the fear. 'I can talk to you about a British drug trial in Kreektown, Nigeria.'

◆ ◆ ◆

1:05 p.m.

It was well past noon when I was finished in the enquiry. I stepped out of the hall, expecting at any moment to be stopped. At first I walked very fast, then I ran, outstripping the claque of journalists seeking private quotes, stopping only when I found the red sign of a tube station. I found a tube map and worked out the fastest connection home. I was about to catch the escalator underground when I saw the headlines of the evening papers: a state of emergency had been declared in Nigeria.

Sontik Republic had seceded.

I stopped in an internet café to read up about my hometown's new country.

◆ ◆ ◆

I GOT home at dusk, and Amana was nowhere in sight. I plugged in my phone and spent a troubled two hours, waiting for and dreading a knock at the same time. I had no idea what repercussion my impulsive speech at the subcommittee would have, but I had broken cover in the most public manner possible. I phoned her number over and over again, but it rang out. At 9:00 p.m. I left the room and travelled once more to Humphrey's house. She was nowhere in sight, and I rang my brother's bell with no expectation that he would open the door. I was not disappointed.

I was sick with worry. On the bus back, I decided I had lost the battle for independence and called Tobin Rani. It was a strange call in which I could say nothing about anything, and it was over in three minutes. But it was a start. I got into a darkened home at 10:00 p.m. I searched my pockets and found some coins—and the card Jan Brill had put in my hand after my presentation. Behind it he had written, *Shall we discuss our common interests over dinner perhaps?* I binned it and fed the meter some coins. I switched the television on. The Nigerian crisis was on the news, but I had Amana on my mind. I had my phone in my hand, trying to decide whether I dared phone the police. I shut my eyes to consider my dilemma.

FELIX FRASER

Meillerie | 13th January, 1986

We had been driving on Jan Brill's property for a few minutes and were still a mile from his chateau. This was usually the point at which the megalomaniac Dutchman delivered a self-adulatory version of the Euro Property Investment Guide, but he was clearly not in the mood today. He gunned the Bentley up the narrow road. Jan's answers to my questions were grunts, and the music was turned just high enough to make conversation uncomfortable. I wondered why he had come to get me at the train station, if he meant to spend the drive time glowering. Eventually we broke through the valley and drove parallel to the ridge. To the left, the breathtaking view that added hundreds of thousand of euros to the asking price of his estate. To the right, more of the same, the view broken by a stand of trees. The chateau appeared eventually, always a mild surprise. More castle than house, it stood cold, old, forbidding—until we passed through the portals and entered into a desperately modern, self-conscious atrium with all the intimacy of a basketball court.

Jan barrelled through, scattering the clot of staff in his way. They read his mood and wordlessly dispensed with the ceremonial hospitality I had enjoyed on my earlier visits. I followed him, rolling my chair down a portico and into the study. The door snatched itself shut behind me. The room's main window was north-facing, sacrificing some natural light for a view that more than compensated. He dropped into a chair and, setting his back against the view, glared at me.

'Just what's going on, Felix? First, you resign and fall off the face of the earth. Next, you are popping up at AGMs, playing the pity card on my directors! This is not the kind of job you can take a gap year from!'

'I'm back now, all right?'

'Well, it's not all right with me, if you don't mind! I'm entitled to some security. I do business with reliable partners.'

'So, do you want to sack me? Or just nag like any old wife?'

'Speaking of wives, how much of our business did Laura know? What could she have told her boyfriend?'

I paused. My hell was not going away, did not burn cooler with each passing year. Experience had taught me that rage made it worse, so I tried sarcasm. 'I wasn't in the room during their sex.'

Jan's glare sharpened. 'I know you're touchy, any man would be—but you were the one who hired his wife in the frontline. And I'm the CEO who has to decide whether Tobin Rani is a threat to my business plan.'

'I never shared off-balance-sheet transactions with Laura.'

'Could she have found out?'

I paused again. I had learned the lesson of convenient lies, and Jan was no fool. 'Yes.'

There was a long silence, in the course of which he flicked a drawing pin around his desk with a letter opener. 'They served Geneva on Friday.'

'Who served Geneva what?'

'Court papers. Some ambulance chasers are suing us in London. Not sure if they are working with Tobin. They'll probably serve Trevi this week.'

'Those villagers? You've got to be kidding.'

'They've got some bleeding-heart foreign NGOs jumping on the wagon. They're suing for a billion sterling.'

I began to laugh. Then I saw his face and broke off. 'That's ridiculous.'

'Well, forgive me if I don't share your amusement, but the prospect of a Megatum liquidation isn't comedy material.'

'A billion pounds is a joke.'

'Not by Western jury standards. That ethnic group is endangered. They belong in a museum or something, anywhere they can be kept alive forever. Think about that: a lifetime of treatment and twice-weekly dialysis for your victims. Plus punitive damages, compensation . . .'

I was silent, sobered.

'So lay it out for me. What are you going to do?'

I took a deep breath. 'It's a bad break; I'm not sure there's a way out.'

'Lay it out for me. Worst-case scenario. How many of them will die?'

'From what we know now, there is an eighty percent probability that everyone who was vaccinated will acculturate—'

'Spare me the bullshit. How many will die?'

'All of them.'

He did not blink. 'Time frame?'

I spread my hands. 'No way to be sure. My team was kicked out of Nigeria, so we have no more monitoring on the ground, but I'd say within five to twenty years.'

'That's a heck of a lot of variation there.'

'There are a heck of a lot of variables. In Kreektown conditions, they'll be dead in a couple of years. If they had access to teaching hospitals, they'd live longer. If they got the best medicine money can buy . . .' I shrugged.

He spun his chair away from me and looked out onto his valley. The beauty of the scene did nothing for his mood. 'Call this a vaccine? I'd take my chances with the virus!'

'It happens with the best! With Thalidomide . . .'

'Well, excuse me! I didn't realise we hired the Thalidomide professor!'

I began to reply, then I shut up. We had been down this street before. There was a reason why he was working himself up all over again. I folded my arms and waited.

'So what's the way out?' he asked.

'I don't know.'

'That's what I like to hear,' he said snidely, 'for a professor to confess those three lovely words of ignorance.' He leaned back and crossed his legs, holding my eyes in a glare. It wasn't just the Menai problem that was riling him. It was the way I had rolled up into the AGM three months back and his puppet directors had tossed his proposed director aside and postponed the board elections to qualify me. I had not expected to return to the board, but I wasn't just a director, I was chief executive of Trevi once again. To be fair, Jan Brill had not opposed my candidature, but this was our first one-on-one meeting since then. It was time to see whether the CEO of Trevi and the CEO of Megatum could agree on a way forward. 'This is what we are going to do,' he began.

I cleared my throat. 'How about some of your estate wine?'

◆ ◆ ◆

THE STEWARD had poured the wine, but Jan Brill had been talking for five minutes, and I just stared at it. 'This is crazy, Jan,' I whispered.

'It is survival. Right now, Bhopal is chipping a tombstone for Union Carbide. Menai won't do that for Megatum. We're gonna bite the bullet.'

I turned my joystick and rolled away, but the farthest I could go from Jan Brill was fifteen feet, up close to the only other window in the room, a small four-foot-square hatch that opened to the greenish blue runway shielded from the road by the designer stand of trees. A Lear jet sat at the near end, waiting, anxious to be in another of a half-dozen patches around the world where Jan Brill had his business hubs. Beyond the wings of the jet, the sun reflected off the surface of Lake Geneva.

I told myself I was not like this, driven by an insatiable greed. I had established it for myself, beyond all doubt, when Laura gave birth to the Negro bastards. I had liquidated all my assets into one card account, called up Raven, talked him into it, and legally lost everything I owned in two nights at the casinos, just to frustrate Laura's divorce lawyers. Plus, I had done it all without an XP9 high. I had a different type of passion, perhaps not so much passion as vanity, the same vanity that drove every scientist that ever lusted after fame in his field. But it had a limit. I took a deep breath and turned to him. 'I want no part of it.'

'I know.' He was speaking fast, avoiding my eyes. 'That's why I got this Dalminda fellow.'

'Dalminda? Who's he?'

'He's a footloose chap I use from time to time. He's burnt his boats in the West. He's game, that's all you need to know. He'll sting Tobin, he'll get close to him, gain his confidence, and find out what he knows about us; and if I sign the cheques, he's game to be planted in Nigeria . . .'

'Game for what? Does he know the details of your plan?'

'Don't take that tone with me!' he snapped. 'Just who do you think you are? Your hands are redder than mine! You made the vaccine! You injected them! I'm only trying to clean up your mess.'

'My "mess" was accidental, Jan. I was shaving years off drug-development time in the course of business and the public interest. This is planned genocide—'

'Don't play word games with me, Felix. Save that for your jury in heaven. Business or genocide, you gave them the death sentence. You were happy to use them as rhesus monkeys and now you're pulling conscience rank on me?'

'I never sat down and planned to kill anyone.'

'I did ask you for a way out.'

I rolled back slowly. I lowered my voice. 'There is another way.'

'Let's hear it.'

'Let's negotiate with them.'

He drained his wine glass. 'Negotiate with whom exactly? Those NGOs are sharks. The poor villagers are going to die anyway; guess who's going to be stuck with all that money?'

'If they sue in Nigeria, we can control the legal process, dictate the outcome, and set the level of damages awarded.'

'Great, but they have sued in London . . .'

'They haven't. Those people are villagers. They don't do Lagos; how much more London? Some do-gooders have sued for them. We can dummy up a Menai NGO of our own and fund it at arm's length. We can find a dozen compliant Menais to sign on. They'll sue in Nigeria, class action or whatever. We'll roll over, pay a fraction of our UK legal fees in damages, and that will be a bullet in the head of the London case . . .'

'Hmm. What kind of damages are you thinking?'

I shrugged. 'Last year, a high court in Lagos gave the equivalent of five hundred pounds in damages for an unlawful killing case. You do the numbers. Life is cheap in their courts. There's a judicial enquiry, under Justice Omakasa or something. We can spread the money around, judges, ministries . . . then, all your UK lawyers have to do is stall, until the Nigerian case is done.'

'Sounds too Perry Mason, Felix. Lawsuits take time. You've lost your spirit; maybe you should retire for good.'

'And you're a loose cannon. I'm a shareholder, and I don't appreciate the kind of political risks you're taking with my money and my company.'

'Look, we are working with a window of opportunity here. Your plan would close that window.'

My heart raced. 'What window? What opportunity?'

'They're all there in one place right now, sitting ducks. The health boffins are trying to spread them out into cities where dialysis machines are available. When that happens, the Dalminda option disappears.'

'Tell me about this Dalminda option.'

He took that for acquiescence and relaxed. I saw then that his foul mood had come from the fear that I would not go along with his plan.

'It's what I said: very basic, really. There are always crises in that neck of woods anyway; it's just a matter of spending some judicious pennies, like tossing weapons into a playground to ratchet up the body count. There's no smoking gun, no traceback . . .' He leaned over and pulled out a file from a cabinet recessed into the wall. Newspaper cuttings spilled out. Border clashes, armed robberies, family feuds, fuel riots, it went on and on. 'I'm talking attrition. Wildcat action. Nothing new to Nigeria. Nothing that wouldn't have happened without us.'

I cleared my throat. 'I understand they're rather peaceful people. There's no theft, little violence. There's never been a police station in the village. Ever.'

He was confused. 'What's that got to do with anything?'

I raised the file. 'This is irrelevant to the Menai problem. I boned up on their profile. They didn't fight in the Nigerian Civil War. They don't have feuds. If you toss guns into this particular playground, they might use it to make hoes.'

He laughed mirthlessly. 'Go back to your test tubes, Professor, and leave human nature to me.' He sat up and rubbed his hands briskly. Our meeting appeared to be over as far as he was concerned; he seemed anxious to be rid of me. He yawned and put a grey attaché case on the desk. He pushed it across. 'I got the eighteen-day notice. You need to build up your antidote numbers for . . . what?'

I stared helplessly. Every couple of months we used to meet up for the sort of transactions that could only happen face to face. But the climate had changed! 'You want to continue the MoD programme? Now?'

He waved his hands. 'What game did you come back to join? Monopoly?'

'But . . . the Menai case—'

'—ends the business of war? Right?' he sneered. 'Listen, the course of history was determined by the lab that first built the atomic bomb. Labs still control history. Germ power is nothing without control. We need antidotes . . .'

'The climate is wrong. The only history we can write now is the history of our own imprisonment.'

'Nonsense. Remember Agent Orange? Twelve million gallons of the chemical dumped on Vietnam, maiming and killing millions, but the American finger that pulled the trigger was also poisoned: millions were affected. Why? Inadequate, incompetent testing. You'll be a war hero, not a jailbird, Felix. Every death abroad saves thousands of lives at home.'

'Agent Orange was a sixties mistake. This is now.'

'If North Korea launches a germ pod now, your research will make you the hero of the free world. Focus on that. We'll take precautions, of course. We'll use the Dutch company—and you'll only monitor the tests remotely. You're tainted now, Professor. No more fieldwork for you. They'll send the field samples to your lab in—'

'No!'

He was exasperated. 'What's your problem now? You wrote the Blind Outsource Policy. These things are contracted years in advance. The out-breaks will happen. Somebody is out there as we speak, doing his work. We have no control over that. Now, will you do yours? Will you try to save lives or just cross your legs and play chicken?'

I was silent. He was saying all the right words. I knew why I had come back. After my foolishness at the casinos, I had taken a job at a French research institute and stuck at it for a couple of years before I quit. The research was uninspiring, the supervising chemists dinosaurs. That was when I realised that unless I controlled my own work I would have to retire from research altogether. Then the foolishness with Tobin Rani happened and I got myself a wheelchair. Raven's foresight had preserved my shares in Megatum and Trevi, and although I was appalled by Jan, consumer drug research was a bore. I could not deny my excitement at the possibility of trialling our labs' latest research on weaponised germs. The wheelchair had ended my years of fieldwork, but a good lab was a universe of its own. An outbreak was going to happen somewhere in the underpoliced half of the world within eighteen days, with a severity that would get even the liberal press to harass governments to authorise experimental drugs . . .

I took my glasses off and wiped them carefully. My fingers trembled, the consequence of twenty years of XP9 doping. Or the pure, elemental excitement of the scientist. I had used my own body for medical research as well. I was not doing to anyone something I wasn't ready to try on myself. My shaking hands decided me.

I reached for the case.

HUMPHREY CHOW

Abidjan | 14th April, 2005

The next morning we sat on a two-hour-long queue to see *le député de directeur* at SOCAR. He had a massive office at the Plateau and met us halfway between the door and his desk, by which time he had lost the official frown he reserved for business callers. He steered us to a comfortable suite of sofas. 'Bienvenue,' he said with a laugh and rang a small bell. 'So you are our runaway husband?'

'This is Izak,' she said as we shook hands.

'Humphrey Chow,' I supplemented, 'short story writer.'

'Surely you should know your husband's name!' roared our uncle Stephane. His laughter was explosive and infectious—except for those at the receiving end. Even Estelle was looking slightly miffed. Not yet regretting the visit, but getting there.

A uniformed messenger answered his bell and took our orders for soft drinks.

Estelle's second cousin had lately become his second wife. He was considered a good catch by the in-laws for his potential patronage value, and that was before his recent posting to Abidjan. This was Estelle's first opportunity to sample the quality of his connections. He was only six weeks old in his new office, but he had been speaking of himself in the plural—and the third person—since. He was expansive and willing to impress.

He asked after six relations by name and Estelle asked after eight. Fifteen minutes passed. Three telephone calls were taken and three declined. I became alarmed at being the cause of the haemorrhage of so much official time, but Estelle and Stephane were quite relaxed. He laughed again. 'This life is a war,' he observed as we sipped our drinks. 'So how can we help you today?'

That was Estelle's cue, and she took it. He looked at me with more interest when she was through. 'No wonder your accent is as blunt as an envelope opener,' he mused, kissing his mobile phone speculatively. I was encouraged to witness the reappearance of his serious frown. He thumbed the trackball on his phone impatiently. 'So who do we want right now? a very good psychiatrist, a very good neurologist, or a very good—'

'—policeman. A very good policeman.' Estelle sniffed, and I was startled to hear a sob break out from her. 'Someone has been trying to kill my husband, and we want to know why.'

The tears brought an edge of focus to his trackball thumb, and his frown became a gladiatorial sneer. 'And who is this assassin?'

'Dalminda Roco,' she asserted. I began to equivocate, but she stopped me with a look.

He procured the spelling of the name on a busy notepad. He called someone on the phone and asked after four acquaintances before relating the health of another five. Then he got down to the business at hand. The name Dalminda Roco was spelt and pronounced, as were Izak Baptiste and Humphrey Chow. After another round of acquaintance enquiries, he was back with us.

'Stephane Ousmane will get a response by evening,' he said. 'You must visit us tonight, we absolutely insist.'

◆ ◆ ◆

4:00 p.m.

Estelle had to buy some software for a new workstation she was setting up at the café, so we stopped at the Marche de Treichville. There was a tattoo parlour next door, and I wandered into it to pass the time. Then there was the moment of disaster when I turned to her from a DVD stall and accidentally called her 'Grace.' She took it well.

'Tell me about Grace,' she said, adding, 'and don't start slagging her off. I don't want you bad-mouthing me, either, to your third wife. How old is she?'

'She'll be thirty-eight in June. She was my agent, helped me publish my first book.' I paused, then said, 'Her mother was my psychiatrist as well. She was treating me when I first got in from Abidjan . . .'

'It was all business, then.' She grinned. 'Just like me.'

◆ ◆ ◆

5:10 p.m.

Stephane's wife, Bintou, was on hand, making it impossible to talk business. We were pressed into an impromptu barbecue with steaming bowls of kedjenou on the side. His visiting children seemed older than the new wife, but she acted older than her husband. The atmosphere was friendly, and the jokes were adult and rollicking.

At 6:20 p.m., a steward let in a senior uniformed policeman, who refused to meet my eyes. Stephane retrieved a little of the formality of the earlier day as he received his guest, introduced him around the company, and disappeared into a private study with him.

They were away for thirty minutes. When they emerged, it seemed that the policeman had shared some of his gravity with our host. Stephane saw off his guest and took Estelle and me into his study. It was a regular room but cramped in comparison with his office. His own chair was draped with a lion skin. As soon as I was seated, he spirited Estelle into yet another room.

They were gone for less than ten minutes, and she returned alone, shaken. 'We have to go now,' she whispered.

The whispers continued throughout the house. It was as though a storm had washed out the party atmosphere of the hour before. We said curt goodbyes, there were no greetings sent to aunts and nieces, and we were suddenly kerbside, waiting for a taxi on rue de Samba. I shivered in a wind pregnant with storm.

'Dee, what happened in there?'

'You can stop whispering now,' she said. 'They haven't heard back from Interpol on Dalminda Roco, but the local police have plenty on my husband! Guess who also thinks your amnesia is fake? You're prime suspect for the murder of a prisoner. He died the day you disappeared. During the war they had more pressing problems than the death of a prisoner, but things are settling down now and their file is still open.'

'*Bamou.*'

'Thank God you remember,' she said icily. She pulled some pictures from her bag, averting her eyes while I looked. 'What was the quarrel, Izak? They said it could only have been a drug quarrel. You were a drug lord on top of everything?'

'Of course not!'

'So he was your boyfriend? Are you like that, Izak?'

'Estelle!'

'Well, they said you were always alone with him in your office. You had your own code language. It was either business or love.'

'It was neither! He did this to himself, Dee, you've got to believe me. He got a letter from a sister, Rubi . . . I have a story based on it in the next Balding Wolf! He just jumped up and brained himself!'

'And suddenly you forgot me, forgot everything, and took off for a brand new life with a brand new wife in London? Izak! I'm not a fool!' The taxi pulled up, and she turned abruptly and walked towards it. When I started after her, she turned, a single, angry finger pointing at me. 'Don't follow me.'

'I'm innocent . . . Dee.'

'And don't call me that.'

'I am. I really am.'

'Guess what, you'll have to prove it. They're reopening the file. The old commandant's gone, and there's a new man in the desk. He'll look the other way tonight because of Uncle Stephane, but tomorrow, they're coming for you, and you'd better not be at my house.' She jerked the door open. She looked at me implacably. 'Goodbye, Izak.'

I returned her glare for a frozen moment. Then I asked quietly, 'Is it too much to ask? To love me unconditionally?'

It was the right thing to say. She paused for a moment, and when she entered the cab she did not shut the door. We did not talk through the journey home. The Hub was busy that night, but she seemed to drift above the work, finishing the installation on her workstation and road-testing it. Upstairs, I watched her undress and sit silently up in bed. We stayed that way for a while. We listened to the house settling down for the night. The nocturnal surfers were quieter than mice. Occasionally, we caught the rumble of conversation from the television in Mishael's room.

Presently, Mishael closed up shop. An unseasonably heavy rain had begun to fall, breaking the ardour of congregating mongrels. It covered the panes of the windows with a fine beadwork of water. It poured steadily for twenty minutes, then tapered off into a steady drizzle. Next door, a teenage girl and her father bailed water from a large drum, collecting roof runoff for household chores. Lightning flashed, streaking the sky momentarily, showing the chocolate bronze of their wet bodies.

I rose and followed her onto the deep balcony, where she had spread a thin mat. We sat on it, wrapped in separate blankets. A copy of *Balding Wolf* lay on the mat. A bored breeze fanned through the balcony, browsing the pages of Phil Begg's debut issue. My limbs slowly grew leaden. The tentative silence grew, became safe. She hugged herself. I sat inches away, but we did not touch. We were delicately strangers all over again.

'Unconditional love,' she whispered. 'How did you know exactly the right thing to say? During those years, I imagined all sorts of things . . . including . . . yes, terrible crimes, and all I thought was, Why didn't you just tell me . . . ? We could have got through *anything.* We were married just six months . . .'

I wiped away her tears. 'I didn't do it, Dee.'

'I believe you, but reading your story in tomorrow's *Balding Wolf* won't prove anything.'

'It will make things worse. I invented a . . . fictional explanation for the suicide . . .'

'You need to find out the truth for the police, for me . . .' She sighed. 'Where's this sister of his?'

'Back then, she lived in Kreektown, in Nigeria.'

'Guess where we're going tonight.'

I stared. From the bathroom, Mishael snorted.

'Is there any such thing as a private conversation in this house?'

He laughed, 'When you married my sister, you married me.'

♦ ♦ ♦

SHE WENT to pack, and I took Mishael aside. In a few minutes we had a strong alliance going. It was a heated argument: I was anxious to keep her safe but happy to lose the argument, but about 10:00 p.m. she caved in. That was when we spread a map on the table. The best way to miss the police dragnet was to head for the border that night. I would take a Kumasi bus at the crack of dawn, cross into Ghana, and fly into Abuja through Accra Airport on Friday. Mishael left to get a cab.

'I'm going to regret this,' she predicted.

'No, you're not.'

'You're going to the most populous country in Africa to look for one woman. You have one first name, and you don't have an address.'

'I know her hometown, and they are an endangered nation. Only a few hundred left. How difficult can that be?'

'That's a very small needle. It could take you forever. We should be together forever.'

'I won't put you on the line, Dee; people die around me. I'll be back, soon.' I kissed her slowly. It was all we had time for. 'And you,' I said, eventually, 'did you . . . remarry?'

She stiffened. 'I was wearing your ring, living with my brother, so that's not the question you meant to ask, was it?'

'No.' I said miserably. She waited, but I was silent.

'What if you forget me again?'

I undid a button to show the name tattooed on the base of my neck. It was still sore. 'I'll never forget you again, Dee.' She gave me a long, tremulous hug. I took her hand. Her fingers were wet and squiggly, live things with a nervous mind of their own, but I managed to slip her ring back on, just as the taxi pulled up outside.

'Wait,' she whispered, and ran downstairs, barefoot. A moment later, the taxi driver pulled away with a muffled oath, and I heard her shouting with her brother. It went on for a while, a good-natured sporting.

She came back into the room as the main door slammed downstairs. There was a mischievous grin on her face. 'You might lose your head in an accident,' she explained. 'There's a better way to help you remember.'

'. . . the taxi?'

'Crazy man. He wanted an arm and a leg. I've sent him off. Mishael's gone for another cab.'

She stopped in the centre of the room. She said, shyly, 'I warned him not to come back within an hour . . .'

I took her clumsily then, kissing her ears, her cheeks, her lips, wondering whether sixty minutes was enough for us to get to the bed.

ZANDA ATTURK

London | 15th April, 2005

When I opened my eyes again it was 6:00 a.m. and I was alone with an earnest weatherman on television.

I grabbed my coat and broke out of the room, trying the phone again as I went. I headed to the newsagents that Amana haunted. Her phone was dead now. The vendor had not seen her in two days. I began to tick off every place we had visited. I hadn't eaten in twenty-four hours, but I wasn't hungry. By the time I returned to Humphrey's house I had reached a personal nadir. I squatted on a stair, unable to bring myself to knock. The euphoria of my speech for the Menai nation had quite ebbed, and I was overwhelmed by a loneliness deeper than words. I climbed on a double-decker bus and went up onto the top deck. I sat there for hours while the bus went in and out of termini, until the bus pulled up in Victoria and two policemen came up to escort me off the bus.

When I got home the landlord was waiting. He was angry that I had left both radio and TV on all day. It had wrecked his siesta, he said. Also, as there were many other people wanting the room, did I want to pay for another week or what? I didn't exactly see the queues, but I told him I still had a weekend to run and would let him know on the morrow. I went up. There was no sign of Amana. Through spasms of hunger I could still think clearly, and I realised I would have to call the police. I read the papers: there were worse things that could happen to a lone woman in London than deportation as an illegal immigrant.

I pulled out my phone to make the call, and it slipped to the ground. I made no move to pick it up, as I listened to the radio news of the standoff between Miss Amana Udama Bentiy, first-ever female candidate for the throne of Nanga, and the kingmakers' choice, Elder Rantan.

A flood of relief swept through me, followed by blinding anger. It did not last. A vengeful hunger followed me downstairs to the fish 'n chips shop, where I tamed it with a meal in a paper bag. Then I glared at the man who had just taken my last currency note. My hunger had been replaced with a sick, complicated feeling in the pit of my stomach. This was exactly what I did not want to be: crippled by the disappearance of somebody from my life. So much for my clear emotional strategy. I had to return to Nigeria. I had to see her again, even at the risk of arrest and execution. There was just the small detail of a passport and a ticket home.

I phoned Freddie Jacks. 'About that job,' I told him. 'I've forgotten the question I had in mind.'

◆ ◆ ◆

Notes from the National Historian
Nigeria Archives, Abuja

15th April, 2005

A man in his mid-twenties, matching the description of the wanted vigilante Badu, was arrested by airport security on the 15th of April, 2005, upon debarking from an international flight into Lagos. He was travelling under an assumed name. He was easily identified by the 'Wanted' posters displayed in the airport building.

Log Two

SLEEPCATASTROPHES

Kreektown | June/July, 2003

Namalie Kama
Dede Orando
Emini Barde
Sama Adeda

Births
Nil

Extant Menai population: 120 (NPC estimates)

GABRIEL IDOWU

The Presidential Jet | 16th April, 2005

The president of the Federal Republic of Nigeria was crying, and his special assistant for protocol was not very happy about it. They were in the presidential jet on the last hour of a marathon flight to New York. The president had spent thirty minutes on his position paper for the meeting with President Bush, forty minutes on a telephone call to his daughter, and the last half hour on a magazine that was now causing him, surreptitiously, to dab his eye with a fold of his resplendent purple robe.

Dr. Idowu did not like that. Only the tough got anything from the cowboy in the White House. He wanted his president in a hard-hitting and savvy frame of mind, not in a soppy and sentimental one. He wondered how the dodgy-looking *Balding Wolf* magazine had found its way into the presidential space. It was not like Mr. President had walked past any newsstands lately. All it would take to start a scandal about the presidential hairline was a photograph of him reading the magazine.

Idowu picked up his copy of the position paper, circled a passage at random, and crossed the aisle. 'Your Excellency, sir,' he began.

'I want a national award for this writer.'

'Sir?' Idowu was flabbergasted.

'This man, he got it completely. Did you read his speech at the House of Commons? I want an honorary national award for him. Put him on the list.'

Idowu took the magazine proffered by his boss. He was still seething at the list Oga had sent down: he had suggested eight of his people and five had been bumped off. Idowu was scheming to revisit the list. 'He is Chinese!'

'Is that not amazing?' said the president, pressing the service bell. 'My own writers are disturbing me for contracts, and look at that: a Chinese! This story is the best memorial for those Menai people—may their souls rest in peace. What do you think?'

'An excellent idea, Your Excellency,' began Idowu cautiously, because the best way to antagonise Oga was to tell him his ideas were harebrained, 'although, of course, these Chinese . . . the politics of it . . .'

'What politics?'

'Well, you know . . .' Idowu floundered, but he was a history PhD, and even when he was floundering he still impressed. 'He might reject the award for political reasons . . . like Benjamin Zephaniah rejected the Queen's O.B.E. That would be quite embarrassing for Mr. President . . .'

'Tea,' said the president to his hostess. To his aide he made a face. 'That was a colonial O.B.E. This is my award.'

Idowu hesitated, wondering how far he could push this. 'But just last year, Chinua Achebe rejected your award—'

'Exactly.' Mr. President grinned broadly. 'So we'll give it to a Chinese writer. That will teach him a lesson. Foolish man.'

◆ ◆ ◆

TWO MINUTES later, the hostess was serving a three-course meal to an agreeable appetite. A hostess had once been reassigned for actually serving a cup of tea when 'tea' was requested. Dr. Idowu inputted 'Humphrey

Chow' onto the honours list on his laptop, and another of his contacts dropped off. That was too much money to refund. He decided to try again. Mealtimes were good for bedding in ideas. He crossed the aisle with the infernal magazine. 'Bush might be worried about the Chinese influence.'

'What Chinese influence?'

'You know, cropping up everywhere, oil contracts, construction contracts . . . and now, our honours lists . . .'

'Hmm.' Mr. President used the napkin delicately. 'What do you suggest?'

'Well, maybe a nice letter, with a decent cheque, something like that.'

'Excellent idea,' said the president sarcastically. Idowu flinched. It was not a good sign. 'For *your own* presidency.'

NANGA-NOMINEE AMANA

Ubesia | 16th April, 2005

I learned more about my mother's past in the previous two days than I had throughout my life with her. These long conversations with Dr. Maleek, Uncle Justin, and others who knew her at my age did not exactly transform my opinion of Eva Udama, but I would someday visit her grave and take flowers. I was thinking of Eva this morning when my chambermaid roused me with more urgent reasons to visit Abuja: she brought news of Badu's arrest. He was on trial for his life at a tribunal in the federal capital.

Zanda's arrest hit me like the bolt of a crossbow. My private quarrel with him evaporated. I saw how like my mother I was, after all: how my life could be twisted forever by one love affair gone bad. Uncle Justin arrived soon after for consultations that 'could not be postponed.' I balled the itinerary he had prepared for me in my palms.

'I'm sorry, Uncle Justin. Cancel my programme here. Zanda needs my personal attention in Abuja.'

'Impossible. Amana, your stool is *not* secure. You must meet with the chiefs ahead of the kingmakers—'

'This is more important.'

'You can't think like a girlfriend anymore! Your nation is in crisis! A secession is in progress! Leave Zanda to me, I'll do what I can. Focus on your nation. Your duties—'

'Uncle Justin . . .'

'Yes?'

'You could have brought Zanda back with me, spared us this trouble in Abuja . . . He was the one that led you to me.'

'That was your decision! You said he betrayed you, you—'

'I know. That was a lover's fury. It was personal then, and it is still personal now. Remember that visit you made to Ma'Calico's with Nanga Saul? I'm glad he did not delegate it! I would not have honoured his will, if he did. For thirty minutes he . . . held my hand. It made all the difference. I have to be in two places right now, and it is not hard to tell where I will go. There are roles that even a nanga cannot delegate: the duties of a parent to a child, of a wife to her husband . . .'

'You are not yet married, Amana.'

'Exactly, Uncle Justin,' I said softly. I pulled off the headdress and laid it on his shoulder. 'A sad and lonely nanga is no asset to her nation. Take charge here, Uncle Justin, I'll be back as soon as I can.'

He followed me to the door. 'There is war in the streets, Amana. How do you propose to get to the highway, to get to the airport?'

'It is time to find out if I am the warlord of the Sontik. If the people on the streets are my people!'

His lips settled in angry lines, and he raised his voice as I started back to my rooms. 'I cannot do what needs to be done! You may win a husband and lose a nation!'

I smiled at him as he stood in the doorway. I hoped it was the unperturbed-exterior smile. 'Your best is all I ask, Uncle Justin. If we all win our families, we can never lose our nation.'

I liked how I turned the tables on him, giving him one of those irritating pep talks with which he had tried to drown me since I arrived.

In my chambers I stripped off the rest of the ceremonial regalia of the nanga and scandalized my chambermaids by pulling on a jean skirt and jumper. I ordered up a chauffeur for one of my father's unmarked cars for the trip to the airport. I had to start thinking of them as my cars—but that would come. In the perpetual comparison of Nanga Saul and Nanga-Nominee Amana, I would always fall short. It would be my duty to make comparison irrelevant by making my own way.

By the time I got downstairs, Uncle Justin had arranged an escort of guardsmen. I left for the airport, worrying about Zanda and thinking on the father I barely knew, and on my first and only meeting with him.

ELDER RANTAN

Ubesia | 18th March, 2005

The Nanga's Residence sat on the last remaining acres of green in the heart of Ubesia, with Era Creek forming a natural boundary to the south. Inside the darkened bedroom lay Saul Bentiy, ailing traditional ruler of the Sontik, with Justin Bentiy, his cousin and seal bearer seated by the drip stand beside him.

When the nurse opened the door, Elder Rantan and three other elders filed solemnly in. They wore the ceremonial traditional gown of the male Sontik, which stopped several inches shy of the ankles. Around their shoulders sat their luxuriant togas.

They bowed stiffly and murmured, 'Che Nanga.'

'Greetings, my chiefs.'

Elder Rantan was irritated by Justin's presence, and by the plastic chairs arranged for them beside the Nanga's bed; they were too plebeian for a future Nanga. 'Open the curtains!' He ordered.

The nurse hesitated, but Saul Bentiy nodded and she pulled away one curtain to reveal a stretch of Era Creek. 'Leave us now,' said Saul Bentiy.

As the door closed behind her, Elder Drosa looked pointedly at Justin, voicing Elder Rantan's own opinion. 'I thought this was a meeting of the Throne Council. It is not for nothing that the Sontik say that the cousins of the Nanga are as far from the throne as the children of the peasants.'

'My cousin cannot aspire to the throne,' said the Nanga slowly, with just a little of his old fire. 'You cannot teach me the customs of my realm. But I might need my seal bearer before this night is done.'

Elder Rantan drew aside the other drape and lounged on the upholstered sill. Such rudeness would have been inconceivable when the Nanga was still truly alive. The entire south wall of the bedroom was a window, and Elder Rantan looked through it at the vast real estate that was the Nanga's official residence. The private marina stretched for a kilometre along the creek. In the distance were the mangrove shrouds of virgin creek country.

The sight of the luxury boats bobbing on the Nanga's private jetty brought an involuntary sneer to Elder Rantan's lips. The personal wealth of Nanga Saul would be a bridge too far, and Saul's girls could keep it. With the governor's patronage, Elder Rantan was no longer quite the destitute elder.

The prize was the Nanga stool itself, not to mention the potentially huge spin-off from the secession. The imminence of great things stirred Elder Rantan's blood, making him reckless. 'Why have you called us here, Nanga?'

'It is time to appoint a new nanga, Elders of Sontik.'

An involuntary sigh pulsed through the old men. 'You have not given us much choice, Nanga Saul,' said Elder Drosa softly, leaning against the bed.

'Children are from God,' replied the sick man.

'Nanga,' said Elder Rantan, 'do you have a son we do not know?' The other elders tensed at the insult. Saul Bentiy was silent, and the men looked at him, more with pity than apprehension. He shook his head, his thin smile still in place, and Elder Rantan continued dispassionately, 'That's a pity. It was the need to give his kingmakers a better choice that made the old emir of Antira desperate in his last days: marrying wives he couldn't have satisfied and having sons he couldn't have sired.'

Beside the Nanga, Justin Bentiy rose abruptly and walked out with an expressionless face, his fury apparent only from the report of the shutting door. Elder Bishop pursed his lips, and Elder Rantan wondered whether he also was offended by the insults. If so, he remained silent, too much of a pragmatist to antagonise the rising power in the kingdom. Already, Governor Obu had issued Elder Rantan with a limousine that was longer than Nanga Saul's.

'God has seen fit to take my sons before me,' said the Nanga quietly.

'Perhaps we can choose a nanga among your daughters, then,' suggested Elder Rantan, to genial laughter.

'There's no nanga among my daughters,' replied Nanga Saul. Five hundred years of Sontik history did not have the precedent of a female Nanga. They knew that none of the Nanga's daughters had the spirit to break that tradition. Lantanya ran his business well enough, but she did not have the steel to tame the contrary Sontik.

'Children are from God,' snapped Elder Gomes in his reedy voice. He was the secretary of the council and a sickly man whom his fellow elders had ceased to pity, for in the fifteen years that he had sat on the Sontik Traditional Council, despite his perpetual ailments, he had buried four other elders fitter than he was. 'We have a serious matter to hand. We are here to suggest a nanga. We have clear traditions when there is no candidate from the Nanga's loins.'

'Indeed,' said the Nanga. 'Who is the choice of your council?'

'Rantan,' Elder Gomes answered bluntly.

'You know my personal wishes.'

'We have gone this route before, Nanga,' said Elder Gomes. 'We are all pledged to Rantan. You know that when you join the fathers—may that day be far from us!—the kingmakers will choose anyway. It is a body in which we have great influence. Appoint a successor today and give some direction to the Sontik nation!'

The sick man closed his eyes. There was a long pause, in the course of which they feared he had fallen asleep. 'Will you give me a pledge, Rantan, before the other elders, that you will not support secession?'

'No,' said Rantan. He was not beyond lying but saw no reason to.

Nanga Saul opened his eyes. 'It is in God's hands, then. Draw up an appointment. I will sign it.'

A sigh passed through the old men. There was a rustle from Elder Gomes as he opened up the scroll that had been prepared months previously.

The Nanga sighed. 'You have vexed my seal bearer. Look for him; I cannot make an appointment without my seal.'

But Justin Bentiy was nowhere to be found. After twenty further minutes of milling around, the nurse returned with reinforcements: a starched sister who hailed from the Yoruba nation. In her eyes, the powerful Sontik elders were just another gaggle of old men. She drew the curtains shut and ushered them firmly out. They left the scroll unsigned on the table by the Nanga's bed.

'You could have done without the insults,' grumbled Elder Drosa, as they filed out. 'It would have been finished by now.'

'I'll come tomorrow and pick it up,' said Elder Rantan, 'I'll sack the peacock. He knows it. That's the first thing I'll do as nanga.'

JUSTIN BENTIY

Ubesia | 18th March, 2005

Justin Bentiy came in from an inner room as soon as the elders were gone. Still simmering with rage, he paced the length of the room.

'The seal,' said the Nanga quietly. He looked exhausted from his day, but evidently he wanted to get this distasteful assignment done with.

Justin walked across to the bed, taking a rolled leather pouch from his pocket. He drew up the bedside table on which the Nanga ate all his meals. He spread out the scroll, securing the ends to hold it flat.

'You heard everything?'

'Yes, Nanga.'

Justin lit the candle. He raised the end of the bed so that the Nanga was almost sitting up.

'It is unavoidable.'

'I know, Nanga.'

He angled the taper over the document and let a gob of red wax drip onto the bottom of the parchment. He gave the seal to the Nanga, who poised it over the molten wax.

'There will be war,' Justin said.

'I know.'

'Hundreds, thousands will die. Nigeria will fracture, your life's work . . .'

'I know. It is in God's hands now. It always was.' The Nanga brought the seal downwards. Justin held his bony hand millimetres from the wax. The hand stayed flaccid and limp, but new steel entered the thin voice. 'Justin, I'm not dead yet. Don't ever stand between me and my office again.'

Justin knelt by the bedside. He clutched his hands. He licked his lips. He whispered, 'Before this final office, I have a confession.'

'I'm listening.'

'The Nanga will forgive me for reminding him of the one woman that could comfort him after his wife died.'

The old man's eyes flicked to a wall panel with photographs. His hand opened and closed, trembling the drip line. 'Evarina Udama . . . Why do you speak of her now? She's almost thirty years dead.'

'No, Nanga. She only died three and a half years ago.'

An age passed. Two rheumy eyes glistened and Justin saw in the old man's eyes the irony of a nanga who thought he had ruled a Sontik kingdom of millions like a lion for decades, whereas he did not even, truly, rule his own household.

Nanga Saul smiled thinly. 'I'm listening.'

'Evarina was not a saint before she met you. There were some . . . men who tried to blackmail her with her past. They tried to use her as their snitch in your palace, and when she refused, threatened to publish, to scandalise your office . . .'

'That was why she killed herself?'

'That was why she tried to kill herself.'

'The newspapers said she died . . .'

'Indeed. Her body was never found. Many people saw her park her car and jump off the bridge, but a trucker found her down the river that evening. She was hidden in hospital in Lagos for six months, with Dr. Maleek's help.'

'Evarina Udama. For twenty-eight years you kept her away from me?'

'For twenty-five years, she kept herself away. From the Nanga and from the enemies of the Nanga.'

'You could have told me! You could have—'

'No, Nanga. If she showed up in the palace and did not betray you, there would have been pictures in the press that would have diminished the Nanga—and forced her out of the palace, anyway. She chose a small village near Abuja and disappeared. We thought it was for the best. Forgive me, Nanga, but we did what we had to do, to protect the Nanga, to preserve his authority. For twenty-five years. And we looked out for them, for you, as best we could. Not one day while she was alive did she or your daughter hunger . . .'

'My daughter?'

'Yes, Nanga, you have a daughter that you do not know. Evarina was pregnant when she jumped.'

There was a long silence in the room.

'You have proof of this?'

'I was there when Amana was born. There is no doubt about it.'

'. . . Amana. My mother's name.'

'She was named for your mother, but she has your spirit.' From his pocket he hastily pulled out another envelope, this one flat and thin. He pulled out a six-by-seven photograph and held it out to the traditional ruler. The woman in the picture was looking across the camera, wearing a bored look and the hint of a scowl. It was the best of dozens Justin's PA had taken over the years, and it was not a very flattering one.

'She is not . . .'

'. . . beautiful like Evarina, no. She has your spirit and charisma. And your leadership—in university she mobilised thousands of students to confront both the university administration and the Students' Union and shut down the university! Amana's beauty is mostly inside. She . . . she will make a better Nanga than any member of the council.'

'There cannot be a woman Nanga.' He sighed. 'Rantan will rule, but I will meet my daughter. Bring her here, now.'

Justin licked his lips. He wiped his face in a nervous gesture. 'You must understand, my Nanga. This woman has your spirit. She is the Lion of Sontik, but she loathes her father. If you must talk to her, she cannot yet know about you and her mother—'

'Why?'

'Your money sent her to jail.'

There was a look of utter loss on the old man's face. 'I think you have a lot to explain, Justin.'

'Three decades' worth,' he agreed.

'Where is she?'

'Kreektown.'

'Then I will see her from a distance. Take me there. Now!'

'My Nanga . . .'

'You have kept my daughter from me all her life. If you delay me one minute . . .'

'Nurse!' Justin shouted nervously. The door opened immediately. 'Prepare the wheelchair. The Nanga is going for a drive.'

ESTELLE BAPTISTE

Treichville | 17th April, 2005

'Oublie-le, tu ne peux plus rien pour lui maintenant.'

'Yes Mish. Like I forgot him these past two years.'

'We thought he was just an ordinary murderer, but no. He's a full-fledged terrorist!'

'He's ill.'

'And you don't need that kind of sickness in your life Estelle. It's hard enough.'

'Can you stop for one moment? I lost my soul when I met that man. Can you understand that?'

'I see that now. But let's move on from there. Jesu! How can a woman be so intelligent in everything and then so stupid in one thing!'

'Don't you talk to your elder sister like that!'

'Well, sorrrrry!'

'You promised me your war compensation, Mish. I need it now.'

'I promised it for your PhD, not for this madness.'

'I need it now, for travel, hotel, lawyers—'

'No!'

'Buy me out, then.'

'You want to throw away your whole life for this man?'

'Okay, I'm going on holiday, all right? Just buy me out. You've got the money in the bank. We both agreed we can't raise our families in the same house.'

'Nigeria is not a holiday destination! I won't do it!'

'You'll have me out of your hair.'

'I don't want you out of my hair. I love fighting you.'

'Now I know you hate me. You promised me this money, but when I really want it, you won't give it.'

'You always wondered why he disappeared. Now you know: he was a killer, a terrorist. You saw the pictures. You heard the evidence! What can you do for him?'

'Be there? Be his wife? It's called unconditional love.'

'No! Unmitigated disaster! And when he's shot by a firing squad? What will you do then?'

'He won't be. I'll get him a lawyer, I'll—'

'No!'

'Fine. I'll go to a loan shark. I'll put down my half of the business, and when I don't come back, you'll have a new partner.'

'Wait . . . I can't do it, Estelle, and I'll tell you why: you're proud. When you lose everything, you'll step in front of a bus rather than come back to sleep under my roof and admit you were wrong.'

'You're right, I'm proud, okay. But . . .'

'If it doesn't work out . . . if you lose everything, promise you'll call. Promise you'll come back home.'

'So you can rub my face in it?'

'Just promise.'

'It will work out, but I promise.'

'You crazy idiot.'

'You mean bastard.'

The siblings hugged for a long minute, then she ran to pack.

LYNN CHRISTIE

London | 20th April, 2005

Although Grace and I worked out of the same building and on the same floor, for my performance review we met at Stag Bistro, six minutes from the Liverpool Street tube station and ten minutes from our office. IMX was the nutter of the agency circuit. Company policy frowned on plastic bowls with apples and sandwiches. It was naff to do Tesco sandwiches in the tea room for lunch. The working lunch was the way to go. It also meant that the pounds piled on faster. Following Grace's lead, I ordered a wooden platter of rocket salad and ground some black pepper over it. Grace's omnipresent diary was by her platter, open at today, as she pointed a stick of celery at me and came straight to the point.

'Your desk is thinning out, Lynn.' She crunched off the end of her pointer. 'You aren't going to like what I'm going to write.'

'I know,' I said shortly. But I had worked long enough at IMX to know that Grace didn't have the authority to fire me. I went on the offensive. 'Do you want my resignation?'

'Hell, no. I just want to know what you plan to do about it. Any poaching in prospect?'

'I wish I had, Grace.'

'I know it's confidential, but you can trust me. If you land a platinum author it changes everything, and people *like* you, Lynn. Is there anything you can tell me, off the record?'

'Come on, Grace, I may have only ten writers, but they're high-maintenance bods. I've got my work cut out keeping them on the wagon. Give me another quarter.'

My ten writers were another reason why I was difficult to sack. I had recruited four of them and was on very good terms with all of them. There was no settled science about it, but I liked to think I could leave with most of my slate.

We chatted through lunch and had something to sign at the end of it. It was a good location: we managed to spot and exchange cards with a writer prospect, a *Guardian* cartoonist, and two tabloid reviewers, so maybe it wasn't such a barmy policy after all.

'Well,' she said, pulling up her handbag.

'About you and Humphrey.' I rolled my ring casually. 'It's not . . . done and dusted, is it?'

She made a face. 'Humphrey and I are *prehistoric* history. As for IMX and Humphrey, now, *that* is done and dusted.'

'What do you mean?'

She briskly opened her diary, which also did duty as a mobile filing system. She was the only agent in IMX who didn't do electronic diaries. She pulled out a standard author-dumping requisition—only it had Humphrey

Chow's name on top of it. She tapped her long red fingernail on Malcolm Frisbee's green signature dated the day before. IMX's chairman had to approve the disengagement of any author. This *was* a done deal. Humphrey Chow final accounts were probably being churned out as we spoke. There wasn't going to be an exit interview 'lunch' this time.

I was stunned. 'Why? What happened?'

'He's been on our books this long because of me.'

'Maybe he was, but he's paying his way just now. His *Balding Wolf* contract . . .'

'*Please.* Begg is anxious to pull the plug. He still feels bad you pulled that switch on him. And if Humphrey isn't on *Balding Wolf*, what's he got? Another year of maybe-someday?' She broke off to answer her phone, and it occurred to me that I had just spent the longest phone-free, pager-free meeting with Grace Meadows ever. She spent the next three minutes talking shorthand with her secretary, scratching out and making new entries in her diary. When she finished, she looked up at me vacantly. 'What was I saying?'

'Begg.'

'Yeah, Begg. Listen, Humphrey's gone AWOL. Shaun can't raise him on the phone. He made the last deadline by a whisker. Frankly, this team can do without that extra aggro.'

'All writers miss deadlines. That's the nature of our game—and he hasn't actually missed one yet.'

'He will. Consider this damage limitation. Did you hear about the last sighting of Humphrey, at Waterloo Station?'

'Well . . .'

'He was barefoot, dragging the hoarding from a Chinese takeaway shop. It cost PR plenty in the favour bank to keep that picture out of the *Mail*. He's on the way to a major breakdown, Lynn, if he's not there yet. This is in his best interest. The pressure can't do him any good.'

I was silent. They were hanging out Humphrey to dry. If IMX kept him on, *Balding Wolf* would not dare pull the plug. Plus, I had initialled three foreign language rights memos for Humphrey's stories before passing the account to Shaun. They would all go belly-up without the *Balding Wolf* deal. 'How could you?' I said quietly.

She glared at me coldly. 'You dumped him on Shaun yourself, didn't you?' It was out in the open now. 'And don't you dare suggest that I'm anything but professional in my dealings with our authors!'

She swung around and rose. I didn't offer to walk to the office with her.

◆ ◆ ◆

2:14 p.m.

Ida was working the mail cart when I got back in. The floor was still running at lunch strength, with five agents scattered over twenty-four desks. Grace Meadows was in her glass cubicle, on her telephone to Australia. I wasn't in a mood to work, but I opened the mail anyway. Ida had passed me a Humphrey Chow letter. Our secretaries hadn't caught up with the reassignment yet . . . I rose to take it over to Shaun, and the High Commission crest on the letter caught my eye. I hesitated, sat back down, and read the letter anyway. My heart began to race.

I phoned Humphrey Chow. All his numbers rang on and on, tripping over to voicemail. I disconnected and reflected for a moment, then I rose. I followed the dispatch trail up to Accounts and found Humphrey's requisition on Smith's desk. The youngster was busy outputting the final accounts. I settled for a photocopy.

I took the lift upstairs to the chairman's suite. Every quarter, Malcolm told the agency conference that his office was open to everyone who needed a one-on-one. Today I had the opportunity to test the boast. In my first agency, an associate could walk into a black-tie meeting and whisper into the senior partner's ear. Frisbee had a bank of personal assistants to preempt that exigency, and the earliest appointment I could secure was the chief's walk-to-the-car-park-chat, that evening.

I had an hour before the last courier deliveries of the day left IMX.

I slipped into the toilet. Withholding my number, I called the IMX switchboard on my mobile. I asked for the chairman's office.

'Malcolm Frisbee's office,' said June. 'How can I help you?'

'I am John Grisham's private secretary,' I lied breathlessly, pressing my nose bridge to nasalise my voice. 'Can I speak with Mr. Frisbee?'

'He's in a meeting. Could I call you back in—'

'Don't bother, John Grisham will *not* be free to be called back. Tell him it's sorted . . .'

'One minute, please . . .'

Within thirty seconds, I was speaking one-on-one with my chairman for only the third occasion that year. 'Hello,' he boomed. 'John Grisham?'

'*Jane,*' I said. 'This is Jane Grisham of the *Guardian*. Would you have the name of Humphrey Chow's new agency? We'd like comments on the breaking news of his major national award.'

'You are speaking to his agency.'

I allowed myself to sound confused. 'My sources said you had ended—'

'Not true,' snapped Malcolm Frisbee categorically.

'Perhaps we'll wait for your press release . . .'

'Within the hour,' he said.

'I'll monitor your website,' I said and hung up.

I paused in our open-air lounge and smoked a well-deserved cigarette. Instead of pinching it dead at the halfway point, I smoked the day's ration straight. Then, with the last drag, I blew a perfect smoke ring: a halo for Guardian Angel Lynn. Then I gave myself the treat of taking an unnecessary file into Grace's office to discuss, just to be there to see her face when the memo came down.

ESTELLE BAPTISTE

Abuja | 20th April, 2005

After this latest nightmare began, I had read everything I could find about Badu. I could not believe this was my husband. I was both afraid and excited.

I hated big countries.

In Abuja, there were people everywhere I turned. The airport was like a bus station; the bus station, a marketplace. And when I got to the tribunal on that first day, I had never seen that many people in my life; and they were all chanting, 'Badu! Badu!'

I made my way through the crowd to the car park, and there I found my lawyer waiting, as we agreed. He was not looking very happy with me.

'What's the matter?'

'There's a problem.' He took me through the police cordon. We walked down a wide corridor and through a library. Finally we stood in front of another lawyer and a short woman in a jean skirt, who had been waiting impatiently for us.

'What's the matter?' I asked again.

'We have an issue with representation,' said the other lawyer.

'Look, I don't speak law-English, what does that mean?'

'What it means,' explained my own lawyer, 'is that you ladies have employed two different law firms to represent Badu in your capacity as spouses. Now, you told me clearly that you are Badu's wife—and I believe you. And all I need is for you to prove to these . . .'

He saw my face and stopped. His voice softened, and he seemed to realise that he wasn't yet in court. 'Sorry, madam, but do you have your marriage certificate . . . ?' He trailed off.

'Do Nigerian women carry their marriage certificates around in their purses?'

'Listen . . .' began the other woman, but I'd had enough. This new wife was too young to be Grace Meadows. It seemed Izak had a wife for every country, and I had left my jurisdiction.

Mishael would never let me forget this. 'Just shut up,' I said and walked away.

They could have the bastard, sickness and all.

I heard my lawyer calling me, urgently. I supposed he would not want me to give in without a fight, with all those fees and television appearances at stake. I heard footsteps coming after me, and I ran. He could keep my deposit; no one would ever be able to say that they saw Estelle crying over Izak again. I ran all the way to the guest house where I had spent the night. When I stopped at the reception, she caught up with me. We stared at each other until my key arrived, but we were panting too heavily to attempt a conversation without looking silly.

I did not know how I looked, myself—after running like a witch overtaken by dawn through the streets of Abuja—but looking at this third wife, all I could think was that Izak was both mad and blind. I could not believe I had sold my business to pay the legal fees for this serial philanderer with such poor taste in women. I took my key without a word and walked upstairs. Why she followed me, I did not know. I had left Izak for her. If these Nigerian girls were willing to fight to the death over a penniless terrorist, I wondered what they would do over a tycoon.

My bed was unmade, as usual. The TV was on. The coverage was still on Badu. We sat on opposite sides of the bed, panting for several minutes. I was the first to recover. Or maybe I was simply the angrier one. 'Shouldn't you be at your husband's trial?' I snapped.

'We're not married.'

'Then at your boyfriend's trial! Or your lover's trial! Or . . .'

'That's what I was trying to tell you. I didn't realise he was married. Nothing's happened between us, okay? He was my friend and I did what friends do.'

I looked at her suspiciously. 'What do friends do?'

'I mean getting him a lawyer. But since you're his wife, and you're here, of course my lawyer will withdraw. I apologise for the mix-up.'

There was a tense silence in the hotel room. I was looking at every angle of every word. These Nigerians were dangerous. Of all the countries in Africa, why did Bamou's sister have to live in Nigeria?

'Your English sounds . . . French?' she asked.

'Ivorien.'

'When did you get married?'

'2002 . . .' Was this just idle conversation? Was she trying to deflect me? 'Are you saying there's *nothing* between you and him?'

'Nothing at all,' she said, but she was looking at an irrelevant picture high up on the wall. 'Absolutely nothing at all.' She stood up quickly. 'Now, I will go and tell my lawyer to withdraw.'

She walked quickly to the door—almost as quickly as I had run away from them at the tribunal. And I was not a child. I could swear that my husband had been deceiving this woman, the way he deceived Grace. But, suddenly, she was not walking quickly any more. She was standing, staring at the television, mumbling, 'Is that a yellow shirt?' She approached the television slowly. On TV, Izak was coming down from a Black Maria. He wore chains on his legs and wrists—and a yellow shirt and jeans. 'Is that a yellow shirt?' she asked again, louder this time. There was something in her eyes and voice that worried me. Izak was definitely not wearing a black blouse, and I was not sure why the colour of his shirt had suddenly become an issue. I found myself hoping she had not locked us in. I stood up and moved slowly towards the door myself. It was too late. She turned from the television and stared at me with crazed eyes. With a sinking heart, I realised that whatever madness was affecting Izak was infectious after all. After our hour of passion yesterday, only God knew when I would lose my own senses!

'What's your husband's name?' she asked.

'*What?*'

'What do you call him? What's his name?'

'Izak.'

She stared blankly.

'He also calls himself Humphrey Chow,' I added.

She smiled, and her face changed. She became a different person, and I saw how it was possible for a man to actually lose his head over her. She crossed the room in a leap. I raised my hands in self-defence, but she was only trying to embrace me. 'Did you know that Humphrey Chow has an identical twin brother?'

It was my turn to stare. She pointed at the TV. 'Do you recognise that tattoo on his neck?'

'That's my name.'

She nodded. 'That's your husband, no question. My boyfriend is his identical twin, Badu.'

'Boyfriend? I thought you said . . .'

She grinned mischievously. 'If you ever tell him I said "boyfriend," I'll kill you. Where's your stuff, Dee? You're family. You're moving out of here now.'

SLEEPCATASTROPHES

Kreektown | December, 2004

Clama Mfala
Daudi Mfala
Netia Mfala
Tima Amaga
Kali Situme
Apo Ulama

Births

Nil

Extant Menai population: 87 (NPC estimates)

ZANDA ATTURK

Ubesia | 21st April, 2005

The streets were still tense, with flying stones and eddying teargas. Her own courtiers were harried and nervous. Amana, though, exuded a calm, seemingly unfeigned composure. She seemed like someone born into the title and office. I felt achingly clumsy, uncomfortable. I smelled of palm oil from the barge that had smuggled me onto the jetty of the Nanga's

Residence. I had thought about this meeting over and over. None of my scenarios even came close. There was the *formality* of the first sight of her—when the very possibility that she could tarnish the stature of the office of Nanga by actually smiling at the sight of me, how much more rising to receive me, had become ridiculous in hindsight. Then there was the *processing* of her train into a private reception room and the coldness of her first words when we were finally alone. 'Your brother was arrested in your place. What are you going to do about it?'

It was as though nothing had happened. As though we hadn't last seen ourselves some days earlier in the stairwell of a Putney apartment block; as though she hadn't abandoned me in London and I hadn't travelled six thousand circuitous kilometres to see her. There were many things I wanted to say, but I had difficulty with the imperial clothes. I had not thought I would, but I had difficulty with the imposing throne. She should have used a regular chair for this private audience, but she did not. *She should have risen to greet me!* I stood there, like any other Sontik subject . . .

There were new truths about us that I'd discovered, on the plane flying into Lomé, on the barge chugging in through Era Creek. Yet, when I opened my mouth, I couldn't help but respond to her curtness. 'I could always turn myself in.' She stared levelly at me until I snapped, 'You aren't suggesting that, are you?'

'You couldn't have planned this better, could you? It beats killing him yourself. He will be executed, and the real Badu will be in the clear, free to live his life the way he wants.'

'You can't blame me for this! I didn't plan it!'

She glared her judgment. Something gave way inside me, and I turned to go.

'Zanda.' Pride crackled like static in her voice. It was not the cry of a moderating lover in the middle of an escalating quarrel. It was the call of imperium—but I was a lover, not a subject. I stormed out. The doors were ten-foot-high ironwood as thick as a trunk and quite unslammable. Outside, the emptiness surged again, and I recognised a battle greater than any Badu had ever fought.

I went back directly, glad for the crestfallen look I surprised on her face.

Her office was the elephant in the room. It was such a stretch, a cavernous, impersonal hall, two metres of her father's damask train on the floor between us. This boil would take some lancing. I walked across it. The ceremonial fan, the ceremonial spear, the ceremonial sword—I pushed them over. I could have skirted them, but it was important to lance that boil and I pushed them over . . . and then I was standing over her, her face now restored to imperial anger. Again, I was past caring. I had risked apprehension at the border posts, death on the streets; there was not much worse her courtiers could offer.

I took her by the upper arms and lifted her roughly.

'Are you crazy, Zanda?' but she was whispering. She could have been shouting for the palace guards. I felt a surge of adrenaline.

'Wrong question,' I whispered in return. Something still held me back. Her headgear. With it on, her resemblance to her father became uncanny. I still felt I was holding the Nanga, not Amana. I seized and pulled it off.

'You are *crazy*,' she said anxiously, her eyes darted to the entrance to her private hall.

'No, but I don't do royalty either.'

I kissed her then. She was rough at first, biting me quite hard, then I felt her giggle, and grip me, and I knew it was going to be all right then.

A noise disturbed us, and we turned around at the same time to see the distraught servitor with a tray of refreshments for me. There was a look of horror on her face. She turned and fled, quartered oranges falling in her wake. We broke apart with alacrity, swiftly restoring the insignia and regalia of the Nanga as best as we could.

◆ ◆ ◆

I TOOK a deep breath. 'You could have told me before you left. I was sick with worry.'

'I was on the chartered plane before I got over my fury with you, for keeping such a secret from me. He thought I hated him. I would have come before he died, known him as a dad . . . we could have planned it so much better. You never learn, do you?'

'I'm sorry. I have, now.'

She sighed and turned to more practical things. 'Your brother, Zanda.'

'*You* are the Nanga of the Sontik. What are you going to do about him?'

'I am only the Nanga here in the private residence. I am the dark horse candidate opposed by my own half sisters: the female, jailbird, illegitimate daughter candidate. All I have going for me is my father's will. My main rival is already entrenched in the palace court. He's the favourite of the governor-president, the favourite of the kingmakers—and they select tomorrow.'

'When does your DNA result come in?'

'There's no chance of it coming in on time.' She shrugged. 'And even if Nanga Saul himself were still alive, what could he do for the most wanted prisoner in Nigeria? I guess the real question, Zanda, is *what is Badu going to do?*'

I bit down on my retort and turned away. It was a question I asked myself also. Badu seemed a bottled spirit bled from the old Zanda, who had turned his back on his Menai roots. With Zanda out of denial, the 'spirit' of Badu had become diffused, like a laser beam spread out to light a room. Badu couldn't cut it any longer.

He couldn't do crazy anymore.

'I'll tell you what I can do,' she said. 'What I have done. Come.'

She swept off her cape, and we went deep into the lair of the Nanga. Away from the public rooms, the residence was more utilitarian, almost Spartan. She walked fast, and I followed, trying to come to terms with the eerie bows that were the automatic response of the courtiers and servitors we met. Her half sisters and the rest of the Sontik nation could wait for the kingmakers, but in here, where the last desire of Nanga Saul was law, she was unquestionably the Nanga. There was a half smile, an arch of the back, and a glide that was the Nanga. She was acting the part now, and I followed in her wake. We left the main house and crossed a lawn fringed with dwarf palms. I smelled the creek, heard the gulls of creek country cry. We approached a wooden chalet on two levels, with a spare, broad balcony running across the front of it. To the south, a jetty ran alongside the creek. We mounted to the first floor, and she knocked quietly. I sensed her excitement as a key turned in the lock. The door stood open. Her smile broke her court facade as she entered a room with an ancient sofa and a garrulous television. Across the room, a corridor opened into an alcove with an unmade bed. All this I took in as my eyes returned to rest on the nervous woman by the door. She was staring at me with wide-open eyes. 'Izak . . .' she gasped, her voice heavily French-accented.

'Zanda,' Amana corrected, with a proprietorial grin. 'Your husband's twin.'

I stared in some confusion. 'Grace?'

'No! You spend too much time on Google! This is Humphrey's *real* wife, Dee!'

I stared. Dee ran to me, ripped away my collar, and stared with horror at my neck. Then she backtracked with her hands cupped around her mouth. As she dissolved into tears she was moaning, 'Izak . . . Izak . . .' and I wondered who *that* was. Did Tobin have triplets after all? It didn't seem quite the scene Amana had planned, and she held the woman close. 'Don't worry,' she said, glaring at me. 'Humphrey will be out soon, Badu is here now.'

'Don't worry,' I said, confidently. 'He's Humphrey Chow. He was in England throughout. His alibi will be cast-iron—'

'Have you read the papers?' Amana asked with some exasperation. 'He hasn't said a word since he was picked up.'

'Why?'

'He's ill,' wept Dee, 'and, as to alibi, sometimes he doesn't even remember we're married.'

My fists tightened until my fingers began to ache. I turned away, avoiding Amana's eyes. It was my first realisation that my brother might die for my deeds. When I heard her footsteps following, I raised my hand. They stopped and I passed alone out onto the broad balcony. I stood there, against a stone totem, staring into the mangroves of creek country. I could not put my sense of loss into words. What was it about me that was so invested in aloneness? I thought of Humphrey in his cell, Tobin in the desert . . . Tume in his grave . . .

TUME ATTURK (ANCESTORMENAI)

Kreektown | 16th April, 1980

Night had fallen and Tume rose slowly, knee joints cracking from stiffness. He had lain motionless since early afternoon, passing a sleepless six hours with the resoluteness that had earned him the sobriquet 'Gentlebones.' When he could no longer see the Nomsoks' kitchen from his doorway he sat up and pushed his feet into boots. He left the house through the back door. Since deciding on the robbery, he had avoided using the front room, under which his mother lay. That decision itself had surprised him, in the speed with which his previous idea of himself had caved in to a biological need.

Only weeks had passed since he arrived, but he had found the corner of his universe that was attuned to his heartbeat. Yet as his money ran out, he fell into crushing want. His father's shop had allowed him to indulge the dreaminess of youth. Now, nothing insulated him from starvation. And it was especially galling, with Malian in the picture, the shy daughter of an Uromi trader, who had lately caught his eye.

His big idea was to kit out a restaurant for the oil workers that drove past Kreektown for Ubesia each day. All he needed was the capital to do so. The pressure of Malian's pregnancy focused his mind. He spent three days on his back in Raecha's house, digging deep for the desperation he needed. His inspiration was the 1975 coup that had brought General Murtala Mohammed to power. Soldiers had broken into Nigeria's State House and stolen power. They were toasted and feted across the world. In 1976, though, more soldiers, led by Lieutenant Colonel Dimka, tried to break in and failed. They were strung up and shot as bandits. With sudden clarity Tume realised that his breakthrough required a grievous and catastrophic wrongdoing. Afterwards he could settle into a rich and moral lifestyle.

He just had to make sure his originating act of banditry succeeded, like Murtala Mohammed's.

The robbery was a fiasco. The setting was the expressway. He had fallen in with two men from Ubesia, but he'd had no idea there were bullets in the pistols they had brandished as mere props. When the shots rang out, he had frozen. At the sight of blood he had abandoned the operation and fled three kilometres through the forest until he got to the Agui, where he threw up. Then he followed the river home.

It was difficult to reconcile the death and destruction he had caused only a few kilometres away with the drowsing village. He found himself wishing fervently that his two partners were dead. If they were caught they would bring the law to his door. He stripped and fell into bed.

He woke up, conscious that something was wrong. It was still dark, but his door stood open. There was an intruder, but he was not in the doorway. He turned his head slowly, and there, in Old Raecha's chair, was the oldest man in the world. His eyes were sunken but steely, as though his life was distilled in those orbs. He wore a cloth cap, and his entire body was encased in a thin red robe. Tume jumped to his feet.

'Mata . . . I did not hear you come in.'

The old man did not blink.

'I . . . I . . .' he faltered. The old man was an eerie presence in the room. Tume had seen the Mata just twice in his life: during the restoration festival that co-opted him into his ethnic nation, and during his mother's sleepcatastrophe. But he remembered his mother's teachings and stumbled into the kitchen, coming out with a pitcher and a cup. He poured for the old man. Minutes passed. Then the old man took the cup and raised it to his lips.

'Amis andgus.' The voice was more resonant than Tume remembered.

'Andgus ashen,' Tume said in response.

'All the wellbeinghealing in the world . . .'

'In this cup of water.'

The old man did not blink.

'In this gourd of water,' corrected Tume.

The old man drank deeply, Tume following suit. A little tension seeped out of the room.

'The sky covers the world like a skinwall, but it is a mirror.'

'Is it well, Mata?'

'Not for you, it isn't, not for your victims on the blackpath.'

Tume clenched his teeth. It was nothing supernatural, he told himself, nothing mystical. Something had gone wrong and they had fingered the stranger. It was deduction, and he only needed to keep mum to get through this. He shrugged. 'What?'

The old man stared. The minutes passed. Tume offered food, made conversation, but failed to evoke a reaction. In the twentieth minute, Mata Nimito spoke, simply, accusingly. 'I saw you.'

'Yes, like you saw the eclipse on the day we arrived.' The words were out as soon as he thought them; they had escaped him like a fart. Despite Wuida's efforts, Tume lacked the instinctual reverence the Menai had for their Mata. He had not grown up under the moral authority of the sage, and once the words were spoken, their aural stigma darkened Mata Nimito's eyes.

The Mata rose slowly, raising himself on his singate. His eyes were wells of pity. 'The eclipse was you, but the ancestors are wrong. For once. You are not worth saving; you are not one of us. Despite Raecha's bloodlife, you are not one of us. A lamb that foraged with goats cannot graze with sheep.' He walked to the door, ignoring the Menai ritual of leave-taking.

'You cannot drive me out the way you did my mother. This is my grandfather's house. I have rights.'

Mata Nimito turned and stumped his way back until he was standing before Tume. Defiantly, Tume refused to stand, and when the old man raised his hand he did not flinch. He had made corpses that night, and there was nothing this waif of a man could do, to make him flinch. He caught the strong whiff of age, of tawny leather, of mottled hide. Then the thin digits settled on his head, shifted, became comfortable, and then, blindingly, Tume thoughtfeltsaw himself bound and gagged and blinded, convulsing in a hail of bullets; he tasted blood as he chewed his own tongue. He had never tasted terror so liquidised, so forcefed him through clamped open mouth, and he thought he screamed his pain but the blinding fire of the sound only echoed in his skull . . . then the Mata's digits lifted and Tume was back in his Kreektown house, sitting defiantly before an ancient, red-robed antique on feet. Wondering at his stinging tongue and the alien taste of blood.

'I won't drive you out,' the old man said softly. He turned for the threshold once again, and this time, he did not pause there.

Tume rose, but his knees were so weak that he fell back down. The image had been so real, and it had connected powerfully with his unease the night before. He had known in his guts that it was his last operation, but he had not suspected it would be for such a terminal reason as a firing squad. He scrambled to his feet again and stumbled to the door. Mata Nimito had disappeared into the night. Tume felt an overwhelming desire to flee, but Malian was intricately knit to Kreektown, and he was irretrievably knit to her.

It was 3:20 a.m.

By 3:30 a.m. he was at the Mata's pavilion. He had to wait another twenty minutes before the old man arrived. There were no pleasantries, and the old man walked past into his pile of masonry, which was half recessed into the ground.

As Tume stood there, flashes of the horror of the evening's operation passed through his mind. He thought of Wuida, of Ahmed, and he thought of all those tales his mother had told him of the Mata. Presently the Mata emerged again, this time dressed in a white shift. He carried a sheath.

'What do you want, fartfaecal son of Wuida and the Fulani Trickster?'

Tume dropped wordlessly to his knees. He had never practised the ritual, but he knew it, inerrantly, in his bones. He leaned forward and kissed the Mata's feet. 'I want to belong.'

'You are not one of us.'

'The bloodlife of brotherhood is not always convenient.'

The Mata sighed grudgingly. 'Wuida taught you well.' Twenty minutes passed. Tume's time sense slowed further as he sank into a slow ebb of centuries. A roost of chickens clucked excitedly in the undergrowth to the south of the Mata's enclosure, as a nocturnal snake hunted eggs. 'Rise,' he commanded.

Tume rose. The place where the Mata's fingers had touched him throbbed. A swell of remorse swamped him, and he felt the sway of ancestors, he smelled Wuida, he smelled the Raecha that he had never known . . .

'Undress.'

'What?'

The Mata did not speak again. Clumsily, Tume stripped until he was standing naked, his clothes neatly balled at his feet. A cool breeze riffled the enclosure, stoking his gooseflesh. Mata Nimito glanced at him and shook his head again. 'If the ancestors were right, if your circumcisionhead and recital are spectacular, then you will serve me, and you will catch my sin-gate when I fall. I will pay enough for your needs but not for your greed, but you will learn.' He paused. 'Will you pay the price?'

Tume's heart began to pound. He nodded.

'You cannot make a sound,' said the Mata. 'It is the most painful thing you will ever feel, but you cannot make a sound.'

Tume nodded.

'It is more honourable to flee a circumcision,' mocked the Mata, softly, 'than to scream in the middle of one. Flee, coward.'

Tume shook his head.

'I will cut slowly,' warned the old man vindictively, 'painfully, for the souls that died at your hands tonight.'

Tume nodded. Hot tears coursed down his cheeks. He felt his disgrace rear, felt his mother's shamed gaze burn.

'And if the pitcher of your mind remains reprobate, I will pour no knowledge into it. You will live and die the Mata's cleaner, nothing more!'

A whisper. 'Yes, Mata.'

Mata Nimito unsheathed the knife and pulled out a bag of cotton strips.

◆ ◆ ◆

THE MILITARY policemen arrived just before 6:00 a.m. Their stony ser-geant had seen it all before, but he was still taken aback at the sight of a naked man with a red bandage around his penis and a lump of wood being whittled in his hand. The old man lay on his back, in a trance, his narrowed eyes trained on a drift of cirrus clouds in the lightening skies. Neither man responded to the sergeant's shouts, the old man because he couldn't, the young man because he dared not. The policemen searched the house and the environs with stabs of bright torchlight and were regrouping at the enclosure. Despite the early hour, Tume's body was irrigated by rivulets of sweat. His muscles vibrated in tiny, involuntary spasms, accentuated now in fear, as he bit down on his tongue and whittled away.

A hush fell on the military policemen as a senior officer entered the clearing. The sergeant hurried over.

'What's this?' barked the officer. 'Break time?'

'Their ritual, sir. One possible suspect, but he won't talk.'

'If he won't talk here, he'll talk in the station.'

By now the officer was standing before Tume. He studied the young man, and his frown grew dubious. He prodded Jonszer, who had been conscripted into the role of guide, 'How long has he been standing here?'

'Sometimes'—Jonszer shrugged, inscrutably—'he can be here two daynights . . . and if he talk before daybreak, he start again.'

There was silence as that sank in.

'What did he do?' asked the officer. 'Another man's wife?'

Jonszer shrugged again as the policemen picked and prodded over the curios in the Mata's pavilion, finding nothing more of interest. Minutes later, they drifted away, speculating on every possible crime except the obvious one.

The endurance test stretched on all day. By evening Tume's eyesight was a red-veined vision. His circumcisionhead stood impaled on a spike before him. His mind was ravaged by the gore and the ghosts he had made, and he lived for the next slaking of thirst from the long-armed gourd of the old man. As the daylight failed, the Mata's mananga struck up a tanda ma, and the menfolk donned their ceremonial dress sewn of Menai weavecloths and found the path to the pavilion. They inspected the circumcisionhead and took their places.

Snatches of the circumcision song they knew, but the spirit of the circumcised inspired its arrangement, and they listened raptly, knowing it was the Mata's own history he sang, and theirs. Once again, the spirit of the mananga possessed the Mata.

'*Amie Menai anduogu,*' he started, cuing the chorus with a note on the mananga.

'It is of Menai stock I sing,' they repeated.

He continued

> '*Near the spawn of Rawadi,*
> *is the plain of our Kantai,*
> *that was berth for the People*
> *for a generation and some*
> *in the days of Mata Doa.*'

> '*It is of Menai stock I sing.*'

> '*On the dawn of Indu day,*
> *the boys that would be men*
> *would climb and watch the sun clearing*
> *the eastern rump of Jabal Jinn.*
> *They would prime their knots of wood*
> *in the soakingpool as the sun*
> *went down the western rump of Jabal Jinn*

and darkness claimed the hills
that GodMenai gave the Menai.'

'It is of Menai stock I sing.'

'With the last fingers of light,
Mata Doa would circumcise each boy,
giving the bloodied blade to him.
Darkness can hide a face
but not a scream.
There were no screams that night.
Mata let blood down the line,
taking foreskin one by one.'

'It is of Menai stock I sing.'

'The Menai boys on the cusp of manhood
willed their trembling hands to still,
willed the blades that caused their pain
to become sixth fingers,
to carve, of the knot of wood,
a face to awe Mata.'

'It is of Menai stock I sing.'

'From night to dawn,
they carved from feel,
those Menai boys.
If they slept they did not snore,
if they cried they did not weep.
Their dreams were wood
Their nightmares were of wood.'

'It is of Menai stock I sing.'

'He viewed the heads, Mata Doa did,
that would henceforth sit on plinths
in household tynes.
"It is not spectacular, but it will do,"

he said, as he walked down, making men,
"It is not spectacular, but it will do,"
then he stood before the trembling Nimito
and said nothing.'

'It is of Menai stock I sing.'

'They scrambled home,
the Not-Spectaculars,
bursting with pain,
and pride.
They were walking wounded,
but men. They were new Menai men.'

'At the edge of the keep
Nimito's father watched.
He feared the worst.
A thousand boys had gone up Jabal Jinn
in the years of Mata Doa
and come down adequate.
Had Nimito carved so bad a face?
Would he spend another night on Jabal Jinn?
His father feared the worst.'

'It is of Menai stock I sing.'

'Nimito stayed seven months
and came down old and far away
dressed in a robe of red
and the tanned leather of a mountain buck.
His left earlobe was swollen
and a thin bone skewered it.
His father saw his royal bib and bowed.
His brothers saw his royal bib and bowed.
Menai saw his singateya,
a splitting image of the old Mata,
installed now on a singate the height of men,
and bowed.
"Mata is dead," Nimito announced.
"Long live Mata," they said.'

'It is of Menai stock I sing.'

'The burial took a month.
The anointing took another month.
It was time to move,
it was written in their blood—
to migrate on the death of an old Mata,
to follow a new Mata to found a new Menai,
but the new Mata was little Nimito.
It was hard not to see he had barely left his teens,
he had barely grown a beard.
And the Keep of Kantai
was the only home they knew.
They did not prepare,
they did not break camp.
they did not kill and skin and
smoke their smaller beasts.
They anointed Nimito Mata
and went back to their farms.'

'It is of Menai stock I sing.'

'Moons waxed and waned.
The new Mata left his mountain house
in the peak of Jabal Jinn
and toured and scoured
the land for a future home.
Then
fifteen hundred and twenty years after
the flight of the Crown Prince,
as my father counts the years,
the Mata's horn preceded dawn
and they heard the clear report.'

'It is of Menai stock I sing.'

'It was the signal they had feared,
and they stumbled angry from their homes
and stood, rooted,

at the sight of the single plume of smoke
that stained the skies of the dawning day;
it rose from the peak of Jabal Jinn.
Mata Nimito had burned his home
and led his goats down to the plains.
Mata had burned his home
and led his goats down, to the plains.'

'It is of Menai stock I sing.'

'There were times in the lives of men
to wonder what might have been
if such and such had not happened.
If the Mata's horn
had blown at noon
when fires boiled their lunches,
when the farms engaged the husbands . . .
but it had blown at dawn
when the spirits of the old Matas
had freshly communed with their souls . . .
before the quicksand of Kantai
had mired them afresh . . .'

'It is of Menai stock I sing.'

'By the time the young Mata arrived,
there were plumes of smoke from homes
whose owners lit the torch themselves,
there were asses piled and readied,
cattle strung and fed.
And the young crop was strafed, and
the old was taken in.
Yet there were many,
many who loved Kantai,
who did not want to leave,
but Exodus was a week in the making,
and when Menai flowed from Kantai
there was not one of her children left behind.'

'There was not one of her children left behind.'

The gathering cupped their hands in solemn applause as Mata Nimito fell silent. The older Menai spoke of Mata renditions that went on for five hours at a stretch, but this was his longest, most intense, performance in recent memory. They touched upraised palms in farewell and drifted home silently, salting away the song in memory.

♦ ♦ ♦

TUME WAS a quick study. He was particularly drawn to the mananga, and within six months it was no longer possible for the villagers to tell whether it was the old man playing or his young servant. He never did set up his restaurant. He soaked in the Mata's teachings and passed his memory tests, and he knew that given wisdom and the salt of the ancestors he would succeed the mata. Nine months passed and Tume married Malian, buried their child, built his own mananga, and was getting bookings to play at functions as far away as Sapele and Port Harcourt.

♦ ♦ ♦

THERE WAS a new excitement in Kreektown. Most evenings, when the mananga struck up they would listen in the village for the first ten minutes, to see whether it was a tune-up or a jam. If Tume was in the mood for a session, generally the village emptied towards Mata Nimito's enclosure. It was years since the Mata last had a successor. There was a time when Tobin Rani had been called to copy the ancient texts, when he may have thought he would be the choice, despite his bloodline. But Tobin soon loved Tume as a brother, and when he was called to fetch his twins in the Sudan, he came for the counsel of the Mata and travelled with Tume and Malian to Khartoum.

BADU

Ubesia | 22nd April, 2005

I woke slowly, knowing what I had to do. That certainty helped me to manage the fear that came with the knowledge. I found a heavy-duty torch in the main kitchen and an extra BL-5C phone battery. I left the chalet and walked down to the sweep of water where the outboard motors were moored. The guard was smoking a wrap while he twisted souvenir bicycles and motorcycles from copper wire. Every now and again the lantern flickered as a moth found the flame and perished. Three mosquito coils around him spread their sulphuric smell like a mantle. He pressed a toke on me, and I took a long, unaccustomed pull, so that when I finally stepped off the jetty I wasn't sure whether I was running on bravery or dope.

I did not know the waterway home. I had taken the ferry many times between Kreektown and Ubesia, but I had never boated there myself. Yet the stars were out, and despite the cloning waterways of creek country, there was never a chance of my getting lost.

The journey was up-creek against the current, with a wind behind me that made the surface of the water choppy. The outboard motor tore a sacrilegious hole in the silence of night. I tied up at the deserted Kreektown jetty, waiting a few minutes for the silence to return to its previous tenor. I sat there, bobbing on Agui Creek, allowing the memories to wash over me. Looking north from the creek, I could just make out the abandoned classrooms of Kreektown Secondary, my alma mater, which we all called Nimito's School. I stepped out onto the ferry stage.

It was now a true ghost town.

During that walk home, Badu seeped out of the urn in which he lived, licking his fury into the spaces of my life, burning away frivolities, firing the pliable clay of my weak vexes until it became a ceramic rage. An ugly bitterness soured my tongue, poisoning my anticipation of the future with the irremediable pain of my past. As I walked down those benighted streets I heard the laughter of my rested youth, heard Malian's warm banter, felt Tume's presence . . . and I heard all that in the creak of a door on a broken hinge swinging out of the way of errant breezes, saw all that in the desolate holes of windows, in the burnt-out homes, and in the feral dogs that growled from the windowsill of Ma'Bamou's house.

My rage was laser-thin again. Those two feet that walked Kreektown's ashen streets left deep footprints from the weight of nation on my shoulders. And yet, I was no longer *free* . . . Badu could no longer *do* without reservation. There were all the possibilities of Amana, all the responsibilities . . .

I walked into the Atturk house and stood in the threshold, in the darkness, breathing deeply, receiving. The rage of the Menai's crown prince filled me and I turned and exhaled it into Mata Nimito's skies. It was wide enough, deep enough for all the troubles of mankind. I fought the beast of Badu with the equanimity with which the ancient Nimito had faced the inevitable end: he was there again, the poetic spirit of the Mata, counselling peace to the vengeance of his crown princes. I fought until I was shaking with the fury of it. Then I turned, disconsolate, into the claustrophobic house.

It had not been torched. I snapped the light up and down, through the small house. I was alone with the rodents and bats that screeched through in flaps of night, snagging insects with each pass.

I stood silently, waiting. I had learned the hard way that memories fled when I searched actively for them. They would be nowhere in sight when I hunted desperately. When I reached out slowly, they were often there at hand. Without trying to remember, I turned around in the dark, around and around . . .

I went towards the well in the courtyard. Halfway there, I stopped. It was obvious and it was wrong. I sighed.

I went to the grave of the dead judge and dug up his phone once again to swap in the new battery pack. On my way out, I ran my hand over the jamb of the door; there, in the crevice where I used to hide my savings, was Badu's last video card. I smiled. It was time for Adevo to earn Patrick Suenu's money all over again.

I was hurrying after that. I ran to the jetty, jumped in the boat, and spun it around and roared out into the middle of the creek, gunning the throttle hard until I could feel the vibration right through my body, I sped through the mangroves until it opened up, the creek, with wider spans of skies and sweeps of water. As I neared Ubesia, I killed the engine and let the boat drift awhile. With steady hands, I thumbed on the phone and scrolled the call log to her number. I dialled.

She answered on the third ring. Her voice was thick with sleep, but there was no grogginess there. 'Who is this?'

'You know,' I said quietly. And waited, and waited, for her to run out of curses.

I had drifted a mile before she lost her voice. I had learnt far more about the Omakasa family than I cared to know.

Hoarsely, she demanded, 'Why are you calling me, you freak?'

'To give you a chance to . . . say what you've just said.'

'And that makes it better? Murderer, ease your conscience if you like, you'll still hang for it. I'll come and watch the trial—'

'I'm free,' I said casually. 'They got the wrong man.'

There was the faintest of pauses. 'I see. This call is to get your accomplice released! The effrontery! You take me for a fool? He'll hang, and they'll get you, too, now that I know you are still free.'

I shut my eyes. The boat creaked underneath me. I struggled to keep my voice indifferent.

'I don't have accomplices. Pitani knows that.'

'Pitani identified . . .'

'Pitani was wrong. They arrested a mentally ill British writer who has never been to Nigeria before. Google Humphrey Chow—and look, I really don't care. But when they hang him, you will also have blood on your hands . . . except that, unlike me, the blood will really be innocent blood.'

'Why did you call?'

'You want to bury your father's body?'

She was silent for an age while I drifted several yards down-creek.

'Listen, your father took a bribe and sentenced the Menai to extinction. I am not sorry I killed him, but I have nothing against you as a person, and some folks like a place to take flowers. Do you?'

'Yes,' she breathed.

'I'm sending Pitani's video out today. I'll include the location of the judge's body.' I paused. 'You won't hear from me again.'

'Wait!'

I waited. 'Hello?' I prompted eventually.

'Giving me a rotting body changes nothing,' she said, softly, with incandescent malice. 'You'll still burn in hell.'

I looked at the phone quietly. Then I put it to my ear again. 'In that case, I'll give your father your regards. You just try to save yourself.' I broke up the phone a final time, stowed the battery, and dropped the rest of it overboard. I was trembling under the weight of responsibility for the deeds of Badu, fighting the overwhelmingly seductive desire for schism, to bury him deep and slab over the memory of what he . . . of what *I* had done . . . But I had done just that for years—slabbed away my people and their fate, only to feed the venom to a Badu. I was not walking that path again. I let the viciousness of her rage wash through me. I sloughed that into the inky creek as well, as well as I could.

There was an agreeable aroma in the air, and I realised I was the object of curious scrutiny. I had drifted into a darkened grove whose giant trees locked fronds, like fingers, over my head. A line of huts built on stilts hugged the east bank of the creek. On the makeshift verandah of one of those huts a young man seared fingerlings on a wood fire. He had a small, ironic smile. '*Oyibo,* come chop,' he said.

I tied up my boat on a stilt and clambered carefully up to his balcony. The walls were thin. I did not know how many families were asleep, and it did not seem the time for conversation, but his name was Kofi Brass. And the fish was good. 'Fine boat,' he said enviously, tossing picked-over skeletons of fish into the creek. The fish were leftovers from his anaemic catch, and we took them fresh from the net beside him.

'Fine fish,' I said.

He was young, but he sat hunched over like an old man, his vest white and luminous in the light of the small fire. He put a thumb and little finger to his ear and mouth. Sympathetically, he asked, 'Your wife?'

I nodded, guardedly, wondering how much of my conversation he had overheard. He was about the age I was when I fled the delta. I wondered at his past. I wondered at his future . . . if Badu would leave him any . . .

It was 6:00 a.m.

NANGA-NOMINEE AMANA

Ubesia | 22nd April, 2005

I watched the boat come in, wondering who it bore: the coward I resented and loved, or the hero I feared and admired. I did not know whether to be cross or pleased. I had told him not to leave the estate; it was much too dangerous, with all the Badu flak flying . . . yet he had travelled all the way from Europe to me with a price on his head . . . and I knew I would not much care for a man who did as he was told, anyway. I watched him tie up and then climb the stairs that led up to the South Chalets. I dressed swiftly, folding my headdress into my bag. The traditional session for choosing the Nanga was being held that morning, and Justin would be waiting, with his judgmental eyes.

I opened the door and saw Lantanya. I did not know how long she had been standing there. The oldest of my half sisters was also the best educated of us, and she had led their tight-lipped but determined opposition to my appointment. Only her respect for Nanga Saul had kept her from filing a court action. Now she was holding the instruments I had signed the night before. 'What's this family trust nonsense?'

I sighed. 'I told Uncle Justin not to show you that until—'

'Uncle Justin does what he wants, even with Papa.'

'So. Will you do it?'

'Next time you want to bribe someone, give her something she doesn't already *own*. I have been running Papa's business for the last eight years.'

I shrugged. Softly I said, 'But you don't *own* it, Lantanya. Nanga Saul willed control to me.'

She smiled contemptuously at me and I swallowed. Before her, I had been unable to call him 'Papa.' The old resentment began to grow again.

'Why?' she asked. 'Why would you give control of the Nanga's haulage business to us, unless you know the DNA tests will come back negative?'

'That is why I told Uncle Justin not to give them to you now,' I said evenly, 'until I am undisputedly Nanga, until you can take them as a gift, not a bribe.'

She stared at me with intense, intelligent eyes. In the crook of her sneer, a tic jumped intermittently. I shut the door softly behind me. 'Besides, you've run it well for years.' She did not step aside as I tried to edge past her. There were half a dozen inches between us, and I stopped and locked eyes with her. 'And there's no point leading the Sontik, if I can't lead my own family.'

She was silent for a long time. The early dawn was still but for the swish-swish of a gardener scything a lawn. It was true that I had never missed having siblings: not until the reading of the will, when I stood in the same room with three grown half sisters in whom I saw uncanny fragments of me replicated and remixed. The last time, there had been so much distance, and I had despaired over the hard words and the mean emotions that swirled between us. This dawn, there were just those six inches, begging a truce of words. I put my arms around Lantanya, but I had misconstrued her involuntary proximity: I was hugging a statue with breasts of adamantine.

'You trade a wealth you cannot keep for a throne you cannot get,' she said quietly. 'My father may have been senile in his old age, but even a DNA result cannot make you my *sister*.' She turned away. At the head of the stairs, she paused. Her voice was measured and determined. 'There has never been a female nanga, ever. And if there were going to be one, it would have been me.'

In another moment I was alone in the corridor. I was angry, but only at myself. First, I was jumping all over Estelle in her Abuja hotel room—like a short-model Ma'Calico auditioning for a Big Brother house; now I was trying to cuddle up to the sitting CEO of the multinational Bentiy Haulage. I had to get my head back in gear. My name was Amana Udama, not Evarina Udama—and Ma'Calico was dead. No one was ever going to fall helplessly into the arc of my embrace. If I could keep one man there for all of his natural life, that was more than enough. For all the rest, I had to take care of business—in *businesslike* fashion. If love made the world go round, it was my duty to cure its dizzy spells.

ESTELLE BAPTISTE

Ubesia | 22nd April, 2005

I wrapped myself in self-pity, in a blanket, and watched him through the curtains where he squatted on the balcony. I kept repeating the refrain that had kept me sane through the previous day: *ThisisnotIzak. ThisisnotIzak.* It did not help. They were not the same person—Zanda's Nigerian accent broke the spell as soon as he opened his mouth—but I could not stop staring at him, and between my desire for him to be my husband and for my husband to be free, I was going crazy myself. In Abuja, Izak's trial was still going on, but with the state of emergency affecting flights and travel by road too dangerous, I could not get there.

I rose. I had to walk, run, get away.

I snatched a bag and a shawl and skittered to the door. I was out on the balcony, then on the stairs. I clattered down the first flight, onto the landing, and stopped. He had not moved. Something about his attitude stopped me, and I walked back slowly until I was standing between him and his view. His eyes were open and unseeing, blinking steadily. I sank slowly down until I was sitting on my heels, like him, at eye level. His face was scrubbed clean of emotion. I peered into his eyes, trying to see into that place where the brothers lost themselves.

I touched his face. I saw him slowly come back to himself. I saw the focus of the eyes seize my face, I saw the muscles of his face force a smile that did not reach his eyes. He swallowed, raised his brows, took my hand.

It was the closest I had ever been to this brother.

'Where were you?' I asked.

'What?'

'Just now. What were you seeing?'

'You think I'm crazy too?'

I grinned. 'I think you are . . . *passionnant* . . . too.'

He did not talk for a while. Then his eyes glazed a little. 'Maybe I should give myself up, Dee—'

'Please don't call me that.'

'Why? I thought . . .'

'It does something to me, when I hear it from you. Only Izak calls me that. And Amana now; she will not listen. My name is Estelle.'

'Estelle,' he said softly, which was almost as bad, 'I don't know what I would have done this morning . . . if . . .'

'If what?'

'A young lad invited me to share his breakfast. A part of me was going to kill him if—'

I laughed quickly. This was not the sort of confession I liked to hear. 'I've felt like killing Mishael—my brother—a thousand times.'

His smile disappeared. 'I've done more than feel.'

I squeezed his hand. Nervously. 'Did you kill him?'

He shook his head vigorously.

'Is that progress?'

His eyes glazed again. 'I couldn't kill Pitani either. The inspector general. I remember . . .' He took a deep breath. 'Don't worry about Humphrey, he'll be out soon. I've taken care of it.'

We looked down at the same time, at the bottom of the stairs. We had not heard her approach until her heel clicked the bottom step. He let my hand go. There was a cold smile on her face. 'The trial is on TV,' she said.

We stood slowly as she came upstairs. I had done nothing wrong, so why did I feel guilty?

He walked past her. 'I have a few things to sort out,' he said, just as coldly.

Then he was gone.

◆ ◆ ◆

WE WATCHED the trial in the small living room. She sat with arms folded, legs crossed, withdrawn. It was the third day of the trial at the special tribunal. The crowd was still outside, screaming, *Badu! Badu!* Inside the tribunal sat my husband, in the same chair, staring as blankly as his brother had, a few minutes earlier. Some policeman stood in the witness box, giving evidence. Suddenly I knew they were going to kill him. Mishael had been right. I hated this country, especially this woman who played the saint, only to act the adolescent because I held my brother-in-law's hand. I wished I had stayed in my hotel in Abuja, instead of coming to Ubesia to be trapped so far from Izak. I grabbed the blanket, entered the bedroom, and slammed the door against her. I fell on the bed. I piled the bedclothes over my face and wept.

Yet, deep inside, I *knew*. When I held his hand, I was wanting him to be Izak. I was wanting him as badly as I wanted Izak. *Mon dieu.* For years I had had to live without my husband . . . and now there were two of him? There ought to be an instruction manual on how to love one of twin brothers.

EX-ALHAJI QUDUS

Lagos | 22nd April, 2005

Ex-Alhaji Rasaq Qudus's current church was a converted warehouse, so its architecture was not quite cathedral. Yet the head pastor was nothing if not creative. A new facade had risen to disguise the original garage entrance. The street front now boasted massive roman pillars and a marbled porch that led into the church hall, which unfortunately still looked like a warehouse.

Qudus headed for the administrative offices built into the east wall for his appointment. Normally conscientious church workers hung around the television in the reception, watching Badu's second tape of Pitani's confession. Qudus had watched it four or five times already since its release that morning, but he still felt that surge of relief as he watched it again. He cut a rotund figure, the sort of physique that was flattered by voluminous robes. That afternoon he was wearing a yellow lace agbada, heavily perforated for ventilation, with black stones sequined into fish patterns.

Finally he was shown into the office of the head pastor, who did not appear to be looking forward to the meeting. 'What can I do for you today, brother?'

'You see . . .' began Qudus. He spoke as always, with glacial dignity, opening up gaps in his sentences long enough to make a cup of tea, and drink it. He wanted advice on which wives to send off and which one to keep. He had accumulated four spouses during his life as a Muslim. Now that he had converted to Christianity, he wanted to get his house in monogamous order.

The pastor's answer was straightforward.

Qudus did not like it. 'But MamaRisi is the oldest out of all of them,' he protested, 'and is only three girls that she born for me . . .'

'That is absolutely irrelevant to God!'

But Qudus hadn't finished his sentence. '. . . and she swears that, unless it is her dead body, she can never enter church . . . now, as for my number four . . .'

This time the pastor let him finish. The answer was no longer straightforward, and he promised to pray about it. The pastoral interview was over . . . but Ex-Alhaji Qudus did not rise. The unease that followed him in had not lifted, and it seemed that the weighty question of the four wives had been little more than a smokescreen.

The ex-alhaji pulled out his blue notebook—which housed a wealth of connections and the telephone numbers for godfathers and godsons, for business contacts and mistresses—and leafed absently through it. He did not need any contact details; it was a power gesture that he indulged regularly. 'Say, for example, that somebody's money, you know, his . . . business, his everything . . .'

'Yes?'

'Say, for example, that it is base on a big sin . . . you know, a *really* big sin . . . If that, then what?'

'What is this *really* big sin?'

Qudus laughed incredulously. 'I don't know! I'm not the person! I'm just asking!'

'It will depend on what,' said the pastor a trifle testily. If he desired to be more forthright, he did not give in to the temptation: Qudus was central to the construction of the church's true cathedral. 'Tell your friend to come for prayer and fasting. There's nothing beyond God.'

'That's what I told the man,' Qudus agreed. 'That's what I told him.'

♦ ♦ ♦

EX-ALHAJI RASAQ Qudus's first wife had never been in any real danger of divorce. Indeed, all his junior wives had been chosen and married into the family by MamaRisi. Apart from the fact that he practised his religion du jour with judicious utilitarian variations, she knew things about him that ensured her place in his heart till death parted them.

For a while it had served him to sit down at prayer with the Muslim colonels and majors of his acquaintance. That time had gone with their eviction from government. The president and his circles were now pretty Christian, but Qudus was loathe to strip himself of the alhaji title he had acquired at such cost, even if he had to put a prefix before it to fit into his new religion; and he certainly was not going to break up his family.

He did what he had to do and got on with business.

What did trouble him, though, was that original sin. It was such a vile memory that now, fifteen years on, it still woke him up in a cold sweat even in the chilliest harmattan season. The thought of it only had to cross his mind in a village meeting for him to hack up into his face towel. For all his pragmatism, his personal faith was a very real one. His personal God was not domiciled in any one mosque or warehouse church. He was powerful, with patrician aloofness, neutral to the little, crooked businesses that oiled His tithes and offerings but red-eyed and brutal on matters of Good and Evil.

Qudus had an Evil Secret, and one of these days he would find the guts to confess it to a pastor and have the horror of it prayed out of his life.

At the entrance of the church he glanced quickly around, pausing to allow two suspicious Rastafarians to walk far enough away. The Badu business had really gotten on his nerves. He had done business with both Omakasa and Pitani. When the second video ended without mentioning his name, it was like a personal deliverance from God Himself.

He had thought the nightmare would end with Badu's arrest, but the video had been released while the man was standing in the dock! Or perhaps there were now many Badus—which was much worse. He wondered whether to skip town, like his mentor Penaka Lee usually did at the first sign of trouble. Yet he had once been abroad, hadn't he? And that had been the most miserable week of his life, a week in which his blue book of connections was quite impotent. He now knew that there was no life for him outside his beloved Nigeria, where anything could be made to happen. Slowly, he realised that he had only one real option: to go public himself sooner rather than later, or to be dragged public by and by.

Going public! It had a resoundingly cathartic ring to it. Going to church so regularly without having something sink in was impossible, and that Christian formula of sin/confession/forgiveness was persuasive. It had bleached the inky blackness of South Africa's apartheid via truth and reconciliation. It had even cleansed the travesty of the Rwandan genocide. Of course it was out of the question with a sin as noxious as his own Original Sin . . . but in the matter of the submachine guns . . . he looked carefully around before hurrying across the car park to his car . . . in the matter of Daniel Sheldon, and the arms he had helped to distribute in Kreektown, it might simply be a matter of going public early and becoming a heroic accomplice who outed more reprobate criminals, or waiting to be outed by a Badu victim—or worse still, becoming a Badu victim himself! He glanced quickly around his car, wiped his hands carefully with his face towel, and balled it into a pocket.

Then he pulled it out and folded it carefully, as his mentor Penaka Lee always managed to do with his filthy handkerchief, even when he was hiding in the boot of Qudus's car.

After all, what was the worst that could happen? It could never be as bad as becoming a houseboy again. He eased himself into the Ikeja traffic and tried not to remember his houseboy days.

PENAKA LEE

Lagos | 21st April, 1990

'Qudus!'

'Sir!'

Penaka Lee tried hard to not to laugh. He told his estate managers that he wanted stupid but clean houseboys in his homes around the world, but this was ridiculous. Not only did Qudus woefully fail his exams, he looked like someone who failed exams woefully. And with his great stomach he also looked anything but smart. Yet Penaka could afford to be generous. The man was in his late thirties and came with the house.

'What's that scrap heap in the carport?'

Qudus sidled closer to Penaka Lee. There was a proud, oily grin building on his face, and from behind him he produced a cheap bottle of gin with an aged and mottled label. 'Is mine, sir.'

'And what exactly is it doing there?'

He raised the gin with a nervous smile. 'Is for you to bless it, sir.'

'Sorry?'

'Is a big Nigerian custom, sir. Is my first car. Is just for you to bless it.'

Penaka Lee smiled his displeasure. 'Remove it immediately,' he said, without heat, and walked upstairs. From his bedroom he watched the deflated houseboy drive the Peugeot, which had to be at least thirty-five years old as well, out into the street. There had to be something wrong with his PR if things like this could happen, he thought. He could indulge silly local customs in the course of wooing a prospect . . . but for a houseboy? Preposterous. He shook his head and turned to other matters.

The Nigerian project was coming to a head.

◆ ◆ ◆

IT WAS the perfect time for a coup. He had found the right soldiers with the bloody-mindedness to take it on, and the right business team. The country was ready—the military dictatorship was unpopular, had more than outstayed its welcome. A coup would literally be greeted with dancing in the streets. He had put down some money for Corus. It was the group's most ambitious project since the death of their previous leader, Lord Risborough, and Penaka was anxious to pull it off. Nigeria was a big prize—to get a walk-in pass to the office of the president. And it was very doable. He knew it.

He only had to talk some sense into the strategists of the coup plot. They had planned to announce the coup by excising the northern states from the federation. The northern states had the largest numbers at all levels of the army, and he knew that such addled thinking would ensure that the excised states fought the coup right to the wire. He was trying to get them to delay the 'remapping' of Nigeria until the takeover was successful, but it was tough going. Yet there was still time to change their minds: D-Day was weeks off. They still had some battalions to seduce into the plot.

He had scheduled to leave the country by the weekend. There was no sense in taking risks. As he soaked in the bath, he made his calls around the world. An hour later, he turned his attentions back to his Nigerian affairs. He called his local manager and told him to sack Qudus immediately. A stupid houseboy would not understand Penaka's mail, even if he read it, but a resentful one could spit in his food. He liked to keep his life simple like that.

'Why, sir? Did he steal? Did he—'

'Do you need a reason?'

'No, sir, but . . .'

'Good.'

He replaced the phone and fell asleep in his bath.

◆ ◆ ◆

QUDUS RECEIVED his termination letter and reacted most unpredictably. Penaka had prided himself with his experience of the world, but Qudus redefined the word obsequious. He was still volubly prostrate on the carpet when the commercial service of the radio trailed off into martial music and a rambling voice announced a 'new government.' Qudus got off the carpet as Penaka collapsed onto it.

Penaka's telephone shrilled. It was his coup contact: the plot had leaked, a prospect had tried to go to the government, and the plotters had been forced into a preemptive strike. Penaka heard out the interminable radio broadcast. The fools had stuck to their plan to excise northern Nigeria from the federation. He knew there and then that the coup was doomed. It was impossible to hide his involvement from his houseboy, but by then that was the least of his problems. Rockets began to explode from the direction of the presidential barracks. He was only three miles away from the barracks and six hundred metres from Flag Staff House. The two generals who ran the country were supposed to be killed at those locations, and if the coup failed he would be the first to be pulled into the net of retribution. He called the airport, and although commercial flights were cancelled, he put his pilot on standby.

He grabbed a briefcase and bolted outdoors. His drivers and the rest of his staff had fled. Penaka got behind the wheel and swung the limousine through his unmanned gates. Outside the house, the shells exploding at Dodan Barracks on the outskirts of Ikoyi became more threatening. He saw a military checkpoint ahead and lost his nerve. Swerving into a side road, he barrelled down empty streets, heart thumping, and doubled back to his house. Qudus had brought his ancient car back to the house for safety, parking it right in the carport.

Penaka Lee stole upstairs without a word. The phone lines had been cut, and he spent the night on his satellite phone, calling international contacts. They confirmed his intelligence. Dozens had died in the attempted putsch, but the coup plot was broken. The government was in control and the plotters were being rounded up by the minute, undergoing interrogations. There could be no help for him if he was taken. The military police arrived with dawn. He heard them only because he had been wide awake all night. They parked on the street, swarmed over the fence, and were crossing the lawn before he was able to tumble down the stairs. He crept through the laundry chute and disappeared under the chicken wire covered with passionflower vines in the back garden.

The soldiers set up guard in the house and made themselves at home. He heard their voices as they drank his beer and wine and sometimes saw their uniforms through breaks in the lush foliage. He knew it was only a matter of time before he was caught. He sat there in his urine and sweat, embedded in the manure of his garden, and only the certainty of the death penalty for coup plotters stopped him from bringing forward the inevitable moment of discovery.

As evening fell, Qudus brought his car alongside the servants' quarters and loaded it up with personal effects. Then he opened the trunk and motioned to his former master, who crawled in on all fours.

Qudus lived with his wife and three daughters in a large room in a riverine Lagos slum. It was a near-bestial life of unimaginable squalor. Only the fear of the death sentence kept Penaka there, listening to Qudus's bogus plans of disingenuous cross-border escapes. Penaka spent four days in one of Qudus's castoff, moth-eaten garments, listening to his lifetime ambition of becoming a managing director of a manufacturing company. It was inconceivable that any jail could offer worse conditions.

Eventually, the penny dropped and Penaka promised to make Qudus's ambition come true. Things started to move immediately thereafter. To seal the deal, Qudus drove his children out of the room, gave his wife a beat-up Polaroid camera, and tugged at his roped trousers, which promptly fell down his spindly legs. 'You have to kneel down and suck, for insurance,' he told his former boss. When Penaka, dumbfounded, only stared, he grumbled, 'Me myself, I hate it more than you.'

In the event, it did not seem like he did.

That same evening, after the worst moment of his life, bar none, Penaka Lee was back in the trunk of the scrap heap he had declined to bless. He crossed the Nigerian border at Seme and caught a flight to Europe from Accra's Kotoka International Airport. He was ensconced in his accustomed luxuries in a matter of hours and developed an amnesia concerning the occurrences in the immediate aftermath of the Orkar coup plot, an amnesia that was cured by a BBC broadcast on the execution of forty-one of his fellow coup plotters in Nigeria. He had caught that broadcast at a board meeting in Lausanne and had dashed to the toilet to throw up. Soon after, a photo album with only one picture arrived from Lagos. That same week, he set up a front company for his former houseboy's business in Nigeria, although he did not dare return, himself, until after the death of the begoggled General Abacha in June 1998 and the return to democracy the year after.

◆ ◆ ◆

THAT LEG up was all that Qudus had needed. By the time Penaka visited Nigeria again in 1999, Qudus was much larger than the sum of his shares in the ceramic factory. Although he was only functionally literate, he was also invested with a serpentine cunning. He did not know the first thing about balance sheets or equity assets, but it was not possible to dupe him twice. And one thing he knew better than anyone else was how to look a tenders officer straight in the eye and ask, with sleepy-eyed mischief, 'Okay. . . so how much do you want?'

GABRIEL IDOWU

Abuja | 22nd April, 2005

Dr. Idowu hurried through the corridors of Aso Rock with his file, in search of his president, finally tracking down his quarry in a state lounge with the wreck of a buffet in the background. Although there was no meal in progress and the president was consulting with his advisers, Idowu's frown deepened: he did not approve of briefings on national emergencies conducted in dining accommodations. The large television was overloud, and the company was motley, but there was no question of attempting to relocate the briefing.

Besides, he had other, more pressing issues for the president's ears. Unfortunately, there were some three dozen other aides, ministers, party chiefs, and waiters in the room, all of whom took rather too literally the challenge of getting close to the ears of the president. Dr. Idowu sighed long-sufferingly, wrapped his starched robes closer around him, and pressed forward.

Chief Eleshin was raging, 'We're back on CNN!'

He was assistant deputy director general in the Office of Presidential Remediations. He did not often sit in audience with the president himself, and he was not sleeping on his opportunity. 'Your Excellency recommissioned a billion-dollar refinery last year, and nothing! Now there's a small riot in Sontik State and we are headline news! Racist news!'

'Change the channel!'

'Yes, change the channel!'

Halfway to his destination, Dr. Idowu sighed in exasperation. Perhaps they were going to vote on it.

Someone changed the channel to a local station, and a rapt silence fell on the room as Charles Pitani's naked top filled the TV screen. It was the dreaded second video. Pitani was kneeling in what appeared to be a poultry cage. His eyes were teary and scared, and he was speaking in a shrill wheedle most unlike the authoritarian bass the Nigerian public was used to. Pitani spoke for fifteen minutes. As his confession progressed, handkerchiefs were used liberally, and one after the other, six of the president's aides and ministers abruptly left for the toilet and failed to return. Sure enough, Pitani went on to mention their names and deals moments after they left.

The confession ended, and the survivors in the room sighed as one. 'Is this not terrible?' asked Mr. President, looking around, his face a study in betrayal. 'I am surrounded by crooks!'

They nodded gravely, scandalised by the Disgraced Six; then they returned to national security discussions.

◆ ◆ ◆

'WAIT,' SAID the president, as a TV report caught his eye. President Bush was in his garden, addressing a press conference with the prime minister of Tuvalu.

'Look at that!' roared an apoplectic Chief Eleshin. 'Mister President has a reception in the White House with George Bush and nothing! Now, look at that! Prime minister of *Tuvalu! Where* is Tuvalu?'

The president looked at Eleshin irritably. He did not say anything, but Chief Eleshin fell silent. The key to a long, sycophantic career was never to sound sycophantic. Striking the right balance was always a problem, and he had clearly fallen overboard. Another invitation to dine was now most unlikely.

'Let's see,' said the president modestly, to a silent room. 'Maybe he will mention our conversation.'

President Bush declared, 'The challenge facing the free nations of the world today was captured in these words of the American poet Robert Frost:

> *"Some say the world will end in fire,*
> *Some say in ice.*
> *From what I've tasted of desire*
> *I hold with those who favor fire."*

'The challenge before today's summit of island nations is to fashion a solution that can accommodate progress while avoiding the destruction of our precious planet . . .'

'Take off the volume,' commanded the president, bored, and the hub-bub of security consultations returned to the room. The war briefings were hindered, however, by the absence of a critical brigade commander on an extended toilet break. Moments later, the president frowned. 'Ofo, am I missing something?' His military assistant was still gaping at the television.

Ofo started, 'No, Your Excellency, I was just . . . it was nothing.' The volume on the TV set rose a notch with the return of presidential attention. 'I like Robert Frost myself, that's all' he explained. 'That quotation was the beginning of the poem "Fire and Ice," that's all.'

'Another soldier-poet like my old friend Mamman Vatsa,' joked the president. 'I hope you're not a coup plotter like him,' The room broke up in explosive laughter at the very idea of another Nigerian coup plotter after Sani Abacha. It was just the icebreaker required after the tension of the second Badu video. As he wiped his tears, the president asked, riding the crest of the successful joke, 'I liked that poem, too; how does it end?'

Ofo took a deep breath. His voice was hoarse.

'But if it had to perish twice,
I think I know enough of hate
To say that for destruction ice
Is also great
And would suffice.'

'It's not as sweet as George Bush's own,' sniffed the party chief, who detested all military men with a passion.

'Yes,' agreed Eleshin, 'American poems need American voices to sound sweet.'

◆ ◆ ◆

DR. IDOWU took advantage of a senior national security adviser's toilet break and attained his objective. 'Your Excellency, about that award list . . .'

'Award list? At a time like this? Didn't you hear of the secession?'

Idowu ignored the warning burr; he was sure of his material. 'There's still time to drop the Humphrey Chow man, Your Excellency, to prevent a national embarrassment. He's not Chinese, he's very, *very* Nigerian.' Idowu opened his file. The information was graphic, with a minimum of writing: two large photographs and an Interpol poster. It was laid out to be grasped at a glance. He dropped his bomb: 'In fact, *his real name is Badu!*'

'*What?*' The press around the president became moderately rude as the aides strained to see the pictures.

'This is the publicity picture sent by his agency in London,' said Dr. Idowu, jabbing, 'and this is the police picture of Badu.'

'It's the same person!'

'*Exactly,* Your Excellency. Should I drop his name—'

'And he said he's Humphrey Chow?'

'It is not a matter of "he said," Your Excellency. In fact, he was travelling with a Humphrey Chow passport! No wonder he was writing about Menai people in *Balding Wolf.* He is Badu!'

'But who identified this person as Badu?'

'Charles Pitani, the IGP,' said Idowu, hardly seeing the relevance. 'He is the only person who has seen Badu and lived to—'

'—the *former* inspector general?' sighed the president. 'How can you trust an ID by that criminal? I am surrounded by *morons!*' There were no assenting nods this time. 'Get me the attorney general!—And don't touch my awards list!'

UCHE OFO

Abuja | 22nd April, 2005

'This is not a good time,' said the voice on the phone.

'I know, sir. I have a watch myself. I just have a message for you: *Do not engage.*'

The reply came loud and angry. Ofo held the phone away from his ear until the worst of the tirade was past. Then he spoke again, quietly. 'I don't care if you are going to have five hundred flat tyres in your brigade, all I'm saying is: *do not engage, sir.*'

He cut the connection and pushed himself deeper into the sofa. He looked around the deserted anteroom and closed his eyes. What he had just done was tantamount to treason, but for the first time he had to admit to himself that he was a whore for power. There was no other way to explain the thrill he had felt when the American president, the most powerful man in the world, opened his mouth and parroted words that he, Uchechukwu Ofo, had instructed. He knew how difficult it was to get his own president even to stick to a script, and he was doubly in awe of Penaka Lee.

His job as a presidential assistant had given Ofo new insights into the asymmetries of power. He relished his ability to issue orders to a brigade commander who outranked him formally, just because he had the ears of the president. But he knew that if he lost his current job he would not only lose that power, he would slide down the power pole with a velocity greased by the vengeful superiors he had slighted. Working with Penaka was an investment in new centres of power.

And revenge for his boss's thing with his wife.

He hesitated, looked around once more, and called Belinja.

ZANDA ATTURK

Ubesia | 22nd April, 2005

The selection meeting of the kingmakers was under way at the Great Court. There was rioting on the streets and federal government cars were burning, but the federal troops scheduled to arrive since dawn were nowhere in sight. The secessionists had the streets.

Around the Royal Palace, a more quiescent crowd milled, awaiting the announcement of the decision of the kingmakers. The cool reception of Amana's convoy, despite Nanga Saul's blessings, was a sobering reminder for me that Amana was only recognised within the Nanga's Residence. She was still very much the dark horse. The battle for the position of Nanga had coincided with the popular secession movement, and Elder Rantan was riding the wave of the movement for all it was worth.

In the Great Court, the thirty-strong Kingmakers Committee had gathered. In addition to Elder Rantan and his fellow elders of the council, chiefs from the fifteen Sontik wards were in attendance. Amana Udama Bentiy joined them silently, looking at that moment very much like a short-lived women's emancipation and sensitisation project by a deluded Justin Bentiy & Clique, and I slipped into the rear of the gallery with her courtiers.

It was a short selection process, all the horse trading having been done in earlier private meetings. Governor Obu, the president-in-waiting of the Sontik Republic, had tagged his endorsement of Elder Rantan onto that morning's TV denunciations against the murderers in Abuja who had killed his wife. The continuity announcer on Sontik Republic TV used the titles *Elder* and *Nanga* interchangeably for Rantan. The speeches commenced. The back-to-back endorsements of all the elders in the council also contributed a sense of inevitability to Elder Rantan's candidacy. From the rear of the room, I watched Justin Bentiy's frown deepen. It was going to be a rout.

I looked at my watch. The speeches were going much faster than I had expected. Finally, the expected text came through from Adevo, and I hurried out into one of the deserted reception rooms. I flicked through the channels. With some alarm I realised that Sontik State TV, which had quickly rebranded itself as the Sontik Republic TV station, was jamming the Nigerian Network programming. I knew then that they were not going to hook up to the Pitani video, and I returned to the Great Court as Amana rose to speak.

She spoke confidently, but in contention with rude hecklers, she sounded more plucky than regal. By the time she finished, a note of frustration had crept into her voice. It was not a speech that could dam a flood. Elder Rantan's was a cross between a secession and an acceptance speech, and he sat down to loud applause.

It was time to vote.

And yet, the applause for Elder Rantan seemed dutiful to me rather than enthusiastic—the din sounded requisitioned, like a bully's due. It was that feeling that prompted me, sometime Menai shoeshine boy, to intrude upon the most sensitive of proceedings in the life of the Sontik nation.

As I stepped forward, I felt again that intoxicating charge of blood that had gone to my head when I addressed the Parliamentary Subcommittee on the Pharmaceutical Industry in London. I climbed onto the raised dais and plucked the microphone from a startled protocol officer. From the kingmakers' ranks, a shout went up: 'The candidates have spoken—no one else may speak!'

'Unless he is Badu,' I said, quietly, recognising—as soon as the unplanned and suicidal words were out—the entire rationale behind the written address.

A hush fell on the audience. 'Who are you?' demanded Elder Rantan.

I ignored him, thinking quickly how to rephrase myself. 'The real question is *who* the Sontik nation selects as Nanga.' I raised my voice. 'Badu's second video has just been released, and this council's vote will decide whether the new Nanga will rule from palace or prison . . .'

Someone switched on a television in an alcove by the Great Court. My bluff had been called and I was about to be exposed. I stepped down from the dais as the kingmakers surged, as one body, into the alcove, hunting channels anxiously. I tried to leave the room but was headed off by security men.

◆ ◆ ◆

EYONO

Sontik Republic TV, Ubesia | 22nd April, 2005

10:00 a.m.

The tape had finished playing, but the mind of the general manager of the TV station was still in turmoil. Eyono pressed the replay button, with the air of someone who had missed something important. *He needed time to think!* He had been a member of the 'X' Committee. The new TV logos, the jamming strategies, everything had been carefully planned months in advance. Like most other Sontiks, he was pro-secession, and he was not so naive as to imagine that Governor Obu was a saint.

Yet the order and magnitude of the corruption revealed by Pitani was nauseating in the extreme. And with both Obu and Rantan in cohorts with the disgraced IGP, it was clear that the new country would be far worse than the old, for the small citizen. Already four countries had recognised Sontik Republic. The US was still hedging, but they had not repudiated the secession either. The State Department statement had merely called for 'peaceful means to resolve the crisis.'

It was a critical time in the secession. Obu was already more corrupt than Sese Seko. Once he was entrenched in power and with an army at his behest, he could be as murderous as King Leopold and no one would be able to do a thing about it.

The general manager had lately been dreaming about Obiang and Equatorial Guinea. Perhaps this was the meaning of the dreams: Sontik was to become a petrorepublic small enough to fit into Obu's hip pocket like Equatorial Guinea had fit into the swag bag of the Obiang family since their independence.

The video still had several minutes to run, but the general manager's mind was made up. He rose. Ugly mutters of *thief, barawo, jibiti* rippled through his office, which was packed with workers—from messengers right up to deputy directors—who had filed in spontaneously to see the long-awaited video. He already knew the mood, but he asked anyway: 'Fine! This is a democracy! To broadcast or not to broadcast?'

The room exploded, *'Broadcast!'*

His head swelled. Downstairs, the governor's mercenaries held the gates of the broadcasting house against the feared onslaught of the Nigerian Army. Yet a new front manned by a citizen's army had opened up right in his office. He knew he was setting his head securely on the block. They all supported him now, but if the gamble failed and they all ended up in Sontik Republic, it was still going to be *his* head. He thought about his young family, his innocent wife . . . then he thought about Sonia, the only good thing in the State House, who had clearly been killed by her own husband to stoke pro-secession fervour . . . and he stopped thinking and nodded to his producer.

Without fanfare, the graphics of the television station morphed from Sontik Republic TV back to Sontik State TV, and the second Badu video went live in the breakaway republic.

His telephone shrilled immediately, with a call from the *office of the president of Sontik Republic.* 'He has gone to piss,' snapped his angry secretary, not bothering to pass the call through.

TOBIN RANI

The Oasis at Gozoa | 22nd April, 2005

As soon as I stopped, David woke up, roused by the change in the rhythm of the truck. He rubbed his eyes sleepily and looked at his watch. It was 3:00 a.m. 'Why are we stopping? Still many travelling hours before dawn.'

'I'm not sure. There are, like . . . sleeping camels ahead.'

He peered at the map, then at the satellite screen. 'There's nothing there. Probably a Bedouin camp. Just skirt around it.'

I gestured behind me. He glanced back and sighed: the Mata was awake.

David sank back into his seat resignedly and shut his eyes. His six-hour driving shift had ended only two hours earlier. The long month on the road had made him a testy travel companion.

We travelled at the Mata's pace. He spent most of his time either asleep or in a trance, but when we travelled, his eyes were trained on the horizon and the stars. I stroked the fingers clenched into my shoulders until they relaxed; then I took his thin digits in mine and turned around. Usually the Mata would be stretched out on his back. The truck was modified with a huge moonroof. I had thought we would have lost him by now, but he was still there, confounding the roadmap I had worked out with David with his directions, *menya, menyi* or more usually *ese,* every hour or two. When the crop of camels had materialised in the wash of my headlights, I had tried to detour, but his hand had pinned me down.

'*Enie Mata?*' I tried again, to be met by silence.

I sighed and, turning off the headlights, killed the engine.

◆ ◆ ◆

I WAS woken up by the slamming of David's door. It was first light but too early for me so I let him go, although I did not get to sleep again. Presently, he came over to my side of the truck. 'It's just a Tuareg camp. Ten, twenty tents. We should have gone around. That's four to five hours travelling wasted.'

'There's more where that came from.'

We made camp that morning and made friends that afternoon. It was an oasis, of sorts. The well was good for two to three months of the year. It was mostly mud just now, and the clan was moving on in another day or so. That evening we shared a goat roast with our hosts, a six-family Tuareg clan. The Mata ate his smoked fish in the silence of the tent I shared with him. He had not said a word all day, but I was not concerned, for I knew he was also spending time with ancestorsMenai. Sometimes he would spend a day in silence and then answer a question I had asked the night before. He was the Mata.

As night fell we said our goodbyes to the Tuareg, who had entertained themselves with David's phrasebook-assisted 'Arabic,' and broke camp. We usually left the Mata for last. He was in a trance, but my gentle attempt to lift him snapped him right out of it, animating him again: *'Ajia! Ajia!'* I had to stop. All my remonstrations came to nothing. After fifteen minutes of this I rose, heart pounding, and turned to David. 'I'm sorry. We have to spend another night.'

'You've got to be kidding,' he said angrily, and we had our first real quarrel.

I got him well away from the Mata and tried to get his voice down. 'Listen, David, I don't know if I told you this before: the Mata *can* speak English. He just *won't.*'

'Yeah, pull the other one.'

'Just keep your comments civil, in his presence. He understands every word.'

'Just damn well put him in the truck, and my comments will get civil again! This is the Sahara desert, Tobin. I didn't sign up to sit and die in the desert with a senile old man!'

'He's not a *corpse* yet. I can't *put* him in against his will!'

'What *will?* He's dying! He's *senile.* It's called *dementia!* It is a natural fact of life, not an abuse against your holy clanfather! And I'm hanging around the desert on his instructions?'

We didn't exchange another word all through that long night.

ZANDA ATTURK

Ubesia | 22nd April, 2005

After only a few minutes of the video, Elder Rantan's more thuggish supporters had switched off and borne away the television set, wresting the meeting back to its original agenda. The selection conference of kingmakers quickly degenerated into protracted bickering as Elder Drosa manoeuvred desperately to supplant Rantan as a compromise candidate of the elders' council.

Elder Drosa's secret ambition took me by surprise. I had counted on some shame, had anticipated that Rantan's own ambition would shrivel up and die, leaving the coast clear for Amana. Unfortunately, Elder Rantan had defaulted into bully mode, possibly figuring that the nangaship was his best chance of escaping prosecution from any Pitani revelations. It was a life office, and although it did not give him constitutional immunity from prosecution in Nigeria, once selected he would be in a position to ensure that it did in the nascent Sontik Republic. So he dug in. Amana's star seemed to fade as the din in the hall grew. When the ballot was finally cast, Elder Drosa's name was also in contention, and Amana only managed a distant third place behind him. As Elder Rantan rose to his feet in victory, Justin Bentiy swept out of the Great Court without a word.

At the very edge of the hall, where I had been detained on Rantan's instructions, I could hear the proceedings, but from where I sat on the floor, I could not see much. I had spent hours on my buttocks, and my lower muscles were cramping.

As the main door opened for Justin Bentiy, a tidal wave of noise crashed into the hall. The patient crowd outside the palace was patient no longer. The whooping from Rantan and his supporters subsided as the main door closed, reducing the din. All eyes turned towards the forecourt of the palace, where a new throng was massing, fed by a never-ending flood from the streets. The Great Court fell silent as the chanting grew louder, despite the insulation of the air conditioning.

'*Odu—gbedu! Rantan—gbedu!*
Odu—gbedu! Rantan—gbedu!'

The ebb of euphoria, and legitimacy, from the newly elected Nanga was a physical thing. I rose tentatively, and this time I was not pushed down as before. The main doors opened again, admitting a shaken Justin, assisted by two palace guards. The late Nanga's cousin was unsteady on his feet, with his blood-spattered clothes at a sartorial low. Things deteriorated rapidly: Through the windows, we watched the mercenaries from Sekurizon abandon their riot vehicle and escape in a motorised canoe. The dozen palace guards who had been holding back the mob on the outside suddenly broke into the Great Court without ceremony. They shut the door with dispatch and put their shoulders against it.

Someone with a phone to his ear shouted, 'The State House is burning!' The sequestered television set was restored from the cleaner's cupboard. This time, there was no resistance. The general unease grew.

NANDA-NOMINEE AMANA

Ubesia | 22nd April, 2005

At the foot of the dais, in the central well of the Great Court, I stood up slowly. I had not said a word for the couple of hours leading up to the final ballot. Now, I said simply, into the restive silence, 'It is time for the new Nanga to meet the people.' I merely stated the obvious—the warlord's frightened drummer was waiting with his talking drum, near the entrance to the balcony.

Yet it was an inconvenient truth; Rantan was not about to step onto a sacrificial slab. The kingmakers glared at me stonily.

I turned and walked towards the balcony.

'Stop her!' shouted Rantan, and a phalanx of palace guards formed between me and the balcony.

I stopped two paces from the uniformed guards, just as the first missile lobbed from the crowd struck a window on the south face. We all jumped as one, but the pane held. On the dais, the television gabbled breathlessly, but its seismic revelations were unable to hold the full attention of the kingmakers.

From the upper gallery, Lantanya rose precipitately and walked down, cutting across the dais and heading towards the standoff between me and the guards. The money from the haulage business had always been the Nanga's, but Nanga Saul never signed a cheque himself: that was Lantanya's to do. The guards would never have dreamt of taking their financial embarrassments to the paramount ruler. Lantanya brought the weight of that authority to bear as she snatched the Nanga's beadwork from the ceremonial stool by the dais and marched toward the door where I stood.

Elder Rantan, certainly recognising the ritual significance of the beadwork, yelled again from across the hall, 'Stop her!'

Yet she was storming *towards* the guards. Unlike me, she did not slow as she approached the line, did not doubt her own authority, and the guards directly in her path wilted and stepped back, not looking at anyone in particular.

A few more paces, and she was at the door of the balcony. She stopped then and turned around, her hand on the knob, her steely eyes on me.

I had not exchanged another word with Lantanya since our less-than-friendly parting earlier that morning. I met her eyes, but the stern expression on the face of my half sister, who had earlier asserted her superior stake to our father's throne, gave nothing away. The beadwork was gathered proprietorially in the crook of her arm . . . yet she was clearly waiting for me. Beyond, the shouts and the jeers, the thud of missiles landing against the doors could now be heard. I approached the balcony. I saw a flicker of uncertainty in my sister's eyes.

'Are you sure?' Lantanya whispered.

I had only one certainty: I was taking my only shot at our father's stool, and courage was the only powder in my cannon. Yet I also recognised the chasm beyond the door, where the price of failure was not just disgrace but death. I nodded slowly.

There was a shout of protest from Rantan's kingmakers as Lantanya pulled a cordless microphone from her bag and put it in my hand. 'Your campaign speech was too fast,' she whispered, swiftly slipping the beadwork over my head. 'Slow down now, be *royal*. Our father was a king.'

'Thank you, Lanta.' I donned my headdress and gave her my bag to hold.

I saw Zanda break away from his demoralised captors and hurry through the hall to protect me, but I stepped out onto the balcony alone. A warlord of the Sontik who needed to be protected from the Sontik was not their warlord.

In more propitious times, Nanga Saul had held regular court with his public from that balcony. During the annual Marinko festivals, adulatory throngs bearing palm fronds would dance beneath the balcony and he would wave his fan to acknowledge their praises.

The balcony was dressed for the presentation of the new Nanga, yet the waist-high rostrum behind which I stood was no protection for the boos, jeers, and cries of 'Gbedu!' which now found a focus in me. A plastic bottle struck me. Then a stone. I did not flinch. Instead I walked forward until I was right against the rostrum, inches from the railings. With my left hand, I seized the rostrum in a death grip. With the other, I held the microphone. I tried to smile. It was still far too noisy to attempt to speak, even with a microphone, so I waved, slowly, incongruously, at the largest sea of faces I had ever seen in my life.

A stone struck my chin, reporting like a small grenade as it bounced off the microphone. I knew I ought to flee for my life, but I did not flinch. That was the telling blow: as the weal doubled my chin and the blood spotted my clothes, the jeers began to recede. Imperceptibly at first, but soon more obviously, the throng began to morph from mob into audience.

I stitched a smile over the pain. I was running on adrenaline anyway, but I smelled Lantanya's fragrance as I settled the beadwork comfortably on my bosom and the headdress on my head. I dabbed at my chin tenderly.

The mood of the mob was still uncertain. They had come to lynch the gbedu and did not quite know what to do with a strange woman in the garb and place of the Nanga. The mob had come hungering for an inexpressible change . . . and when it found the vent, all its energy was channelled into the chant.

When the new cry went up, I recognised the roughboy who first raised it up in front: Domu, who had won most of my first salary as the DRCD rep in Kreektown. I had used his tricks to earn back my losses many times over, but it was on my inauguration that he made the real payback:

'Che Nanga Amana! Che Nanga Amana!'

Lantanya had come closer; she snapped her fingers and the warlord's drummer hefted his talking drum onto the balcony and fell into the rhythm, tensioning the sinews of the drum underarm, to modulate its voice. Within moments, the chant was resounding in the timbers of the Great Court. The palace guards turned slowly, from the hall to the balcony, as though acknowledging a new anthem, a new power in the Sontik nation, whose authority flowed from the ultimate repository. Within minutes, all the kingmakers rallied behind me, the people's Nanga, on the public balcony. Their embarrassing vote of the expired moment was something they were suddenly anxious to bury deep beneath their public and vocal support for the newly acclaimed Nanga. By the time Elder Drosa pushed his way into the balcony, it was standing room only, behind me.

ZANDA ATTURK

Ubesia | 22nd April, 2005

I remained in the Great Court, watching Elder Rantan watch the television. The hairs on my skin had stood on end when the chant for Nanga

Amana had begun. Then the television had shown Rantan's house burning. Starting with the five chiefs who had voted for her, one by one all the kingmakers had left the hall and gone to stand with her.

I felt limp with relief. Sinking into a chair, I did not stir for another hour as I listened to the speeches from the balcony. When Amana eventually stepped out with her train, I was alone with the television. Her grin was lopsided from the weal on her chin, but I grinned back helplessly. Suddenly I no longer had a problem with the headgear.

I rose and bowed from the waist. 'Che Nanga.'

From around her, the chorus came unanimously.

PENAKA LEE

Ubesia | 22nd April, 2005

It was not a good sign when the president of a new country began to get, from his own civil service, messages like *they have gone to piss* or *they are smoking cigar outside.* Obu got five messages of this ilk in five minutes; that, more than anything else, told Penaka Lee that the game was up.

It had been looking pretty good until Pitani took over the airwaves. It was a good thing for Obu that Sonia did not live to see this video. In between reruns of the second Badu tape, the backstabbing TV station kept showing the streets.

Mobs were interesting animals. Before Penaka's eyes, the raging lion turned into a bumbling Saint Bernard.

Before 11:00 a.m. the streets were burning with secession slogans. There was a period of two hours when it was a free-for-all, but by 2:00 p.m., the fire of secession seemed to drain out of the mob. The crowds doubled in numbers, but the fervour was gone. They were putting out car fires! The banners Penaka had printed at great cost lay thick on the streets. And then the chanting! After a while, he realised it was coming more from the lawns of state house than from the TV.

He opened the window a crack.

Gbedu! Barawo! Jibiti! Ori!

'Shut the goddamned window!' swore Obu. 'The air conditioner is on!'

'What are they saying?' Penaka asked.

'Go and ask them!' he snapped rudely and stormed out.

'They are saying the same thing in four languages,' whispered a cowed secretary. Her eyes were red, and her frightened phalanges were in danger of dislocation.

'What languages? What are they saying?'

'They are saying *thief* in Sontik, Hausa, Yoruba, and Igbo.'

Penaka knew then that it was definitely over. He crossed the office and looked out the other window. That was a more peaceful prospect, and he needed all the peace he could get to leverage his special gift of decision making. He prided himself on being able to smile under most conditions, and he was smiling now.

The lesson from this debacle was clear, he reflected: these Africans lacked the pluck to liberate themselves. They could talk it, but that was about it. Penaka had to figure out how to transfer this insight into the Katanga operations. The strategy of outright independence would have to be scrapped, as too high risk. The sieving basket of the Congo could lubricate Corus without putting Penaka's life on the line again. Low-boil conflicts were more sustainable . . . no more outright takeovers. Just the occasional spanner in the works—to keep the systems shambolic enough for lucrative milking.

Penaka called his PA twice, and although he could see the limousine in the car park, the PA did not take his calls. Penaka did not call a third time. He could recognise a resignation when he read one. He closed his eyes.

I am Penaka Lee, lean hunting lion in the African savannah. The wildebeests out-number me by far, are much heavier, with scything horns that can rip me apart—but they have fear scripted into their genes. I have to manage that fear. It is good when I see it in their eyes as I bear down on them. Not so good when they run amok, with me still in the path of their mad stampede. I have to wait until they are back in grazing mode, focused on their grass before I can hunt again. Once again I am caught down-hill in the course of a major stampede. I have to get out, fast, or be trampled to death.

The secretary's weeping was affecting his concentration. Across the rear lawn, two veiled women waddled up the fire escape towards the top floor and the helipad. The obese one was dressed in a floral native wrapper. The more effeminate woman, struggling with heavy bags and bringing up the rear, was wearing Major Lamikan's boots under her boubou. The yellow governor-president was making his getaway.

Penaka let him go. Ten years earlier, he would have gone chasing after Governor Obu in a flap, but a civilian helicopter was not the place to be in these angry times. Not with the containers of rocket launchers Daniel Sheldon had pumped into this delta through Penaka's contacts. It would be far safer to find a comfortable passionflower vine somewhere and ride out this storm. Penaka could only hope this particular calamity ended with a whimper rather than a bang.

'I like your braids,' he said to the whimpering secretary. She had clamped both lips together with her teeth, but they were still trembling. He was smiling as usual, and she reciprocated through her tears. Penaka left the window and turned to her. He took her right hand. Their fingers were unencumbered by rings. 'Do you live around here?'

TOBIN RANI

The Oasis at Gozoa | 23rd April, 2005

Next morning the friendliness of the Tuareg set off the hostility between David and me. I could not wait for night to fall. The heat of day was a fiery trial. My joint pains grew. My thoughts and dreams and memories fried together in my head. I sat there in a pool of self-pity, moistening my lips with my allotment of hot water, marvelling that people would live this existence by choice, that my ancestors had thrived like this. The Mata refused to eat, and I feared that his end had finally come. We declined the Tuareg invitation to a meal, but they declined the declination, inviting themselves into the circle of our anaemic camp, with a meal of flatbread and cheese and a stew to stir disgruntled bowels. We joined them with ill grace, adding our tins of milk and smoked fish to the evening feast. The Tuareg patriarch asked after 'our father's' health and told us about his own ailing mother in their main settlement in southern Libya.

Night fell. David packed his tent wordlessly, strapping his stuff in the rear of the truck. Then he sat down and watched me.

This time I opted to load up the Mata first. I opened the tailgate and drew out his stretcher. When I went to lift him up, a chill ran through me.

He was not in a trance. His glassy eyes stared through me. And he began to sing.

David rose. Beside me, he asked gruffly, 'What's he saying?'

I translated:

> *We were not Tuareg but we lived with them,*
> *Somewhere in the evening of our trek.*

Their ways were not our ways.
Their taboos amused us,

Until we lost the dozen daughters to their men.

'It happens.' He shrugged. 'Well, are you coming or what?'

I went on my knees and locked eyes with the old man. I had disobeyed him in the past; some of my trips from Kreektown were over his opposition. Yet there were life-and-death matters in which I followed him blindly. I realised that this was one of them. I would not have started out on the journey otherwise.

I rose reluctantly. I turned to David. 'One last night, please.'

He turned wordlessly and strode to the vehicle, his present silence more ominous than his previous rage.

I hurried after him. I gripped his arm. 'Hear me out, David.'

'I'm listening.'

'Have you asked yourself *why* you made this trip at all?'

'Have *you* asked yourself that question?' he exploded, his finger half-way into my lung. 'Why are you carrying a dying man thousands of miles across a dangerous desert?'

'Death is the crux of life, and I'm his burial detail.'

'Just listen to yourself!'

'We're burying a nation, David, not just a man . . .'

'*You* are burying a nation. Let me spell this out for you, Tobin Romantic-Airhead Rani. We're bang in the middle of Chad Republic. We are next to a muddy well which will be dry for the next nine months. We are sitting ducks for armed bandits. We have a sandstorm coming, we have five days' water in the truck, *and we don't know where the bloody hell we're going.* Let me ask you just one question: are you ready to die for this old man?'

I thought of Kreektown without the Mata, and suddenly the world seemed pointless. 'Yes.'

He stared at me levelly. 'Well, I'm not. I came here to *live*, not to die.' He pulled down two kegs of water and a jute bag crammed full of tins, another full of citrus fruits. He dragged down the mananga; he pulled down our bags, ran the stretcher home, and slammed the tailgate shut. Then he jumped into the driver's seat and tossed the paper maps and a field compass on the sand. He fired up the truck. 'I'm serious now, Tobin. Are you coming or not?'

'Please.'

'Good thing the Tuaregs have extra camels.' His lights swept half of the night away, returning startled coins for the eyes of the camels in the distance. The 4×4 described a large circle and headed in the direction from which we had arrived two days before. I watched him go, with our wheels, the satellite phone, and half the supplies, certain he would turn back, angry, raging . . . but he went on. The camp was on a promontory, and I could have stood for an hour and still seen the dot that was David growing fainter still.

◆ ◆ ◆

I TOOK the maps and compass into the tent, leaving the supplies and mananga where they lay. I fell down beside the Mata. The comforting smell of old leather filled my lungs.

'*Beni mute Davidi?*'

'*Beni mute,*' I confirmed.

'*Emuni,*' he breathed; and I wondered what was good about the situation. Then his eyes dilated in alarm, and I looked down to see that I was lying on a burial shroud. In Menai lore, there was no greater harbinger of bad luck. I chuckled and stretched out deliberately on it, and after a while Mata Nimito laughed as well: how much worse could things get?

Eventually, we lapsed into a sober silence, and I knew he was also thinking about the maker of his unfinished shroud. Outside, the wind began to rise, and I went to haul the supplies in.

WEAVER KAKANDU (ANCESTORMENAI)

Lagos | 18th March, 2005

When I got Jonszer's message from Kreektown, I struggled to finish, really, I did. But the evening came and my fingers were heavy with sadness and they stopped trying. My head was saying weave and weave on, try! For the greatest of all Menai, weave and weave on! But they stopped. That old rabbit was chewing and chewing my insides, but that was not the reason why my eyeswater was running. All the eyeswater from a war is too salty to quench even a small child's thirst, so what's the point? Me that am expert in many different designs of marriage cloths, but for years now, is only burial shrouds that I weave! May GodMenai forgive my sins.

So I remove the thread from the koma and push the ajila back into their storage holes. I pack the body of the jamaya carefully, the way my father taught us, the way his father taught him, the way I taught my ancestor-daughter and have tried to teach these boys and girls that government brought me to Lagos to teach so that the Menai's weave won't die out like the Menai. But to teach them is to cry, because—may GodMenai forgive my sins—to watch them with jamaya is punishment . . . and the way they call the jamaya 'loom' is the worst thing, to call me 'man,' when my name is Kakandu . . . jamaya that is the mistress that makes wives jealous. Jamaya that is the lover that vexes husbands, and that is how it should be. My fingers play her without tire from sunbirth to sundeath. Between a jamaya and her owner there is no divorce. That is how it is. She breaks and he repairs her. She is dull it is polish. That is how it is.

Yet the worst is how they talk, those students they sent to punish me in my last days. A weaver is a person whose jamaya does his talking: *chakata-chakata-chakata,* and the koma is flying in and out, building the cloth one line by line by line . . .

No . . . the worst thing is my memory! May GodMenai forgive my sins! I remember how after two or three hours the head of our kamira will slow down—*kata-kata-kata*—and we will push the jamayas into the centre of the room and the snuff will come out and the roast corn and eighty or ninety knuckles will crack and one quiet joke, one nineteen-year-old memory—remember that time that Daudi won the pools and ordered six manos for his wife? One for every year of marriage? Ah!—another old man's joke, and ten minutes, twenty, will pass and the head of our kamira will pull up his jamaya and *chaka-chaka*—which is how one jamaya sounds when it is weaving alone, because no matter how fast you are, you must slow down to reverse the koma and that is that.

So one jamaya making cloth is one old man talking to himself. But three? Five? Eight? May GodMenai forgive my sins! There is no song in this world like the sound of eight jamayas singing. Before my legs grew long enough to pedal a jamaya I used to sit and watch my father—whose hands were the fastest hands in Menai—and I've seen grandpa and his brothers and my brothers and my father's brothers weave, so I know what I'm saying—I used to sit and watch my father throw the koma and listen to the song. So the head of our kamira will put away his snuff and suck the last corn from the holes in his teeth and . . . *chaka-chaka* . . . and slowly by slowly the rest of us will start, the laughter and the jokes and the clearing of the throat and the sucking of the corn from the teeth and the cracking of the last of the knuckles will continue for a while but all that will pass until suddenly, I am like a child in the middle of a room with a low roof and the song of eight jamayas . . . *chakata-chakata-chakata* . . . and on and on like that forevermore!

◆ ◆ ◆

BUT NO more. May GodMenai forgive my sins. It is the pride of the weaver to attend the marriage or baptism or party of his customer. To see how people are praising the skill of his weave and the beauty of his design. These past few years my work has gone down graves. I spend my life making cloth that my customers will never see. I am weaving food for termites. The fellowship of the kamira is broken. It is a long time since I knew that as the last weaver, I, Kakandu, master weaver of Menai, will not have a burial shroud himself . . . but now that the last Mata has died, who will play my tanda ma?

I stand and go.

Although I am bent, I am not old. My neck and back are the weaver's. My bowlegs are the weaver's. A neck bent over jamaya, legs pedalling ajilas, for forty, fifty years, will they not bow? I am not old but it is time. When Grandpa's hands grew too slow to throw his koma, he was not too old to sit in Menai's kamira, hands running over the latest cloth, to test the weft, to stretch and knob and roll the bale, and he was sitting there, in the fullsurround of perfection, listening to the song of eight jamayas, and that was where he was on the day of his sleepcatastrophe, when the head of our kamira pushed his jamaya away. There was no *kata-kata,* which is how a weaver slows to stop, it was just *cha!* and his koma was tumbling across the kamira, and we followed his eyes to the wall where Grandpa's head was bent lower than a noviceweaver's looking for his mistake, and the weaver's song ended in a sigh. And that's the road to GodMenai: a songcorridor of six or seven jamayas. I cannot go back to the loneliest sound in the world, the sound of one jamaya. Especially one that goes *chaka-cha chaka-cha.* I won't stutter any more, or wait for the rabbit to eat his fill and close Menai's last kamira.

◆ ◆ ◆

THERE ARE more important things, like the voice of the girl.

She is hawking bread on a wooden board. She is too thin to be Salia, but it is Salia's voice, so I follow her. What else is there to do? I follow her. And may GodMenai forgive my sins.

I don't come too close. A dream is not searched with suspicious eyes. A dream is followed with trusting eyes. I follow from far. Ajima soa

kocheya. It is warmhot . . . even early like this before the sun is coming out, it is warmhot. Like as if the ground kept the fire from yesterday's sun like leftover soup. All around, traders and students and workers are passing, but my eyes are for the hawker. She is singing, with Salia's voice:

> *Buy bread,*
> *Buy bread,*
> *Buy sweeeet bread,*
> *Buy sweeeeet butter bread.*

Salia! I still remember the weight of her as I laid her down in her bedroom grave. She is going again.

My eyeswater is flowing. Why is this? I am not an old man. Menai does not count forty- or fifty-something as old. To die at fifty is a curse. But the rabbit is biting, and although I know it is not her, it is good to dream. To use that sweet bread voice to bring my daughter back to call me to the house of Old Menai. Because only my daughter can call me into the wadigulf of the great taboo that has no name.

Chakata-chakata-chakata-cha chakata-cha.

She stops before a basket of onions. And I stop. I see her hand go up and bring down a bar of bread and a blade and a can of margarine. Her fingers are quick and wiseknowing. She cuts the bread still in the wrapper. That is how she cuts it. She spreads the margarine and gives the bread to a hand coming out of the basket of onions. She does all this with the board of bread on her head, her head moving side to side to balance her load. We continue. Her rubber slippers slap-slapping the road, the motor park conductors crying,

> 'Oshodi, Oshodi, Oshodiooo!
> Oshodi, Oshodi, Oshodiooo!'

. . . then I hear Mata Nimito's voice singing in my head and I freeze. It is my circumcision song!

> *Aya simino ganumu*
> *There were times in the lives of men*
> *to wonder what might have been*
> *if such and such had not happened.*
> *If the Mata's horn*
> *had blown at noon*
> *when fires boiled their lunches,*

when the farms engaged the husbands . . .
but it had blown at dawn
when the spirits of the old Matas
had freshly communed with their souls . . .
before the quicksand of Kantai
had mired them afresh . . .

By the time the young Mata arrived,
there were plumes of smoke from homes
whose owners lit the torch themselves.
There were asses piled and readied,
cattle strung and fed.
And the young crop was strafed, and
the old was taken in.
Yet there were many
many who loved Kantai,
who did not want to leave,
but Exodus was a week in the making,
and when Menai flowed from Kantai
there was not one of her children left behind.

There was not one of her children left behind.

The weight of taboo presses me, heavy, heavy, I cannot breathe. Mata Nimito's skies read my mind, they frown on me. I am hot. GodMenai! There is no shelter from his searching gaze, from the knowledge of ancestorsMenai.

The nylon shine of bread wrappers disappears in the crowd . . . I see it far away, running across an expressway.

Mata's voice dies away. Who will sing my tanda ma? I that have shrouded hundreds of Menai in their graves, who will shroud me, the last Menai? For what am I living now? And I am running, running, I can see the breadwrappers of the bread of the breadhawker running. I can see the eyes of traders and bus stop girls and soldiers and bus conductors, opening wider and wider, I can hear their shouting. And the breadhawker turns, and it is not . . . it is not . . . it **is** my daughter Salia, may GodMenai forgive my sins, whose fingers threw a cheerful koma, who sold her mother's sweet butterbread in Kreektown Square, and she is laughing . . . no, she is crying . . . and I am running to comfort her through the doorway of the runninglorry.

TOBIN RANI

The Oasis at Gozoa | 24th April, 2005

I did not sleep until morning. I lay there, counting the seconds between every wheeze of the old man's laboured breathing and allowing the bleakness of my situation to sink in. Some sound and fury my life had been, yet I was as lonesome as an eagle in the Saharan sky. With my nation and language dead, and my sons estranged, it was hard not to think of life as pointless, too. The hours drained; the wind speed grew.

There was a call from fifty metres away. I looked out of the tent. The Tuareg were packed and ready to go, with impossibly clumsy bundles strapped to their camels. There was concern on their faces, but without David and his phrasebook, very little communication between us. There was another consultation in Tamajaq and then a blue-clad young man brought over a goatskin. I tried to pay and watched anger replace his gap-toothed smile. I watched them go in an undulating file. Presently the boy returned and dropped a hoe wordlessly near the tent. He had not retrieved his smile, and the gesture to make my grave-digging easier seemed suddenly more sinister than friendly. They passed from sight, and eventually I fell asleep.

The burning heat woke me up. The sun was halfway across the sky. I rolled into the cooler shade of the tent, discovering a tangled blanket where the old man had lain. I rose immediately. I looked around and headed across to the oasis.

It was different without the Tuareg. The land continued to rise to the northeast, and there was nothing to date the landscape—nothing to say, looking towards the highlands of Darfur, that I was not standing eight, nine centuries in the past. On both sides, the land fell away steeply. To the southwest, a rising wind had erased the tracks of David's truck. I walked down the main causeway of packed dirt. There was something eerie about the boulders that towered over me, the clumps of brown date palms and rows of stringy cacti. I walked slowly, not so much seeking the Mata as *seeing*, with new eyes, this patch of earth that so transfixed him. Then I saw him by the entrance of a cave, under fading rock art with the imprimatur of the Menai, reminiscent of the art on his Kreektown adobe house, and I *knew*.

'The Oasis of Gozoa?'

He nodded.

My mouth dried up. This was the root of the great taboo. He sat up-right on a granite platform, his singate between his legs, in the extremity of the oasis, in that place that bordered soil and sand. I walked around him slowly, marvelling at the surge of life that had brought him to where he sat, staring glassily into his skies.

I hurried back to the tent, where I filled a jug with water. I returned and sat by him. I offered him a drink, and we toasted, studying the same skies that had spoken to our ancestors. Ten minutes passed. Under that mon-strous sun he was wilting, but something was happening to him that I did not have the power to stop. He was more with *them* than with me.

I hurried back to the tent and broke it down. I was panting and breath-less. My joints were killing me, but I was *alive,* energised. I carried the pins and ropes and wands and canvas across the oasis and rebuilt the tent around the Mata, wheeling the mananga across when I was done. When it was installed at the entrance of the cave, I collapsed by him and poured another cup of water.

'Amis andgus.'

'Andgus ashen.'

I *saw* the root of our tradition of the water toast, that sharing of water that was primal, central to hospitality. That word, untranslatable into English: *andgus*—a portmanteau of wellbeinghealing. In the desert, the drink of water that greeted the traveller was the greatest gift of all, com-bining healing, blessing, love, wellbeing . . . No one could say the words *Andgus ashen,* and truly mean it, who had not had a scourging desert thirst slaked by a gourd of life-giving water.

The Mata spoke: 'I see this horizon of sand with the eyes of Mata Asad, whose singate knows me. Fields of grain and herds of long-horned goats. Thousands and thousands of Menai roofs as far as eyes can see. A town four times as large as Kreektown ever was. Home of the People for a hun-dred years and five.'

He fell silent, and I stared wordlessly at the desert, imagining an oasis fed by a lake rather than a seasonal well, imagining how Kreektown would look in a century or two.

'Ajanu,' he said.

Slowly, I began to play. I was rusty, and I knew it. It had been years since I last played the mananga, but it was not possible to forget. I thought I did okay, and I knew he was old indeed, for he did not, as in years past, snatch the instrument and show me how it was done. Instead, he sat, his legs folded beneath him, teasing out, to the beat of my tanda ma, the words of a historysong I had never heard before. I was so engrossed in the history that I looked up only when the Mata broke off. He was staring at David Balsam who was paces away.

'I thought you left with the Tuareg,' he joked nervously. 'I almost turned around.'

There was a split-second surge of relief, and then an incontinent rage took over. I leapt over the mananga and slammed into him. We rolled in the dust.

'Stop!'

We froze. We sat up, stunned. The Mata had spoken English. It had slipped from him like a fart, and now he continued, embarrassed, 'Brothers don't fight like jackals. *Ajia!*'

'This is not my brother.'

'He is.' The Mata's English was languid, so overlaid with the burr of his encrusted Menai that it sounded like a third language. 'The only brother you have left. We are Mata . . . we *make* Menai.' He extended his cup to David, who crawled over, dazed. '*Amis andgus.*'

'*Andgus ashen,*' said David shakily.

'We are not so senile now, no?'

'I . . . *am* sorry,' said David.

I rose and walked to him. I took his hand and pulled him up. 'Sorry, I lost it.'

'Where did you learn to fight like a thug?' he grumbled.

◆ ◆ ◆

DAVID TOLD us he had run into a drilling caravan and had bought fresh provisions. He brought the truck around and pitched his tent in its shadow. Then we had the first meal of the day. We ate silently inside the tent, away from the wind, which was now stinging with sand. I finished my meal, took my drugs, and sat back, reluctant to stir. The Mata had eaten more than he had in several days, and he was expansive and more animated than he had been in months. In my exhausted depression, I began to believe that he would outlive me as well.

David passed around drinks from a cooler. '*Anobi,*' said Mata Nimito gratefully. 'May you have your hundred and ten.'

'Hundred and ten what?'

'Years,' I explained. 'It's a Menai blessing: we're greedy for life. We believe the normal human life-span is a hundred and ten years.'

'If there's a hundred-and-ten-year blessing, is there a curse as well?'

I began to shake my head, but the Mata was speaking. 'In the old days, there was a curse on the thief and the murderer: he cut his life-span in half. In the old days, crime was rare.'

'Was there any way of . . . ending the curse?'

Mata Nimito took a handful of dust and let it filter through his fingers.

'That means *no*,' I interpreted. 'Yet if the old curses still worked, all those children we buried in the last ten years, I'd have cursed them all, given them another forty years of life at least!'

There was a sober silence as the wind died. Finally the Mata took up his singate. I rose to help him up.

The sun was two hours away from death when I followed him to the entrance of the cave. He recited three stanzas from three separate historysongs, and then, orienting himself by the sun and the rock art, he measured ten paces into the cave. Then he took an eleventh.

'It should be ten,' I whispered, 'by the songs . . .'

'*Noriegamu.*' He agreed with a grin. 'But Mata Asad was a short man. *Esua aroko.*'

I nodded, although I desperately wanted to shake my head instead. I took up the Tuareg hoe. It was impossible not to feel Mata Nimito's excitement, but I had been labouring all day, and I was not looking forward to the exercise. With his singate, he marked a rectangle on the packed earth just inside the cave, where there was just light enough not to need a lamp, and I began to dig.

David entered, incredulous. 'That's rather morbid.'

'It's not the Mata's grave.' I panted. 'It's the grave of Crown Prince Alito, the last Prince Menai. Mata Asad buried him here.'

'And when was this?'

'Four hundred and sixty-one years ago.'

'You can be so sure?'

I did not bother to reply, reserving my energy for the task.

David went to the truck for a shovel. 'Looks like a long tradition, this,' he said when he returned. 'Burying your dead where you live.'

I sat down while I caught my breath. 'We seek that union between the dead, the living, and the yet-to-be-born. But we live on three different planes—so all we ever get is a . . . a . . .'

'. . . *federe saga* . . .' said the Mata.

'. . . a marketmeeting—' I translated.

'—a market*junction*meeting,' the Mata corrected. 'Not satisfying. But, very soon, all Menai will *live* in one room. Perfect unity, the silver lining of extinction.' He turned slowly to me. His milky eyes were moist again. 'We will be waiting for you, my son.'

'I'm coming soon, my father,' I said quietly.

David stepped in and spelled me. We went at it in five-minute shifts. We were four feet in when the Mata called a halt. He picked some ceramic beads from the mound of sand disgorged from the grave. Panting, we followed him into the sunset outside the cave. He rinsed the beads and held them up so we could see that they matched perfectly with the beadwork on his bib.

'The royal beads,' he murmured. The excitement was gone, and in its place, the sobriety of a funeral. 'Don't disturb the crown prince further.'

He unwrapped a bronze singateya and placed the centuries-old insignia of Menai royalty in the half-dug grave. As we buried it, he stood over us, chanting the names of the Menai suicides since the death of Crown Prince Alito. Ma'Bamou's name stunned me, dropped me to my knees, so that David had to finish filling the grave alone.

By the time I stepped out of the cave, the Mata was sitting as before, staring at the dying sun. I was now physically, mentally, and spiritually exhausted, but I approached the mananga. There was work to be done.

'What now?' whispered David. He was sitting silently, no longer the impatient professor.

'Intercession,' I said softly. 'Suicide kept the souls of our dead from the conclave of ancestorsMenai. The Mata wishes to bring them into the fold.'

'I read Dr. Fowaka's monograph. Suicide was unknown among the Menai; you didn't even have a word for it . . . ?'

The Mata laughed quietly.

I took a deep breath. 'A thousand years before the first words were grunted in the English language, Menai had names for fifty stars in the night sky . . . and we don't have a word for "suicide"?'

He shrugged. 'Just quoting a Menai scholar . . .'

'The true Menai scholars are Menai, and they are dead. We rest words we have no use for.'

'Kamogo,' whispered the Mata, and I flinched. Hearing it spoken was still disturbing.

'That,' I said to David, 'was the tabooed Menai for "suicide." Mata Asad tried to close the suicide door of despair. After he buried his crown prince, he made both word and deed taboo. But now, now that we have lost the battle of extinction anyway, Mata Nimito will end the taboo, will bring them all in . . .'

'My faithful Jonszer,' murmured Mata Nimito. 'AncestorsMenai will be hell without him.'

'From Crown Prince Alito to . . . Ma'Bamou—' I broke off.

'*Ajanu!*'

Obediently I began to play, and slowly my tiredness and despair fell away. Soon I was firmly in the tanda ma groove. I played with my eyes shut, finding the panes by a resuscitating skill as the Mata cycled through funereal historysongs. Then his voice sank into a hum, a wordless moan. Under the mesmerism of the tanda ma, the centuries-old 'Taboo Song' began to swell, with a brand new ending:

> *Bronze!*
> *screamed their cormorant,*
> *and the sun was standing still.*
>
> *Bronze!*
> *roared their warriors,*
> *their nostrils flaring wide.*
> *And even Crown Prince Alito*
> *knew his time was running out.*
> *They cut him from that morning*
> *until the day he nearly died,*
> *but he did not say a single word.*
> *It was I that betrayed us.*
> *For the love of Crown Prince Alito,*
> *I yielded up our forge.*
> *On the morning of Arimela*
> *I broke the Menai vow,*
> *I took the enemy cormorant to*
> *our forge in Mauve Valley.*
>
> *You could feel the sun slow down and stop,*
> *above Gozoa's pond.*
> *It was the arsenal of the Menai.*
> *I, traitor, took them there.*
> *I, Mata Asad, took the enemy*
> *to the forge in deep hiding.*
>
> *They gave me Crown Prince Alito,*
> *or what remained of him.*

They gave me a grieving Prince Menai
that weighed me down like stone.
The Settlers' eyes trailed me like sin as I
strapped him to my camel
and went the low way up
to the Menai keep on high.
I bore him till the sun went down.
He did not say a word
and he did not weep a tear
and he did not make another sound.

Till he killed himself at night.

Until he killed himself at night.

Hear me and weep, O Great Menai.
This was your valiant Prince,
slain by his own hand, buried
like offal in Gozoa's barren cave.
Was there a singateya by his head,
for spirit guests to know?

No . . . Until today . . .

There is just that grave,
ten paces south of the Menai cross
in the Mata's keep on high,
where he awaits his tanda ma,
in vain . . . Until today.

On the low pass
in Gozoa's pond
where Prince Alito died.

On the low pass
in Gozoa's pond
where Prince Alito died.

I continued to play for a few minutes after he fell silent. When I opened my eyes, there was a full moon in the night sky and the Mata was stretched out on his back. David was kneeling anxiously over him. 'He's . . .'

'. . . not dead.' I sighed, stretching out myself. The analgesic of music had worn off, and I felt like a marathoner stumbling across the line. 'He's just popped over for renewal in the land of the ancestors. You and I don't have visas, so you'd best get some sleep!'

David chuckled. 'His trances do rejuvenate him, don't they?'

But I could not take my own advice. I lay there for another ten minutes, trying to imagine what could have driven a woman of Ma'Bamou's faith and fortitude to the great taboo.

MA'BAMOU (ANCESTORMENAI)

Kreektown | 18th August, 2002

I switch the gas off and close the doors. When I reach Tamiyo's Peugeot I wait for many minutes, before I go back to make sure I have switch the gas off. Then I go to the bafroom to check that the windows are very closed. They are very closed. I take me and Namodi's photograph from the wall. But is too big for Tamiyo's car, after all my other loads have entered in. So I take it to my bedroom where Namodi and Felimpe are sleeping, and I leave it on their grave, under my bed. That's when I leave my house for maybe the last and final time.

Travelling with Tamiyo is a journey I have done many times before. For eighteen years now, he's the driver of my monthly journeys to Cotonou to buy my okrika. But today's journey is different, somehow. My body is telling me to look at that house very well, because, well, nobody knows what song the agogo will sing next market day. The only thing we can know for sure is what it is singing now. Me that sold okrika during the war! And when people say, how can? I ask them whether they have ever seen any soldiers fighting naked. Yes, I sold khaki and okrika during the war. The snake is not dancing for us, that's just how she walks. Yes, with these two eyes I have seen war, but this thing is different, somehow.

This one is very different.

It is not yet five-thirty in the morning when we left Kreektown. Is a journey I have done many times before. We will travel for two hours to Benin, then the car will drink fuel, then we travel another two hours to Ore. This is where we will eat. Is funny really, but somehow the food in Ore is sweeter—in my mouth, oh—than the food in all those other towns we can pass. And

Tamiyo, if he likes, will take a little more fuel. Then we will travel a little more and stop at Sagamu, not to do anything, really, just to rest the car, because this is a Peugeot that is old enough to be called 'uncle' even.

This is where our today's journey will be different from all the journeys before-before. O Menai. Because today I am not going to buy okrika. We will not continue to the bush road to Benin Republic. We will branch here and enter Lagos. To the place where I am going to live, at least for another week. Or two even. (More than that, may GodMenai forbid.) To see what this cloud is carrying that is following Menai, whether it is rain or something else.

Whether it is rain or something else.

Kreektown is silent as we drive away: me, Tamiyo, and his wife, Sade. Whether it is silent because it is empty or because it is sleeping is another thing. Me, I did not go to anybody's house to say goodbye. There is no need for foolish things like that. This world is not a place for doing foolish things. This thing is like a war, O Menai. And when war comes is not the time to go around saying goodbye. After all, eyeswater is not for drinking, so what is the point of purposely making it?

We pass a army lorry on the road, entering Kreektown. Sade talks to me quickly-quickly, but I have seen them already. We left in time. That is one disgrace that would have killed me dead before my time, true: for soldiers to drag me from my own house to take me to a government dormitory. Something I did not see, even during the civil war. Is better for me to go for a one-week holiday and live with Sade and her husband. Or two weeks even. (More than that, may GodMenai forbid.) Because for many days now they have been going street to street, catching human beings like fowls . . . but is better not to think about things like that. After all, eyeswater is not for drinking.

Sade claps her hands, three, four, five times. 'It's a hard thing, but what can government do?'

'They can leave us alone,' I say.

'The sickness is too much for the health centre, you know that yourself.'

'Urubiesu simini randa si kwemka.'

'What's that, Ma?'

I am laughing a little, which I did not know was possible, for a woman who buried her husband inside the bedroom only three weeks ago, who is leaving her house of forty years. 'Is too difficult to translate!' But because it made me laugh, they ask and ask me, so I say, 'You know how it is when you're in the middle of a dream, and you know you're dreaming, and you're eating something nice—or maybe not even eating, maybe just doing something very nice, and you're thinking: Biesu! If only I can just take this thing that I'm eating, or doing, and bring it into the real world! Ah! Then you can say: Urubiesu simini randa si kwemka!'

They laugh a little, but I can see that it is not coming from the laughing-place. That's the thing. Only Menai can see it well. Tamiyo is looking at Sade. He shakes his head. 'But . . . what is happening is not very nice, even!'

'That's the thing,' I say, and I am not laughing anymore. 'I'm wishing I can take it into a dream and leave it there.'

The car begin to go very fast. Sade put her hand on her husband shoulder but the car continue to go very fast. 'God punish Trevi,' he is cursing, and his voice is not very strong, although it is still too dark to know whether is because he is crying or not. But I can see that although he is not Menai, he has seen it very well.

'Ami,' we pray.

◆ ◆ ◆

WE PASS Ubesia very quickly. I can see the memorial they built for the six Kreektown childrens. And I remember that day that I was dressing quickly-quickly to take Felimpe to hospital, and Namodi shout to me that no need! That she has die! Then my blouse fall from my hand, and I carry Bamou's daughter that I take as a baby from her mother's dying womb. And not remembering that I haven't even cover my breast, am carrying her on the road. And am crying calamity. And there's no Menai with blood in their body that can hear calamity and not answer. And when they see that I have no blouse, that's how they tear their own shirt and blouse off: is not something we planned . . . is a madness of sadness that crazed Kreektown that day. Because what's the use of dress to a dead person? And are we not all dead, O Menai, that bury our children before ourselves? And when they see that I'm carrying my dead, that's how they carry all the other five children that are waiting for burial too. And when I tire, the young men carry Felimpe, until I look back at the governor's house and see that GodMenai has opened the hearts of my country and there are more people with us than all the descendants of the Menai, even! That's when the spirit of Felimpe stopped crying and I took her home and buried her.

And how will I know that Bamou will blame his own mother and will run away from me forever, because I could not keep his daughter from the call of sleepcatastrophe? But am I GodMenai?

Am I?

At the petrol station in Benin they were looking for my tablets inside my green portmanteau when they found the sigilisi box. This is a funny thing: they don't know what it is! This world is a really funny place: there are adults that don't even know sigilisi! So we stop everything and I taught them how to play the game. And—that's the thing about sigilisi—we didn't go anywhere again for another one hour. They like sigilisi. Hah! Maybe living with them will not be . . . but it is better to be going step after step. To be living day after day. Is better that way.

The road is very bad. Every time another hole in the road scrapes the bottom of the old Peugeot, I am feeling it, almost as if the car and me myself are the same! At the end, even Sade is angry with me. 'If it happens to us, you will do even more than we are doing for you, so what's all this "sorry-sorry" for?'

So I stop saying it, but I still feeling it.

By the time we reach Ore, my stomach's rabbit is biting—of which, even when I was in labour with Rubi and Bamou, nothing more than termite came out of his stomachsac, upon all the pain. Today, I just smile and keep quiet, to hide the pain from my friends, because what can they do for me, except to say "sorry" and feel bad too?

◆ ◆ ◆

SO EVENTUALLY we reach Lagos. And from the things that happen there, and from the things I saw, I can just say that of the two of us, Namodi is more lucky, that he has die already. Only ten days have pass, but already, Sade is saying every evening how, is it not funny that the shop beside her own is empty and how the nearest okrika shop is more than two bus stop away. Yet, am not a child, and I know that people who are on two weeks' holiday don't open shops.

And one thing I want more than anything is to sit in a market where my maybebuyer will say to me, 'Worie,' instead of 'Good morning,' and I will answer, 'Dobemu.' I hungry to walk down the street and children will say to me, 'Kpabi,' and I will say, 'Anobi.' And I will do my eyes as if I don't recognise them (which is how to make a child happy that she have grow so tall since last week) and they will give me their timi-torqwa, counting back only two or three generations, until I say 'Ubiesu! So Anamu was your grandfather!' or 'Oho! Chame's daughter! How you have grown!' (But all that is pretend!)

But all I'm doing, every day after day in Lagos, is speaking this English, like a stammerer.

Until even Sade saw that there's a river inside me that must to flow, and that river is my language. So, when Tamiyo left for work she locked her fruit-and-ice-water shop and we took a bus to Ipaja, to the hostels where they are keeping Menai.

The Lagos walls are the hardest thing. Kreektown doesn't build walls. For what are we building it? Around this hostel is the same: walls and walls until it is looking really like a prison, not a house to help Menai. There's a gateman there, with his book that we have to sign. So I sign and we enter.

It is not empty, but not full either. I see Asiama, Nurufe, and Egoni, with all their brothers and sisters, and we hug and greet and hug and greet and cry a little . . . but nobody brings water to greet us in the Menai way. Is not many weeks they left Kreektown and they have forgotten that already? There is no adult there. Asiama was in secondary two in Kreektown, now she and all the other children are waiting for new schools to take them.

'Where's everybody?' I ask.

'In hospital,' Asiama says. 'I will take you there.'

Am happy for that walk. Small by small, the rivers begin to flow again, that small Menai I spoke with Asiama. There's a language you can speak that melts the frozen words in your head into rivers for your mouth, so that the thoughts of grandmothers you never met can flow from your lips. Asiama's own mother have die and she is too serious for her age, but already her Menai is becoming heavy on her tongue—the way she is telling me, 'Anuisi gobemu expressway lote.' So what is wrong with anuisi gobemu numakta lote? Even her hairstyle is not the type that Etie would have plait for a secondary two girl . . . but this is Lagos, not Kreektown, and in the middle of a war is not the time to be looking at a poor child's hairstyle. So I enjoying talking to the granddaughter that I have not have since termites began to eat my Felimpe in March 1990.

I was still talking to her when I notice that she was not listening again to me. Even Sade's mouth was open. So I turned and followed their eyes, up, up to where they were looking at the wooden poles surrounding a house that was building up into the sky. Then, Asiama was crying: 'It is Masingo, it is Masingo!'

'Masingo? Where?'

Then I saw her, and I think I hear her crying calamity at the same time! To hear somebody shouting in Menai! In Lagos! And for that shouting to be calamity! So we ran towards the house, even me with my iron stick and the shorter leg I have carried from my mother's womb.

'She ran away from the hostel yesterday,' Asiama was crying as she was running. 'We haven't seen her since yesterday.'

To pass through that crowd was trouble. Somebody has drag a old mattress to under where she was standing, but she was at the top of the fifteen storeys, so we began to climb. This was more climbing than I have climb before in my life, but this was Masingo up there in the sky. There is nobody alive who tells stories like Masingo. You can hear the same story every night for six days and they will come out like six different stories. And this was her standing at quarter-to-abomination?

GodMenai forbid!

So I struggled and struggled until we reached upstairs. Even there was full of people, no space to pass. But we scream her name and scream her name and she stop her singing. So the people standing around can see that we know this woman, so they let us pass, all those people, until I was standing there, not even ten steps from where she stood on a plank they tie for painters on the outside of the building. She was holding a iron rod. She only has to leave the iron to fall, but I call her. 'Masingo, sepete?'

She left the dormitory, but she didn't know the way back to Kreektown. In all the motor parks she went, nobody even know the name 'Kreektown,' or the people call Menai! Lagos was not a one-motor-park village like Kreektown or a three-motor-park town like Ubesia. She was not like me that travel many times to Cotonou, that even speak a little English as well. She was Masingo, and apart from the day we march to Ubesia with the bodies of our childrens, inside Kreektown was all her life.

'I'm the last Menai,' she is crying.

Why does everybody saying this all the time?

'You're not, Masingo. See, I'm here as well! And Asiama is here as well.'

'We're not enough!'

So I tell her all the lies that can bring her back to the concrete of the house. And little by little she stop her crying and begin to walk back. Because that is what adults do, O Menai: tell the little lies to the children until they are old enough to know that this life is war itself. And although she is almost forty herself, she is still a child to me. 'Amusia natna asikoro muezin,' I say.

'Netie?' she ask.

And me, poor me, I have to swear to her with the name of GodMenai. Because words are tie together in the belly of the lie. Say just one of them, and she will drag her ugly sisters out, one after the other: 'I just coming from Kreektown and I will take you back,' I lie. 'Everybody is going back now. They are building a hospital now . . .'

Finally she walked down the shaking plank and reached me, and every-body was flatclapping and Masingo held me tighter than Bamou and Rubi have ever held me in this life. O Menai! To hold them one more time, before I become a taboo ancestor who will never fellowship with Grand-Menai! How sweet can another man's church and country be, to make children forget the breastwaters of their own mother like this?

'Anobi, anobi, anobi . . .' But why is she thanking me? Then they took her from me, the police and others, and strange languages wash over us like dirty water, enough to comfort Masingo for today and for tomorrow. But I do not want to see her face when she knows that I lie to her. That I lie to her in the name of GodMenai.

I feeling warmer than I ever feel before, like a woman that has give birth. But this is the fate of women: sometimes we die in childbirth. Like Bamou's wife. I let my walking stick fall. The iron cries on concrete. It does not hit the mattress. By the grace of GodMenai, me myself, I won't.

JUSTICE SHITTA

Judge's Chambers, Abuja | 25th April, 2005

Shitta J. had just received a nolle prosequi and was having trouble breathing. It was a powerful piece of paper. Once signed by the attorney general, it could end a federal prosecution anywhere in Nigeria and set the defendant free—whatever the evidence or the state of the trial. In Shitta J.'s twenty-year career on the bench, he had seen only three. He was just about to sign a ruling to reject Badu's bail application and remand him to prison custody when the fourth arrived, with Badu's name on it.

It took his breath away.

Since he was alone in chambers, he had no need to pay lip service to politically correct notions of judicial restraint, and he flung a law report across the room with an oath. *Politicians!* He thought of the past few days of sleeplessness, the trial within a trial he had conducted, the garrulous arguments and submissions by amicus curiae, flamboyant senior counsels, and ambitious younger lawyers—while his caseload piled up in his regular court—and a black rage welled up in him.

It was not just the premature end of the biggest case of his career, it was the sheer cynical termination of an open-and-shut case, and it boiled his blood. That a judge was nothing more than a paperweight to be flung to and fro by irresponsible politicians! Bad eggs like Omakasa gave the entire bench a bad name, and now that he had set out to do a thorough job, he was being stymied at every turn! If he had been born in a country with a proper inquisitorial system, he could have directed investigations himself as an examining judge, and once a strong case was made out, no politician masquerading as an attorney general with his eyes on a general election could jump in and end it!

The legality principle would have taken care of that.

He rose and felt around in a drawer for a kola nut, a habit he had fallen into during his youth service in Aba. He found a lobe and he chewed it without pleasure. He glanced at the clock. In thirty minutes his tribunal was due to start. The circus was already waiting, the lawyers, the journalists, the public . . . Yet it was all over! He shook his head. He should have followed his father into the rice importation business. With a sigh, he dropped into his thinking chair and shut his eyes.

He had achieved a respectable reputation as a fair and fearless judge, but he had a simple judicial routine, really: when he had taken in all the facts of the case, he let his mind see the path to justice, and then he looked for the law to take him there. It was as simple as that. Occasionally there were gaps in the law, but he always found creative ways to build a bridge to justice. He did not allow technicalities of law to make an ass of him. He left that for the court of appeal: to follow him across the bridge or to slip through the gaps into opprobrium. He simply did the right thing by his own conscience. His thinking chair helped. He never sat there for any other purpose, and it was a great aid to concentration. For him the Badu case turned on a simple question of vigilantism: whether the law could sanction mob law, permit over a hundred million people to abduct and lynch their own personal devils at will.

And it didn't matter if Omakasa J. was the devil himself.

The principle was so fundamental that Shitta J. realised he had found the issue on which he was prepared to resign from the bench! As he reflected on the facts of the Badu case that had emerged from the briefs and affidavits filed so far, the thought of placing his entire career on the line for a principle gave him a rush of power. Having decided where the justice of the case lay, what remained was the legal path there . . . He tossed the rest of the kola into his mouth and crunched speculatively. He had to demystify the attorney general's power of nolle prosequi . . . It was possible—without precedent but possible . . .

On a strict interpretation of the law he ought to strike out the case as soon as he entered the tribunal. But . . . what if a legal power was exercised for an illegal or improper purpose; could it not be invalidated? There were authorities for that general proposition of law. In the light of such over-whelming positive identification by two dozen policemen from the Abuja and Ubesia divisions, from Sergeant Elue, *and* from Charles Pitani himself, surely there were prima facie grounds to impute bad faith . . . He would ask for arguments from counsel on the point, and *then* he would rule according to his conscience.

Badu would not walk free.

Not on his watch.

He made up his mind and locked down his decision. After rising from his thinking chair, he made a beeline for his desk. He had only fifteen min-utes before court sessions started, and it was possible to set a watch by Judge Shitta's court sessions. He signed his ruling denying the bail. He was ready to take on the presidency, in a battle that his superiors at the court of appeal and the supreme court would most likely hang him out to dry for . . . but he was ready.

He dressed and rang for his registrar, who took his papers and led the way to the judge's entrance of the tribunal, where the clock over the en-trance showed that it was still eight minutes before the hour. The adrena-line from the nolle prosequi had thrown off his internal clock. He paused. He could not resume a minute early, but the anteroom had been furnished for just such an exigency: a suite of chairs in which he could lounge and view a muted television. Shitta J. took one of the chairs for the eight-minute wait. There was an Ubesia press conference on TV. He had seen it the night before and did not pay much attention to the history-making female Nanga. Instead his eyes wandered over the strangely attired Sontik men and women behind her.

That was how he saw a face that took away his breath, for the second time that morning. The man standing behind Nanga Amana was in his mid-twenties, of medium height, mixed race, and clearly a clone, a dop-pelgänger of the man in his holding cell downstairs! Judge Shitta's eyes worked like a forensic camera, and he knew, devastatingly, that the open-and-shut case before him that morning was wide open again and that the overwhelming identification evidence on which his convictions were based were suddenly, fatally undermined.

If he were the attorney general, right there and then, he'd have signed a nolle prosequi.

The timing of the newscast hit him like a religious experience, and he reflected on the benefits of being a Nigerian judge in an adversarial sys-tem who was supposed to sit dispassionately, well above the fray, without investing his ego and emotions in an investigation, who could decide the justice of a case purely on the state of the pleadings before him, nolle prosequis inclusive. When the orderly finally plucked up the courage to interrupt his reflections, Judge Shitta had made a different kind of judicial history: he was fifteen minutes late for court.

ESTELLE BAPTISTE

Abuja Tribunal | 25th April, 2005

'What is this Nollywood proboscis? I love it, you know, I really do, but what is it?' I asked.

'Nolle prosequi,' the lawyer answered, looking worried. 'It is a technicality.'

We were waiting in the registry for the paperwork for Izak's release, but he was not looking like a lawyer whose client was about to be set free, and that worried me. The excitement of seeing Izak in a few minutes rushed to my head. I leaned toward him and asked, 'Is it your fees?'

'What?'

'I will still pay your full fees,' I promised, but he only scowled.

'Look,' he said, nodding at the window. Outside were hundreds of people waiting to catch a glimpse of Izak. 'You see those policemen?'

I looked again, this time noticing the policemen. 'Okay.'.

'They are also waiting for your husband.'

'I don't understand. Their prosecutor just *nolled* the case . . .'

'It is a technicality. Sometimes, someone eats a bribe and files a nolle prosequi . . . did you pay a bribe?'

'No!'

'So maybe they think there is a mistake in their case, or maybe they have new evidence and want to file more serious charges, or sue in another court—with a nolle prosequi, they get a second shot. So the defendant steps out of court and they arrest him again.'

I looked again, and it *was* true, the policemen seemed more interested in us than the crowd behind them. My excitement evaporated.

'Don't cry, madam,' warned the lawyer.

'I'm not crying,' I said.

'Look, this is what we will do. Stand here, as if you are still waiting for your husband. I will arrange with my friends here and sneak your husband into the car park through the bailiff's section while the police are watching you. We will take him out in a tinted car—is the Nanga still coming?'

'Yes. They missed their flight, but they are still coming.'

'Great. Nanga Amana will pick you up, and I will call and tell you where to meet us. Madam! You have to look like someone whose husband has just been freed; don't cry!'

'I'm not crying,' I said.

The lawyer left. I stood there, pretending to be a wife whose husband had just been set free. I hate this country. I was still waiting when a policeman walked up to me. 'Are you Mrs. Baptiste?'

I nodded dumbly.

'Please come with me.'

My throat dried up. *Estelle Rosemarie Baptiste, you see your life? You will be shot with your husband!*

He did not handcuff me. Instead he led me politely through the crowd until we were in the car park. The lawyer's SUV was sitting there, sandwiched by police trucks in front and behind. As we approached, Izak opened the rear door. The policeman who had arrested me was looking at me with worry. 'Madam, don't—'

'I'm not crying,' I snapped.

Then I was inside the car, in Izak's embrace. He did not tell me not to cry. My lawyer was well brought up and did not look at us. He drove behind the police truck, and soon we were speeding down the empty roads of Abuja with the second police truck behind us. 'Which court are they taking us to?' I whispered.

That was when Izak gave me an envelope with the crest of the Presidency.

'We're not going to court,' explained the lawyer. He was no longer looking worried. 'Your husband is late for his national award, so they sent a police escort from the Presidency.'

HUMPHREY CHOW

Hilton Hotel, Abuja | 25th April, 2005

Karma was what I had thought, standing in that dock. To have missed standing trial for Yan Chow's murder, for which I was guilty, and Bamou's death, about which I knew something, only be tried for the death of a judge I had never heard of . . . *Karma,* I had thought and had held my peace.

This is the real peace, though. Sitting here with Estelle. It had been three hours since I left the court and the shock of detention, and the sense of sudden freedom had not yet worn off.

We had arrived at the conference centre on time, but the event had been postponed for an hour, another hour, another hour, and then adjourned to 7:00 p.m. in the evening because of compelling affairs of state on the president's diary.

'Probably overslept,' grumbled the old man next to us, jumping angrily to his feet. 'I could have spent all this time at a fuel queue!'

'Maybe we should go back to Abidjan,' I whispered to Estelle. 'The lawyer thinks—'

'Nonsense,' she said. 'Come, you need a proper bath to wash off that prison smell.'

We headed for the hotel proper. Even outside the court, people stared as I passed. Is this notoriety or fame? Do I have to claim Badu's deeds to get to keep this face recognition? And—more to the point—does this mean I can now sell a hundred thousand copies of my next book?

At the reception I reached for my wallet, but Estelle pulled me towards the lift. 'Come, we have a room already.'

That was the point at which I became suspicious: earlier, she had made and received a couple of mobile calls out of earshot. But if I cannot trust Estelle, I do not have anything. I followed her to the lift, and we rose to the fourth floor. She led me by the hand. Her fingers were wriggling again, and I knew she was excited.

I felt cautious. I had no need for excitement now. What I needed was peace, not a surprise party by the Abidjan community in Abuja.

She knocked once, and a short woman held the door open. There was just one other woman in the room, so I knew it was not quite a party. My mouth went round. I recognised the door opener, but the place was wrong . . . I felt the searing pain of Dr. Borha's death again. My shock showed in my voice. 'You! You're the paparazza!'

'You have a great memory, Humphrey Chow.'

'His name is Izak,' said Estelle.

The paparazza grinned. 'Come here, Humphrey "Izak" Chow.' She hugged me. Tight. I didn't know how to handle this. Something was going on beyond my control. What was she doing here, so far from Putney Village? She let me go and hugged Estelle as well. 'Have you told him?'

Estelle shook her head.

'Told me what?'

'Promise me you won't freak out, Izak,' Estelle said.

'My name is Amana Udama Bentiy,' she said, 'ex-paparazza. This is Sheesti Kroma-Alanta.'

Slowly, formally, I shook hands with the second woman. When she stood up, I could see that she was heavily pregnant. Her hand was limp, but her eyes were cold steel. Yet it was not just steel I saw in her eyes but also peace. *'Worie,'* she whispered.

'Dobemu,' I replied, without thinking. *'Eriana de.'*

She hugged me then. When we came apart, I realised that she was struggling not to cry. I remembered how Bamou had responded when he heard his language spoken.

'You were born a twin, Humphrey,' said Amana abruptly.

'I know.' They stared at me with surprise. It was clearly not the answer they were expecting, so I explained: 'When I was a teenager I broke into a Social Services cabinet. I saw my brother's death certificate.' I grinned. 'I was five minutes older.'

There were no reciprocating smiles.

'The certificate was a forgery,' said Amana quietly. 'Your brother is alive and well.'

It was my turn to be stunned. I sat down on the bed. Amana put a letter in my hand. *Dear Son,* it started, but it was not written to me. The minutes passed, and I set the letter aside.

'Are you ready to meet Zanda?' Sheesti asked softly.

I shook my head. *Tobin Rani was my blood father.* I took Estelle's hand and walked out of the room. We walked down the corridor, to the lifts, in silence, and there she stopped me with a long embrace. The coins dropped slowly into place. I played back the days and months and years with my father, Tobin Rani. Everything began to make sense, especially the way he had looked at me, especially the jail sentence he had served for me. I felt bereft. I had hugged him many times but never as a father. I had a People, but they were almost extinct. *I had a brother,* but I had grown up lost, alone . . .

I *have* a brother.

'Have you met him?'

She nodded. 'Izak,' she warned, 'he's your *identical* twin.'

I processed that. 'Badu?'

She searched my face with alarm, her fingers massaging her tattoo. 'Yes, but it's not how you think. You know how you do things and go places and don't remember them? Give him a chance, *please.'*

We walked back to the room. The ladies had not moved a muscle. 'I'm ready now,' I said.

'Zanda,' said Amana hoarsely, and the bathroom door opened slowly. My image looked out from a mirror, and growing a mind of its own, stepped out carefully, bearing the vase of himself across the room. I saw how my clumsy embarrassment was not my fault but that of my genes. He offered me a glass of water. '*Amis andgus,* Humphrey,' he said.

I took the glass. My eyes did not leave his face. I drank. '*Andgus ashen.* It's been a long time, younger brother.'

'You may have come out first,' he said with a grin, 'but in Menai culture, the senior twin sends the younger out first to scope out the world.'

The ladies laughed, and I knew then that even though my brother was the most dangerous terrorist in Nigeria, he was all right.

Then, for the first time—outside the womb, at least—we hugged.

ESTELLE BAPTISTE

Hilton Hotel, Abuja | 25th April, 2005

I love this country. Within ten hours my husband had gone from a courtroom where he was on trial for his life to a cocktail party to mark his national award. I looked at my watch. It was 8:00 p.m. Mishael was probably standing in the kitchenette, buttering a baguette and shouting at the surfers in the café to keep the noise down. I grinned in spite of myself. I was in the Congress Hall of the Abuja Hilton with my husband, his strange family, and maybe seven hundred other awardees, spouses, and friends.

If I was not having the time of my life it was because I was worrying about what would happen next. Finding Rubi was the least of our problems. Sheesti had her telephone number at the Sacred Heart Convent in Ikot Ekpene. We still had not spoken to her, though, because she not broken the vow of silence she took in November 2002 when she got the news of her brother's death. She had not forgiven herself, poor woman, for breaking the news of their mother's death by letter. Still, they would soon know the truth in Abidjan. She would testify by letter, and Bamou's murder investigation would close. Izak was a free man. I should have been enjoying the occasion.

I was not.

I was beginning to recognise the onset of Izak's illness. He had not said a word for five minutes, and I saw the muscles of his face grow rigid. A distant look entered his eyes. Take a bow, Estelle Baptiste! This is the public stage of your *international* disgrace! That Fuju Club freakout was just a trial run. *Dieu du ciel!* . . . I raised my eyes to the ceiling. They filled with tears as I said a silent prayer.

When I looked down, Izak had disappeared. I looked around desperately, and he was cutting across the hall in the direction of an overloud group of men who had attached themselves to a minibar. I left Amana and Zanda abruptly and hurried after my husband.

There were not many Europeans in the room. This one was loud and friendly and wore a blue dashiki—which looked pretty good on him. Izak pushed himself into the man's circle just as I got to his side. He did not do anything crazy or over the top, just offered a handshake. I took Izak's other arm. My heart was pounding with relief as they shook hands warmly. I realised that maybe I was the one freaking out.

'Are you Dalminda Roco?' Izak asked.

The other man made a face. *'Dalminda Loco?* What sort of name is that?' He seemed offended to have been mistaken for a mad Dalminda, and he reclaimed his hand to his chest and stared hard at Izak. Indeed he seemed the very opposite of the character described in Izak's bomber story. The introductions broke down then; he did not give his name, and Izak did not introduce us. The cocktail clot around us melted away and reformed elsewhere. It is easy to look miserable at a cocktail party: just stand by yourself and don't talk. We looked miserable, as Izak slowly retreated into himself. His eyes followed the European who was not loco around the room.

'He said he's not Dalminda Loco,' I said impatiently, trying to distract him. 'Let it go!'

'Roco,' said Izak. *'Roco.'*

◆ ◆ ◆

DURING THE presentations, the man Izak had mistaken for Dalminda was called up to the dais. His name was Daniel Sheldon, and he was introduced as a company director and a philanthropist who was patron to many Nigerian charities. My husband went up for his own award without crisis, but he barely looked at it.

Afterwards, there were photographers outside. I tried to bring a smile to his face for the pictures. 'Just smile, Izak! You must have been mistaken . . . he's a philanthropist.'

'Terrorist, not philanthropist.' He gestured at the award I was holding proudly to my breast. 'You are real, I know that, but as for this award, this ceremony, this Sheldon, I'll wake up tomorrow and it will all be a dream.'

I glared at him. 'At least you can make some money for us when you write it up for *Balding Wolf!*'

That seemed to do it. It still was not a proper laugh, but it was enough. The bulbs flashed and that was the picture in *The Punch* newspaper the very next day.

◆ ◆ ◆

Ubesia | 26th April, 2005

I had never before seen my husband cry. When we attended his parents' funeral soon after our wedding in Abidjan, he did not shed a tear. Yet when I returned to our bedroom, he was alone in the dark. And when I drew the curtains apart, his eyes were red.

'Izak! What happened?'

Of course he tried to 'be a man'! There was a faster way to find out, so I stormed off to the grill bar beside the marina where I had left the brothers laughing barely an hour earlier. Zanda was still there with Lantanya, and Sheesti was just arriving. 'What did you do to my husband?'

'He's just gone to the loo,' said his brother. 'He'll soon be back. We have an appointment with Sheesti—'

'Well, he's in the bedroom *crying!*'

Zanda rose, worried.

'We were just listening to a recording,' said Lantanya. 'Then he said he had to use the loo . . .'

'What recording was that?' asked Sheesti.

'Our torqwa,' said Zanda. 'I recorded Mata Nimito's recital of our ancestry . . .'

Sheesti took his hand and mine and pulled us down onto the bench. She has a quality about her, this woman, like calamine lotion on a back prickly with heat rash. When we were sitting again, she said quietly, 'He'll be fine. It's a normal response to your first torqwa. It's a shock to go from not knowing your parents to knowing your ancestors from a thousand years ago.'

She took Zanda's phone, and in a moment we were listening to an old man's voice singing in a strange language. Sheesti started. I saw goose pimples on her arms. She took my hand and placed it so I could feel her baby kicking. 'He likes Mata Nimito's voice.' She smiled.

'I want to meet this man,' I whispered.

'You will. I'm back from London in four days. You must come with us to Khartoum.'

TOBIN RANI

Sudan | 27th April, 2005

We had made camp at dawn, and I was so tired from driving the last shift that I slept until the sun was overhead. I woke hungry, to the aroma of a simmering soup, and found the Mata and David on deck chairs under the shade of the tailgate. David was learning to count in Menai. 'Better late than never,' he laughed, passing me a plate.

We ate facing the Keep of Njakara; it was still a hundred kilometres away, a scenic range of hills that had materialised overnight on the northern horizon. The granite outcrop was cobalt blue, with a private retainer of clouds on a plateau of date palms, and it overlooked silica-rich dunes that glistened in the sun. David scratched his new beard. 'I'm not complaining, you understand, but I'm hoping we're not digging up five-hundred-year-old mummies in this mountain.'

The Mata smiled, and his eyes moistened. *'Ariemo mai Njakara nasuti kaisoko.'*

I looked at the range with new eyes. I had gone to sleep before the sun came fully up and had not really taken in the view. In awe I said, 'Our greatest poems from antiquity describe the beauty of the Keep of Njakara. Mata Nimito always wanted to see it before he died.'

Minutes passed. 'Was it worth the journey, Mata?' asked David softly.

'Anobi, Tobin ba Davidi,' sighed the Mata gratefully. 'Journey? It is worth living through three centuries to see this sight. Once upon a time, we ruled all this.' His finger pointed from the eastern end of the range to the middle, then slowly came to rest in his lap.

As I translated the Mata, I thought it odd that he claimed just one half, when the Menai historysongs claimed the entire plateau. Perhaps he was finally losing his memory. Then I looked sideways and saw the smile with which Mata Nimito had left for eternity.

He was a hundred and ten years old.

DAVID BALSAM

Sudan | 27th April, 2005

It was a moment of no particular significance, the sky beyond the Keep of Njakara remaining the featureless azure of the previous week, a bland blue soup variegated by the flimsiest strands of white. David watched his companion closely, waiting for the outburst, the breakdown, but it did not come. Tobin washed and rubbed down the Mata's thin onionlike skin with a fragrant oil. Then he robed him in red and shrouded him in Kakandu's last weave.

'Are you okay?' David asked.

'I'm fine. I've been mourning him since I was a boy.'

Then he zipped up the last Mata in his body bag.

'We don't have much time now, in this heat.' It was the end of the quixotic quest for an ancestral Field of Stones, but David felt no vindication, only a strangely disorienting loss. 'Where do we bury him?'

Tobin glanced around the desert. 'Any old place,' he said quietly. 'Any bloody old place.'

David pulled out the log. 'I'll call it "under the shadow of the Keep of Njakara," right?'

Tobin ignored him. David took the spade down from the truck, moved the Mata's deck chair, and began to dig. Tobin made no effort to help. During his first rest stop, David sat amidst the pile of the old man's clothes that Tobin had thrown down from the truck. He picked up some rolled-up leather scrolls and looked at them with quickening interest.

'This is impossible!'

'What?'

'Is this . . . a Menai script? You have *writing*? Mata Nimito could read this?'

'Our writing is older than the Latin alphabet. Everyone raised in the way of the Menai can read and write it.'

'I know exactly where the "Field" is.'

'*What?*'

David rose and scrambled toward the truck. He reached inside for the satellite phone and the paper maps. 'This script, I'm positive, belongs to the Meroe family. The civilisation of the Meroes disappeared from history about eighteen hundred years ago, but thousands of writings in their script survive in museums across the world.'

He pulled up the map on which we had sketched our hopeful journey. He powered on his tablet and scratched his head ruefully. 'You know that empty patch we thought we were heading for? My GPS may consider it empty desert now, but a century ago, it was a city of dead kings. Begrawiya. If the Mata's stories are accurate, he was heading to the pyramids of the Meroe kings.'

Pause. 'And the Meroe kings are . . . ?'

David stared. 'Now you surprise me. They had a kingdom . . . the Egyptians called it the land of Kush. The height of its majesty was 200 BC. For Christ's sake, they conquered Egypt at one point! Their kings were called the black pharaohs!'

'Oh. That Meroë. I know about them. I'm just confused about the connec—'

'You *know about* them! You're fifty, for God's sake. What did you teach your children? All you know is Menai this and Menai that! The Meroes also built pyramids—far more than the Egyptians. They have over two hundred in Begrawiya. They adopted the Egyptian script, but they had their own written language!'

'And these scrolls?'

'As a curator, I'd place them in a Meroitic gallery today.'

Tobin took a deep breath. 'You never said so.'

'I never saw them.'

Tobin paused. 'What are we waiting for?'

David grabbed his phone. Waving the maps, he said, 'These maps are not historically annotated. I've been out of the field for years, I'll need to call colleagues in England. Put the Mata in the truck. Move your ass and clean up here. I have to make contact with Khartoum.'

◆ ◆ ◆

TOBIN HAD been driving for three hours, and David had been working his phone intermittently all through the drive. He pulled gloomily at his beard.

'There are any number of places we could take him . . . Dongola, Karima . . . but they are all historical sites. Pyramids and all. We couldn't drop a bubblegum wrapper there, much less bury an old man, even if he is your great Mata.'

'I'll talk to them.'

David laughed humourlessly.

◆ ◆ ◆

DAVID BRACED himself against the bumps of the desert floor as he studied the scrolls. He cursed and slammed his hand again and again against the dashboard of the truck.

'What now?'

'I met the holy grail of African archaeology, a living expert of a close relative of the Meroitic script, and I let him slip through my fingers! Am I a retard or what?'

'I guess we are agreed on one thing then.'

◆ ◆ ◆

DAVID SNIFFED. He rustled through his maps. 'We have more immediate concerns. We need to have the old man embalmed.'

'Not if we're burying him today.'

'Be realistic. Karima is still twelve hours away even at your speed. On the strength of these scrolls, there is a ghost of a chance we can give the old man his last wish, but we still have weeks and weeks of paperwork and political lobbying to get through!'

A minute passed, and Tobin eased off the accelerator. 'What are you saying?'

David pointed at the map. 'That's a tarred road. Bede is only a hundred miles northeast. It is not much of a deviation.'

'Not much chance of a mortuary there. Folks tend to bury the same day or the next in this neck of the woods.'

'Worth the chance. Besides, it looks big enough for fuel. We're running low.'

David plotted the coordinates into the GPS, and Tobin followed the new course.

Eventually, they found the highway. There wasn't much tar left on it, but they made forty miles per hour steadily and travelled northeast. The land was deserted, lifeless. Bustards and eagles drifted in the clear skies, but apart from that, they were alone in the world. Two hours into the road they found out why: it terminated on the lip of a wadi with a steep cliff on the far side. The bridge across had been swept away.

◆ ◆ ◆

ABANDONING THE GPS, they spread a physical contour map on the bonnet. David located the wadi and traced its course. It ran eighty miles south and only twenty-five miles north. They looked north. The northern miles, furrowed by ridges and pitted by pustules of black tar, did not seem motorable as far as the eyes could see. David put a point on the map and drew a six-inch-diameter circle around it.

'The fuel circle,' he said grimly.

Tobin drew a concentric circle with double the radius. 'The water circle. I shouldn't have washed the old man back there, but I thought we were going home.'

'We are now,' David told him, 'unless we're really lucky.'

◆ ◆ ◆

A LATE lunch lightened their depression.

'There's one circle we didn't draw,' said Tobin, 'the trek circle. We could camp here, cross the ravine on foot, and walk overnight to get fuel. It's only sixty more miles to Bede. We could make it by dawn.'

'I love that word, *only*—' He broke off, and Tobin turned to follow his gaze. They both rose as a small herd of goats emerged from the wadi.

◆ ◆ ◆

THE TEENAGE goatherd's English was rudimentary, but the word *water* was enough. They drove after him at the pace of his goats, into the motorable bed of the wadi and another two kilometres north to his village, announced from afar by the limbs of a great baobab. It was a sprawling settlement with a few hundred homes and an overhead tank fed by a borehole. Yet both the village and the dirt road that served it were invisible on their maps, electronic and paper alike.

'No fuel station here,' sighed David.

They did not get much welcome either. The looks that greeted them were not as friendly as the goatherd's. But the villagers let them fill up their water tanks from the hose at the borehole.

An old woman approached on a cane. She seemed to carry some authority, as her circuit of the truck attracted more than the usual amount of attention. Speaking volubly, with some violence, she bore down on David and Tobin as they finished bathing in a line of communal stalls whose walls ended just above the neck.

'Wonder what she's saying,' muttered David, beginning to wish they had trekked to Bede.

'Our grandmother says,' said a coal-black youth beside the goatherd, '"Where do these idiots always going with so much stuff?"'

The two men exchanged glances over the dwarf walls. Then they stared at their new interpreter.

'What's your name?' Tobin asked.

'Deen.'

'You want to know?' He struggled into his clothes. 'Come.'

◆ ◆ ◆

THE MATA'S body brought on a thaw. The villagers found something noble in the carrying of an old man—who had died on a trip—across the Sahara to his ancestral home. Suddenly David and Tobin found themselves invited to a meal, which grew in impromptu leaps into a funeral feast.

The village was New Aria. It was less than ten years old. The New Arians had migrated south when their old settlement was burnt in the war between rebels and their government. They spoke tearfully of their ancestral home, vowed to go back, and then laughed and brought the subject back to the burial of old men.

It was a sad little place, a soft underbelly of the parched desert. Dozens of juvenile economic trees too young for shade or fruit. A crop of camels crouched under a shelter built of palm fronds. A village square of packed earth darkened by donkey droppings. Several trucks, sturdy and virile despite their age, sat ready for the next cross-Saharan trip, which would take place on the morrow. Bales of hay, of dried spices, of fodder. Uniformly lanky children with wide-eyes, modest women, earnest men . . . David's wandering eyes were dragged back to the feast by the old woman's wagging finger.

'Our grandmother says,' said Deen, 'he must sleep here.'

'We will,' said Tobin. 'Tell her she is very kind. We will go tomorrow.'

'No, no, your father, we will dig grave for him. Our grandmother says, the body he will smell. No good at all.'

A dust cloud appeared in the distance, just ahead of a roar of engines that precluded further conversation. The younger children grew excited, crowding into the square, where two minibuses apparently driven by frustrated rally drivers arrived in a scream of tyres. The menfolk debarked whooping and sharing sweets.

They were wary of strangers, too, but easily won over, and they cheered at the prospects of a party. More interpreters emerged from the new arrivals, who all worked in Bede. As the night wore on, three more buses arrived. The funeral bow acquired yet another string as music was added to the mix.

Feeling a little inadequate, David and Tobin went to their truck to root for food to contribute to the feast. David uncached some packets of yoghurt, and Tobin hauled out a cured joint of beef. As they made their way back, they heard the unmistakable sound of a wooden xylophone. Tobin stopped momentarily, then hurried down to the square. Aziondi, one of the new arrivals, was playing a thirty-six-pane wooden xylophone strikingly similar to the mananga. The xylophonist petered to a stop when he noticed Tobin's reaction. The whole assembly was suddenly muted.

TOBIN RANI

Sudan | 27th April, 2005

Their amazement grew as I produced the Mata's mananga. I set it up opposite the New Arian xylophone. The natives touched it and marvelled. 'Do you buy in the souk?' asked Aziondi.

I shook my head vigorously. 'From our father's father's fathers. And yours?'

Aziondi nodded. 'The same.' He turned and uttered a sharp cry. A youth ran off, and the assembly sat down to wait.

David and I, though uncertain what we were waiting for, sensed that the time for questions was past. We sat down, feast forgotten.

Ten minutes later, a tall middle-aged man arrived on a scooter with the messenger behind him. The grey in his hair was mostly powdered grain. His gown was dirty white. But he wore a coal-black necklace and carried himself with an air of quiet dignity. He seemed to have been well briefed and walked slowly around the mananga, inspecting it closely, then sat in the chair produced for him. He addressed a question to Deen, with a steady stare at us, and got a blast of quick-fire Aria from a dozen sources. He raised his hand and into the ensuing silence said in English, 'Please play.'

I drew the mananga's arms from their sockets and looked into the Mata's skies. Not for the first time, I wished that I, and not Tume, had been the chosen one, but I was descended from the lineage of the crown prince, and that lineage could never produce a mata. Three times Mata Nimito had chosen, and all three had predeceased him. Perhaps had I never gone away to Dundee, had I married and settled early, the end would not have come, at least in this lifetime.

I turned my thoughts away from regret then, and the skies turned from grey to grey, from a darker shade of white to a lighter shade of black. I was not dying, I was living. Mata was not dead, he was sleeping. The Menai were not extinct, could never go extinct . . . here were brothers after all. Perhaps had David and I followed the wadi south—or even further north—we might have found another hive of cousins. The blood of Menai was diluted, yes, but sprinkled throughout Africa. And, through Laura, Europe. Even the Tuareg with the dozen daughters . . .

I drew the right arm from the upward sweep of the panes down, slowly, once, twice, finding the pane I wanted by ear, testing it, and only then looking down and beginning to rain my thoughts on the mananga.

I knew then why the Mata often spoke of himself in the plural. It was never he alone that spoke, that remembered, that gave the torqwa. It was the whole agglomeration of his ancestry giving tongue to the moment.

As I played, I felt my spirit buoyed, felt a skill alien to my lived experience, connecting, through a mananga designed by matas older than Nimito, to burn a rhythm in the air. As for the music that issued, I had not thought myself capable of the joy of it, with Nimito's cold body in a zippered bag. So I played, with expiation, knowing my life would end. So I played, with abandon, knowing my music would never end, calling the desert sands that held my ancestors' bones to witness, calling the Arian blood that was kin to Menai to boil . . .

DAVID BALSAM

Sudan | 27th April, 2005

Eventually Tobin faltered and Aziondi's instrument picked up, and the musical sparring began. Young men, excited by the challenge, pulled up their instruments, musicians launching off one another's apogee to hit supernatural heights, until every living soul within earshot was caught up in the fervour of it.

Save for David. He watched from a distance, the only person who was not dancing. His spirit was anchored to a weight that music, however elemental, could not shift. As he looked at his watch, it struck the hour.

He was fifty-five years old.

TOBIN RANI

Sudan | 28th April, 2005

By the small hours, the small children had drifted off to sleep. The small
tea fires were dead, and xylophones and ancillary instruments lay around
like the discarded implements of a sated sex. People slept where they lay.
There were houses aplenty, but the flat roofs and open air seemed best
suited for sleep. The dawn arrived, borne on an insectless breeze from
clear skies. In the distance, a small generator coughed into life. The sun
was low and cold, but experience had taught us, David and me, that it
would be a brief respite.

At first light, kettles and cups of tea appeared, followed an hour later by
trays of food. Presently Aziondi was making conversation, pointing at the
seated man stuffing a famished hand of *ful* and flat bread into his mouth,
'This is our Djatou; Djatous they know everything, but him don't know
you.' Then he laughed uproariously.

The mocked man smiled long-sufferingly. 'Who are you?'

I dipped a cup in the large gourd of yoghurt. I was hoarse from the previous night's singing, but my spirit was ecstatic. 'I will tell you a true story.'

Deen turned and called, and there was a drawing together of mats. He
interpreted my words and was corrected by Aziondi. There was an angry
exchange over translation rights, fevered by the prestige of the occasion.
When that was settled, I began.

'All this I am saying is true, or my name is not Tobin of Menai,' I started,
unconsciously slipping into the formula.

'*Aga, aga, aga.*' The echoed response startled me. Distant doors opened
and closed, and my audience grew.

'In the beginning, we were the Kingdom. We paid no tribute to anyone. Nations brought gifts to us. Our hero was Crown Prince Xera. Even
among the tall and brawny people of the Kingdom, Xera stood out as he
grew. It seemed unfair, at least to his younger brother, Mera, that the first
in line to the throne of the Kingdom was also the most handsome in all
the land. He was to be king when his father died. And his father ailed. But
he was yet to marry.

'There was but one lass whose wit and fame, whose rising height,
whose beauty could appose, without embarrassment, all the charms Xera
could bring to a wedding feast. That girl was Aila Numisa, third daughter

of the chief of Tarasa, who lived well beyond the suzerain power of the king of the Kingdom but not beyond the shroud of his fame. Perhaps you have heard of Tarasa?

'As was their tradition, Prince Xera set out with a large caravan to impress his in-laws. Hundreds of slaves, courtiers, craftsmen and artists, camel loads of gifts and more. And his Mata as well, for in all their travels, the princes went with their Mata, their . . .' I looked at that worthy, '. . . their Djatou? That is the way the stories of the ancestors come down to their descendants.' Nods rippled through his listeners.

'They travelled two weeks to the wedding and were a full week in festivities. On their way back, they were met by a desperate rider, a bloody messenger from the Kingdom, bearing news that invaders from Egypt, their age-old rivals, had overrun and destroyed the Kingdom. Everyone the groom's party knew was dead. The invaders were even then riding towards the marriage party to exterminate the heir to the throne. Our hero was to flee for his life. He wanted to return to fight for his honour, to wrest some vengeance for the blood of his fallen people, but wisdom prevailed. He fled for his life, for the life of his new bride and her train from Tarasa, for the life of his faithful courtiers, his bronzesmiths, his warriors, his counsellors . . . for the life that the People could live through their seed.

'He fled southwest to the valley of Ser, where he lived out his years. That is why the leaves of the trees of the valley of Ser are ash. They were changed by the grief and the curses of our hero, the Crown Prince.'

A small voice asked a question whose translation threw me briefly. I shrugged. 'I don't know. We called ourselves the People. We called our country the Kingdom. It was the only kingdom, of its mammoth size. When there is only one thing, the thing does not need a name. It is like asking the name of the sun.'

The boy nodded. He fully understood.

'Our hero grew old. In his nineties, when his hands were only good to crack walnuts and hold a walking stick, a caravan stumbled upon the valley of Ser and told of the Kingdom of the great King Mera. The betrayal was exposed. The subterfuge was known: Egypt never came. His father merely died, and Mera had won his brother's throne by wile.'

A sigh rippled when that was translated.

'Our hero's heart was turned to bile. He called a gathering of his people in Ser. He was too old to fight, but . . . *GodMenai!* . . . could he curse! He cursed the Kingdom and its usurper, Mera, *until he should return to rule.* He called his Mata to witness, he called his son as heir. He took his son's oath that he would grow an army to reclaim in war the throne stolen by cunning, on which day alone the curse upon the land would abate.

'Our hero died. His son, taking his oath to heart, uprooted his people from their peace in Ser and raged south and west like a cloud of anger, conquering and absorbing smaller clans and villages, growing an army that could confront the Kingdom. He won many battles, but he lost enough to keep him too small to confront the great army of his cousins in the Kingdom. He grew old and weak. His hands turned from cracking heads to cracking walnuts. He passed on his princehood and his bloody oath. Thus, each new princehood of Menai was founded on the curse of the mother Kingdom.

'The years of the centuries came and went, and the Menai sickened of blood. Sickened of an oath that set new princes on the trail of bloody war. Sickened of a curse that went northeast to bait a Kingdom they did not know. In the years of the great Mata Asad, the Menai lost their last prince. And they did not crown his son. They did not renew the oath of war. The Menai embraced peace.

'But peace did not embrace Menai. The curses we had sent northeast came back to roost. Our neighbours drove us on. We were the feared rooster that could never be allowed to roost. The palm of vengeance grows slowly in the desert sand, but grow it does. Rivulets of blood flowed down to us from our centuries of war. A hundred years in this oasis, eighty years by that wadi. A generation in this valley, three seasons in that jabel. We took the path of peace and migration. Until we journeyed right up to the lips of the sea, beyond which we could flee no further. Until Mata Nimito led us to Kreektown, to our final camp.'

I paused deliberately and brought the cup of yoghurt to my mouth. As I drank I looked at my audience, watching the last translation take root. I thought I detected hostility and reserve and wondered whether, perhaps, I should have held my peace. Yet it was too late to stop.

'In that truck lies Great Menai, the last Mata. In his hand lies singate, uninherited. In his brain, wisdom undecanted. All the stories are dead, all the dreams and the histories as well, but he had one wish before he died.'

'What?' asked the Djatou in a level voice.

'To break the curse of violence on the Kingdom and her spawn.' I let my hand rest lightly on the desert sand.

'The living cannot undo the curses of the dead,' said the Djatou harshly. 'You do not have that saying?'

Their grandmother raised her voice volubly and at length. The Djatou disputed with her. When they quietened, he looked at me uncertainly.

'Our grandmother says that a dead king can *conquer* a city and undo his own curses when he is buried.'

'How is this so? Please explain.'

'Your Mata was a wise man. If a king dies in battle but his army wins the war, he is buried in the conquered city's mausoleum of kings. In that case, it is not the living that *undoes* the curse. It is the satisfied spirit of the dead king that *rests* it.'

I turned and met David's eyes. To the Djatou, I said, 'Your grandmother is a wise woman. So she knows the legend of the Kingdom, then?'

He sniffed. 'There are many versions of it around. In some versions we are children of the kingdom of Kush.' He sneered. 'Look at us now.'

I sighed. 'I am glad you do not think our errand foolish. I am a descendant of Crown Prince Xera. That is who I am. And now, we leave to seek the burial ground of the Kingdom . . .'

Once again the old woman interjected strenuously. When she finished she rose and blundered off into the distance without waiting for the translation to be made. The Djatou waved his hand in exasperation. Aziondi took it up: 'She says, "What Field! What Field! A grave is a grave is a grave and the spirit of your great Mata is good salt for our land! Come, I will give you a grave!"'

◆ ◆ ◆

THAT MORNING, the minibuses did not go to Bede, and the entire village mustered for the Mata's funeral. As the sun rose, they sank a grave to the music of an Arian dirge. Beneath the boughs of the great baobab, they sank that grave, between a fork of roots. They broke up the ancient mananga and laid Mata Nimito on a bed of its wooden panes. They set him deep, in a grave as snug as a womb. They laid his singate by his side and the bronze singateya by his head. They spread his red robe at five feet and broke his beaded bib into pellets at four. They slabbed him in sand, with the trunk of the baobab for headstone.

I looked up, to rein in my tears, and saw New Arians as far as my eyes could see: a field of kindred souls instead of the stones the Mata had resigned himself to. A choir of Arian manangas cued themselves, and the sorrow fell from me like a spent sentence. Mata Nimito was dead, but GodMenai was clearly still alive: for instead of rotting in a necropolis of pyramids, the Mata had been brought home to manure a hive of cousins. This kind of death was also a kind of life, complete with children to play on his grave. The Djatou embraced me and stepped aside for the queue that had formed to condole the chief mourner.

DAVID BALSAM

Sudan | 28th April, 2005

They stood together, the Djatou, David, and Tobin, finishing their bowls of camel milk as the minibuses pulled away from Aria. Fuel kegs emerged from outhouse stores to refuel David's truck. The professor glanced north at the darkening sky as the Djatou took his leave of Tobin. 'We have a lot to talk about, my brother across the centuries.'

'Indeed, Djatou.'

'I will mix my dough and put my boys to work. I will be back soon.'

'I will be here.'

The Djatou shook David's hand formally and mounted his old scooter, which growled slowly away. David took a last look around the flat country-side and the flat-roofed homes. 'It is a peaceful place to live,' he conceded.

'And die. I'm ready now.'

There was a giggle, but when David turned, a veiled face at a nearby window retreated shyly into a darkened room. He smiled. 'Maybe death is not yet ready for you.' He gave up his empty bowl with a smile to a waiting child. 'There is sky aplenty, but you are no cloudcaster. What will you do?'

Tobin shrugged. 'Live. I've spent all my life trying to save the Menai from death.' He gestured at the young children in a semicircle staring at them with unrelieved curiosity. 'My students. At last my PhD might be useful.' He offered a leather scroll. 'Here's a memento of your trip. The historysong of Crown Prince Alito's death. Perhaps you can figure it out for yourself.'

'You once called me your spirit brother. Will you lie to me?'

'No.'

'I spoke to Professor Reid on the phone. He saw the script you wrote on the walls of your London prison cell. I know you can read this.'

'Of course.'

'Teach me.'

Tobin sighed. 'I am under oath to GodMenai. Unfortunately, a lot of African knowledge was protected by secret society oaths. When we began our migration, our writing was one of them.'

'Perhaps this explains the extinction of Menai?'

'True, though if we forced our language on our vassal states these past millennia, we would have erased other tongues too, like any other colonial language—'

'You could teach me: the Mata made me an honorary Menai.'

Gently, Tobin said, 'Sure. But you will have to take the oath first. Then what you do with the knowledge will be your own problem.'

David swallowed. His breath came in shallow draughts. He knew that he stood on the lip of the discovery of his career. He reeled from the shockwaves of temptation. Another book beckoned, the book that would open up not just the world of the Menai but that of the mythical Meroes before them, that would finally rest the plagiarist demons of *Genesis of Mythical Africa*. Yet he was just gone fifty-five . . . and not quite sure he would survive the day. His inadvertent sabbatical from London had taught him a new respect, and fear, for his ancestral land. He hesitated.

'We have a saying that is not just a *saying*,' said Tobin.

'What?'

He lifted a fistful of sand into the air and let it filter through his fingers. When the fine grains had settled fully, he dusted off his hands. 'Concerning the old oaths, it used to be said that when you can retrieve every last grain of the sand spilled from your hand—and not an extra grain, then you can break the curse that flows from a broken oath.'

David looked down at the sand. He remembered his singateya. Then he took a deep breath and let it go. 'This is a good memento of the Mata, thank you. I think archaeology is overrated anyway.'

'Indeed.'

David turned to the truck. He took out his phone.

'Did you find what you were looking for, David?'

'I don't know. But yesterday was also like a private party for me.'

'How so?'

'I am fifty-five today.'

'That is great! Here's my birthday gift: come back here in three months, and these kids will be able to read, write—and teach you the Menai script . . . even if I'm no longer here.'

'And the oath of secrecy you have to swear them to?'

'You heard the grandmother. The Mata's burial here breaks all the curses on them. The kids will have a new deal.' He hesitated and then said with a wink, 'Although a small "ethnographic" schoolroom will help.'

David laughed out loud. 'So you'll trade your truck for a school? Deal!'

They shook hands on it and then embraced clumsily. David climbed into the cabin. 'There is no dialysis centre for a thousand miles, if you ever need one . . .'

'I know.'

He was silent for a moment, then fired up the engine. 'I'm really sorry it had to end like this.'

'Don't be, *Davidi*. Everything ends.'

◆ ◆ ◆

HE SPED across the shifting desert floor in the largest country in Africa, driven by the sandstorm and a rage for life. Steering by GPS alone, his fingers clamped the steering wheel, and as visibility fell, he pushed down on the accelerator, as though he could overhaul his demons and the sand djinn by speed alone. He lost the satellite connection and his tracking went offline, but he didn't slow down. Loud music blared from the speakers, but his nerves stayed taut. Then, as the hour struck, as he crossed into the new day, he took his foot off the accelerator and let the truck roll to a stop. He sat up for the rest of the night as eddies of sand tried to bury him, thinking that in a sense he was dead after all, for there was no way he could go back to being the Professor Balsam who had arrived in Nigeria back in February.

When the sun rose, although his doors were jammed solid, the wind was still and the sky was clear. He was hot, wet with sweat, and stripped down to his underwear but alive and only four hours from Khartoum. He slid open the moonroof and hauled himself up on the top of the truck, gasping at the purity of the air after the staleness of the cabin. He sat there soberly, looking out on a world with a virgin sand cover on which no human foot had trod. He felt like a man emerging from his own grave, at a failed funeral where no one had even turned up. He thought back to the hero's burial given to Mata Nimito by people who had never met him, and David felt a new lease on life, not to write another book but to live such a life that his real death would be a catastrophe for his communities . . . a sleepcatastrophe . . . . He dropped the shovel over the side of the truck and jumped down after it, losing his footing and rolling onto his back.

' . . . GodMenai!'

The word was out before he realised it. He shook his head ruefully, picked himself up, and began to dig out the truck.

He had a school fund-raising to organise.

SLEEPCATASTROPHES

Kreektown | March/April, 2005

Kiri Ntupong
Asala Turo
Farmer Utoma
Jamis (Jonszer) Biri
Mata Nimito

Births
Nimito Kroma-Alanta

Extant Menai population: 24 (NPC estimates)

PENAKA LEE

Geneva | 28th April, 2005

The private guests milled between the poolside topless ballet and the centrepiece spitted lamb on the mezzanine. A steady stream of signature dishes emerged from the kitchen of the French chef flown in the night before. The wine bar did not disappoint. As for the celebrant himself, there was no sign.

Penaka had reached that station in life where he was not particularly bothered by people's opinion of his hospitality. He felt like being alone, so he retreated into his basement gallery and shut the world out. The concept of home was somewhat diffused for a man of his circumstances, who kept four private houses around the world and several more well-used guest houses. Yet, year on year, he did spend more time in Geneva than in his other homes, and his most valuable collections were in that one basement.

He did not need to rise from his sofa to enjoy them now. He could look around, as he did, and see the Picassos, Monets, and Dalis that had disappeared from museums and galleries around the world.

His heart quickened once more as he turned to a central plinth. Monica Parkerson had finally delivered the unfinished Benin bronze that had possessed him ever since he first saw it in Conrad Lord Risborough's house back in 1979. It was difficult to explain Conrad's reluctance to part with it (he had sold more valuable things) or Penaka's own desire to own it (he owned far more valuable pieces). He could only describe it as destiny. For all the presence of his one, spectacular, Dali, it did not quite have the same magnetism of his latest bronze. Perhaps part of the value of the bronze was the twenty-six years it had taken him to acquire it.

Yet the wait was over now. It was *here*.

His lips slipped into his perfect grin. Forbidden pleasures thrilled the most. He thought he would take down the bronze, touch and caress it . . . do with it all those things that seven billion people could not, but he was suddenly *tired* of it all. And he wondered whether, in the unlikely event that he entered heaven and was sentenced to an eternity of pleasures much like his current life, he would be able to, you know, after a thousand years or two, resign, sleep indefinitely, or something. He yawned and stretched, settling deeper into his sofa. Upstairs on his mezzanine, the specially screened guests at his fifty-fifth birthday oohed and aahed around his more public art, waiting for an introduction into the collector's secretive world.

PHIL BEGG

London | 28th April, 2005

'Boss, it's an email from Nigeria; I think you'd better take a look.'

'I've got no time for jokes, Gene,' I snapped. I was up to my ears in sign-offs. 'Our printing window in Melbourne closes in five hours!'

'It's no 419 letter, Phil. It's another Humphrey Chow story.'

'He didn't!'

Gene nodded. 'He's just made the deadline by minutes, but we've typeset the standby story already. What do you want me to do?'

'Run with the standby. We haven't checked the e-mails, okay?'

'You're the boss,' he said, in that tone that suggested I wasn't, really.

◆ ◆ ◆

I WENT back to the third issue of a magazine the market didn't need, which had to be published because the third-largest media group in Europe had to have a foot in the Men's Lifestyle 30-to-49-year-old demographic. It was a tough job. The money paid the bills, but the ulcers were hell. Issue two had sold 150,000 copies, and we had managed to give away another 80,000. That was a lot of recycling stock, but our ad projections were based on a 300,000 sales threshold and, yes, I was under pressure.

♦ ♦ ♦

PRODUCTION WAS going to plan; the PDFs were done and ready to go. Our printers were on standby. Heads were down in the proofing room, and the adrenaline was surging everywhere. Then someone found a booked, full-page ad that had been accidentally spiked. I had to decide between devastating the psyche of *Balding Wolf*'s 230,000 real readers by canning their biweekly DIY Hints section in the interests of ad revenue. So it was pressure, but it was nothing I couldn't handle; then I entered my office and found Gene lounging in the easy chair.

In an ideal world, he would probably have gotten my job ahead of me, but he had headed up one failed launch too many. That was how the market worked. He was overweight, ran on Coke and coffee, and no longer needed combs. He was neither sexy nor hip, but he knew the job; and if there ever was a wolf who was balding, here he was. I had picked him as my deputy because I knew that if I was sacked he would not get my job, and if the magazine went bust, it was back to freelance features in the daily rags for him. He would work harder than I could to keep us in business; but he was also ten years older than I was, so I expected some insubordination.

'Do we have a problem, Gene?'

He put a printout on my desk. 'He hit six thousand words on the nose, plus he resurrected Dalminda Roco. I didn't really like his Bamou phase.'

I glanced at the clock. Australia was printing in two hours and our Kent press was scheduled to roll shortly afterwards. 'So? We have an understanding on Mr. Chow.'

'We did, but I read the story, didn't I?'

'We've got a safe Pushcart winner—'

'We've got a *bland* Pushcart formula, that's what we've got; and if it's gongs you want, his last story for us won a national award in—'

'—Nigeria. Yeah, right. Listen, the name 'Dalminda' kills the story, okay? I'm not going to be hauled in by the terror police for Humphrey again.'

'He's gone and set Dalminda in Nigeria. It's a whole new fictive take on political farce with a twist in the tail of a Swiss godfather that makes the

Italian mafia look like a bunch of frat boys. The *New Yorker* called his last story 'elementally edgy.' They'll have to trot out the thesaurus to review this one. I can swipe the stories around in ten secs, without nudging the layout out of sync—'

'This is not a layout issue. The police think Dalminda is a real person. We are talking potential lawsuits—'

'What? *Al-Qaeda* sues IVC? That type of lawsuit?'

I glared at him.

'Okay, I was out of line there,' he grunted. 'But, hey, the only call the publisher's made on this issue is to ask if we got a Chow story.'

I realised that admitting that one was out of line was not exactly the same thing as apologising, but I didn't press the point. I sighed, took the printout, and dropped into the chair opposite him. 'The publisher won't be happy to get a call from the police after we go to press.'

'Are you kidding me?' Gene said, rising. 'If we can get the *Sun* to report your arrest, that's an extra fifty thousand copies sold.'

'That's the name of the game, isn't it?' I grumbled, 'Go away, Gene, give me five minutes.'

◆ ◆ ◆

I TOOK twenty minutes, in the event, but when I was done, I gave him the call. 'Okay, Einstein, change "Megatum" into "Mutagem" or something, but go ahead, run the Chow tale.'

Epilogue

SHEESTI KROMA-ALANTA

London | 28th April, 2005

She was in the courtroom in London. It was another colourless day in the Menai Society's litigation against Trevi Biotics and Megatum. The bar was swamped by a shoal of seasoned counsel to the defendants, who had just that morning filed a fresh box of interlocutory applications trying to halt the case until the House of Commons investigations were completed. The lead QC rose to address the court. The timeworn engine of justice revved up.

Sheesti's phone pinged, and she pulled it out discreetly. The bright LCD gleamed with Tobin Rani's poetry in text message. She moaned softly, and the phone slipped from her fingers. As the QC started his address, she began to weep softly. She tried to rein it in, but something gave, deep inside her, and she broke all the way. Clutching her womb, she dropped her eyelids on the film of tears and began to sing Mata Nimito's calamity. There was consternation in the courtroom. Denle, who had picked up and read the message on the phone, held his wife close and did not try to hush her, did not try to move her. When their alarmed lawyer leaned over, he passed her phone wordlessly to him. Then the swelling song straightened her spine, and he rose with her, her haunting voice and susurrant Menai raising gooseflesh across the English gallery.

When the stewards burst into the court, her phone was before the judge, who was standing, with his courtroom, as still as all the dead Menai who had once upon a time mourned a living Sheesti Kroma-Alanta in Kreektown's village square.